The Calling of the Grull was originally released as serial chapters, with a new chapter every month. Here is what readers had to say.

"The author really brings you into the past and makes you feel the story.... A fantastic story brought to life. I read the first one and quickly bought the next two and can't wait for the next installments." - 5 stars Amazon

"Most interesting read so far.. On to read part two... Highly recommended." - 5 stars Amazon

"This is an exceptional series, very well written and entertaining. The story takes you back in time when clans of people still lived in huts and caves. This clan lived very close to a river and after a flood took nearly everything, they had to travel to find the home of their ancestors. The story tells of their adventures and hardships along the way." - 5 stars Amazon

The Calling of the Gruill

Jonni Jordyn

<u>**Other books by Jonni Jordyn**</u>

<u>**The Lost Art of Magic Series**</u>
The Lost Art of Magic
The Untold Prophecy
The Old Child
The Orb of Destiny
<u>**The Mother of All Viruses Series**</u>
The Mother of All Viruses
The Queen of All Viruses
<u>**The Chronicles of the Grull Series**</u>
The Calling of the Grull
The Hammer and the Chain
The Beat of a Different Drummer
The Diva of Mud Flats
Something About Nobility

This book is dedicated to Tweety, who sits with me every morning and never complains, as I write and revise the coming month's chapter in this series.

Update: I have lost my Tweety, since the first edition of this book and series. She did sit with me for years without ever complaining. She is missed.

Contents

Yet, None are Master

1 **The Stone**
  Hard and strong
  Everlasting and ancient
  Is humbled by the water
  Shaped and tumbled
  Weathered and worn

2 **The Wood**
  Fresh and pliable
  Hard and sharp
  Consumes the water
  Splintered by stone
  Burned by fire

3 **The Fire**
  Hot and dangerous
  Wild and untamed
  Shapes the wood
  Or consumes it
  Defeated by water

4 **The Soil**
  Soft or hard
  Liquid or solid
  Shaped by the water
  Hardened by the fire
  Shattered by the stone

5 **The Water**
  Fluid and undefeatable
  Diverted by the stone
  Stirred by a stick
  Captured by a clay cup
  Boiled by the fire

6 **The hut**
  Stone and wood
  Mud and brick
  Harmony
  Home
  The sum of all

- Jonni Jordyn

The Calling of the Gruff

Jonni Jordyn

Chapter One

The Sacred Soil

All was lost, yet all was not lost. Dark clouds still broiled overhead, dropping torrents of rain, day and night, onto the mountain slopes and spilling into the creeks and tributaries that fed the mountain rivers. The rivers overflowed their banks and divided the land with new rivers that dug into the mountain, unearthing old roots and felling the trees. These new rivers carried the debris down the mountain and deposited all of it into the main river, the river of life, the river that had cut the valley and provided food and water to the people for as far back as they could remember. This was the same river that now flowed over its banks and destroyed their homes and crops. The murky flooding water was relentless. It swept away babies and children as heartlessly as it did the old and the infirmed. The river of life was now the river of death.

This wasn't the first time in memory that the rain had fallen for twenty-one straight days. All winters have periods with storms day after day, but nobody remembered it ever being so heavy with no breaks between the storms. None of the ancient songs told of such a great drenching, or the flooding which followed so heavy a downpour. It had been one continuous storm that swelled the rivers beyond their capacity and was now wiping their village off the Earth.

Kendo saw the water when it was attacking his hut and would have gathered his belongings to carry them to high ground, but his duty was to his people. He waded through the rising water, seeking out the women and children that clung to anything still connected to the ground. He carried the Staff of Justice, which was given to him by his father as a symbol of his leadership, but now was little more than a stick of steadiness as the chest-deep water rushed by and threatened to carry him downstream with it.

The hunters mirrored his actions and searched for survivors in the drowning village. The water was already over the children's heads and was reaching the necks of the women. They carried them out one by one and took them to high ground. Kendo and the hunters could not save them all, but they left no one behind that the river had not already claimed.

Kendo looked upon his medicine woman. Her wrinkled face was wet and smeared with mud. She spoke comfort to the people while she treated their cuts and scrapes. He could not imagine how the people would have survived if they had lost the grizzled old woman and all the knowledge she carried with her.

Mora's duties were to maintain both their physical health and their spiritual well-being. Right now, their physical condition required most of her attention, but she kept one eye to the heavens and the mountains while she tended their injuries. She could not explain what was happening; not to herself, and not to the people. She had no words of understanding for her people and could only offer hope. There were no ancient songs to guide them.

Her predecessor might have suggested that the Gods were cleaning house and needed to wipe the village out to remove those who were not worthy, but she was not him. She would not go into a tirade to scare the people into submission. She simply did what she could for their wounds and told the people that the spirits would reveal themselves when the time was right.

When the last of the people had been evacuated, Kendo and the hunters surveyed the remains of their village. He could see timber and pieces of thatch roofs floating down the river. Their livestock was gone. They were too busy evacuating the people to save the goats and chickens. Kendo's heart hung heavy in his chest as he asked, "Does anything remain to be saved?"

The hunters tried to fight the despair, but the village was decimated. Any huts that weren't torn down outright had disappeared completely beneath the muddy water. "Nothing," one said, "all is lost."

"Not all," said one of the younger hunters. "My sling remains on my side."

"As does mine," said another.

"So, we start over," Kendo said. "We have our minds, our strength, and two slings. Kendo thinks it is enough."

"We have more than that," Mora said from behind. "We have the love of a good stout people, and we have Kendo's leadership to see us through this."

"Kendo's leadership," he echoed, unconvinced.

The hunters agreed with Mora's words and sang out, "Kendo! Kendo!"

"Well then," Kendo said, "if the people's trust is in Kendo as you suggest, then Kendo will lead us up the mountain and we will find new homes."

In truth, the tribe had more than just the two slings. One of the cooks had saved a cooking skin and a flint, and the water porters salvaged three partial skins of fresh water.

Kendo turned to Mora and asked softly, "How are the people? Can they travel?"

Mora nodded her head and said, "The people are tired and cold. Walking will warm them but will also make them more tired. The mothers may not be strong enough to carry the babies all the way. Ragna's baby burns hot and may not survive. The people need shelter from the storm so they can gather their strength, but Mora believes the people can travel until we find it."

Kendo bit his lip before asking the next question. It was a harsh question for such a moment as this, but as chief, he could not shy away from the bad news. "Of those the river has taken from us, have we lost anyone that we cannot replace?"

Mora felt the pain in his question and bowed her head as she answered, "The people have many losses. Mora will feel the loss of Soba, our best seamstress, but we are fortunate that Soba's apprentice survives. Mora does not see Boora among the people. Mora has spent many years training Boora and fears she may not have enough life left to train another apprentice."

Zho, who led the hunters, said, "We have lost two of our elder hunters who trained our young, and one of our more promising young hunters also is missing, but we have enough hunters who survived. Also missing is...is ..." He lowered his voice to a whisper and said, "Kendo's..." He couldn't finish his sentence, but Kendo knew he meant Kendo's son, who was destined to accept the Staff of Justice as the people's chief one day.

Mora continued, "And let us not forget Troon who was oldest of us. Troon no longer hunts or works, but he is wise in many things. Even Mora has asked for Troon's advice in many matters."

"As has Kendo."

"Mora misses Troon. We can remake the tools and we can remake the weapons, but we can never remake the memories Troon takes with him. Mora also worries that we have lost more than just our people today. The river has taken all of Mora's medicines. It took years to collect them all. Mora fears that without the medicines, we may continue to lose more people than just those the river has taken."

Kendo nodded, then turned to the hunters and said, "The people cannot stay here. Zho, assemble eight men to climb up the mountain and scout ahead of us for shelter. Kendo fears that the people will need the strongest men to remain behind to help carry the women and children, so take with you some of our younger hunters and apprentices. Kendo wants them to stay in pairs. We cannot afford to lose any of them."

Zho nodded and started off, but Kendo stopped him. "Zho, tell them the people will continue up the mountain. Kendo does not want them out alone after dark, so they should return to us even if they find nothing. Watch over the apprentices."

Zho nodded again and trotted off.

"It is still early in the day," Mora said. "Let us hope they find something before dark."

Kendo then walked among the tribe and picked out two girls, one of eight years, and the other almost old enough to marry. He held their hands up for all to see and announced, "Here are Mora's new apprentices. We must all help them learn her crafts. Let us hope that in what time Mora has left with us, the two of them, together, can learn as much as Mora has learned in her lifetime. Mora can start by showing them what herbs to collect along the way up the mountain."

Kendo turned to the remaining men and said, "We must team up the best we can. Those of us who are still young and strong should be able to protect at least one woman and one child. The older children can walk alongside the rest of us. Babies must be carried, but if the passage becomes difficult, we may also need to carry the women and the elders."

"You needn't worry," said Brahg, the largest and strongest of the tribe. "Brahg is here to carry Kendo."

Kendo tried to laugh, but the mood was too somber on this occasion. He placed his hand on Brahg's shoulder and said, "It is good that we try to keep our spirits light. This is a dark day, and we have a difficult road ahead of us. Kendo is truly comforted to know that your heart is as big as your back. You are easily twice the man of any of us. Let us hope you do not hurt yourself on this journey, for Kendo fears there are too few of us to carry you up the mountain."

"As you say," Brahg replied, "Brahg is twice your size, so Brahg will take two women and two babies."

Kendo smiled. "Thank you, Brahg, but let us give you two women and only one baby that they must care for between them."

"Good thinking," one of the remaining hunters said. "Brahg also has twice our appetite and might be tempted to eat one of the babies."

Brahg blushed and laughed while administering a well-earned punch to the arm of the hunter who had spoken.

Pela, who has long carried a crush for Brahg, said, "If Brahg is that big, Pela will gladly go with Brahg."

Several of the women giggled and Brahg blushed again.

Kendo took his staff and started up the mountain. He led his people along a goat trail that took them up through the foothills at the base of the mountain. The hunters had taken this trail many times, but there was a place further up the mountain, where the land was sacred and the hunters no longer ventured. Perhaps this would be their destination. Kendo would let the spirits guide him.

After weeks with no sign of letting up, the rain finally subsided. The tribe took this as a good omen that they were doing the right thing by leaving the valley behind and climbing the mountain to find a new home. The ground remained wet and muddy in those spots where the water collected. The storm may have finally passed them, but the season of storms was not through with them yet.

Dark clouds gathered in the distance and would find them before dark. Thick vegetation lined the sandy trail. Mora was already identifying the plants along the trail for her new apprentices. The path led them up to a small plateau, where it nearly disappeared into a thick, green meadow and then climbed out on the other side and was lost from view again between two tall, rocky spires. The mountain rose up, across the field, in a large pile of tumbled boulders.

Kendo pointed across the meadow and said, "Hopefully, our hunters can find caves in those rocks."

Mora gasped when she saw where he pointed, and said, "Those are the Gods' toes. I've never been here, but I've heard the songs, and I'm sure of it. Our ancestors once lived high up in those mountains."

Kendo paused to look upon the great pile of stones and ponder what lay beyond. He could see great white peaks that rose up into the heavens until they were obscured by the clouds themselves. "Kendo wonders why the ancestors left their homes in the mountains to live in the valley that no longer wants us. What will we find when we get there?"

Mora knew of no song that held Kendo's answer and simply shrugged and shook her head.

Kendo entered the meadow with his people in tow. They trampled a wider swath than the goat path as they crossed the field. Mora guided her two new protégés through the meadow and pointed to the leaves and roots she wanted. Yona, the apprentice seamstress, presented them with bags she had stitched together during the walk up there. Her own clothes no longer protected her legs, but the bags would be more useful to the tribe than her extra hem. The two girls went forth and collected as many ingredients as the new bags could carry.

Kendo was only halfway across the large meadow when two of the hunters hailed him from the base of the Gods' toes. They had found shelter there, as he had hoped they would. Kendo turned to Mora and asked, "Do Mora's songs tell us if the Gods' toes are too sacred for us to camp there?"

Mora simply asked, "What God would not offer shelter to His people?"

His people.

The phrase echoed in Kendo's mind as he turned around to look at his people. He worried about them. Mora might say he worried too much about them, but he didn't believe there was such a thing as too much. He worried about them both individually and together as a tribe. Too many were taken in the floods and they could afford no more losses. He felt the pain of every loss as much as he did his own son, who was last seen bravely trying to pull an elder from the wash, but was carried away from them down the river.

Kendo looked beyond his tribe at the wide path of crushed grass and trampled wild flowers that stretched across the meadow, and it soothed his mind to know that the remaining hunters would see it from far away and find them easily.

The cave wasn't large enough for the tribe to settle in, but it provided shelter from the storm. Its massive tumble of stones was ancient, and the crevices between them were mostly filled with dirt and debris that served to keep the bitter wind out of the interior. The people huddled in groups to keep warm while the stronger boys and girls gathered wood for a fire. The two hunters who had found the cave were already out in the meadow searching for rabbits while some of the women were gathering grasses and broad leaves for a soup, but their usable water was growing scarce.

Mora taught each of her new apprentices different skills to prepare the collected herbs by drying, cutting, and grinding them. Yona collected more hems from the tribe and assembled small pouches to hold the prepared ingredients.

The hunters found no game, but they did not return empty-handed. They brought with them the other six hunters, whom they had found on the other side of the meadow. There would be no meat tonight, but the soup would be warm, although the women gathering the ingredients would not vouch for its flavor, and with the lack of water, it would not be as plentiful as they would like. The soup and the fire would keep them warm through the night, but there would be no songs of victory and triumph. Silent prayers and bowed heads filled the cave, accompanied by the soft crying of the children and infants, who eventually fell asleep, leaving only the sound of a soft rain falling outside.

Brahg insisted on the first watch, or Kendo would never have slept. This was no time for them to fall prey to a hungry bear or mountain cat, but it was also no time for their leader to go soft from lack of sleep. Kendo insisted that he should be wakened to take the second watch, but Zho and Brahg had already conspired to nod their heads and pretend to agree with him, but let him sleep while Zho took the watch in his place.

Kendo quickly fell fast asleep. He dreamed of the river carrying his son away, but his nightmare was interrupted by the piercing cry of a lone eagle high in the sky. He stepped out of the cave and searched the skies. The full moon illuminated the ground around him as well as the bird he saw high overhead. It was a pure white eagle flying in a circle, looking down upon them from its great vantage above them. It must be an omen.

He started to call for Mora, but the eagle broke from its circle and flew over the mountain until it came to rest on a large boulder far up the ridge.

Kendo had never seen a white eagle before. He'd never even heard songs about one. He climbed the ridge for a better look. The ground was soft and his feet sunk into it like sand, but it held his weight and, with effort, he scaled the mountain to the base of the spire where the eagle had waited.

The eagle looked at him and spread its wings, showing Kendo how big it was. It flapped its large white wings but did not leave. Kendo had never seen such a wondrous site until he looked beyond the spire and saw a small village in the base of a valley. The eagle left its perch and circled over the village.

Kendo studied the steep descent, looking for the best path down, when he heard Mora calling him from behind. He turned around but couldn't see her. The sun peeked up over the eastern rise and dazzled his eyes. He closed his eyes and shielded his face from the sun. She called again, and when he opened his eyes, he saw only her eyes staring into his.

"Good morning," Mora said. "Kendo's people grew restless, and Mora thought she should wake you before you were left behind."

Kendo blinked and nodded his head. He looked around for Brahg, but couldn't see him. Only Kendo and Mora remained in the cave.

"Is Kendo ok?" she asked.

"Yes," he said, "Kendo had a vision."

"Oh?" she asked. "Now Kendo wants Mora's job?"

"No," he said softly, "it was a leader's vision. Kendo has been shown our path. The people are to climb the mountain and return to the home of our ancestor's."

Kendo got up slowly. The badly needed sleep on the hard rocky ground left him stiff and sore, but a new day was upon him, and he had a new sense of mission. He stepped outside the cave and saw that morning had brought the first blue skies they had seen in weeks.

A brisk breeze blew down from the mountain and carried away the mist, which now rose from the wet ground. Kendo felt a new energy. Any anger he might have felt for being allowed to sleep was overshadowed by the love he felt for, and from, Brahg and Zho.

Yesterday, Kendo may not have been sure where he was taking his people, but today he was absolutely certain. His vision had shown him the home of their ancestors. He recognized the fabled Valley of the Sun from the songs his people had sung since he was a child. They had just spent the night in the Toes of the Gods and now he would lead them up the sacred mountains of their ancestors.

They had no meats or grains to break their fast, so he wasted no time starting up the mountain. The wind coming down the mountain was chilly, but the sun was bright and clear. Together, the two elements served to dry their clothes and over-skins.

Kendo followed the path along the edge of the meadow, then turned sharply into a canyon that led up the mountain. A lazy river, fouled with dirt and mud, flowed at the base of the canyon. Kendo did not know if the river belonged there. After the rains they had had, rivers flowed many places where they had not before, but as long as the river flowed past them, he knew they were still going up the mountain.

The people followed Kendo into the ravine. Many of the children grabbed handfuls of sweet grass as they left the field behind and followed the adults up the rocky incline. The canyon snaked around right and left while climbing ever higher. The cliff walls narrowed until they closed in on them enough that they could almost touch both sides if they stretched. At the end of the canyon, a spring flowed from the top and fell into the river at the base of the valley. Mora and one of the water porters tasted the spring water, but it was heavy with bad salts and minerals. Mora shook her head. This was not water for filling their skins.

Kendo surveyed the distance to the top. It was nearly a vertical climb. Getting out of the canyon would be difficult. Many of the women and children would need to be carried, and the men may have to make several trips.

Kendo tied his staff to a chord that hung from his waist and took Mora on his back. He led the people this far, so he would climb up first. Mora was small, and her frail, old body was light. The climb started easy enough, but each step up grew harder, and her weight grew heavier upon his back. He thought the wetness of the rock would make it slippery, but it actually made the stone soft and brittle. He reached up with his hand to take hold of an edge and tested his weight against it, then raised one foot up to find an edge of its own before heaving himself up and allowing his weight, and Mora's, to lean against the wall.

Brittle stones broke off below his feet, leaving the two of them dangling from a single handhold. The tribe gasped as they stepped back from the base of the cliff, ducking the loose rocks that showered down upon them. The hunters were more accustomed to making their way through rough country such as this, and shouted up advice for Kendo to go to his left or right, but ultimately, he had to rely on his own judgment and take what he thought were the strongest handholds he could reach.

At the top of the climb, he crawled over the ledge and lay flat on the ground while Mora climbed off of him. He stood up next to Mora and looked at what lay between them and their ancestral home. He was still bent at the waist, breathing heavily, but pointed ahead of them and said, "Kendo has never seen an all-white meadow before."

"Nor has Mora."

"Is this real or is it a vision for two who have come so close to death as on the climb?"

Before Mora could answer, Brahg reached the top with a woman and a child on his back and said, "Brahg would like some help."

Kendo returned his attention to his people and helped lift the woman and child from Brahg's back. Kendo then started climbing over the ledge to go back down, but Brahg suggested, "Kendo should stay and help lift the women and children off of the other's backs as he helped Brahg."

Mora reached for Kendo's arm and nodded her agreement.

The sun was halfway from mid-day to the western range when they finally carried the last member of the tribe to the top. Kendo took Brahg's arm personally and lifted him across the ledge. Kendo patted him on the back and said, "Brahg did good. He should rest now, as should all of us."

Brahg looked up at the advancing sun and shook his head. "Brahg will rest when it is dark and we have shelter for the night."

Zho signaled for a couple of the hunters to join him and said, "Zho, too, will rest when we have food and shelter tonight. The hunters will scout for some place while we hunt."

Kendo nodded and took the lead again. They still climbed, but their path was no longer steep. The ground changed from rocky sand to a slick, shiny stone that crunched under Kendo's feet. He walked out into the white meadow. His feet felt unsteady, so he planted his staff hard on the ground. As he planted his left foot and brought the right one up, his feet shot forward and he landed flat on his backside.

Laughter echoed off the cold mountain walls. Kendo picked himself up off the ground and brushed the cold, white dirt off his backside. He surveyed the paltry remains of his tribe as they doubled over, laughing at his misfortune. It was the first time they had laughed since their homes and crops were destroyed by the floods. On any other day, he might have admonished them for laughing at him, but not today. What would be the point?

They now climbed the sacred mountains, searching for the fabled homes of their ancestors. All of them were tired, cold, and hungry. They could use a good laugh and he laughed along with them, but he couldn't laugh too long. They needed to find a new home and something to eat.

"It is good to hear you laugh, my friends, but we must climb these mountains to find the home of the old ones; a land which has not only been told to us in our sacred songs, but was shown to me in a vision from our ancestors. Kendo fears we do not have so much time to laugh at an old man's clumsiness."

Kendo turned and headed once more across the meadow, and once again, his feet skidded out from under him and he crashed to the ground. He shook his head and said, "This land is hard to walk on."

Ragna said, "Perhaps you are doing it wrong."

Kendo brushed himself off again and asked, "Does Ragna suggest Kendo does not know how to walk?"

"No," Brahg said, still laughing, "and nobody here is suggesting that Kendo does not know how to fall either!"

The tribe erupted in laughter again. A young boy fell to the ground and rolled around laughing, then leaped to his feet and yelled out, "Hey, this white ground is very cold, but it is also very soft."

Kendo responded, while still rubbing his backside, "It is not so soft as you might think, little one."

Mora beckoned to the young boy, "Bring me some of that white ground."

The boy scooped up a handful and took it to the gnarled old woman. She took a pinch of it and tasted it. "Ooh, it is very cold," she said, "but it tastes like no other dirt I know. In fact, it has no flavor at all." She turned and pointed into the tribe and asked, "Ragna, does your child still burn?"

"Yes, Mora, he does."

"Bring him to me." Mora took a handful of the white dirt from the boy. It was even colder than her first taste. She rubbed it into the baby's forehead, but it disappeared.

The crowd hushed. They had never witnessed such powerful magic from Mora before. She kissed the baby's forehead and said, "He feels better. If he gets hot again, rub some of the white dirt on him like I did." She turned to the boy and said, "Give Ragna the rest of your dirt."

"I cannot!" the boy cried out. "It is gone!"

The tribe was stunned.

Kendo stepped into the hushed crowd and announced, "This must be sacred dirt. That explains why it is so white. We are not allowed to own it, but the spirits allowed us to soothe the baby with it. Kendo thinks we must be close to our destination now."

Mora asked, "What if we are not allowed to walk on the sacred dirt? Is that why you fall?"

Kendo stood tall and said, "If we are not allowed to walk on the sacred dirt, then we will humble ourselves before the spirits of our ancestors, and we will crawl on it."

A loud crack, followed by *oohs* and *ahhs*, was heard on the other side of the tribe. The crowd parted and two of the tribe's hunters approached, each carrying a snowy white rabbit.

"So," Kendo said, "it looks like we shall have some meat tonight. How much water do we have left?"

"Very little," the water porter said. "The floods spoiled our river, and all of the streams. We could not refill our water skins."

Kendo frowned and asked the hunters, "Has anyone seen any sign of water?"

"No," a hunter said, "not since we climbed out of the stone canyon, and Mora did not like that water."

"Nuro thought he saw a lake," said another hunter, "but when we walked down to it and touched it, we saw that it was made of stone."

Kendo scanned the valleys below them. "If only we could find some water, we could use these rabbits to make enough stew to feed us all."

Mora could still taste the dew from the baby's forehead on her lips. "I think," she said, "that the spirits of our ancestors have provided sacred water for our stew."

Kendo looked around but saw no water.

Mora waved her arms to indicate the white dirt that lay everywhere. "When I put the sacred dirt on the child's forehead, it turned into water."

Kendo looked at his medicine woman, then at the starving tribe, and asked, "Can we use sacred water to cook our food?"

Mora asked, "Can we turn down a sacred gift from the spirits?"

Other hunters returned with news of shelter in some boulders nearby where the tribe could set up camp for the night. The mood was much lighter during this hike. Others found it challenging to walk on the white ground, but no amount of slipping or falling would ever erase the image of Kendo landing so masterfully on his butt.

The men searched the cave for signs of wild animals while the women started a fire and began preparations for a feast of the rabbit meat. Yona made new slings from the rabbit skins, and a soft white cap for Ragna's baby. The tribe was finally ready to sing songs of conquest and survival when Brahg thought he heard something outside the cave.

He grabbed a large stick and blocked the entrance to the tribe. It was dark outside, and the moon had yet to rise. "Zho!" he half yelled, "bring a fire stick. Brahg heard something outside!"

Zho came up behind Brahg, holding a long stick from the fire. "What did Brahg hear?"

"Brahg does not know. It is too dark to see clearly."

Zho waved the fire in front of them. The flickering flame cast eerie dancing shadows, bringing the whole ground to life.

Brahg took a small step out of the cave and said, "Who is there?"

They both cocked their heads to hear an answer, but hearing none, Zho suggested, "Perhaps Brahg should ask it in bear talk."

"Bear talk?"

"Sure," Zho said, "Hoorahrah! Hoorahrah!"

Hearing no response, Zho said, "Now Brahg should try it."

Brahg cleared his throat and growled, "Hoorahrah! Hoo..."

He stopped when he heard Zho laughing at his side. "Ahhh," he said, "Zho teases Brahg."

Then they heard more laughter from outside the cave. Brahg brought his stick to the ready, and Zho stepped to the side and held out the fire for a better look.

Brahg growled, "Who is there?"

This time they were answered by the bleating of a goat. Brahg stepped forward and raised his stick. "Who approaches?"

"Easy, Brahg," said the voice from outside. "It is Joog, son of Kendo, and Troon, and three very lost little goats."

"Joog!" Brahg exclaimed. "You are alive! And you found us!"

"It is good," Joog said, "that Brahg leaves such a wide trail for us to follow."

Tears fell from Kendo's eyes as he welcomed Joog and Troon. This was surely an omen. The tribe entered into their ancestor's lands and now they had Troon, who knew the most of their ancestors, and Joog. Together, Joog and Troon were the future and past of the tribe, and now, with Troon's memories, the tribe's past would also be their future.

Kendo escorted Joog and Troon to the center of the celebration, where they could be warmed while telling their tales. Everyone ate stew and shared stories long into the night. Tomorrow would be a new day like no other!

Chapter Two

The Giant Goat

Of all the feasts held since the dawn of time, last night's feast would certainly be remembered as the tamest. There were no spirits to feed the men's courage and exaggerate their claims. The songs that were sung lacked the gusto of more memorable feasts. It was a somber memorial rather than an exuberant celebration. The tribe's gratitude for those that survived could not overcome the immense loss of those who perished, but it was a feast, and the people put their best faces on. The night would still be remembered for the retelling of the many sobering acts of heroism. Thanks were paid for the many lives saved that day, and prayers were said for all the souls who were lost. The night ended young, with the sound of an exhausted tribe sleeping deeply after a trying day.

A mild breeze whistled through the mouth of the small cave and stirred Kendo and Mora. They cracked their eyes open just enough to see the pale light of the moon reflected off the snow and into the cave. The remains of the fire in the center of the cave flickered against the walls as a few dying embers glowed red hot in the breeze and flamed up, then popped and sputtered back to an ash-covered glow.

Mora smiled and whispered, "Mother Earth sleeps with us."

"Yes," Kendo said, "and she snores with us, too."

They closed their eyes and slept with the warmth of the Earth's love, even while the ground was still hard and frozen below them.

Kendo woke with the sunrise. Seeing him sit up, one of the mothers started waking her children, but Kendo shook his head and said, "Let them sleep a little longer."

He got up and went out to see their camp in the daylight. Zho was already up and making a new spear. The ground outside was as brilliant white as Kendo remembered from the day before.

He crouched down and felt the white powder with his hands and said, "This is a very different place from the home where we grew up."

Zho looked up from the spear he was sharpening and asked, "Does Kendo think this is the home of our ancestors, or is it the place where their spirits go after death?"

Kendo stood up and brushed the cold white crystals from his furs. He stared at the water forming on his hands and said, "Perhaps Mora will know, but Kendo thinks there is too much magic here for this not to be the home of the spirits."

A small chunk of ice fell from a tree and landed squarely on Zho's great black mane. He ran his hands through his hair, and they too came out covered with water. "Zho hopes the spirits do not object to our presence."

Kendo walked a few paces to the clearing in front of the cave and scanned their new world, starting at the cliffs that brought them here and ending in the mountain peaks where he believed they were headed. "The people can stay here a day," he said, "but no more. We can drink the sacred water that the spirits have provided for us, but we must scout for a river where we can build our new home. Kendo thinks it is still further up over the next mountain top. We still have far to go and it would be good if Zho could find meat for the journey while Kendo scouts ahead."

Zho thumped the new spear against his chest. The slender rod easily flexed as it slapped against his ribs, then sprang back to its original shape. He held the spear up to his eye and stared down the length of its shaft, saying, "Zho will take two men and hunt for meat. Perhaps we will even find a river with fish."

Joog exited the cave and followed his father's gaze up the mountain. "The home of our ancestors is still far," he said. "Joog will climb half a day and scout ahead while Kendo rests with the people." Kendo started to argue but Joog said, "One day Joog will lead the people. Today is a good day to test Joog's skills on the mountain."

Kendo smiled and said, "Joog needs no such tests, but Joog may practice leading and take Marl with Joog. Marl is young and strong and too full of energy to spend the day cooped up here."

Joog nodded and said, "Many thanks, Father. We will return for supper."

Zho selected Brack and Koro to join him on the hunt. They were each good with slings and they were pleasant to travel with. The sky was regaining some of its blue tint as the sun peeked over the east, but the land surrounding the mouth of the cave was still in shadow. The cave they spent the night in was nestled at the base of a mountain, which now stood between them and the rising sun. To the north were the mountains Joog planned to scout. The valley to the west was their best chance of finding a river where Zho hoped he might find a chance to try his new fishing spear.

The hunters had often debated whether it was best to be facing the sun or to have it at your back. Zho would have preferred to face the sun. He believed that the shadows they cast made it easy for small game to spot their movement when looking into the sun, but he admitted that it was far easier for them to aim their slings if they weren't blinded by a morning sun that was low on the horizon.

They crossed a narrow meadow that lay directly outside the cave. The meadow was blanketed with a deep layer of snow, something for which they had no name and only knew as the sacred dirt. Their feet sank nearly to their knees as they crossed the meadow and occasionally up to their thighs. It was cold and wet, and though they had trained themselves to withstand the elements, this was even colder than the spring rivers they would stand in when catching salmon.

Just beyond the meadows was a stand of trees that extended clear up the next rise to the mountain. The trees were not good for their slings, but they were a good place to find game. The snow gathered in thick layers on the trees' branches, sometimes drooping the branches down under the weight, but the snow was only shin deep on the forest floor beneath these trees. A gradual slope led down ahead of them. Zho knew this was a good sign and might lead to a stream.

He concentrated on the sounds of the forest, listening for rushing water when Brack dropped down low and swung his sling around his head. Three swings and he let out a mighty hurl, but the stone brushed against a limb and went off target, cracking thunderously into a thick tree trunk.

"Rabbit?" Zho asked.

"No," Brack said, "squirrel."

Koro slapped Brack on the back and said, "Bad luck. Let us hope the squirrels in this strange land are not vicious beasts wishing vengeance upon us. Especially if we haven't proper room to use our slings."

"Shhh," Zho said as he pointed to the limbs of the tree Brack had hit. The squirrel had ventured out onto the limb and was watching them.

Koro snickered and whispered, "Koro thinks the squirrel is laughing at Brack."

Brack dropped down again, and this time choked up a little on his straps before he swung his sling. One... two... three swings and he let loose. The stone flew cleanly past the squirrel, slapping against twigs and landing with a dunk and a splash.

Koro said, "The squirrel still laughs at Brack."

Zho slapped Brack on the back and said, "Well done."

Koro laughed heartily now. "See? We all are laughing now."

"Aaaay," Zho said while poking Koro's arm, "Does Koro not pay attention?"

Koro was puzzled.

"Did Koro not hear what Zho heard?"

Koro shrugged and looked at Brack, who was equally confused.

Zho waved them off as he would children and stepped ahead, leaving them behind as he said, "Brack found water. Zho heard Brack's stone splash."

"But Koro hears no river."

Zho led them through the trees and onto the bank of a large pond with a great beaver mound in the center. Now that they were clear of the trees, they could hear rushing water on the far side of the pond.

Brack and Koro immediately started circling around the beaver home. It had been a long time since the tribe had had beaver. Brack especially liked their moist tails. While they circled the beaver mound, Zho followed the opposite shore around to the stream. It was a fast-moving stream, heavy with water and crystal clear.

When he reached the beaver's dam, he crossed the mouth of the pond to get upriver. He pulled his spear free from the straps that tied it to his back and approached the edge of the stream. He saw large boulders deep under the surface of the rushing water. They pinched and twisted the water into swirling eddies. Those boulders were perfect places for fish to rest from the current, but they were far too deep for him to reach with his spear.

He walked up the river past the rocky section to a bend where the stream widened and he knew he could find some calm, shallow water on the outside of the bend. He stood as still as stone and stared into the water. Only his eyes and the pulse points in his temples and neck moved. If there were fish, they would show themselves, and they did, but they were only fry, about half a finger long.

Brack and Koro saw his stance and kept their distance until their patience wore thin.

"If Zho sees nothing by now," Koro said, "then there is nothing to see."

"This is good water," Zho said. "The fish are here. Zho sees the hatchlings."

They followed the river further up the mountain and stopped when Koro crouched down and froze. He scanned the cliffs on the opposite side of the river but said nothing.

Zho crept up closer to him, being sure to keep sling distance away, and whispered, "What does Koro see?"

Koro pointed up to some rocky cliffs and said, "Up there, where the sacred dirt does not cling. Koro saw movement."

Brack and Zho scanned the area, and before Zho could say, "There!" Koro had already swung his sling and loosed a stone. The rock screamed up the cliff and hit the animal squarely on the head with a hollow thunk that reverberated off the cliff and sounded like a woodpecker striking a tree trunk.

"What is it?" Zho asked.

Koro shook his head and said, "Koro does not know what it is, but Koro hit it."

"Yes," Zho said, "Koro hit it, but it is too big. It just stands there and laughs at Koro."

Brack laughed too and said, "Koro's aim is true, but it is so far away that Koro can't hit it with any power."

Zho said, "Zho still wants to know what it is. Did you hear the sound Koro's stone made against its head?"

Brack said, "It looks like a giant goat, except it has that thing on its head."

"Yeah," Koro said, "It reminds Koro of the time when we were little and Joog put the cow skull on Joog's head and asked Koro to hit Joog on the head with a stick."

"Brack remembers. Brack also recalls how Koro wanted to wear the skull when Kendo learned of it and chased after Koro with Kendo's staff."

Zho said, "A giant goat could feed all the people without needing stew to make the meat stretch, but Zho thinks we need a larger weapon."

Koro asked, "Didn't our people used to have slings that could shoot spears? Could those spears take down a giant goat?"

"Yes," Zho said, "they were called bows, but that was a long time ago. We lost our craftsman before you were born and nobody is left who remembers how to make them."

The ram tired of watching the strange two-legged creatures and swiftly scampered up the cliff.

"Did you see that?" Brack asked. "He flew up the mountain like a spirit. Maybe they are sacred giant goats and we shouldn't hunt them."

"If we can drink the sacred water," Zho said, "then the sacred goat can fill our bellies. Let us return and tell Kendo what we saw."

Koro shrugged and asked, "Do we return empty-handed?"

Zho grunted his agreement and said, "We can skirt around the forest trees and back to camp. Perhaps we can find a rabbit slow enough for one of you to hit."

Joog was a natural born climber. As a baby, he climbed over rocks and logs before he could even walk. Racing up the mountain was in his nature. It was something he would have done just because it was there and not out of any duty to the tribe. It was fun to him, and he knew Marl would be the perfect companion for the trek.

Marl was a couple months younger than Joog and he was a good match athletically. They liked to challenge each other by swimming up and down the river. A slight smile stretched across Joog's face as he remembered their most recent race, until he also remembered the great flood that took their homes and did not want to relive his memory of swimming the river, so he turned his attention back to the task ahead of him.

Normally, on a hike like this, they would have packed dried dates, figs, and jerky, but all the village's supplies were at the bottom of the river. Mora's apprentices had collected some berries and nuts. The berries weren't quite in season yet, and the nuts were probably left over from last fall, but they accepted them graciously and started out.

Marl sprinted up a deer track that looked like it might lead them straight up to the mountain peak, but Joog called him back, saying, "Marl! No racing today. Let us conserve our strength for later."

Marl sighed and said, "Joog is right. We can climb at your father's pace today."

Joog couldn't completely resist a little smile, but stopped himself and said, "This is serious. Today we climb as men and leave the boys behind with the women."

Marl scratched his head and said, "Marl would rather let the boys climb the mountain while we be the men with the women."

Joog threw a nut at him and asked, "Does Marl ever stop clowning?"

Marl made a funny face, performed a cartwheel, and said, "Never."

Joog pointed over to a stand of trees that followed along the track. "Joog is going over there to look for a walking stick in those trees."

"Marl is going, too. Marl has never seen a stick walk."

Joog shook his head and sighed. "Joog thinks it will be a very long day and wonders why Joog brought Marl along."

Marl was serious for a moment and said, "Joog brought Marl because Joog knows that if danger finds us, Joog can rely upon Marl to be there at Joog's side instead of running home to Marl's mother."

"Just so long as Marl is there to help and does not laugh if Joog falls."

"Like Joog's father!" Marl laughed deep from his belly.

"That's not funny!" Joog objected.

"Oh, that's right!" Marl exclaimed. "Joog was not with us! Joog did not see it. When we climbed out of the canyon the very first time, Joog's father was the first to walk on the white dirt, and Kendo slipped and landed on Kendo's backside! Twice! Everybody laughed; even Kendo laughed."

Joog let a chuckle slip out and said, "Joog would have liked to be there for that."

They entered the stand of trees and found a pair of fallen branches. The twigs were brittle enough to come off easily, but the branches had large deposits of sap on the bark. Joog attempted to clean his stick off by rolling it around in the snow, but Marl took his and whacked it against some large rocks jutting out of the hill. He thoroughly knocked the snow off the outcrop of rocks, but did little to remove the sap.

"Joog! Come see what Marl has found."

Joog's branch was still tacky, but it was no longer gooey. He picked up his stick and marched the few paces to Marl. The rocks that Marl had exposed were dark grey with sharp edges.

"Marl has found slate! This is good."

Joog felt around the slate for a loose piece. He pulled off a piece a little larger than his hand. He looked for another good piece and picked at it with the slate he held until he broke off another piece. Marl had never seen slate before and followed Joog as he carried the stones out into the sun where it was a little warmer. He took one of the stones and chipped at the edge of the other until he made a decent edge. Then he switched the stones in his hands and chipped the other rock until both had edges.

"Here," he said, "now Joog and Marl have decent weapons."

Marl took his slate and scraped the pitch-covered bark off his stick. It was tedious work, but he scraped at it relentlessly, from top to bottom, until he had a pile of bark at his feet and all the clean, white wood was exposed. Then he stood back, breathing heavily, and admired his work.

Joog whistled and said, "Marl is smarter than Marl looks. That is a fine looking walking stick." Joog showed Marl his stick where he had taken his stone and similarly scraped the bark off the area where he planned to hold his stick, leaving the bark on the rest of the stick intact. "Fortunately, Joog is also smarter than Marl looks."

With walking sticks in hand, they set out once again up the deer track. The trail eventually disappeared into a field of rocks that extended out in front of them like a meadow. They stepped carefully through the round rocks, planting their walking sticks securely and watching for loose stones begging to turn their ankles.

Beyond the field of stones, the trail continued, but remained rocky. Boulders, much larger than the stones they just traversed, were scattered along the path, which ended abruptly at the base of a cliff. Joog looked for a route going around the cliff, but seeing none, he tied his stick to his sling and climbed straight up.

Their pace slowed. The climb took its toll, but it wasn't just their strength that was tested. Their breathing also became more labored, and they paused more frequently to catch their breath. Their ascent up the cliff was mercifully short, and the trail continued atop the ridge.

Marl found a large boulder to sit on and said, "Marl does not like this." He took a sip from his waterskin and continued, "We have walked most of the morning, climbing this mountain, and the land becomes more unfamiliar with every step. This land is even stranger than the white meadow below us. There are no trees or flowers any more, and worst of all, Marl thinks the land is cursed. It makes Marl's head spin."

Joog sat down next to him and looked up at the sun. "Joog's head also feels strange, but it is not quite midday yet, and we are almost to the top where we can look down into the next valley."

"Does Joog think the spirits make us feel this way? Do they wish us to turn back?"

"Kendo believes our ancestor's wish us to return to their ancient lands. Joog trusts Kendo's vision, but perhaps the spirits wish to warn us about what lies ahead."

Marl passed the water skin to Joog, who took a few sips. They remained on the boulders while they caught their breaths, then, with a shrug of their shoulders, continued on up the mountain.

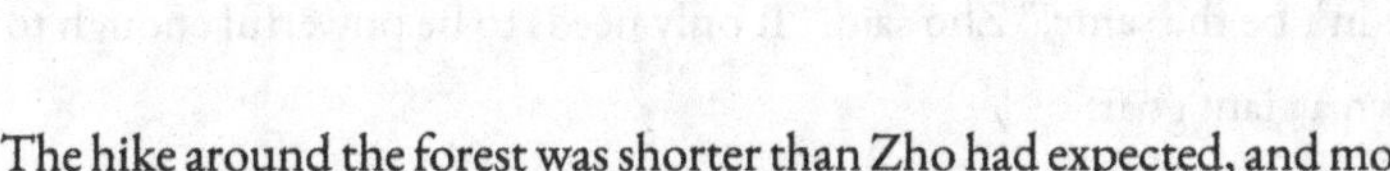

The hike around the forest was shorter than Zho had expected, and more barren than he had hoped it would be. They came across no game since they had sighted the giant goat. Zho's disappointment was short-lived as they arrived in camp and found Troon skinning two rabbits and a pheasant.

"Troon!" Zho shouted. "How does Troon succeed when Zho fails?"

Troon pretended to look hurt and asked, "Does Zho believe Troon is one of the women now? Has Troon not taught Zho better than that?"

Zho laughed and fell to his knees, bowing low to the ground before Troon. "Troon is always the master, but Zho thought Troon's legs were too slow to catch rabbits."

"Troon's body may have lost a step, but not so his mind. These were caught the old way, with traps. Troon thinks these rabbits have never seen traps in their lifetime."

Zho slapped Troon on the back and sat down next to him. The old man beamed with pride, knowing the whole tribe could see the contribution he made. Zho was equally proud of his old master and couldn't hide the pleasure from his face.

"Troon, my master, Zho needs your mind once again. Zho saw a giant goat today. It was large and wore a helmet on its head. Koro hit it with a stone, but it only laughed at him and flew up the cliff like a spirit. It was very fast. Zho thinks we need one of the old weapons to hunt it. Zho remembers Troon was one of the last hunters to use the bow."

"The bow?" Troon asked. "Yes. It is a very fine weapon. Troon kept Troon's bow long after the crafters were killed. It was still on Troon's wall when the floods came. Does Zho think we should send someone to go find it?"

Zho thought about it. He saw the twinkle in the old man's eyes and had no doubt he missed his bow. "No, but Zho wonders if Troon could describe it to our builders so they could learn to craft one just like it."

"There will never be another bow exactly like Troon's."

"It needn't be the same," Zho said. "It only needs to be powerful enough to bring down a giant goat."

Troon shrugged his shoulders but nodded his head. "Perhaps, but Troon thinks the bows are not easy to make, and our builders may find it difficult, but Troon will try to describe it for them."

"Excellent!" Zho said. "If Kendo agrees, Zho thinks Troon should talk to the builders immediately."

"Very well," Troon said as he stood and handed the rabbits to Zho, "let Zho finish these and Troon will talk to the builders."

"But," Zho said, "Kendo..."

Kendo had been standing behind Zho and had seen the spark in Troon's eyes. He put one hand on Zho's shoulder and said, "Kendo approves. Don't forget the pheasant."

Joog and Marl were still short of breath as they climbed, but they had already seen the mountain peak from the spot where they had rested and were too close now to waste any more time resting. The last leg of their climb was rocky, with a few pockets of snow and ice caught in the shadowy interior of piled jumbles of boulders. The air seemed to get cooler as they climbed, but the sun was warm and plentiful. This section of the mountain had little to shade it and soaked up the sun's warmth, radiating it back to complement the chilled breeze.

The distance for this last part of the trek was not great, but they each had to dig deep to find the strength to complete the journey. Both boys reached the top and bent over at the waist, sucking in as much air as they could. Joog stood tall and tried stretching his belly to pull in more air, only to bend back over until his breathing eventually eased on its own.

Marl was the first to recover. He stood and marveled over the land beyond the mountain. "Wow," he said, "has Joog ever seen a more beautiful view?"

Joog pulled himself upright again and joined him. They stood at the top of the peak on a small plateau, large enough for no more than two huts across the narrow way and four along the long axis. One end had a ridge that extended down a small valley, then back up to a neighboring peak.

"No," Joog said, "Joog has never seen anything to rival this." He stood in one spot and turned all the way around. He could see down all sides of the mountain from here. It was truly the very top of the mountain and felt more like he was on top of the world.

Marl pointed down the other side of the mountain to a lake. The emerald green water was nestled between three mountain peaks. Its sandy brown shores were barren of trees and vegetation.

Joog shielded his eyes from the sun and pointed to the West. Marl followed his finger and saw a huge lake between a large and a small mountain. The dark blue waters were surrounded with a thick green forest.

Marl took a sip of water and said, "That looks perfect. Marl thinks the fish will be as big as Joog's leg."

Joog looked behind to the valley they had come from. From this vantage, he could see a pass to the North that would take the people to the large lake without climbing the whole mountain. He pointed below them and said, "Look there. If we guide the people over to that passage, Joog thinks we can pass below that cliff on the other side of the valley to reach the lake."

Marl didn't respond. Joog kept his eyes on the path while he nudged Marl with his elbow. Marl pointed below them and asked, "What do you see there?"

Joog looked and saw the large carcass Marl was pointing at. Two eagles sat atop the dead animal and pecked at its flesh.

"That is a very big catch," Joog said.

"Yes," Marl replied, "far too big for two birds, even two very large birds."

Joog didn't hesitate, but climbed over the edge and walked briskly down the mountain towards the dead beast.

Marl followed and said, "Marl hopes Joog is not planning to take some of that meat back to the tribe."

"Joog just wants a better look. If we are scouting a new home for the people, then it would be good to know there is game to eat here."

"Does Joog forget that something killed it?"

"Of course, Joog can see that something killed it."

"Marl means that something big enough to kill that large beast hunts this mountain that Joog and Marl now carelessly descend."

Joog took his meaning and measured his stride. "Joog only needs to get close enough to see better."

"That's what Marl thought Joog meant."

Wull rocked his daughter in his arms while he shook his head and said, "No, Wull makes houses and boats mostly, never weapons. The hunters make their own weapons."

"But," Troon said, "Wull works with wood. Wull knows more about shaping wood than anyone in the tribe. The huts Wull makes have long wooden poles bent to shape the dome. The boats have wood that is bent round to make the hull. The hunters don't know how to make this weapon. It's made of bent wood like Wull uses to make the boats."

Kendo and Troon both looked at Wull expectantly. He continued to soothe his daughter and shake his sad face while he said, "Wull cannot."

Troon bowed his head and slunk past Kendo.

"Perhaps there is another way?" Kendo asked. "Does Troon recall any other weapons the hunters can use to bring down the giant goat? Can Troon make a large trap?"

Troon's eyes were sad. He thought he could help his people and make himself feel useful at the same time. He looked up at the taller Kendo and said, "No, not if the beast is as fast as Zho says. There are stories of great hunts, with many men and large spears taking down far larger game than Zho's goat, but they were slow, lumbering beasts. The bow is the only weapon Troon knows that can feed the people with this large goat."

Wull's daughter was all he had left after the flood. She was barely old enough to talk, and he clung to her as much as she did to him.

Kendo turned back to Wull and asked, "Can Wull teach Zho how to bend the wood?"

Wull just wanted to find a bed and hide under the covers. His life was over, but his daughter reached up and squeezed his nose. She didn't care that she was hungry, only that she could tell how sad her daddy was. He pulled her close and buried his face in the crook of her neck, then turned to Kendo with tears in his eyes and said, "Wull will build your weapon, even though Wull does not know how it is made."

Kendo wrapped his arms around Wull with the little girl between them and said, "Do not worry about failure. It is understood that the first attempts may not work. Wull can learn from the mistakes and make the next ones better."

Zho gathered the hunters into a circle and showed them the spear he made. "This spear is for catching fish. It is light and flexible. It is thin enough to pierce both the water and the fish, but it would be useless against the giant goat we saw. Zho will work with Troon and Wull to try to learn how to make the bows that our fathers' fathers used, but Zho believes we should still make larger and more sturdy spears to use until the bow is ready."

Brahg wandered over and joined the hunters. Brahg was not one of the hunters, and Zho asked, "Does Brahg need something?"

"Brahg wishes to help. Brahg thinks a giant spear will easily take down a giant goat and only Brahg can throw a giant spear."

Koro said, "Brahg is too big to hide behind a tree."

Brahg replied, "Koro is too skinny to throw a big spear."

"Zho would like to see Brahg throw a large spear, but first Brahg will need to make one. You have all seen my fishing spear. Go now and gather long straight wood for each of your spears."

As they were leaving for the forest, Koro said, "Brahg may need a whole tree instead of just a sapling for Brahg's spear."

Long straight wood was hard to come by naturally and the tribe had lost all their tools. The hunters scoured the forest, looking for young trees that pushed up straight and tall, searching for sunshine in the shade of the elder trees that surrounded them. Such saplings, whose trunks were straight and tall, might make decent spears. Brahg needed a slightly older tree for his spear and soon learned that cutting it down would be more of a challenge than his friends faced.

The other hunters were experienced in making flint points for their spears. Brahg had watched them many times and thought he could do it, but when he tried making an edge from two stones, he mostly bashed his fingers, but did eventually manage to get an edge on a piece of quartz.

He took the quartz and cut a circle around the tree and through the bark. He tried slamming the edge into the tree, which was effective, but hurt his hand. He picked up a large round stone and considered slamming it into the quartz while he held the edge to the tree, but decided that the fingers holding the quartz would not survive. The edge was long enough that he could saw the stone back and forth against the wood and eventually work his way into the trunk.

Brahg's tree was three fingers across and the wood was more mature. It took him longer to cut down his tree than the other hunters did with their two-finger trees. By the time he returned to the circle with his tree, the other hunters had already removed all the branches and bark. Zho welcomed him back and showed him what he had missed. With the branches removed, Brahg's tree was a full nine feet long and towered over the other hunter's five foot spears. He used his quartz to scrape off the bark and the knobs where the branches were removed until it was smooth and comfortable in his hand.

Zho lifted Brahg's spear. It felt twice as heavy as the other spears, but it was straight and had a nice balance. He marked the balance point with some coal and said, "This is where Brahg will wrap the leather bindings to make a handle. It is a good spear, but it is too heavy for Zho. We will see if Brahg can throw it."

Brahg had no doubts.

Joog and Marl descended the mountain until they were close enough to smell the rotting flesh. It was still far below them, separated by a sheer cliff. It was a large, hairy beast with a giant stone skull. Joog had never seen such an animal.

He reached down and felt the heft of his sling, knowing he could never bring down such a great beast with a simple stone. Marl was correct when he had said that something even larger killed it, and Joog could see pairs of puncture marks on the hind legs and long slashes that ripped out the poor animal's throat. It was killed by a very large, and very adept, killer.

"Come," Marl said, "Marl has seen enough. Marl saw enough from the mountaintop. This is too close already."

"Wait," Joog said, "if there is a large predator in our new homeland, we must learn more. What could kill such a large animal?"

"Marl has heard stories of bears growing so large."

Joog leaned out on the ledge to see better and asked, "What bear would leave its meal behind like this?"

"An angry bear that does not kill from hunger."

"Look!" Joog said, "those are not bear tracks."

"Marl sees no tracks."

"Joog thinks Marl stands too far away to see the tracks."

"Marl thinks Joog is too close to the edge. Such a huge bear can not be killed by Marl alone if something happens to Joog."

"Not alone," Joog said, "but if Joog and Marl work together, they could kill such a bear."

"Maybe," Marl admitted, "but only with a great amount of good fortune. Marl is not feeling very fortunate right now."

"Is Marl afraid?"

"Marl fears many things. Right now, Marl fears that Joog will fall over the edge and land in the lap of a very angry bear. Marl fears the bear is too large for Marl to save Joog."

"Marl sounds like a silly girl."

"Maybe so, but if Joog falls, this silly girl cannot save Joog."

"Fine," Joog said, "if Joog falls, then Marl will return for help from the hunters, but Joog will not fall. The ground is solid here." Joog took his walking stick and hammered it against the ground, and it gave way. The ledge fell from under Joog and he slid down the cliff into an open crevice which divided the cliff in half.

Joog screamed as he fell. It was neither a manly nor a girly scream. It was the primal scream of one's soul that is tumbling out of control.

Marl heard Joog's scream and was terrified. His terror grew as Joog's screams were drowned out by a sickening, high-pitched scream. It was a cross between a loud whine and a growl and it hit Marl in the pit of the stomach, bringing shudders to his whole body. He wanted to call out Joog's name, but he feared the unknown monster that he had just heard. He could not leave his friend like this, in spite of what Joog had told him to do.

He crawled on all fours to the new ledge left behind by his fallen brother. He spread his arms and legs to distribute his weight and slid his head over the edge to see down. He could see the crevice where Joog had fallen, but he could not see his brother. He saw something, though. It was long and thin and it slithered like a snake, but it was not a snake. It whipped around in the air and was attached to something hidden from him. Something was inside the crevice with Joog.

Chapter Three

A New Threat

Marl peered nervously over the edge of the cliff. It was brittle and crumbled beneath his hands where the previous edge had already collapsed under his friend Joog and carried him to the bottom of a crevice that divided the wall. He heard something in the crevice with Joog and saw the tip of something that looked like a snake flick out of the crack in and out of his view. Whatever was in there with Joog had a hideous high pitched shrieking cry that made Marl's skin prickle.

Marl pulled some stones out of the ground and tossed them down the cliff, away from the face of the crevice. The snake creature disappeared, but nothing emerged. He tossed another stone, hoping to lure the beast away from Joog, but nothing came out.

Marl whispered, "Joog? Can Joog here Marl?" Marl slapped himself on the head. Of course, Joog cannot hear Marl when he whispers like a little girl. "Joog?" he called out stronger. "Joog? Can Joog hear Marl?"

Joog did indeed hear him, but he dared not respond. The beast paced back and forth across the narrow crevice which stood between Joog and the beast. The opening between Joog and the beast was too narrow for the animal to pass. Joog was buried under rubble with only his foot exposed. The beast stopped occasionally to examine Joog's foot,1 which was wedged in the base of the crack. Joog could feel the beast's breath on his leg as it tried figuring a way to reach it.

He wondered why Marl was still here and not running back for help, but he was afraid to ask him.

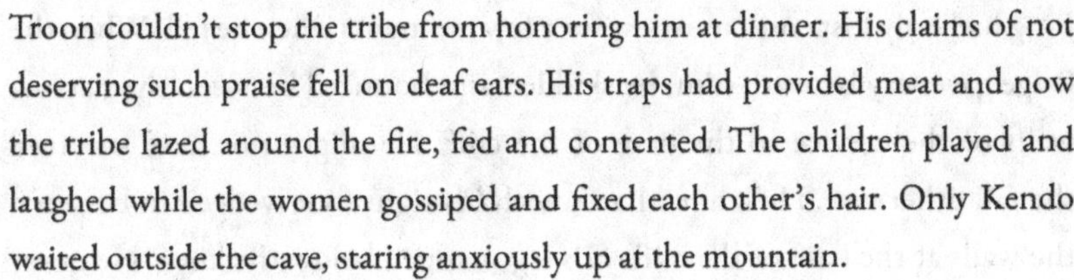

Troon couldn't stop the tribe from honoring him at dinner. His claims of not deserving such praise fell on deaf ears. His traps had provided meat and now the tribe lazed around the fire, fed and contented. The children played and laughed while the women gossiped and fixed each other's hair. Only Kendo waited outside the cave, staring anxiously up at the mountain.

The sun dipped below the western mountains and already the temperature had cooled slightly below comfortable. The slight breeze, which had been a saving lick of coolness during the afternoon, was now a biting sting of cold threatening to numb the toes and fingers.

Zho exited the cave after telling the story of the giant goat for the hundredth time and saw the concern in Kendo's eyes. "Joog's a fine young man and very smart. Zho is certain that Joog is fine. Joog will show up any moment now and we will laugh about worrying so much."

Kendo grunted and said, "Zho is correct when he says Joog is smart. Joog knows when it is time to turn around and return. Joog and Marl are both good trackers. They would not get lost. They should have returned long ago. Something must have happened to prevent their return."

Zho stood alongside Kendo and peered up at the mountain. "Perhaps," Kendo said, "Marl happened. That boy has limitless energy and is absolutely without fear."

"If, as Kendo fears, Marl has gotten them in some trouble, they may wait now for us to come rescue them."

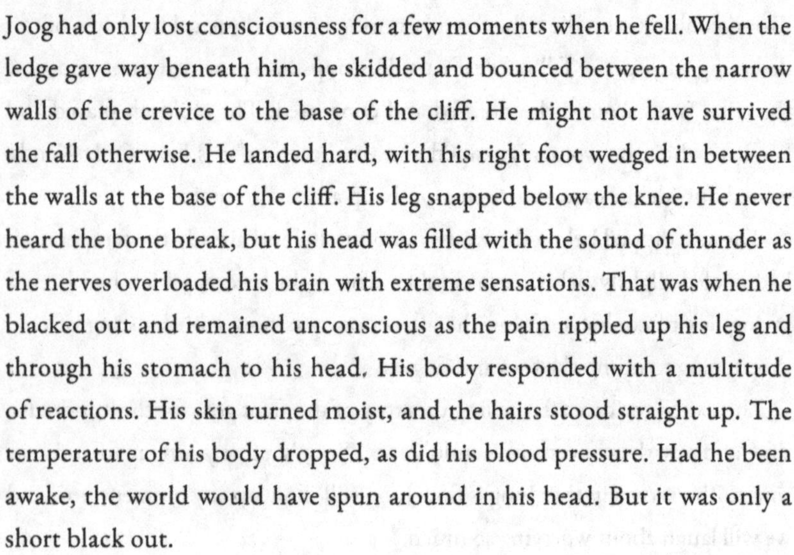

Joog had only lost consciousness for a few moments when he fell. When the ledge gave way beneath him, he skidded and bounced between the narrow walls of the crevice to the base of the cliff. He might not have survived the fall otherwise. He landed hard, with his right foot wedged in between the walls at the base of the cliff. His leg snapped below the knee. He never heard the bone break, but his head was filled with the sound of thunder as the nerves overloaded his brain with extreme sensations. That was when he blacked out and remained unconscious as the pain rippled up his leg and through his stomach to his head. His body responded with a multitude of reactions. His skin turned moist, and the hairs stood straight up. The temperature of his body dropped, as did his blood pressure. Had he been awake, the world would have spun around in his head. But it was only a short black out.

He opened his eyes and looked up into the long crevice. The crevice extended all the way up to the sky or he might not have seen anything. Dust and pebbles still fell down the crevice and covered him with debris. The thunder rolling in his head was joined now by the loud thumping of his heart. Then the pain set in. He felt a warmth at first. It started in his leg and rolled up into his abdomen. His skin was still icy cold, but inside he was burning. Then the real pain rose up in his leg. He was thankful that the pain in his leg didn't follow the warmth up to wrack his whole body.

He tried pulling his hurt leg up to his chest, but it was stuck where it was. He stared up the crevice at the small bit of sky and tried thinking of a way out of this mess, but something hit his foot. He couldn't retract the foot. It was lodged in with the rocks. Something hit it again. His foot felt strangely numb, but each strike brought excruciating pain to his leg. He tried sitting up but could only barely raise his shoulders. A large stone was atop his leg, pinning him down and blocking his view of his foot.

The thunder in his head dissipated enough so he could hear the beast. He heard a low drawn out growl, at first that pitched up into a high whine followed by another swipe at his foot. He wasn't alone. Something was playing with his foot, only he didn't believe it was a game.

As his head cleared, he remembered that he really wasn't alone. He was with Marl, but where was Marl? Joog closed his eyes and grimaced as he remembered telling Marl to go back to camp for help if anything happened to him. He was alone, after all. Another swipe at his foot reminded him that he wasn't alone.

The beast on the other side of the rock was not playing with him. The crevice was too narrow to fit its head or it would have dined on the ugly foot. It tried pulling the foot out of the rubble, but its fore legs were too short and stubby to reach the foot well enough to dig its claws in.

Brahg joined Kendo and Zho outside the cave and announced, "Brahg is ready, as is Brahg's spear."

Zho looked at the large man and wished he had time to train him on the many facets of hunting and the outdoors in general, but he could not escape the truth that if Joog was in trouble of any kind, Brahg's strength would certainly be an asset. Zho put his hand on Brahg's shoulder and said, "Brahg is a good man with a stout heart and is welcome to join us."

Brahg looked to the West. The sun was nearly behind the mountains. "It will be dark soon. We should not delay."

"True," Zho said, "It will be dark, but we cannot track well in the dark. Even walking in unfamiliar land is not safe after dark."

Mora joined the men and said, "Mora heard what Zho said, but the moon will be up soon enough, and it is nearly full tonight. You should have light enough to walk."

"Kendo agrees. Plus, this white soil is very easy to see at night. Kendo also recalls some of the hunters did not like their spears today. Perhaps they would make better torches."

"Perhaps," Mora said, "but I have no spirits to soak the rushes for a torch."

"Then should the moon ever fail us, Brahg will find branches in the woods and we will burn bare sticks to light the way."

More than ever, Zho was glad to have Brahg along.

Marl picked up his walking stick and held it in both hands. He would use it as a club should that beast find him before he finds it. He walked down the ledge away from the crevice and climbed over the side. The sun was almost gone, but the sky was still light. The moon had yet to illuminate the side of the cliff, leaving the valley deep in the shadows and already darkened. He knew it was too dark to safely scale the cliff, but the safer route around the cliff and down to the valley was too far away and would take too long. He couldn't see and climbed down, using his sense of touch instead of sight. His eyes adjusted the best they could to the darkness, but he felt like he imagined half of what he thought he saw. It was a very treacherous climb, and he had to move slowly to keep from falling to the bottom. He wondered if it might have been quicker to take the long path around after all.

He also wanted to be silent and crept down the side of the canyon wall. There was little vegetation waiting at the bottom for him, but across from the base of the cliff, there was a stand of trees. The beast cried out again and his heart raced. It was taking too long. He skipped down the side of the cliff, thinking little of his own safety, but he needed to reach Joog before the beast finished him.

Once he reached the floor of the valley, he crossed into the trees and hid behind them while searching the darkness for the crevice Joog had fallen into.

He was so focused on finding his friend that he didn't sense the eyes watching him from the trees above.

Yona had already sewn new bags from the rabbit skins Troon had trapped. Mora told her what the men would be doing, so she collected some leftover meat to fill the new bags and added some berries she had found near the cave.

It was far less than the men should have taken for an expedition like this, especially being a rescue mission, but it was all the tribe had. Yona gave the rations to Zho and started to say something, but stopped abruptly and turned and ran away.

"Yona!" Zho called to her.

She stopped and turned to face Zho, but her face was to the floor.

Zho lifted the bag and said, "Thank you. Do not fear. Marl is strong. Zho will find him for you and bring him home."

Yona blushed. She had no idea her feelings were so easy to read, but Zho knew what she was thinking. Even Marl didn't know how she felt or that she even existed. She nodded quickly, then turned and ran away again.

At the base of the cliff, there was a wide flat track which abruptly fell off a few feet before it gently led down into the valley. Marl hugged the ground and crawled behind the ledge created where the track had fallen off. He left the trees behind and followed the ledge, peering up over the edge when boulders were available to peek around. As he approached the crevice, he could hear something moving inside. It was too dark to see inside, but he heard the animal pacing. He found a stone on the ground and tossed it against the side of the entrance. It hit hard and bounded off the cliff with a resounding crack.

The pacing stopped. Marl thought he could see a large shadowy figure, but it was too dark to be sure. He tossed another stone and heard definite movement and a loud snort.

Joog did not know what had distracted the beast, but he heard it leave to the entrance. He tried pulling his leg loose, but the large boulder on his thigh kept him pinned in place. He tried sitting up to grip the boulder, but he couldn't exert enough leverage on his pinned leg.

He couldn't pull his foot loose, and he couldn't reach the boulder. He tried pushing and managed to slide his leg further under the boulder, but he still couldn't grip it. He pushed again and felt that he was getting closer, but the beast returned. Now the beast could reach Joog, and this time swiped his paw and sunk a large claw into Joog's foot.

Joog screamed as the beast pulled his foot. The beast tried pulling him from the rubble, but Joog remained pinned under the boulder with the beast's claw firmly sunk into Joog's limp foot.

Marl heard him scream and jumped up from his hiding place and yelled, "Come out here! Marl is ready for the beast in the cave! Marl dares the beast to come out!"

The beast released Joog's foot and sprang to the entrance.

Joog heard Marl and yelled, "RUN! The beast comes for Marl! Go get help!"

Marl ran back along the ridge to the tree line and hid behind a large trunk, still holding his walking stick as a club. He had no idea what the beast in the cave was, but he could hear its steps behind him when he ran. He heard Joog's scream for him to get help, but he couldn't leave him here to die. He peeked around the base of the tree, but the beast had already retreated back into the crevice.

Marl remained unaware of the other beast which still watched curiously from the limbs above.

***

"It is time," Kendo said. "Kendo will take Brahg, and Zho will take Brack and Koro."

"Wait," Mora said. Even with the full moon, Mora did not want the men going out at night with no torches. She wished she had some fish oil to soak some reeds. Larger mammals are also good sources of lard and oil, but they could not afford to sacrifice one of the goats for this. "If Kendo takes Mora and Tela as far as the trees, we will make your torches in the ancient way, from the bark."

Kendo nodded his agreement. The tree line would not delay them, and it is always better to travel with torches at night. "But," Kendo said, "Kendo does not want Mora traveling alone at night. Wull can escort Mora. Wull may even like to see the kind of wood we have, and Kendo will feel better knowing Mora does not return alone."

Mora called for her apprentices. "Tela will go with Mora to learn a new skill. Mora would like Risa to help Troon as needed, but do not be too obvious."

"But Risa wants to go too!"

"Mora fears that Risa is too small still and may be lost in the white meadow."

Risa pouted but understood.

Tela hugged Risa and whispered, "Maybe Risa can get Troon to tell one of the old stories."

Risa smiled and skipped off to find Troon.

The trees weren't far. The troop quickly crossed the snow-laden meadow. Kendo could see the ache in Mora's bones and knew it was from the cold, but he would not embarrass her by saying so.

Once they were in the woods, Mora swiftly started peeling the thin white bark from the trees. The light below the tree boughs was dim, but the moon was rising already and reflected off the snow.

Wull picked his own trees and felt the suppleness of the branches while Tela watched intently at the way Mora coiled the bark around two twigs as she peeled it off the tree. Tela picked a tree and mimicked Mora's moves. Her bark broke frequently, and she started many new strips, but each strip was longer than the one before it.

When each of them had sufficient bark, Mora showed Tela how to wind it tightly around one of the abandoned spears. When the bark reached the width of a fist, she tied a reed around the strip to keep it in place and slathered it with sap from the tree. Then she started a new row just above it.

Tela found that winding the bark onto the spear was easier than peeling it off the tree. In a short time, the men had two good torches. Kendo and Zho each checked their pouches to be sure they had their flint and lightning stones.

Kendo observed the torches and said, "These are fine torches. Good work ladies."

Zho poked Brack in the arm and said, "Does Brack see that? Brack's stick makes a much better torch than a spear."

Wull selected an assortment of branches that seemed to match the size of Troon's bow. He would build a model that very night and use it to measure how much he could bend this wood.

Marl was certain the beast had returned to Joog, so he climbed up over the ridge and lay flat on the ground while he crawled closer to the crevice. There were few boulders and little else for him to hide behind. This would not be a good place to face the creature alone, but he could not leave Joog there while the beast was inside with him.

He crawled as close as he dare, still clinging to the walking stick. It was dark already. The sky was still lit, but the valley had fallen into the shadow of the mountains. He peered around a large boulder into the dark crevice and called out, "Joog?"

Joog heard him but did not want to rile the beast. He could still hear the beast pace back and forth, stopping only to smell his foot. The beast's hot breath on Joog's foot combined with the chilled air and brought shivers to his chest. The sky darkened overhead until it was pitch black where he lay. Even the beast must find it hard to see.

"Joog?"

Joog wished Marl would go get help as they had planned. If he lures the beast out, they could both be killed. Joog closed his eyes, which seemed pointless in the dark, and prayed to the spirits, "Great spirits, please guide Marl away from here to lead Joog's father and the hunters back to this spot. Do not let Marl die for Joog."

"Joog! Marl is coming in."

"No Marl! Get Kendo!"

Marl heard Joog's voice but could not hear his words over the creature's growl. He did not enter the cave, but remained in his hiding place just outside. Perhaps the beast would leave Joog to hunt. That would be a good sign.

Even in the dim light, Joog's and Marl's tracks were easy for the experienced hunters to pick up. Zho followed the signs and found the place where they peeled the bark from the walking sticks, and Koro found the slate they left behind. The slate was a very good find.

The tribe could use the slate. Kendo called the younger hunters, "Brack! Koro! Return to the tribe and tell them to find this spot in the morning and collect as much slate as they can. Then, after you deliver the message, follow the trail back to us as swiftly as possible."

Kendo didn't have to tell them to stick together. It was nighttime in a strange land, and even in the moonlight, it could be a dangerous place. Nobody should ever travel alone in a strange land. The thought struck a nerve with Kendo. If anything has happened to either Marl or Joog, the other would be alone. He forced the thought from his mind and said, "Let's continue."

Zho led the way from there. The sky was clear, and the moon shone overhead, lighting the landscape. The snow made it especially easy to see the landmarks around them. A spark within them wanted to run to the boy's aid, but they couldn't risk missing a sign on the trail. Zho looked mostly down at the ground nearest them while they walked. He looked for broken twigs in the bushes and patches of dirt with skid marks where someone may have dragged a foot. Patches of snow sometimes showed a trail, but whether the trail was made by the boy's boots or by animals was unclear. The white dirt did not hold foot prints very long.

They paced their climb, both to conserve their strength and to allow Brack and Koro time to regroup with them. The trail led them to the base of a cliff. Zho looked up the cliff. It was steep and ragged, but he saw signs of rocks that had been recently disturbed. "It looks like something has climbed up here. Zho can not say if it was them."

Kendo looked along the base of the cliff. To the right, he saw only more cliff and rugged terrain. To the left, the base of the cliff formed a valley with the neighboring mountain. An owl hooted from the forest to his left. He looked up the cliff once more and asked, "Will Zho be ok here alone if Kendo and Brahg go around?"

Brahg looked up the cliff and asked, "Kendo does not want to climb the cliff? Let Brahg carry Kendo up the cliff."

Kendo smiled and patted Brahg on the back, "No, Zho does not sound sure that the boys climbed the cliff and Kendo wants to cover more ground by splitting up. Besides, Brahg already has to carry that log, that Brahg calls a spear, on his back."

Zho looked up the cliff again and spotted a ledge where he could sit. He pointed up and said, "Zho will climb up to that ledge and wait for Koro and Brack. Kendo is right to split up and search around the bottom of the cliff."

It was a short distance back to the cave. Brack and Koro were young and fast enough to sprint back. Brack stopped when they reached the point where they had emerged from the forest and said, "This is the way we came, but the tribe is over there. We crossed the white meadow into the forest, then came this way and found their trail."

Koro nodded his head and sprinted the direction Brack had pointed. The sooner they reach the cave, the sooner they can head back and catch the party.

When the boys ran into the cave, Pela saw them first and her first thought was for Brahg. Mora knew of her interest in Brahg and when she saw Pela's reaction, she put her hand on the girl's shoulder and calmly asked, "Brack? What has happened? Is Kendo ok?"

Brack was bent at the waist panting, but Koro held his palms up and said, "All are fine. We followed Joog's trail and found a slate deposit. Kendo wanted us to tell someone where to find it."

Troon heard Koro and said, "Excellent. Show Troon where."

Troon was already heading out of the cave when Brack said, "Wait. It will still be there in the morning. Rest now and take some boys at sunrise."

Koro added, "Let the young ones do the work while Troon supervises. Teach them how it is done."

Pela filled a wooden cup with water and took it to Brack, who was still breathing heavily.

"Thank you," Brack said. "Brack wonders if Brahg knows how lucky Brahg is?"

Pela's eyes widened and her cheeks flushed. Does everybody know her mind? Everybody except Brahg? She left the cup with Brack and ran to a dark corner of the cave.

Mora picked up a slender switch that she used as a stylus for drawing in the dirt and whacked Brack on the shoulder. She looked him in the eye and said, "Mora doesn't want Brack to blab what Brahg needs to see with Brahg's own eyes."

Brack winked and said, "Of course not. Koro. Come. Let's go."

Mora followed him to the entrance and said, "Mora means it! Don't tell Brahg!"

Brack turned around and backed out of the cave, saying, "Brack won't spoil anything. A hint only."

"Just a hint," Mora said as Brack and Koro started running back up the trail. "Nothing more!"

The base of the cliff was barren and rocky. Kendo hadn't noticed just how barren the land had become until it descended back into the valley and into the tree line. The steepness of the cliff, which had been nearly vertical, relaxed some but still presented a daunting grade. Kendo followed the curve of the cliff as it dropped back into the forest and then rose again to a ledge with the trees on his left and the cliff rising on his right.

Brahg lumbered behind Kendo. His huge form towered over the elder leader, and the great spear straddled across his back made his size even more impressive. His great size wasn't in his girth, but in his height and in the breadth of his shoulders. His neck and arms were as big around as most men's legs, and he was as strong as he was big. Though he was not as nimble as the smaller men, he wasn't saddled by his size, either. He followed Kendo with his arms slung over his spear, holding it securely on his shoulders.

Kendo pointed along the line separating the cliff from the forest and said, "Look how the forest ends here and rises no further. Kendo sent Joog to scout the land of our ancestors. Joog would not scout for a desolate land of rocks. Joog must have gone this way and followed the forest."

"Perhaps," Brahg said, "but those boys are young and very quick. They may have climbed to the top for a better view. They would not look for our new homeland in the mountain's rocks, but Brahg thinks they might look down on this valley from up high and see best where we might go, like the eagles would see it flying overhead."

Kendo looked upon Brahg with new eyes. There was much more to the man than everyone assumed. He may ask his council again in the future. He smiled broadly and said, "Brahg surprises Kendo sometimes."

***

Zho climbed the cliff to the ledge where he had said he would wait. It had definitely been disturbed recently, but he couldn't tell any more about how the rocks had been dislodged or by whom. If it had been daylight, he might have seen something more, but the moonlight, though relatively bright, was too dim for details. He didn't believe there was anything significant left to learn, so he found a comfortable spot and sat down to wait for Brack and Koro.

The temperature had cooled since the sun had set. A slight breeze pulled off what little warmth he could create and left him chilled. Sitting around idly, thinking about what he might or might not see in the daytime instead of climbing the cliff, didn't help any.

It wasn't far to the cave, and he knew the younger hunters wouldn't dawdle. They would be here soon, but waiting for them made time run slow. An owl hooted in the forest below and a flock of birds lifted up into the sky and undulated over the trees. Kendo and Brahg probably disturbed their peace. At least they were doing something. If those boys don't hurry, Kendo and Brahg will find Joog before he even scales the rest of the cliff.

Joog and Marl should not be out this late. They would have continued finding their way home, unless something had happened to them, or maybe they were just lost. They could have climbed the cliff and reached the top of the mountain only to see something interesting enough to capture their attention instead of returning to the tribe. They may have found another village. Perhaps there are other descendents of the ancestors. Even so, they would have returned to tell the tribe, or at least sent one of them back to tell Kendo, unless the new people wouldn't let them go. They could be captive and he is just sitting here on a ledge doing nothing when they need him to come free them. Where are those boys?

Zho's mind rambled on until he finally heard footsteps approaching the cliff below, followed by Koro's voice saying, "It looks like the trail ends in that mountain."

"That cannot be," Brack said. "They would not make it so difficult for us to follow them."

"They did not," Zho shouted down to them. "It's about time you two showed up."

Brack stopped to catch his breath while Koro yelled back, "We ran all the way!"

Zho grunted and said, "It is good you are both young still. Now you get to climb the cliff with Zho."

Zho turned and started climbing. His hands and legs had grown cold and stiff, which were not good for climbing. Koro nearly caught Zho as he reached the top. The two of them immediately started scanning for signs of Joog and Marl.

"There!" Zho pointed.

Brack joined them as they started up the new trail.

The ridge at the base of the cliff extended far along the massive wall. Kendo and Brahg followed the ridge, looking for signs of Joog and Marl. The ridge continued to define the boundary between the cliff and the forest. Above the ridge there was little growth, but the forest below the ridge quickly fell into the valley where the trees grew thick and strong.

Kendo pointed a few paces below the ridge and said, "Kendo will search the cliff while Brahg looks down there along the edge of the forest. Look for broken twigs and scrapes in the dirt."

Brahg stepped down from the ridge and said, "The soil is softer below the trees. Perhaps Brahg will get lucky and find a footprint."

"Let us hope so," Kendo said.

Brahg bent over at the waist and stared at the ground as he walked. He still carried his spear on his shoulders with his arms lazily wrapped over the top. He kept to the tree line and studied the trees' bark. Many of the trees had thin spindly trunks with the thin white bark used for their torches, while some had a rough thick bark wrapped around massive trunks. He weaved in and out of the trees, looking for anything out of place. He wasn't a hunter and had never been trained for this, but he had often snuck out on his own and secretly followed the hunters to steal their skills.

He came across a large tree where the bark at the base had been disturbed. He circled around it and saw several places where the bark had been scratched. The marks went up the tree like someone had climbed up. "Joog?" he called out. "Is Joog up this tree?"

Kendo heard Brahg and asked, "What does Brahg see?"

"Brahg thinks someone has climbed this tree."

Kendo came for a closer look, but quickly backed away, saying, "Those are claw marks!" Before he could warn Brahg to back away, a large saber cat lept down from the tree and sunk his dagger like fangs into Brahg's shoulder, but his spear prevented the cat from penetrating deep enough for the kill.

The animal outweighed the large man by half of his weight, and Brahg collapsed to the ground under the beast. The cat's fangs were wrapped around the massive spear. It could not sink them deep enough to mortally wound Brahg, but it had a solid grip and was not letting go. It shook its head, trying to both dislodge the spear in its mouth and sink its teeth deeper into its prey.

Brahg was stuck with his face in the dirt. His spear saved his life by obstructing the cat's fangs, but it also prevented Brahg from rolling over to face the beast.

Kendo ran to Brahg yelling and swinging the Staff of Justice. As he reached the pair, Kendo's staff slammed against the great animal, but the cat would not let go and remained focused on Brahg.

A full moon can be a curse to nocturnal predators. They lose their advantage to see in low light, and larger predators that might not be nocturnal by nature can now see them making them the prey. Even their prey can find an advantage in the moonlight, as they can now see their attackers approach.

The snow leopard is a hybrid, hunting in low light like other nocturnal predators, but preferring to hunt at dawn or dusk rather than the darkest parts of the night. The moon can sometimes extend their hunting time by simulating dusk conditions after the sun has set, but tonight, its brightness on the snow made hunting difficult.

Poor hunting conditions did not deter two snow leopards from coming down the mountain and prowling the edge of the forest. The cats were playful when they were not serious. They followed the forest to a snow filled meadow where they rolled around in the snow, making them that much harder to see. The female rolled twice, then went into a crouch. She raised her nose slightly and smelled the air. Seeing his partner's stance, the male also fell into a crouch and crawled on his belly to her side.

She still sniffed the air while he sniffed the ground around her, then he crawled away from her, still sniffing the ground. There was a new scent in the meadow. The two cats followed the scent away from the forest and saw movement in the mountain. She lifted her head again and whiffed the air. His eyes narrowed on the movement. It danced and flickered like ripples on the lake.

He crawled forward two paces and froze in place. She followed. The flicker did not change. He crawled two more paces. Still, the movement was unaware of them. They inched forward patiently until they were just outside the cave. The fire light danced and flickered upon the snow outside the cave. They coiled their muscles, preparing to pounce. Each twitched, ready to leap in an instant. Nothing emerged from the cave and the moment grew too anxious for both of them.

They leaped into the cave where the male fell upon Troon and gripped his jaws around Troon's throat. It was a practiced move where he clamped his jaws and cutoff the prey's air. Troon was alone at the entrance to the cave. The female leaped between Troon and the rest of the tribe while the male dragged him outside the cave to feed first.

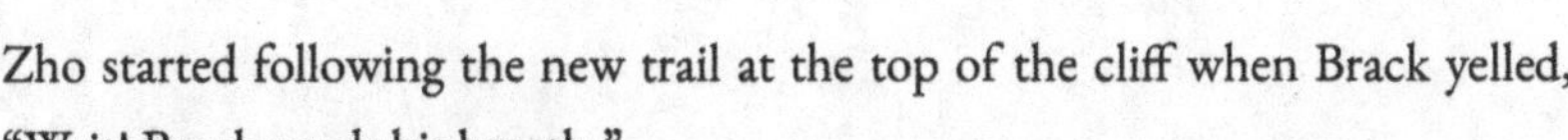

Zho started following the new trail at the top of the cliff when Brack yelled, "Wait! Brack needs his breath."

Koro moved ahead until Zho called him back, "Koro, we can wait. Zho too would like his breath. It is as if the spirits are stealing the air from Zho's chest."

"Koro feels it too, but Koro does not wish to let the spirits have Joog without a fight."

"Aye," Brack said, "Brack's head spins, but Koro is right. Brack will not let the spirits have Joog because they could make Brack sit down like a woman."

"Then we continue," Koro said. "We can move a little slower until Brack's head clears."

"Zho's head would like to stop spinning as well. The spirits are strong here."

The boy's track was easy to follow. It led them up the barren mountain, over rocky ledges and around large piles of boulders. The canyons were all below them and the other mountains grew further away, but they could see sharp ridges that extended like flint edges from one mountain to the other.

As they neared the top, Zho spotted another trail that came down and turned to their left.

"Zho wonders why the boys would not return the same way they came?"

"They must have seen something in that direction," Brack said.

Zho recalled his rambling thoughts while he waited on the cliff for their return and did not want to believe it. "No," he said, "they would not risk it."

"They might," Brack said, "if it were important enough."

Zho still shook his head and said, "No, they would not take chances."

"Perhaps it looked easy," Brack said, "and harmless."

Zho still shook his head until Koro said, "Koro could climb to the top and see what they saw in the time it takes the two of you to debate what you guess may have happened."

Zho laughed and said, "Yes, Koro is correct. Brack and Zho will catch our breaths while Koro goes to see what Joog and Marl saw."

Wull called the two remaining young hunters to grab their spears and form a semi-circle around the leopard. The three of them held their spears well back of the throwing handle, with the points far in front of them. The female held her ground while her mate dragged Troon's body out of the cave.

Flom jabbed his spear at the beast. She bared her teeth and screamed back at him. He took a step forward and tried to stab her, but she was quick and easily batted the spear away with her paw and growled.

"Step back," Wull said. "Flom will only make the beast angrier."

"We should kill it," Flom said, "and save Troon."

"Troon is lost," Wull said sadly, "and if Flom is killed, Vol and Wull will not be enough to protect the women and children."

Flom was angry. He screamed, "Why did we bother making these spears if we are not to use them?"

"Measure the beast," Wull said. "It is almost two of us in weight. It is a predator and has strong hard muscles which our puny spears cannot penetrate."

"Then," Flom said, "what of the bow Troon had Wull make?"

"It is not yet ready. Wull has only made a crude model as a guide. It is not a real bow yet."

Flom couldn't help the tears wetting his eyes. "Can't Wull at least try?"

Wull looked around for another hunter to hold a spear while he tried the bow, but there were none.

Varna saw him looking for help and ran to his work area to grab the bow he had made and some arrows. She returned to Wull's side and notched an arrow.

Wull raised his brows and asked, "How does Varna know to set the arrow?"

"Varna has spent much time listening to Troon's stories. Varna understands how the bow works."

"But Varna is a girl!" Wull said, "Varna cannot use the weapon!"

"Hush!" Mora said. "Do you really believe Troon caught all those rabbits himself? Troon has taught Varna the sling and trap. Mora has no doubt he has also taught her the bow."

Wull just shook his head and shrugged his shoulders.

Varna stepped between Wull and Flom and pulled back on the arrow. "It does not feel right," she said.

"How does Varna know how it should feel?"

"Troon's bow had much more pull. Varna does not believe this is strong enough, but Varna will try." She loosed the arrow, and it jabbed the cat in the ribs but bounced off. The cat leaped straight up in the air and came down on all fours, screaming and spitting.

"Did Wull just hear Varna say she has used Troon's bow?"

Varna notched another arrow and said, "Mora told Wull that Troon taught her to use Troon's weapons. The bow was Troon's favorite weapon."

The cat hissed and swung its paw in the air. Varna let loose another arrow and jabbed it inside the throat. The cat leaped forward and clamped its jaws around the tip of Wull's spear. Flom stabbed at its face, but was unable to penetrate its hide. The cat swiped its paw again and knocked the spear out of Wull's hands.

***

Koro returned from the top of the mountain to find Brack and Zho sitting together, laughing and telling stories. Zho looked up and asked, "Did Koro see anything?"

Koro shook his head and said, "Koro wasted the trip. The moon is bright, but it is not as much light as you may think when you are far away."

Zho rose from his boulder and said, "It wasn't a waste. Zho and Brack are refreshed and ready to continue."

Zho and Brack headed off in the direction of the second set of tracks while Koro was out of wind and fell behind. The trail led them down and around the side of the mountain and eventually joined back up with what looked to be the top of the same cliff they had climbed.

"Look!" Brack said, pointing ahead, "The tracks end there and go over the cliff."

"No," Zho said, "The edge of the cliff has fallen there. That looks like a fresh break. Let's not get too near." Zho pointed to the left of the break and said, "It looks like the cliff broke off from there over to there."

"Oh no," Brack said dejected, "both tracks led to that section and disappear. They have fallen over."

"No!" Koro said behind them. "Look here! Their tracks lead back this way and climb down here."

Zho went to Koro's position and looked at the tracks. "That is only one person," he said. "One of the boys must have fallen when the cliff collapsed."

"Which one?" Brack asked.

Zho shrugged.

Koro followed the tracks over the edge and said, "We can ask the one who made these tracks."

The female snow leopard was furious. She pulled Wull's spear from his reach and coiled to pounce on him.

Varna only had three arrows left, and they weren't very effective. She stepped in front of the defenseless Wull and loosed another arrow which hit the angry cat directly on the nose. Her arrows could not kill the cat, but Varna was sure they must have hurt.

Flom continued jabbing his spear at the cat's face. She ignored most of his jabs, flinching only when he landed a lucky jab on her lips.

Vol had taken to swinging the spear like a switch, swatting the cat like a misbehaving goat.

The cat spun around, swiping her paws in large circles. Her paws were spread wide, easily displaying the sharp claws she possessed.

Varna loosed another arrow that landed near an eye. The cat blinked and turned its face away a moment before coiling again, this time focused on Varna.

Mora joined the four of them, waving a log from the fire. "Give Wull that," Wull growled, "And back away. We can't risk Mora."

Wull took the fire and stepped between Varna and the cat, waving the flame in the cat's face.

The leopard didn't care. Her anger consumed her. She coiled again and was ready to pounce, but when she heard her mate's call, she backed out of the cave, still spitting and hissing at them. His call was far away. She spit one more time, then turned and ran out of the cave. Varna kept her last arrow trained on the cat and followed it to the cave entrance until Wull had retrieved his spear and stood guard at the mouth of the cave with Vol and Flom.

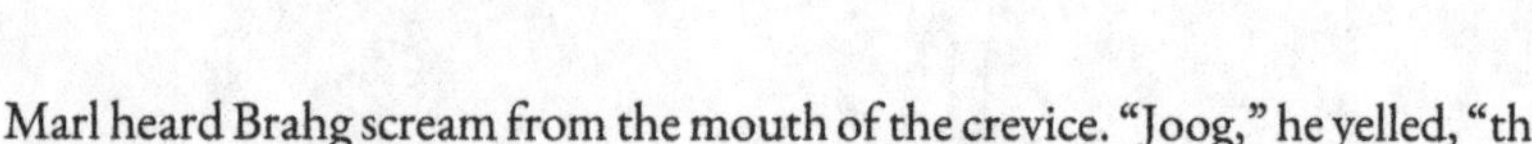

Marl heard Brahg scream from the mouth of the crevice. "Joog," he yelled, "they are here, but they are in trouble."

"Go!" Joog yelled, and as he did, the saber lion inside the cave swiped again at his foot, sinking his claw into the bony mass and pulling hard.

Marl ran along the track between the cliff and the forest.

Kendo hit the cat again and again with his staff, but the beast refused to let go of Brahg's shoulder.

Marl thought he had never seen anything braver than Kendo hitting the giant cat with his staff. He ran around to the opposite side, away from Kendo, thinking he would do the same thing with his walking stick until he saw the cat's mouth wrapped around Brahg's spear. Marl grabbed the end of Brahg's spear and shoved it upward into his mouth. The cat's eyes rolled backwards as it tried to repel whatever was being shoved into its mouth.

Marl heaved upwards, and the spear pulled the cat's teeth out of Brahg's shoulder. Kendo beat his staff onto the cat's nose and Brahg rolled over towards Marl. He jumped to his feet and grabbed the spear, which the cat gladly spit out. Marl returned to his walking stick and froze when he heard Joog scream.

The cat in the cave pulled Joog's leg loose from where it had been caught in the crevice. Joog was still under a pile of rocks, but the cat had pulled enough of his leg out to sink his teeth into Joog's calf. Joog tried throwing rocks at the beast's head, but that only made the cat pull and twist harder.

Brahg was a foot and a hand taller than most men and nearly twice their weight, yet the cat he faced outweighed him by as much as a full grown man. The cat had lost its advantage when it lost its hold on Brahg's shoulder, and now it faced three of the strange two-legged creatures, yet it showed no fear. It stared into Brahg's eyes and hissed at him. Brahg reared back with his spear and shoved with all his might into the cat's neck. The cat reared up on its back legs and swiped at the shaft with its claws. Brahg leaned into the spear and toppled the cat over, but it quickly spun and fell on its feet.

The cat growled. It was not happy about the outcome, but no meal was worth this much effort. It growled and hissed again, then sprang back into the forest and disappeared.

Marl ran immediately back to the crevice. Kendo wanted to ask if Brahg was okay, but Brahg was already racing behind Marl.

Marl yelled out, "Joog! We are coming."

Only then did Kendo realize that he, too, had heard Joog's scream when Marl had arrived.

Kendo yelled out, "Joog! We are here." As he got up to speed behind Brahg, he could hear Koro yelling from behind him, "Koro comes too!"

Brack and Zho spent all their energy running and did not announce their arrival.

Marl ran blindly into the dark crevice and swung wildly, hitting the beast on the rump. The cat dropped Joog's bloody foot and sprang on top of Marl, pinning him to the ground just inside the entrance. Brahg was on the cat in an instant, forcing his great spear painfully into its side. Kendo brought his staff down atop the cat's head just as it had sunk its fangs into Marl's side. Koro entered the cave and saw how ineffective the wooden spears were against the cat and tried stabbing its tender eyes.

The cat was greatly outnumbered, but it was powerful and fearless. Given a chance to escape, it might bolt, but cornered as it was, it would fight to the death and probably to the many deaths. Zho ran into the cave and pulled his sling from his side. He leaped onto the cat's back and wrapped his sling around the soft throat and pulled as hard as he could, which was not hard enough. He tied the cords around the neck and slipped his torch into the loop, and twisted the tourniquet as tight as he could. The cat bucked and twisted, but there were too many hands and bodies holding it down. Zho twisted until the life slipped out of the monster.

Kendo called out, "Joog!" but there was no answer.

Koro tended to Marl, but he could not detect any breath in the boy. He tugged to get the cat's body off of Marl. "Brahg!" he yelled. "Koro needs Brahg!"

Brahg joined Koro and pulled the heavy cat off of Koro's limp body.

Kendo ventured deeper into the black cave and called again, "Joog?"

Zho struggled with the flint to get the torch lit. Brack recognized the sound of the flint and said, "Zho! Let Brack try!"

Brack took the flint from Zho and deftly struck it against the lightning stone and lit the tinder. He blew on the tinder and started the flame to light the torch.

"Joog?" Kendo wandered blindly through the dark crevice until Zho and Brack joined him with the torch.

Brack pointed to the back of the crevice. Joog's mangled foot hung limply from the bloody leg which stuck out from a pile of rubble. Kendo immediately began removing stones from the pile, as did Brack and Zho.

Brahg carried Marl outside the dim cave into the moonlight, where Koro continued trying to find life in his friend.

Kendo pulled Joog out of the rubble and carried him out of the cave. Joog's foot bobbed and twisted as it dangled from his bloody leg. Kendo laid Joog next to Marl while Brahg stood guard over them. Kendo put his ear to Joog's chest. Everyone held their breath until Kendo announced, "Joog breathes."

Koro said, "Marl breathes too, but Marl won't wake up."

Brahg said, "We should return them to Mora without delay. Brahg can carry them."

Kendo said, "Has Brahg forgotten that Brahg too is injured?"

Brahg said, "Well then, Brahg will only carry one of them. We should go now."

It wouldn't have mattered if the crevice had been just across the meadow. The return trip, no matter how long, would have still seemed like an eternity. Kendo knew Joog would lose the foot, but they had no tools to remove it. They wrapped the end of his leg the best they could for the trek back.

Zho took a rock and broke the cat's teeth from its head. He used one of the sharp teeth to skin the great cat and then combined the skin with the spears to make a travois that could carry both Marl and Joog. Brahg laid the boys on the skin, lifted the handles of the travois and said, "Let's go."

Kendo led them back along the route he had followed around the cliff to get here. Zho walked next to Kendo, holding the torch in front of them to keep the predators away. He hoped the light would last until sunrise and did what he could to keep it burning as long as possible.

Koro walked alongside the boys, monitoring their condition along the way. The ridge narrowed and one of the travois' spears dragged over the edge. Brack stepped over the edge of the ridge and lifted the spear to keep the boys level. When the ridge widened again, he said, "Brack can take a turn so Brahg can rest a bit."

"Brahg will rest when we are with the tribe."

Koro saw the blood seeping from Brahg's shoulders and hoped Brahg would not have the forever sleep when they returned.

The sky lightened and the first ray of the morning sun illuminated the opposing mountains just as they plunged back into the forest. The cliff curved to the left, and they started climbing out of the valley up the rise that followed the base of the cliff.

Brack said, "Brahg? Brack can..."

"Brahg is fine. We must not delay."

The sun was above the canopy of the forest and flickered through the leaves onto Marl's face. Marl opened his eyes and asked, "What happened?"

Brack said, "Marl was very foolish to face the beast alone."

"And brave," Kendo added.

"But mostly foolish," Brack said.

Marl tried getting up, but Koro said, "No, Marl may still be hurt. Marl should rest."

Brack quietly caught Koro's attention and nodded his head towards Brahg's bloody shoulders and asked, "Can Marl walk?"

Marl nodded his head and Brack said, "Brack will help you." Brahg didn't stop, so Marl half jumped and half fell out of the travois. Brack put Marl's arm around his shoulder and lifted him up. Marl's chest hurt and he asked, "Did Brahg sit on Marl?"

"Worse," Brack said, "That giant beast fell upon Marl. Brahg and Koro pulled it off."

With only Joog in the travois, Brahg's pace quickened. They cleared the rise out of the valley and leveled off at the base of the cliff where Joog and Marl had first climbed up. It was not far now. They turned for the cave and picked up the pace again. They still had to cross the rocky fields, but it would be smooth and downhill from there.

Kendo thought they might have joined up with their tribe collecting slate, but nobody was there. Zho took a quick look at the slate and said, "I don't think anybody has been here."

Kendo looked up at the sun. It was still early, but not so early that they should not have been here already. "Did Koro tell them how to find this place?"

"Yes," Koro said, "Look at the tracks. Even the smallest child could follow this trail."

"Who did Koro tell?"

"Koro told Troon. Troon wanted to go out in the dark, but Koro and Brack both told Troon to wait until morning and let the boys do the hard work."

Kendo picked up the pace, but stopped short when he reached the mouth of the cave. The snow around the cave was red with blood. Kendo's blood went as cold as the snow as he rushed in.

"Wait!" Zho yelled, "Let us go together."

Inside the cave, Kendo found Wull and Flom holding spears, and a girl holding Wull's new bow. He quickly glanced around counting heads: Mora, Ragna, Ragna's baby...

Zho remained outside, analyzing the blood trail. "Get some boys," he said. "We can follow the trail."

Koro ran into the cave and yelled out, "Grab your weapons. Zho leads us to follow the blood!"

"No," Kendo said, "Tell Zho to come in. Mora told Kendo what happened. The trail is cold. Tell Brahg to bring Joog in."

Koro went to tell Brahg, but he had collapsed outside the cave. Koro yelled, "Mora! Brahg and Joog need Mora!"

Chapter Four

Life and Death

Mora was rattled by the loss of Troon and the horrific battle with the leopards. She had told Kendo of Troon's loss when he ran into the cave, but she hadn't told him the details yet. A chill prickled her skin when she heard Koro call for her. His words were simple, "Mora! Brahg and Joog need Mora!" The tenor of his voice brought a chill to her soul and told her the horror wasn't over yet. She ran out of the cave and past the three guards with no regard for her own safety.

Varna could already hear the gossip start. Troon had warned her that this would happen. He knew that if her secret were ever discovered, she would be shunned by men and women alike. There was no law against a woman handling a weapon. It just wasn't done. The men hunted, and the women gathered. Everything and everybody had a place. She knew this and Troon knew this, but she would have gladly submitted herself to a lifetime banishment before she would have given up Troon. She would not change anything about the time she had spent with him. She ignored the looks people gave her and rushed out into the open to stand in front of Mora with her bow trained on the meadow that faced the cave.

Mora tended to Joog and Brahg. Joog lay in the travois with one foot nearly severed off his leg. The leg was wrapped, and the bleeding seemed to be under control, but Brahg had crumpled to the ground in a heap. She tried rolling the giant man over on his back but could not. Koro immediately came to her aid and helped push him over without her needing to ask.

Varna scanned the field outside. The snow was red with Troon's blood. A brisk wind blew cold across her face, but her sniffles were not from the chill in the air. She forced herself to stand steady, but her breathing faltered and her aim wavered as the bow grew heavy in her hand. She did not want to see her lover's blood that stained the ground, but she could not look away because that was the exact direction the beasts took her Troon. Blinking did little to wash the tears from her eyes. Her heart wanted to roll up and cry, but she could not. She scanned the field for movement. It was imperative that she keep her mind focused, but her grief was too great. She wanted to kill the beasts, but she knew she could not. She cleared her eyes again and scanned for signs of the beasts.

Wull and Flom joined her. Varna took a deep breath. Mora was safe now, and they didn't need her to stand guard with them. Varna stepped out into the meadow and followed the blood. It wasn't far. She only stepped a few paces over a small rise and saw them. The male leopard gnawed on her lover's leg while the female had her snout buried in his abdomen. Varna's legs buckled, and she fell to her knees, still holding the bow, useless as it was, trained on the two cats.

The female leopard looked up and stepped over Troon's corpse to face Varna again. She knew the sting of Varna's arrows, but it was only a sting. The large cat stepped forward, her head above Varna's head. She walked proudly and stared the girl in the eyes.

Pela was hovering over Brahg. She knew he was strong, but she saw the blood seeping from his shoulders and cringed. The wounds were in the back of Brahg's shoulders. Mora wished now that they had rolled him onto his stomach. She leaned over to peer under his shoulder with her head nearly on the ground. The wounds were large punctures. She inserted a finger to probe the wound and Brahg groaned.

Pela sucked in her breath and looked away. Her gaze fell upon Varna, who was on her knees staring into the leopard's eyes. Without thought, Pela pointed out into the meadow and pierced the night with a blood-curdling scream.

Kendo and Zho's first reaction was to run to Varna's aid, but Kendo stopped and yelled, "Wait! If we rush in now, we may force the beast to attack."

"If we do nothing," Zho said, "And the beast kills Varna, is that not also our fault?"

"No friend," Kendo said, "The blame will be Kendo's and Kendo's alone."

Zho remained frozen, watching the encounter between Varna and the leopard while Kendo returned to his son and held his hand, hoping he would return from the land of the dreaming.

Varna hated the leopards for killing her Troon. More than anything, she wanted to kill them, but she could not. The bow she held was not Troon's bow. It was like a toy. Troon's bow was mighty and could easily slay the beast. The leopard would not be looking upon her as it did now if she had his bow. She had no weapon worthy of the beast and if she could not avenge her lover, she had little reason to live. Not in disgrace, but in an act of hopeless inevitability, she lowered the useless bow and stared through her tears into the cat's face. She was ready to accept her fate.

The leopard inched forward. Its breath was hot on Varna's face. The cat snorted and blew Varna's hair off her cheeks so it could sniff her face. It smelled the tears on her cheeks.

Varna could smell Troon's blood that covered the cat's snout. It sniffed her face again, and she wondered if it could smell the hatred in her heart. She closed her eyes and prepared herself. "Varna comes for Troon," she thought, but the cat didn't kill her. It sniffed her again and again. It smelled many things, but it never once smelled fear.

Varna didn't know if the leopard felt respect for her as a warrior or pity for the grieving widow or if it had simply eaten enough, but it backed away and bowed its head, then turned and left with its mate. They ran to the end of the meadow, then turned and ran up the mountain.

Zho ran out to join Varna, while Kendo and Koro carried Joog inside. Zho slowed as he approached her and asked, "Is Varna good?"

Varna wiped the tears from her eyes and said, "No, Varna may never be good again. Varna should be in the spirit world, but Varna is cursed to walk alone among the living."

"Zho does not know what was between Varna and Troon, and Zho does not know why Varna carries Wull's bow, but Zho cannot deny what just happened."

"What happened?" Varna asked, "Troon is with the spirits and Varna is not."

Zho's mind whirled. "Troon was Zho's mentor, yet Zho did not know that Troon had taken Varna as a daughter."

A weak smile snuck onto Varna's face as she said, "Troon was many things to Varna, including Varna's master, but Troon was never Varna's father."

Zho took to a knee as the world spun around him.

"Is Zho ok?"

"Zho is amazed. Troon was Zho's master in everything, yet Zho hardly knew Troon at all."

Varna's heart ached. Still on her knees, she sat back onto her heels and said, "Troon was proud of Zho. Troon said it many times. Troon and Varna would lay in the field at night and Troon would point to the stars and say that was how many things Zho had done to make Troon proud. Zho was the son Troon never had. Troon was happy when Zho took over the hunts,` and Troon was proud when Zho taught the hunters, but Troon's pride would not allow Troon to be a burden on the tribe."

"Troon could never be a burden. As Varna says, Troon was like a father to Zho."

"Still," Varna continued, "Troon would not be a decrepit elder who needs the tribe to feed him. Troon took Varna in and taught Varna to hunt."

Zho sat cross-legged and looked at the girl as if he had never seen her before. "Did Troon love Varna?"

"Not at first. Varna was just the girl who played rough like the boys and liked to climb trees and throw stones at the birds. Troon knew Varna would never have a mate and felt sorry for Varna."

"That can't be true," Zho said. "Zho may not have known of Troon's feelings for Varna, but Zho knew Troon well enough to know Troon would only take Varna out of respect, not pity."

Zho's words brought some comfort to the girl. "Perhaps," she said, "but Varna was only a pupil at first. Love came later. After Troon taught Varna the sling, Troon showed Varna the bow. It was the most magnificent weapon. It was art and using it was art. We shared a love for the bow and that was when we discovered each other."

"What you say is not true," Zho said.

"It is," Varna insisted. "Every word is true!"

"Not the part that Varna would never have a mate. Varna could have chosen from many men and she chose only the best."

The scent of her lover's body wafted past them and brought more tears to her cheeks.

"Let us return to the cave," Zho said. "Zho will send someone to honor Troon's remains. Zho will speak to Kendo as well. Varna should not hide her love for Troon."

Outside the cave, Koro, Brack and Flom tried lifting Brahg to carry him in. "Zho!" Koro shouted. "Zho is here in time to help!"

Zho joined Koro at Brahg's shoulders and each took an arm with Brack and Flom at his feet. Pela stepped out of their way and watched.

Koro counted, "One... Two... Three..."

On three, they each lifted, but as Koro and Zho lifted the giant's arms, the wounds on his shoulders bled and they put him back on the ground. Pela ran into the cave crying.

Koro said, "Brahg bleeds when we lift. We must move very fast. Ready? One... Two..."

Mora came running out of the cave and yelled, "What are you men doing?"

Koro answered, "We try to carry Brahg in!"

"How can men be so shortsighted? Use the skin!"

Zho felt stupid. He made the travois and had forgotten about it already. They rolled Brahg over on his side and slipped the skin under him. Brack lifted the travois. The spears bent under Brahg's weight, but held while Brack dragged him inside. Marl was sitting with Joog when Brahg was dragged in. He was quick to help lift Brahg off the travois and lie him down next to Joog until Yona pointed at his side and screamed. Blood seeped out of the punctures in his side and Mora made a space for him next to Joog.

Zho found Kendo at Joog's side. Part of him hated to interrupt his friend during a crisis like this, but much had to be said and done. "Kendo?" Zho asked, "Joog is in good hands, and Zho would like a word with Kendo."

Kendo looked up from Joog and nodded. His face was tired and his eyes were red. He followed Zho outside the cave, where Wull and Flom still stood guard with their spears at their sides. They continued to scan the horizon for movement, but their stance had relaxed since sunrise. A red trail still stained the ground outside the cave and led to what remained of Troon's partially eaten corpse. Kendo sighed when he saw the blood. He had much more to worry about than just Joog, but it was difficult for him to focus on anything else.

"Varna is distraught," Zho said.

"Kendo saw that. Does Zho know why?"

"Zho knows some. Troon took Varna as a secret student. Varna loved Troon and Zho thinks Troon bedded Varna as a wife."

"What?" Kendo asked. "Troon is old enough to be Varna's father!"

"Troon," Zho corrected, "is old enough to be Varna's grandfather."

"Kendo didn't even know Troon could still bed a woman."

Zho nodded his head and said, "Troon was surely a man among men. Troon was certainly more Zho's master than Zho ever realized. We should do what we can to comfort Varna and we need to take care of Troon's remains."

"Yes," Kendo agreed, "We owe Troon a proper sendoff many times over. Zho really believes Varna was Troon's wife?"

Zho nodded his head and Kendo yelled into the cave, "Koro and Brack! Come at once. Yona and Pela come too."

Koro was assisting Mora by holding Brahg's wounds closed while she examined Joog's leg, but she also heard Kendo's call and said, "Koro has done well and Mora appreciates the help, but Kendo needs Koro now. Go."

Koro didn't want to leave his friends. He frowned a bit and ran out of the cave behind Brack. Pela and Yona reluctantly left their men behind to see what Kendo wanted.

Kendo pointed out into the field and said, "Kendo wants Koro and Brack to retrieve Troon and build a pyre for Troon's body."

Wull stepped forward and said, "Wull and Flom can collect the wood. Wull does not believe the beasts will attack during the day. Perhaps Wull should also build a gate across the cave to keep them out tonight."

Kendo agreed, and the four men ran out into the field. He turned to the women and saw the tears in their eyes. He opened his mouth to speak, then paused a moment. Pela looked back into the cave at Brahg's gigantic form lying limply next to Joog. Kendo softened his voice and spoke as a father to his grieving daughter, "Pela. Yona. Kendo knows you fear for your men..."

Pela blushed. She never concealed her feelings for Brahg and had even spoken openly to some of her closes friends, but she had never discussed her feelings directly with Brahg and now the tribal chief speaks to her about her love for a man who has not yet shared his feelings with her. She stared down at her feet, unable to conceal her embarrassment.

"Do not worry," Kendo continued, "Kendo understands that your feelings are young and need time to grow, but Varna also had feelings for Troon and Kendo has learned that her feelings were not so young. Kendo will not command such a thing of you, but Kendo asks if the two of you can clean Troon's blood from the sacred soil around the cave?"

"Of course," Pela said. In truth, she welcomed the distraction. In her mind, she knew Brahg was in good hands, but her heart was less rational than her mind and would have her pine away uselessly at his side. Yona also agreed, and they set out to scraping the snow off the entrance. The tribe had no experience with snow and their job quickly became a series of experiments as they learned how to remove the cold substance without melting it and making more of a mess.

Brack and Koro carried Troon's remains to a spot that would be visible from the cave once the pyre was built. They laid him on the ground and piled snow in a mound next to him, hiding his remains from the cave for now, then ran out to help Wull collect wood.

Wull worked furiously to bend and twist a young sapling. He wished he had his tools, but could waste no time grieving over the past. "Wull!" Koro said. "Would the slate Joog found make this faster?"

Wull released his grip on the young sapling and said, "It would. Is it far?"

"Near enough to run there and back," Koro said.

Koro took off in the direction of the slate, but Wull said, "Flom! Return to the cave and collect some leather ties that Yona has made from the rabbit skins."

Brack held Flom's arm to stop him from running off and said, "Brack will go in Flom's place. Brack knows the way to the slate and will meet Wull there with the leather straps."

Wull accepted his explanation and ran with Flom to follow Koro.

Mora knew that Joog's foot was lost. The bleeding had stopped, but his blood burned and she feared the black disease would take the leg and she had no knives to remove it. She applied herbs from what they had found to stem the infection, but without her proper stores, she was improvising. She waffled back and forth between examining his leg and checking her medicinal inventory.

Tela saw her return to the inventory stores for the third time and said, "Mora has checked the herbs many times. Tell Tela what is missing and Tela will find some."

Mora sighed and said, "Everything is missing. A lifetime of collecting medicine cannot be replaced so easily."

"Then tell Tela what it looks like and Tela will search the meadow and the forest, but Mora cannot keep going through what we have, expecting it to magically appear."

Mora sighed and said, "Tela is correct. Mora wishes it were possible for Tela to find some in the forest, but Mora fears Tela would only find it if she were to return to the old village where Mora's things were lost, but that is not possible."

"Everything is possible," Tela said. "Tela will find a man to escort her."

"No," Mora said, "Mora was only dream wishing aloud."

Mora looked at the leg again and sighed. There was nothing more she could do with what she had. She turned her attention to Marl and said, "You, my young friend, are very lucky. The punctures in your side appear to have gone clean through you without sending you to the long sleep."

"Then I can help around here," Marl said. He started to get up, but Mora gently pushed him back down into his bed.

"No," she said, "Marl cannot get up yet. Marl will be up soon enough, but Mora has to close Marl's wounds first and Marl must give them time to seal or he will bleed himself to the long sleep."

Marl was too wound up and full of energy to lie idly in bed. His best friend was gravely wounded. To lose his leg at their age was like a death curse. Marl's wounds were nothing compared to Joog's. Joog still slept, but stirred next to him and Joog felt helpless.

Mora smiled and said, "Marl will most certainly be up and around before Joog. Mora is sure that Marl will be a great help with Joog when Joog finally awakes."

"And what of Brahg?" Marl asked.

Brahg had been resting but not sleeping and answered for himself, "Brahg is fine, but Brahg will do as Mora asks."

"Brahg is a good boy," Mora said. "Brahg is lucky like Marl, and after some rest, he, too, will be up and around."

Mora's younger assistant, Risa, returned and said, "Here are the bags Mora wanted."

One of the bags had threads made from rabbit intestines while the other held a collection of thin rabbit rib bones.

Risa watched Mora pick through the threads and said, "It's a good thing Troon caught so many rabbits for us."

Varna lay curled up in a corner of the cave, weeping quietly to herself. Mora glanced up at her and said to Risa, "We are lucky to still have Varna with us, and we are very fortunate that Varna was taught so well to catch the rabbits for us." Mora leaned towards Risa and whispered, "But Varna hears everything we say, so let us not talk of Troon while Varna still grieves for the loss of Varna's husband."

Risa bit her lip and sat quietly at Mora's side.

Mora gave Brahg a roll of leather and said, "Bite down on this. Mora is afraid this may hurt."

Brahg smiled broadly and said, "Brahg will bite down and pretend it hurts, so Marl will feel no shame when it is Marl's turn."

Marl smiled but winced when he saw Mora insert the needle to start the first suture.

<hr>

Three men, including Kendo's son, lay injured on the floor of the cave and another was dead. Kendo stood over his son as Mora worked to clean and sew Brahg's and Marl's wounds. He wasn't the tribal chieftain at this moment. He was a father grieving over his son's future. He kneeled down and took Joog's hand into his. "Kendo is sorry for this," he said, "It is all Kendo's fault. The two of you should never have been sent out into such a strange new land alone. It is Kendo's arrogance that has brought us here. Kendo has doomed us all."

Joog lay silent. He floated in a dream world where he was unable to touch the real world, yet he felt his father's hands. Kendo's words floated past Joog, but Joog's mind could not make sense of them all. Some words floated past him like bubbles in a stream, while other words came to him and he understood them.

He had heard enough of Kendo's words, however, to want to tell his father he was being too harsh on himself, but Joog could neither command his eyes to open nor could he force the words out of his mouth.

"It is not like that," Marl said. "Joog and Marl believed in Kendo's vision. We still do. It was our duty to search out the land of our ancestors. We were honored to follow the white eagle's path to our new home."

"Bah," Kendo responded, "What right has Kendo to believe every stray day dream is a vision from the spirits? Kendo led us here, and Kendo's pride has brought us to ruin."

Marl shook his head, spitting out the leather bit, and said, "We found the ancestral home before we found the beast. It sits on the shore of a wondrous lake with a rich forest surrounding the lake."

"Lay still," Mora said as she replaced the leather in his mouth and continued to suture the punctures in his side.

Marl winced and bit down hard, then spat the leather out again and said, "Kendo has not doomed us. Kendo saved the tribe. It was Kendo's fierce bravery that led the tribe out of the floods. Kendo did not stand above us and direct us to save the people. The river of life turned into the river of death and Kendo dived into the rushing water and pulled our people out with Kendo's own hands. Kendo is a hero."

Mora smiled and nodded her head as she tied the last knot in Marl's side.

"Marl speaks the truth," Brahg said. "Kendo asks what right has Kendo to see a vision from the spirits? Kendo has the right of the chieftain. Kendo cannot allow grief over Joog to cloud Kendo's thoughts."

"Kendo is not only Joog's father," Marl added, "Kendo is father to us all. The beast has taught us a valuable lesson about our new land and already we take steps to adapt to it. Our injuries will heal, and we will learn to cope with them just as we will learn to cope with our new home when we reach it."

Kendo bowed his head and said, "Your words bring comfort, but how can Marl still speak of our new home when we are stuck here?"

"Who is stuck here?" Marl asked.

"Marl is brave," Kendo said, "but Marl must heal before we can travel and by then, it will be too late in the year to build our homes. Perhaps we can continue next spring."

"No," Marl argued, "Only the three of us must heal. Kendo can lead the tribe to the new land and build our homes. We will join Kendo when we have healed."

"How?" Kendo asked. "Does Marl forget that Joog will never climb the mountain again?"

"Do not worry about Joog," Brahg said. "Brahg will heal and Brahg will carry Joog."

"Even so," Kendo said, "We have faced two beasts that we cannot match. We know of no weapons to defeat them."

"That's not true," Varna said from her corner. "Troon's bow could defeat all of them."

"But we do not have Troon's bow," Kendo replied.

"But Wull has already started to build one," Marl said.

"And we all saw how effective that was!" Kendo sounded defeated.

"Does Kendo not see?" Marl asked. "Wull will learn to build the bow, just like we will learn to defend against these beasts. Do not forget that we have already killed one of them, and that was without the bow."

Kendo started to reply again, but Mora touched his shoulder and said, "Mora thinks we have lost a wise elder in Troon, but gained two new elders in Brahg and Marl."

"Elders?" Kendo asked.

"Advisors then," Mora said, "Their counsel is true enough. Kendo should listen."

<hr>

Wull was already sharpening pieces of slate when Brack returned with some leather cords. Flom and Koro collected slate from the hill and stacked the pieces in piles arranged by size. Wull took the slate he had already sharpened and attached the pieces to suitable handles until he had four decent axes and two extra sharp knives for Mora.

"This will do," Wull said. "We can return for the rest of the slate later. We must collect some wood now."

Wull put the knives in his pocket and led them back to the forest where they diligently chopped down trees and collected them in a pile. As the pile grew, Koro and Flom dragged them to the site where they had lain Troon, then returned for more.

When Wull was satisfied that they had collected enough, all four of them dragged the remaining piles of trees back to the pyre site. Wull picked out the straightest trunks and began removing the branches. "These will be for the gate Wull will build."

Flom carried Wull's completed lumber to the mouth of the cave. Pela and Yona were still removing the red snow and replacing it with a clean white layer. Flom nodded and said, "It looks much better."

Pela smiled weakly, but continued working.

Flom returned to the pyre and saw that Wull had prepared more lumber and had also made a pile of supple twigs for him to carry. Brack and Koro built the pyre from the remaining wood. They had plenty of wood and an abundance of kindling.

Wull helped Flom drag the last batch of lumber back to the cave while Koro and Brack continued to work on the pyre. Wull went straight to work building a fence across the mouth of the cave. He used his axe to dig a ditch in the ground where he placed the strongest timbers. Some of the wood was long enough to reach the top of the cave, but for those that were too short, he sharpened the tops into points. He braced a strong piece of wood across the gate and tied it to each of the vertical timbers.

He left an opening in the center of the gate, which would be the door and could only be opened by lifting it and could only be lifted by removing the straps that tied it down. If their beasts are smart enough to open the door, then their tribe would have been outmatched already.

Kendo and Zho came out to examine the gate. Wull grabbed the fence and rattled it. "You can both see," Wull said, "that the timber is solid. We may have no weapons to defend ourselves against the intruders, but this will stand between them and us. Wull is sure of it."

Inside the gate, two women gasped and pointed out towards the meadow.

Zho spun around to face the threat and saw Varna carrying rabbits and pheasant.

"Varna," he said, "Zho did not see you leave."

Her grief was still etched on her tear-streaked face as she replied, "Troon always said that stealth was a hunter's best asset, and Varna was afraid she would not be allowed to hunt anymore. Here is some fresh meat. Varna is sure the men are quite hungry after all their labor."

"Varna did not have to do this," Zho said.

Her face fell and her shoulders slumped as she said, "As Varna feared, Zho does not wish Varna to hunt."

"No," Zho said, "Zho welcomes help from Troon's bride as much as Zho would welcome Troon's help."

"Zho does not speak for all the Tribe," she said. "Varna hears things."

Kendo stepped through the door hole and put a reassuring hand on Varna's shoulders. "Kendo does speak for the tribe and Kendo would never dishonor Troon by turning away help from one of Troon's best students."

"Varna is not one of Troon's best students," Zho said. "Varna is the very best of Troon's pupils. Still, Troon's bride is in mourning. Zho should have hunted."

"Zho was busy," she replied. "Troon would have done this, if Troon were still with us, and Troon would have wanted Varna's help."

Zho accepted the meat and bowed, saying, "Varna's initiative proves once again why Zho is only Troon's number two student." He then turned and delivered the meat to the cooks.

They would honor Troon tonight with a feast for the dead.

Mora accepted the knives from Wull and sat down before Joog's mangled leg. Koro saw the sharpened slate in her hand and the anguish on her face. He knew what she was about to do and sat down next to her. Tela and Risa joined them and sat on both ends.

The cave's natural odor of dirt had already been replaced with the smell of burning tallow and sweaty people. Here, where the three wounded lie, was the smell of blood and the faint odor of death. Many tribesmen remained at the far edges of the cave, preferring to keep clear of the spirits that come to collect the dead.

Mora took a deep breath to steady herself and said, "Mora is glad Koro is here. Mora may need Koro's strength." She leaned over and smelled the damaged leg. "Here," she said, "smell this."

Koro shook his head and said, "There is no need. Koro can smell the poison from here."

Tela leaned over and smelled the wound. "It smells like foul meat."

Risa frowned and grimaced as she took her turn.

"Death is eating the leg," Mora said. "Some of the flesh must be removed, but the bone is in the way. We must cut the bone to shorten it." She looked at the slate knives and said, "Mora has no doubt that these knives can cut the flesh, but the bone may be too hard to cut with sharp stones."

Koro said, "If Joog were a goat, Koro would cut the leg at the knee where the bone comes apart easier, but Koro fears that Joog will not like losing his leg."

Mora frowned and replied, "Joog's leg is already lost. We try to save what remains. This will be unpleasant."

Koro brushed Joog's forehead and said, "Koro is glad Joog sleeps. Koro hopes he does not waken before we are done."

Mora handed Koro the leather that Brahg and Marl had bitten and said, "Use this just in case."

Marl remained quiet at Joog's side. He knew what they were about to do. He turned his head the other way and looked at Brahg. He could not watch them remove Joog's leg, but he could not help to hear them.

Koro opened Joog's mouth and lodged the roll of leather into his jaw. Mora began by severing the thin strip of flesh which had hung onto his foot. Risa gingerly removed the foot and set it aside. Mora then cut away the bottom of Joog's leg. Joog remained asleep as she cut through the dead and dying calf muscles. Risa's insides wanted to heave as she removed the slice of flesh and laid it next to the foot. Joog's bone protruded from the severed flesh. Mora leaned over and could still smell the poison in his leg. She sliced again, two finger widths up and removed the diseased tissue. She could still smell the rotted infection and cut again, two more finger widths up. Joog stirred and bit down on the leather as fresh blood seeped from the new cuts. Koro held his head and whispered comfort into his ears while tiny Risa tried to hold his whole leg down.

Mora sniffed again and said, "Good. We have removed the rot. Now, as Koro suggested, we remove the bone from the knee."

She wound a length of leather around Joog's thigh and made a tourniquet. "Tighten this," she said to Koro.

She sliced a vertical incision up the length of the shinbone to the top of the knee. Joog stirred again and bit down hard on the leather. His good leg stiffened, and the toes curled on his feet, then he passed out. Mora cut around the knee socket but could not loosen the lower leg.

"Let Koro try," Koro said. They traded places and Koro made deeper cuts around the knee socket, then forcefully removed the lower leg bone. Mora used more of the rabbit ribs and gut to close up the leg around what remained of the knee, calf, and shin.

Koro loosened the tourniquet, and the leg bled profusely. He tightened it again. Mora poured water on the incisions and then took a small burning log and blew out the flames. She continued to blow on the ember until it was red hot and pressed it against the incision. "The heat seals the flesh," she said, "and tightens the stitches." She repeated the process all the way down the wound. Koro loosened the tourniquet again. There was some light bleeding, but Mora was satisfied that the stitches would hold.

The sun settled behind the mountains in the west and turned the high wispy clouds a brilliant pink. The tribe gathered in a circle around Troon with the women and children nearest the cave and the men armed with whatever weapons they could put together. The sky darkened and the pink clouds glowed in stark contrast. The ground around them also glowed, casting each of the figures as a dark silhouette against the snow.

Mora stepped forward and said, "It is the time for introductions. Troon is the oldest of all of us and has many friends and family in the spirit world who will welcome Troon, but first we must introduce Troon to the spirit guides. Mora has known Troon the longest of us, so Mora will go first. Troon was only slightly older than Mora. As a child, Mora was witness when Troon first joined the hunters. Troon had a natural gift and excelled beyond Troon's mentors. In the days of the buffalo, Troon was nicknamed the Buffalo Man. After the buffalo had left our valley, and only smaller game remained, it was Troon that learned how to fish the river of life. When the great tiger was forced down into our valley by the mountain of smoke, it was Troon that defended the village with his mighty bow. Troon was a good friend to Mora and even after his hunting days were over, he remained a trusted adviser. Mora misses Troon already."

Mora stepped back, and Zho stepped forward. "Up until a couple of days ago, Zho would have told you that Zho knew Troon better than anyone. Troon was Zho's teacher, but Troon was more like a father to Zho. Even though Zho has accepted most of Troon's responsibilities to train new hunters and lead the hunters, Troon was still Zho's master and Zho could never completely fill Troon's shoes."

Zho stepped back and Tela surprised everyone by stepping forward and saying, "Troon was the greatest teacher Tela has ever known. Troon did not teach Tela to hunt, but Troon always welcomed the children of the village to his hearth with the most wonderful stories from the old days. Tela will miss Troon's stories, and Tela thinks Ragna's baby and all the other babies will miss Troon's stories the most, without ever hearing Troon tell them."

Tela stepped back, and silence followed. The clouds in the west had faded away, leaving a dark sky in the west just as the moon began to peek over the eastern mountains. Nobody stepped forward, and all eyes fell upon Varna. Varna's tear-filled eyes widened as she realized the tribe expected her to speak. Whether they welcomed what she had to say or feared that her words would be blasphemous to the old ways, she could not tell, but she had heard enough to know that not all of them shared Kendo's sentiment.

"Go ahead," Kendo encouraged her, "Varna's words will help carry Troon to the spirit world. The ancestors will know how Troon was loved in their absence and they will accept him into their tribe."

Varna reluctantly stepped forward for Troon's sake. Her voice quavered as she softly said, "Troon was Varna's husband. Varna knows now why Troon kept our marriage a secret. Varna feels love and acceptance from some and is grateful, but Troon was wise to hide our love just as Troon was wise to hide that Varna hunts." She took a deep breath and wiped the tears from her eyes, then continued, "Varna sees the shame Varna has brought onto the tribe and hopes the tribe will forgive Troon for his part. Troon only meant to give Varna's life meaning." As she spoke, the trembling in her voice grew. "Troon was the most loving person Varna has ever known. Troon accepted Varna for who and what Varna was. Troon taught Varna not just about killing, but about living and loving. Varna does not regret spending time with Troon or being Troon's bride, but Varna is lost without Troon and regrets how long it may be before Varna can join Troon again in the spirit world."

Varna stepped back and sobbed uncontrollably. Kendo stepped forward and spoke directly to Troon and to the spirits. "Troon. Friend. We have walked many paths in the time Kendo has known Troon, but now, it is time for Troon to walk a path without Kendo, but fear not, brother. Troon does not walk alone. The spirits will guide Troon and many of our ancestors await Troon, just as Troon will await Zho and Kendo and especially Varna. Safe travels, friend. Be patient with us until we meet again."

Kendo nodded to Koro and Brack. They stepped forward with their torches and lit the pyre. The green kindling started slowly, but spread throughout the base of the pyre. The heat grew, and the branches started to burn until all at once the entire pyre pitched up into a great blaze. Flames leaped high into the air and scattered brilliant embers among the stars. The ground below the blaze sizzled as the snow melted and white steam rose into the sky along with the black smoke and embers.

"Behold!" Kendo proclaimed, "Troon's spirit is carried off by sacred smoke!"

The blaze lit the entire meadow and could be seen for miles in the night. Zho stood vigil over the tribe and wondered if the pyre would keep the beasts away or attract their attention. He played with the weight of the axe Wull had given him and continued to scan the meadow around the fire. The tribe returned to the cave, which was filled now with the scent of roasting rabbit and pheasant. Wull waited inside for Zho, who was the last to return to the cave. He placed the door in its tracks, locked the loop of leather onto the frame, holding the door in place.

For the second time in the last few days, the tribe held a feast in this cave, and for the second time, it was a somber event with little life to support it. The food was meager but good, but they still had no spirits to toast their fallen comrade. The only stories this night were those of Troon, who had touched so many lives that the stories might last until morning.

When Joog had fallen asleep, it was to the terrible pain of the infection in his leg, but now he awoke to an entirely new but equally terrible pain. He kept his eyes closed and did not move for fear the pain would increase.

Zho offered Kendo another piece of meat.

"No," Kendo said, "Kendo has had enough."

"Zho thinks you should take the tribe at first light and find our new home. Marl has told Zho that Joog found a lake and a forest which would make a wonderful location for the village."

Kendo shook his head and said, "It is too soon. Kendo cannot leave Joog while he lies there."

Joog wished for sleep so the pain would go away and he could dream of the better days when he used to swim in the river with Marl. But sleep did not come and the throbbing in his leg eventually escaped his lips as a moan.

Kendo snatched the meat from Zho's hand and went to his son. "Joog! Joog is with us. Here, son, take this meat."

Joog pressed his lips closed and refused the food.

"Joog must eat," Kendo said.

Joog shook his head and said, "Joog will not eat until Kendo leads the tribe home."

"But Kendo cannot leave Joog."

Zho kneeled down and took Joog's hand in his own, saying, "Zho will protect Joog. And Brahg has already volunteered to carry Joog. Kendo must not delay. Take Wull and the tribe to the home of our ancestors."

"Kendo cannot."

"Then," Joog said, "If Kendo refuses to leave Joog, Joog will leave Kendo. Joog will not eat." A tear formed in Joog's eye as he looked up at his father. "Joog will not be responsible for the tribe perishing here. Joog will wish for the final sleep so Kendo will lead the people to the land of our ancestors. In the morning, Kendo will see it is the right thing. Then when Kendo leaves, Joog will eat again. Joog loves Kendo the father, but the tribe needs Kendo, the chieftain, right now."

Kendo hung his head and said, "Kendo will sleep, but Kendo does not want to leave Joog."

In the morning, Kendo went to Joog's side. Mora and Koro were tending him.

Kendo asked, "Has Joog eaten yet?"

Mora shook her head and said, "Joog has not. Mora fears that Joog has lost much blood and will not survive long without food and water."

Kendo hung his head and said, "Very well. It pains Kendo, but Kendo will go." He stood and shouted, "It is time. Pack your things. We leave for the new land. Zho will stay behind with Brahg, Marl and Joog. They will find us when they can."

Mora said, "Mora will stay to tend the injured. Tela and Risa are very fine students, but Mora thinks you may have the makings of a medicine man in Koro."

"Koro?" Kendo asked, "Very well. While we travel, Varna will hunt in Zho's place."

This announcement elicited gasps from the tribe.

Kendo held his hands out at his sides and asked, "Does Kendo's people doubt Kendo's wisdom? Varna! Come forward."

Varna did not come to him and he asked again, "Varna?"

A voice in the crowd shouted, "Varna is not with us!"

Zho circled the cave counting heads and said, "It is true. Varna is gone, as is Wull's bow."

Kendo reeled, "What has Varna done?"

Brack stepped forward and said, "Brack will be honored to hunt in Varna's absence."

Kendo turned to Zho and said, "Kendo now hears Varna's last words in a new light and fears for her safety. Zho must find Varna before it is too late."

Chapter Five

What Was Left Behind

Zho grabbed a spear and an empty water skin. Kendo gripped his arm, forearm to forearm in the fashion men do when one of them embarks on a solitary journey. The two men looked at each other's faces and neither saw confidence in what they were about to do.

"Safe travels," Kendo said.

"Safe travels," Zho repeated. "Travel quickly. Zho expects to find a bustling community and a warm hearth when we finally rejoin the tribe in the land of our ancestors."

Kendo grunted and said, "We shall see. Kendo is leaving the best of the tribe behind and taking mostly women and children to go reclaim the ancient land."

Zho pointed at Brack and said, "Kendo takes two of Zho's finest students. Brack and Koro are both excellent hunters and it would seem that there may be much more in store for Koro's future. Most importantly, the tribe will have Kendo. They are in good hands."

Kendo broke the grip and said, "Zho must go and catch up with Varna before Varna does something rash."

Zho frowned and asked, "Does Kendo truly believe Varna would do harm to Varna?"

"Kendo does not know, but the depth of Varna's grief surprised Kendo. Varna's words were those of a wife ready to follow the husband on the path to the spirit world."

"Well then," Zho said, "Zho will waste no more time talking."

He took off out of the cave and searched for her tracks. The sun had barely risen and the snow already blinded him. He squinted and shaded his eyes with his hands, but it wasn't the sky that blazed in his eyes. It was the very ground where he searched for her trail.

The snow outside the cave was trampled by the tribe during Troon's cremation. It thinned in places, and dirt could be seen where the pyre had burned. Zho also saw dirt coming up from beneath the sacred white soil where the tribe had stood around the pyre and left the impressions of their feet. The pyre was mostly cold and black now, but some embers still smoked in the center. The scent of charred wood hung around the circle, and Zho was sure the odor had climbed the mountain and found its way to the spirit world. He also worried that the scent of Troon's ashes may have floated up the mountain to the lair of the great cats that killed him.

Zho walked in a large arc around the funeral pyre. He found Varna's tracks on the opposite side, where they led to the leopard pair she found feeding on her husband. He saw the leopard look into Varna's face. There was no doubt in his mind that the large cat had seen into her soul and chose to leave her to her grief. He knew where these tracks led and did not believe she would travel in that direction again. He continued his arc until he found another trail leading away from the cave. The tracks looked roughly the same size as Varna's, but it was difficult to be certain. Zho did not like the tracks that were made in the sacred soil. They were much less precise than dirt or mud, but they were easy to follow.

For all the many lessons that Troon had taught her about stealth, he evidently had not trained her to conceal her tracks, or perhaps she just did not care. Maybe her grief hid the love of her tribe from her. Her words were those of an outcast. She had broken with tradition and learned to hunt. When she looked around her at the tribe, she only saw those who were easily shocked by such new ideas and never saw the support she also received. Zho laughed at himself for trying to understand her mind. She was a woman, and she had just lost her man. He could not put himself in her shoes. He could never understand.

The trail led him back in the direction the tribe had taken from the lost village to get here. He stopped at a particularly brilliant snow drift and packed the sacred dirt into the water skin. He may not have liked the tracks in the white ground, but it was very convenient for the spirits to provide them with soil that changed itself into good clean water.

Zho didn't know when she left and couldn't tell how much of a head start she had from her tracks. He was taller than she was and felt certain that he walked at a brisker pace, but the snow was deep in some spots and slippery in others. As long as he had difficult footing, she might be able to keep pace ahead of him. He tried to speed up, but ultimately the ground had more to say about his velocity than his will.

Kendo couldn't hide his heavy heart from his closest friends, but he had to muster up a stronger face for the tribe. It was good for them to do something about their situation instead of sitting around in the cave with nothing better to do than spread idle gossip.

Even after the incident with the leopards, too much talk was spread about Varna and the bow, or Varna and Troon. Troon was dead, three men were terribly injured and one of them had lost his foot, yet still Kendo heard the whispers about Varna this and Varna that. Better to be out on the trail where they can worry about the next encounter with the leopards or the saber cats.

Brack and Koro walked up front with Kendo while Wull and Flom took the rear of the procession. Marl gave Brack detailed directions to lead the tribe through the valley without climbing the mountain as he had done with Joog. The walk was much less challenging technically than the climb up the cliff that brought them here, and they had little gear to carry.

Kendo stopped near the slate deposit so Wull and the other men could pack as much of the slate as they could comfortably carry while the women took turns carrying the infants. Some of the children wanted to run ahead and scout, but Kendo put his foot down and made them tend the few goats Joog had saved.

Zho had seen the leopards head up the mountain when they left the valley. He believed that keeping down in the valley should keep the tribe far away from them, but Kendo remembered the saber cat striking from the trees, and they were just about to enter the valley forest.

Kendo slowed as he scanned the trees.

"What's wrong?" Brack asked, "Does Kendo see something?"

"No," Kendo said, "But it was from the trees that Brahg was attacked. We walked directly beneath the beast as it hid in the branches."

Brack scanned the trees with Kendo while Koro ran back and spread the word to Wull and Flom. Koro returned to the front of the line while Flom discreetly told the other young hunters and trainees.

Pela and Yona ran to the front while the men divvied up the slate so some of them would be free to carry the spears and axes they had made. Pela and Yona approached Kendo but still kept a respectful distance. Kendo was pointing ahead to the valley forest and talking to Brack when Yona pushed Pela forward. Kendo glanced over at the two women and waited. Yona pushed Pela in the back again.

Kendo asked, "Does Yona have something to say?"

Pela stepped behind Yona, who stared at the ground and said nothing. Pela said, "Zho has set out to find Varna. Mora is alone to care for Brahg, Marl and Joog. Mora is too old to be sent to fetch water and forage berries. Yona thinks Kendo should send us back to assist Mora.

"Kendo thought Yona and Pela would want to have nice homes with warm hearths when Brahg and Marl returned to the tribe."

The girls blushed and Yona said, "But we cannot build homes."

Kendo smiled and said, "Perhaps the huts would be a wedding present."

Terror spread across their faces. It was too soon to speak of weddings. They did not want to jinx their chances with their men.

"Relax," Kendo said, "Koro will escort both of you back to the cave to assist Mora.

Koro said, "We must hurry. Koro must still run back to catch up with the tribe before someone scrapes a knee."

"Be smart," Kendo said, "Don't go out at night and stay in pairs when you forage."

Koro and the girls ran back to the cave while the tribe followed Kendo down into the valley. A shallow stream flowed along the base of the valley. Kendo stopped and examined the stream while the water bearers emptied the skins and refilled them with fresh water.

Brack looked nervously along the stream and said, "Kendo's beasts may hide in the trees, but surely their eyes are on the stream where their game comes to drink."

Kendo agreed and said, "Kendo wonders if it would be easier to watch for them from the stream bed. The trees closest to the stream would not support their weight, and we would only have two directions to guard against."

Brack shrugged and said, "Perhaps, if we are lucky, they only hunt at night."

Kendo looked back on the tribe and said, "If we are so lucky, we will not still be here at night." It was too soon to rest and if Brack was correct, they needed to get through this valley before sunset.

The stream flowed over a rocky bed with sand and pebbles filling the shores. The water ran deep and was freezing cold. It wound back and forth, following the contours of the valley. The tribe followed the stream as closely as they could. They could climb over the tumbled rock, but the outside bends in the stream sometimes gathered silt which wanted to swallow them up and was too dangerous to traverse. The women and children stayed closest to the stream while the men stood between them and the trees.

Kendo could see through the trees to the ridge above him where they had found Joog. They were near the same spot where Brahg was attacked, and he was glad when Koro caught up with them. This was a dangerous place, and he wanted to get through it as quickly as possible. The children had boundless energy, but the women, and especially the mothers, did not. They needed to rest, but Kendo could not do it here. It was too close to the same spot where three of their men were attacked.

Marl told them that the valley would take them over a rise and down into the other side of the mountain where the lake waited for them. Kendo hoped the lake waited for them and would welcome them. He also hoped the spirits would watch over them while they rebuild.

Varna wore the bow diagonally across her chest like a sash, but she had no quiver for the arrows and had to carry them in her hand. She left the cave before sunrise while the air was still crisp. The ground was cold against the thin soles of her shoes, but crossing the plateau was still relatively easy compared to the cliff that stood in her way.

She looked down from atop the cliff and thought it looked much steeper than it had when the tribe climbed up it. She walked along the edge of the cliff, hoping to find an easier passage, but they all looked the same. Turning her back to the cliff, she backed over the edge. She gripped a large rock with her left hand while still clinging to the arrows with her right.

Keeping herself as close to the cliff as possible, she slid over the edge, lying on her belly with her legs dangling below, searching for a foothold. Her right foot found a ridge, and she planted her toes against the sheer wall and lowered herself down to find a similar foothold for her other foot.

She couldn't climb down with just one hand and had to slip the arrows into her blouse. They scratched and poked at her belly, but her hand was free to hold on. She lowered herself below the top of the cliff and worked her way straight down. The rocks dug into the soft flesh of her fingers as much as she dug her fingers into the rocks.

She saw a ledge to her left, but it was too far below her to reach yet. She worked her way across the face towards the ledge. Left hand, then left foot; right foot, then right hand. Left hand then left foot, her foothold gave way and her weight pulled off her right hand, leaving her dangling by her left hand. Her face slammed into the cliff while she swung freely from her left hand until she could find another handhold, but the rock she clung to gave way and she slid down the cliff and landed with a crash onto the ledge.

She closed her eyes and hugged the cliff. The abrasions on her hands and face stung while rock and debris rained down around her and fell to the valley floor. This was a stupid idea. She looked up the cliff and then looked down. There was no escape for her.

Tears streaked down her cheeks. She needed Troon, but he was gone and the tears only doubled down her cheeks. "Troon, love, Varna may be coming sooner than we thought."

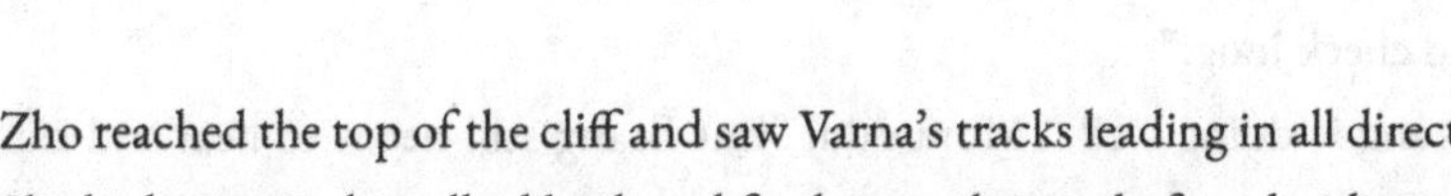

Zho reached the top of the cliff and saw Varna's tracks leading in all directions. She had apparently walked back and forth several times before deciding where she would cross over the ledge. He couldn't tell which spot she chose and instead had to look for himself to find the safest way down.

He chose the far end of the ledge and strapped his spear to his back, then gently eased himself over the side. The foothold was unsteady, and he tried keeping his movements as smooth as possible. Without stopping, he gently lowered himself to the midway point before he looked around for the next route down.

This wasn't how he remembered it. The route they took up the cliff seemed to have a clear pass that took them to the top. Going down, the cliff seemed to have no character at all. He descended at an angle towards his right, which took him further away from Varna's path. As he neared the bottom, he crossed a goat path, which angled him back to his left. The path was only a couple of fingers wide and nearly impossible for him to keep his toes on. He moved swiftly and smoothly until he was close enough that he could jump to the floor of the valley.

Once on the floor, he fell to one knee to catch his breath and thank the spirits for delivering him. Then, not wasting too much time, he followed the base of the cliff, looking for her tracks. He found none and crossed back again in the other direction. There was no sign of Varna, but he also found no remains of Varna from a fall down the cliff. He widened his search by a few steps and followed the contour of the cliff base. The ground was smooth and undisturbed until a small rock slide fell around him and pelted him with small stones.

He backed away from the cliff and looked up. He saw Varna clinging to the cliff halfway up.

"Varna!" he yelled, but she didn't hear him. "Hang on Varna! Zho is coming!"

* * *

"Brahg is fine," Brahg complained. "Brahg does not even feel the wounds. Mora should check Joog."

"Brahg is doing well," Mora said, "but Brahg still needs to heal and eat. Brahg promised to carry Joog up the mountain, so when Mora tends to Brahg's wounds, Mora is also taking care of Joog."

Marl snickered and pushed himself up to a near sitting position.

"Ach!" Mora exclaimed, "If Marl breaks Mora's stitches, who will hunt for us when the provisions run out?"

"Uhuh," Brahg added.

Marl let himself down and said, "But the ground is getting uncomfortable. Marl's back is sore."

Mora handed Brahg's food to Pela and moved over to check the stitches in Marl's side. She nodded her head and said, "Marl can sit up in two days."

"Then Marl can hunt?"

"No," Mora said, "Marl cannot hunt yet. Wait five days and then Marl can set traps if Marl promises to walk slowly."

Marl mumbled something while Mora handed his meal to Yona.

"What did Marl say?" she asked.

Marl just frowned and said nothing.

Brahg said, "Marl wishes Koro had stayed with us instead of Mora. Then Koro could hunt for us while we heal."

"That is a good idea," Mora said, "except Mora thinks Marl believes Koro would let Marl up before Marl's wounds are healed."

"Does Marl see now?" Brahg said. "How Marl can't fool Mora. Mora has gifts from the spirits and sees through Marl's plans."

Marl's frown worsened.

"Eat your fruit," Yona said.

"Marl is tired of fruit. We need meat to heal."

Mora agreed, but they had to make do with what they had. She leaned over and smelled Joog's stump. She wriggled her nose and took a long whiff. Joog stirred and Mora said, "Good morning. Mora does not believe that Joog feels well yet, but Mora hopes that Joog's appetite has returned some."

She held a bowl of berries for him and he gladly accepted. "Joog is starving. Joog will pretend these are diced chicken with onions."

Brahg chuckled and said, "Marl would do well to pretend that too, instead of pretending Marl is well enough to get up already."

Pela and Yona looked at each other, wondering why their men had to act like boys all the time.

Varna's fingers ached as she dug them into the cliff. She longed for Troon and wished more than anything to be with him, but she did not believe he would approve if she just let go. His lessons often taught great patience for the hunter to wait for things to develop on their own.

She pressed her face against the cold rock of the cliff and cried as she pictured Troon teaching his lessons, but she didn't have time to cry over her lost love. The stone beneath her left foot let go and sent her foot dangling without support. She searched blindly for another toe hold when her right foot broke loose and slipped down a hand's width to a thin but solid ledge. Repositioning her hands, she lowered herself the short distance, finding the same ledge with her left foot. She bowed her head and held her forehead against the stone again while she closed her eyes and said a little prayer, "Varna thanks Troon for saving Varna. Varna knows it was Troon that found the safe place for Varna's foot and though Varna does not know why Troon is not ready for Varna, Varna understands now that it is not Troon's wish for Varna to venture into the land of the spirits just yet. Fear not, love. Varna knows Troon will wait until it is time for Varna to join Troon."

"Varna!" Zho called from below as he scampered up the sheer face, "Hold on Varna! Zho comes!"

New tears flooded Varna's eyes. Troon sent his best pupil to save her. Her chest heaved unsteadily, but she held on and calmed her emotions.

"Varna?"

"Yes Zho. Varna is waiting."

Zho climbed to just below her and calmly said, "Zho is here now. It is too far to climb up, so let Zho guide Varna's foot down to a better ledge."

Zho reached up and gently wrapped his fingers around her left ankle, saying, "Trust Zho. Varna will step down to the next ledge with Zho." Even more than she trusted Zho, she trusted Troon's judgment in sending him. Zho guided her foot off the smaller ledge and down to his. She stepped down with him and saw that the new ledge led them diagonally across the face of the cliff down to the valley.

Once on the ground, Varna closed her eyes and angled her face up to the heavens. Troon sent his surrogate son to save her. She opened her eyes to thank Zho, but her face contorted and she threw herself to the ground, spewing her breakfast onto the valley floor and almost onto Zho's feet.

Such a revolting response to the man that had just saved her left her mortified. She never should have shown such weakness to Zho. She turned away from him and kept her face close to the ground.

"Is Varna good?"

"No! Varna is not good! Do not look at Varna like this."

"Do not worry so. It happens to all of us sometime. It was a very frightening moment. Varna should not feel shame."

"It does not happen to all of us!" she yelled. "When did it ever happen to Zho?"

Zho smiled sheepishly and said, "When Troon taught Zho to slaughter and clean a goat, only Zho did not miss Troon's feet."

Varna looked up and asked, "Really?"

Zho just nodded his head and said, "Now perhaps Varna is ready to come with Zho back to the tribe?"

Varna shook her head no.

"It is Kendo's wish that Varna comes with us. We need Varna's skills."

"No," she said, "what we truly need is Troon's bow. We cannot face those beasts with our bare hands and Wull's bow is not ready yet. Varna returns to the old village and hopes Troon's bow has survived the flood."

"Varna should have told Kendo first."

"Why?" she asked, "So Kendo could refuse Varna's request?"

"No," he replied, "Kendo would have assigned Zho to accompany Varna."

"Varna does not need a man to protect her!" As she heard the words escape her lips, she glanced up the cliff where Zho had just saved her, and her expression softened. She tried looking stoic and forced herself to swallow the smile that so desperately wanted to escape onto her face.

"It is a difficult trip," Zho said, "and Kendo would not want Zho to go without someone to protect Zho."

"Now Zho mocks Varna."

"No, Zho joins Varna. We protect each other."

Varna got up to her feet and said, "Agreed, then."

"So," Zho said, "We return to the old village and get Troon's bow. Then we return to find the tribe at the home of our ancestors."

"Or," Varna said, "We get the bow and we find Mora's medicines and we return to the cave where Joog waits."

The sides of the valley rose up to jagged peaks on both sides. The river had cut a narrow gorge between them that twisted right and left. Kendo could not tell how far they could walk along the river before the water might fill both sides of the gorge and they lost the comfort of the shoreline. Brack and Koro stepped ahead for a better look. The canyon sides were steep and rocky, but smooth at the basin.

"The water is fast and deep," said Koro.

"And," Brack added, "the base of the walls are polished smooth from the river. It may be that the river will not allow us to pass."

"Yes," Kendo agreed, "but the valley climb looks very difficult and our women are already tired."

"Rest here," Koro said, "while Brack and Koro scout ahead."

"No," Kendo said, "It is getting late already. Let us put our faith in chance and follow the river. If we come to an end and it does not lead us out of here, we can turn around and return here to camp for the night."

"As you say," Brack replied, "it is late already. It will be dark soon, and this is a good spot to camp in the canyon. The walls should provide protection from the large cats. Only the goats can scale these cliffs. Then we can set out in the morning when the women and children are rested."

Kendo scratched his chin while he thought it over.

"And still," Koro added, "Brack and Koro can scout ahead so we know where to go in the morning."

Kendo walked to the river and reached down to scoop up some water. It was cold and refreshing. He saw movement in the water as three fish scattered to the other side of the stream. He remained very still as he stared into the water.

Koro inched forward and asked, "Kendo?"

"Shhh!" Kendo said as he stared into the deep pool. He remained frozen until he saw the larger of the three fish return. It swam lazily behind a rock, watching for food to drift past it. The two smaller fish rejoined it behind the rock that sheltered them from the current.

Brack joined Koro, but Koro just looked at him and shrugged.

The two smaller fish shot forward and swam upstream to another rock, but the large one remained behind.

Kendo stood and said, "We will setup camp here while Koro and Brack scout ahead."

The most perilous part of their journey was behind them. Next was a long hike, which took Zho and Varna from the cliffs down into the lower valley that opened up into the familiar foothills that surrounded their old homes and the river of life they had left behind. There was no snow here. Their people knew nothing of snow except for what little they learned in the past few days. The lower valley never saw snow and the ground below their feet was comfortably warm compared to the higher elevations.

A stream from the mountains followed the valley and fed into the river of life. The banks of the stream were filled with debris from above. The debris spread widely over the banks and into the forests and meadows that bordered the stream. The further they descended, the more destruction they saw. The floods knocked down trees and destroyed the peaceful floor of the forest. Many trees had no new buds and remained stark reminders of the dark grey winter. Zho had been on a hunting party when he was young that had found a forest which was burned down by fire and was no less barren looking than this.

But not all was dead. Amongst the dying skeletons of trees were those with new growth trying to survive. Some were older established trees with deep roots, while others were younger saplings new to this earth and loath to give up their new life.

The forest thickened at the base of the foothills. Varna recognized these woods. Troon often brought her here for her training with the bow. The trees sheltered them from prying eyes, but they also required her to develop a keen aim. Her pace quickened. The village was near.

They emerged from the forest atop a hill overlooking the village. Most of the elders had homes along the bank. These were prime locations and the most beautiful the village had to offer. These elder's homes were gone. Some had an outline of the floor left behind to mark their location, while others were completely wiped from existence.

Mora's hut wasn't on the shoreline. It was built on a high hill overlooking the village. Troon's lodge was even further back from the village and higher up the hill. It was more secluded, which offered them some additional privacy during their secret marriage. It was also directly in the center of a new river which had splintered from the overflowing stream and now was dry without the floods that fed it.

The thatch roof of Troon's lodge was gone. The uphill walls were caked in dried mud. Varna was overwhelmed with regret as she saw the destroyed hut. Did the Gods disapprove of their marriage or were they angered by her secret training? She did not know which. Tears flowed down her cheeks as she looked at their destroyed home. In her mind, she thought she had stopped walking when she saw the destruction, but her feet kept walking of their own accord, carrying her closer to the carnage until she was upon it. The mud around the hut had dried and hardened. She found a large hole ripped in the back wall where the river had broken through and carried all their belongings away, but when she entered through the hole, she found a wall of furniture and spears had dammed up against the door. The missing wall, where the hole had torn through, was where Troon had mounted his bow. It was gone. She fell to her knees and lamented the loss of the bow.

Zho put a hand on her shoulder and said, "Do not give up now. We must search through the rubble." He stepped to the door and started dismantling the dam. "Some of these spears are still good. Let us start a pile of all those things that we can salvage. We may yet find the bow to be counted among the salvage."

Varna climbed to her feet and joined him. The tears still flooded her eyes and fell freely down her cheeks, but she was able to see enough to tell a good spear from a bad one. She saw no sign of Troon's magnificent bow.

The river coursed swiftly through the twisting gorge. Its pace slowed where the gorge widened and lowered the water to splash over the rocky bottom, then sped again to a swift and dangerous torrent where the gorge narrowed and deepened the water. The banks collected no silt or mud. Smooth pebbles crunched beneath Brack's and Koro's feet as they scouted the length of the gorge, leaving the tribe behind to set up camp for the night.

They never came across a section of river that filled the canyon from wall to wall as they had feared it might, but Brack could see from the smooth sides that the river does fill the gorge after a heavy rain. The steep canyon walls may provide the tribe some protection from the predators for the night, but a heavy rain could spell disaster. Fortunately for them, the skies were clear and did not look like a coming rain storm tonight.

The rise in elevation from the point where they left Kendo was not bad. The women could easily handle the climb, but at the end of the gorge was a waterfall, and there was nowhere left to go except up. They would have to climb their way out, this time without Brahg's help.

The sky darkened, and they were losing the moon, which was already in the west. Brack climbed up the canyon wall to about Koro's height then jumped down and said, "The rock is sturdy enough, but it will be too dark to climb before we would reach halfway."

Koro agreed and said, "Within these canyon walls, it may soon be too dark to see the path back to camp. Already it may be dangerous finding our way."

Brack nodded his head and said, "True. Koro can go first."

Koro laughed, but headed back first anyway.

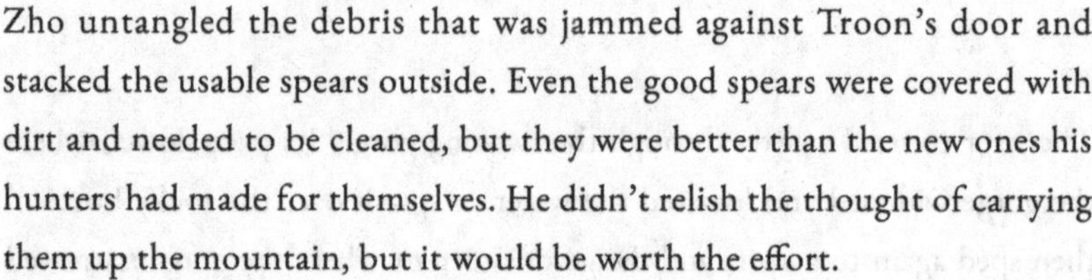

Zho untangled the debris that was jammed against Troon's door and stacked the usable spears outside. Even the good spears were covered with dirt and needed to be cleaned, but they were better than the new ones his hunters had made for themselves. He didn't relish the thought of carrying them up the mountain, but it would be worth the effort.

Varna exited the hut through the hole in the back wall and walked around to the front. She pulled debris out of the mess on the opposite side from Zho, but paused when she pulled out a pair of slippers. They were hard and crunchy now, but had been soft and warm. They were from Varna's first kill and were Troon's favorite slippers. A tear formed in her eye. She wondered when the tears would stop coming to her. She hugged the slippers. In her mind she saw Troon with the slippers, but when her body registered how sharp and scratchy, the leather had become, the image in her mind dissolved and she tossed the slippers on the pile of garbage she had started and wiped the tears from her eyes.

They finished digging up enough of the debris to allow them to pass through the doorway and the bow was not there, but they did salvage a handful of knives to join the pile of spears Zho had made.

Varna stood in the cleared front door looking towards the river and saw ripples in the dried mud where the water flowed around the hut. There was also a tear shaped ripple that flowed through the front door. Anything that did not get trapped in the front door must have been carried down the hill to the river. She followed the ripples that formed outside the door. A thin, hard crust had formed atop the ripples. Her feet broke through the crisp surface and sunk into a soft layer of silt below.

"Varna," Zho said, "it gets dark already. Let us settle for the night. Zho is certain we can search better with the light in the morning."

Varna turned and looked at Troon's hut, but Zho pointed up the hill and said, "Not here. Mora's lodge remains standing."

***

Mora looked over their meager stores. Her patient's appetites were returning, which was a good thing, but their rations were limited and Brahg had a huge appetite. She wasn't a cook, but she could roast meat over a fire and prepared the remaining meat on spits in the center of the cave.

She had already salvaged the rib bones, which made good needles, and didn't want the remaining carcasses to spoil in the cave, so she took them to bury outside in the sacred soil. When she opened the gate, Marl asked, "Where is Mora going in the dark?"

"Mora is just going to bury the bones."

Marl started getting up and Mora screeched, "Stop! What are you doing?"

"If Mora plans to bury the bones, Marl will escort her."

Mora shook her head and said, "Mora is perfectly capable of burying a few bones alone."

"Mora is also capable of making some large cat a fair meal," Marl said.

Brahg looked at her and added, "More like a light snack."

"Do not worry," Mora said. "Mora will stay close."

Pela said, "And Pela will go with Mora."

Brahg objected, "But Pela is even a more fetching meal than Mora is."

"It matters not who goes to bury the bones," Marl said. "Marl does not want every creature within our scent to dig up the front of the cave and lie in wait for us. Marl does not want the bones to be a beacon for hungry predators, and Marl cannot allow Mora to venture off away from the cave in the dark."

"But," Brahg said, "If Mora does not bury them outside, we will have all those creatures trying the gate. Brahg has faith in Wull's gate, but Brahg does not want to test it so. Brahg thinks it would be best for Mora to bury the bones just outside the gate."

"Perhaps," Yona said, "Mora can bury them outside the gate for the night. We can dig them up and move them further away in the light."

Marl agreed, and Pela kept watch just outside the gate while Mora dug a hole. The snow was still thick in the shadow of the mountain and she was able to bury them deep in the sacred soil. They returned to the cave and Mora said, "It is done. As long as the sacred soil does not turn to water overnight, the remains will still be buried."

She returned her attention to the roasting meat and divvied up the fruit. She may have to let Marl out sooner than she wanted so he could trap some more game for them.

Mora's hut was untouched by the flood. While the rest of the village was swept under by the swollen river and even Troon's hut, which was high on the hill like Mora's, collapsed under flash floods, Mora's was dry and complete.

Varna circled the inside of the lodge, examining Mora's many stores, which everyone had assumed were taken by the river. "Mora is going to be so happy," Varna said, "when we bring her supplies."

Zho was too busy starting the fire to search with Varna, but he glanced up to see how many sacks and bundles Varna had found. He wasn't going to be able to carry them all. He was already concerned about how he was going to carry the spears and looking at the additional supplies Varna was collecting, he said, "Zho can build a travois to carry the supplies as with Joog, but Zho can't drag all these supplies up the cliff."

"Varna will help."

"It will be many trips."

"Varna will help! This trip will not be for nothing."

"No," Zho said, "This trip will not be for nothing, but Zho wonders why Varna is so upset. Did Varna really come for the bow? Is that really why Varna left the tribe and came here?"

Varna shook her head and said, "No, not entirely. Varna wanted Troon's bow. Varna thought that getting Troon's bow would honor Troon's memory. Varna also thought that the tribe would forgive Troon for training Varna when they saw Varna using the bow to protect the tribe from those creatures. But Varna also heard how much Mora wished for these things and how much Joog needed them. Kendo had the visions and could not deny the calling of the ancestors, so Varna came back for the things that Kendo would not return to get."

Zho still wondered, as Kendo had, if Varna had really meant to use this trip to join Troon in the spirit world. He started to ask her when they heard a twig snap outside. He reached for his weapon, but it was down by Troon's hut. Varna grabbed two daggers from a box and handed one to Zho.

It was dark outside, but they could hear something rustling around the back of the hut. Zho stepped quietly through the door and paused to readjust his eyes to the darkness. Varna grabbed a tallow lantern that Mora kept by her bed and lit it. She followed Zho out with the lantern in one hand and the dagger in the other.

The sound stopped. Something was there, and it knew they were looking for it. Zho crept around the corner to the back of the hut. Varna went the other direction. She had to circle Mora's chicken pen, which was just a small fence that bordered a yard attached to the side of her hut. She kept low with the lantern out in front. The low flame flickered and barely lit the way. Varna turned the final corner and something in the bushes that jumped out, then darted the other way directly into Zho.

She heard the collision. Zho landed on his backside, but he had the intruder locked in his arms. Varna ran to assist and found him lying on the ground, laughing with a goat in his arms.

"Look at this," he said. "Zho has found dinner."

"It looks to Varna like dinner has found Zho."

"Zho will take it down to the river to clean it."

The goat bleated and Varna said, "Wait. Is the goat still unharmed?"

"Yes," Zho said, "Only Zho was hurt in the struggle."

"Varna doesn't need dinner tonight. We should take it back with us."

"Great," Zho said, "More to carry back."

"Varna does not think so. Troon told Varna a story of the time when they still hunted buffalo. One buffalo survived the trap the men had dug, so they made it carry the others back to the tribe for them."

"Zho has heard the story. Troon said the beast was very difficult to control and it might have been better to slay it and carry it on their backs with the other meat."

"But," Varna said, "This goat is already tame. It will follow us with a simple rope around its neck."

Varna was right. Zho carried the goat and put it in the chicken pen. The goat seemed content to be near them.

"Zho wonders if any more goats survived the flood."

Varna was staring at the goat in the otherwise empty pen and said, "Varna wouldn't mind finding some chickens."

They returned inside Mora's hut, and Zho stoked the fire in the center. He lay down on one of the extra sleeping rolls Mora had for patients and allowed Varna to have Mora's own bed, which was separated by a screen for more privacy.

Varna laid her head on the pillow and whispered, "Varna thanks Troon for sending Zho. Varna knows that Troon will watch over Varna's return. Troon loves Varna and Varna loves Troon."

She fell asleep with her lover's name still on her lips.

***

Brack and Koro could smell the roasting fish long before they could see the light from the fires. The sun and the moon had long ago disappeared over the western wall of the gorge, leaving them in nearly total darkness. They found their way back by listening to the sound of the river and watching the swath of stars in the clear sky overhead that outlined the gorge walls as an inky blackness where the stars were blocked from view.

The scent of food was encouraging and prompted them to step a little faster. They rounded another twist in the winding canyon and saw the glow of fires dancing on the sides of the canyon further down the river. The tribe had set up multiple fires blocking the entrance to the gorge. Each fire had an abundance of fish mounted over it. The people found spots on the ground where they could sit up against the canyon walls, but were still near enough to feel the warmth of the fire.

Koro kicked a river stone which startled one of the nearby women until Koro said, "It's ok. It is us."

The children, energized with full bellies, bounced around in circles, laughing and squealing. One of the four-year-olds ran up to take Koro and Brack by their hands and guide them to the food.

Kendo and Wull stopped their conversation to join the returning scouts.

"So," Kendo said, "Where did the river take Koro and Brack?"

Koro had already grabbed a skewer with a roasted fish on it and was shoving pieces of meat into his mouth. "Mmph blphh rppph."

Brack laughed and said, "Brack will answer for Koro. At the end of the canyon is a steep climb, but no more steep than here, and perhaps less so. It is certainly less high than the climb would be here."

Kendo looked into the darkness up the river and imagined he could see what lay beyond. "So," he asked, "does Brack think it will be best to follow the river and climb up at the end of the gorge then continue following the river?"

"Brack does."

Kendo's eyes twinkled as he looked at Koro and said, "Brack better eat something before Koro leaves Brack nothing."

A shaft of light cast through a crack in the wall, caressed Zho's face and flashed across his eyelids. He snapped his eyes open and sat up. The hut was warm, and the fire was still going.

He scrunched his face as he looked at the fire. It should have burned out long ago. He got up and stretched his arms. It felt like it might be warming up outside.

"Varna?" he asked as he checked around the screen that separated Mora's bed, but she was gone.

"That explains the fire," he muttered to himself.

He stepped out of the hut. A slight chill still hung in the air, but it was a beautiful blue sky and he could tell it would warm up rapidly. The goat in the pen bleated, and then a second goat answered. He spun around and found two more goats in Mora's chicken pen.

"Varna?" he called out, but she didn't answer.

He saw her tracks heading towards the river and followed. The path to the river was littered with rubble from Troon's home. He rounded a large tree at the base of the path and found her in the river bathing. Her back was to him and she didn't see him approach. If Troon had ever come across her bathing, there was no wonder why he would have taken her for a wife. This certainly wasn't the rough and tumble tomboy Zho remembered as a child. She dipped down under the surface for a final rinse and sprang up, shivering from the cold water. She squeezed the water from her hair as she lazily turned towards the shore where her clothes were piled in a wet lump.

"Zho?"

He averted his eyes and said, "Zho didn't mean to intrude, Zho just came down to catch some fish for breakfast."

"With no spear?"

"Zho can still catch the fish the old way."

She laughed and said, "Varna has already caught breakfast. It is here. Maybe Zho can cook it?"

Before Zho could respond, a chicken clucked nearby to his right. He sprinted after it and chased it around a tree.

"Or," Varna snickered, "Zho could try to catch the chicken."

Zho weaved between the trees after the wily bird. He banged his shoulder into the thick trunk of an old tree and bounced back towards the river after the bird. The chicken darted to the edge of the stream, then ducked back under a bush.

Zho followed, but when he planted his foot to turn, he slipped on the damp stone. He twisted to catch himself but only managed to turn himself over and slid into the river, landing face down and prone in the water.

Varna squealed with laughter.

Zho was cold, wet, and humiliated. "Why does Varna laugh so?" he asked. "Does Varna not think that catching the chicken could be important for the tribe?"

"Varna agrees, but now Zho can bathe and perhaps when Zho is clean and doesn't smell so, the chicken won't run away."

"Oh?" Zho asked, "Can Varna do better? Has Troon shared some secret knowledge on how to catch chickens with Varna?"

"No," Varna said, "but the chicken shared its knowledge on how to make Varna bathe."

Zho raised his eyebrows and then pointed one hand at the chicken and the other at Varna. She nodded her head, and he laughed.

"Very well then," he said. "Since the chicken commands it, Zho will move downriver to the men's section to bathe."

"Varna will cook the fish. We can build some traps for the chicken after we eat."

"Does Varna know there are two more goats in the pen?"

"Yes," she replied, "They were just standing outside the gate visiting the one we caught last night. Varna opened the gate, and they went right in."

Varna climbed out of the water.

Zho tried to avert his eyes again, but he couldn't. They shared a common father, even if they were only adopted. She was like a sister to him, yet he still could not look away.

She wrapped a skin around her waist and left her breasts free to dry in the air, then picked up the fish and the rest of her clothing and walked up to the hut.

He watched her hips sway as she walked and didn't break his gaze until she was obscured by the trees. He slapped his palm against his head and reminded himself that she married his adopted father, which made her more like his mother.

She was gone now, and he could have bathed here, but it felt wrong to him. This is where she was, his mother, and he felt deeply disturbed. He moved down river to bathe, but stopped when he saw the grisly remains of a goat on the shore.

The goat's belly was split open, and its limbs were dismembered. Pieces of it had been torn off and scattered around the shore. Zho crouched down in the water. Had it been so long since the tribe had left the river that a predator would have moved in already? He forgo the bath and ran up the hill to the hut.

Varna was inside, humming a pleasant tune. A fourth goat wanted into the pen with his friends and the chicken that was in there with them.

Zho let the goat into the pen and asked, "Did bathing really help Varna catch the chicken?"

"No," Varna said, "the chicken was hungry and followed Varna's fish all the way here."

"And we have another goat," Zho added as he stepped into the hut.

The roasting fish overpowered all the other scents of herbs and powders that Mora had in her stores. The odor of cooking fish wasn't one of Zho's favorite fragrances, but his hunger made it a welcome scent. Varna handed him a serving board with one of the fish and he immediately began pulling bits of flesh from the bones.

A rooster crowed outside.

Zho just shook his head and asked, "Do the animals always flock to Varna? Does Varna hear them speak as well?"

Varna giggled and said, "No. Varna thinks they returned after the flood and their food was gone. They are glad we have returned."

Zho remembered what he saw at the river and said, "With good reason. There is a predator in the village. Zho found a goat shredded apart. We should be more careful."

Varna had been giddy all morning, but seeing the expression on Zho's face, she pulled a shawl around her shoulders to cover herself and said, "Varna needs to look again for Troon's bow."

Kendo had stayed up longer than he should have, watching over the sleeping tribe. It was nearer to sunrise than sunset before Wull and Flom could convince him to get some sleep. Even when he finally did close his eyes, sleep did not come easy. He worried more about Joog than he should have. He should hand the leadership of the tribe to someone else, but who could lead them? Most of the surviving men were too young to lead. Only Wull had the experience, but he would be far too busy building the village to concern himself with any other matters. Kendo's mind raced throughout the morning and even when he did drift off to sleep, it was restless at best.

Wull quietly woke the tribe as the sky lightened above. He shared the leftover fish with everyone as they packed their things and prepared for the day's march. When everyone was ready, he gently woke Kendo and said, "Wull was going to carry Kendo while Kendo slept, but Brack says the climb is too steep. Kendo will have to carry Kendo."

Kendo looked up and saw many smiling faces circled around him and asked, "Did Kendo oversleep? Very well. Let's pack up to go."

The many faces that circled him laughed and Wull said, "The tribe is ready. Here is some fish to nibble on while Kendo wakes his legs."

The sun had not yet shone directly into the gorge, but all could tell it would be a warm day. The sky was clear, and the tribe was well fed and well rested. Even the sound of the stream was filled with mirth.

Kendo rose and inspected the tribe. He looked at Wull and remembered the rambling thoughts that had kept him awake. As if he could read Kendo's thoughts, Wull said, "The tribe is ready. Wull has everything prepared, but only Kendo has the vision which we can follow."

Kendo gripped Wull's arm, forearm to forearm, and said, "We are far too short of elders and leaders. Kendo does not think one leader is enough anymore and welcomes Wull's help."

Kendo took the lead and said, "Brack? Koro? Show us this passage you have found."

Wull motioned for Flom to join him and said, "We will take the rear. Let us keep one eye ahead of us on the tribe, and the other behind us."

After breakfast, Varna and Zho left to search Troon's quarters, but three more chickens had gathered outside the pen. They pecked at the ground, looking for grain.

"Truly," Zho said, his voice filled with amazement, "Varna has magic inside. Varna speaks to the animals and they listen."

"No," Varna said, blushing slightly, "The cock crowed, and the chickens came. There is no magic."

The chickens did not run to escape as Varna picked them up and dropped them over the pen walls. The cock strutted arrogantly along the pen wall.

Zho still thought there was magic within Varna. The rooster came for her on its own. He scratched his head and said, "So many chickens now. Zho wishes Wull were here to build a cage so we could take them with us."

"Maybe," Varna said, "Zho can build a trap and we can use it as a cage."

Less and less did Zho wonder what Troon had seen in Varna. She continued on to Troon's hut and Zho saw the sun light her head and swore he saw a red glow in her hair surrounding her head.

"Zho will build a trap, as Varna says. Then Varna can speak with the chickens when we journey back. But Zho thinks they would simply follow Varna if Varna asked them to."

Varna returned to Troon's hut. They had already dug up the debris that had dammed up the front door, but she checked it again in the morning light and still found no sign of the bow. She followed the stream flow as it was etched in the crusted mud and found another dam atop a ridge that led down to the heart of the village.

This new dam had a lot more mud and debris. Large chunks of thatch from Troon's hut had soaked with mud and turned into hard chunks like stone. She fetched a broken spear from the junk pile and began digging out the debris.

Below the top layer of debris from Troon's hut, she found larger tree branches which must have swept down the flooding stream from above. The tree branches were too big and too deep for her to pull out. She dug down again with the broken spear until she could remove them.

Zho used pieces of Mora's hut to build the trap. They were lucky that her hut was as unscathed as it was. He was able to build not only the traps, but he also built two more travois for them to load up with Mora's supplies.

The day was slipping by and Zho had thought that they would have left by now. It was time to break for lunch, so he went to Troon's hut to find Varna. He found her chipping away at the crusted mud around the tree limbs and said, "Varna should have called Zho to help. Troon may have taught Varna to hunt like a man, but even Troon could never teach Varna to have a man's strength."

Zho gripped the buried tree limb and gave it a mighty tug. It was too deep, but he could not give in after what he had just said. He dug his feet in and held the exposed limb across his back and put all his effort into it.

Varna giggled when she saw how much he wished he had never said anything, then she saw something reflect from under the limb and yelled, "Stop! Hold it right there!"

She reached into the pile under the limb. Zho dare not lose his grip now or the limb would spring back and kill Varna. She brushed away the dirt where she had seen a glint of red and exposed the tip of Troon's bow. She took the spear and began chipping away around the bow.

"The tree is strong, and Zho cannot hold it forever."

Varna understood and climbed out from under the limb and said, "Let it back gently. We will dig out the limb first."

Zho put the limb back in place and wiped the sweat from his brow. All thoughts of breaking for lunch were gone. He grabbed another spear and began digging out the limb alongside Varna.

Mora used the last of the stores to fix breakfast for her patients. Brahg said he wasn't very hungry and gave half his portion to Joog and Marl.

Mora went to the gate and said, "Mora needs to gather some more food."

Brahg sat up gingerly and said, "Brahg will come with Mora."

"No," Mora said, "It is too soon. Pela and Yona can come."

"Brahg will be careful. Mora should have a man with her if danger comes."

"It is too risky for Brahg," Mora said.

Marl added, "Brahg is right. No creature will attack Mora while Brahg is nearby."

"And," Brahg said, "Mora has said before that the fresh air is good for the healing."

"Brahg is big," Mora admitted, "but if Brahg's size were enough to scare away predators, then Brahg wouldn't be in this bed with teeth wounds in his back."

"It was dark," Marl said, "and the creature did not see his face."

Pela threw a berry at Marl and said, "Brahg has a very nice face."

"And perhaps this evening," Marl said, "Marl should set some traps."

"No," Mora said, "Neither of you will be going out today. If Marl does not want to eat nuts and berries for five more days, then Marl can teach Yona to make the traps."

"Yona?" Marl asked. "How can a girl make a trap?"

Brahg shook his head and whispered, "Marl should not have said that."

Mora stepped to the foot of Marl's bed and sternly said, "Did Marl not see Varna bring the meat? Does Marl still believe it was always Troon who fed the tribe?"

Marl was speechless and looked to Yona for support, but she only looked angrily at him.

Joog said, "If Yona brings Joog thin supple twigs, Joog will teach Yona to build a trap."

Yona was thrilled and moved from Marl's side to Joog's.

Pela reminded them, "We still must move the bones we buried last night."

Mora returned to the gate and asked, "Is Yona going to fawn over Joog now or come join us to collect the wood Joog requested?"

Yona jumped up to join Mora and Pela. She looked sternly back at Marl and said, "Yona will return later to take care of Joog."

A cloud of dust gathered around them as Varna and Zho chipped and dug around the tree limb, but it seemed like they would never reach the end of the limb. Defeat began to register on Varna's face, and Zho worked all the harder, swinging the spear violently into the earth. Regardless of how much the bow might mean to the tribe, he knew how much it meant to Varna and would not let her go home without it. Sweat dripped off his forehead as his swings slowed and lost their force.

He dropped the spear and fell to his knees, exhausted. "Again," he said, "We could use Wull's help."

"Or just his axe," Varna added.

Even her voice sounded defeated to him. He feared she might start to cry again, so he took a deep breath and gathered his strength. He got up and went to the end of the limb and tried again to force the limb away from the bow. They had dug enough of the limb out that he could bend it much farther than he had before. Varna took a grip of the limb alongside Zho and pushed with him. The limb bent even more and wiggled in the mud but still held. Varna grunted as she pushed harder; one more step; a step and a half; the branch cracked and sent Zho tumbling to the ground with Varna landing on top of him.

"So," Zho said, "Troon taught Varna a man's strength after all."

Varna blushed and said, "No, Varna does not have a man's strength, but Varna believes that Troon sent Zho, so he could be here to break Varna's fall."

Zho laughed and thought Varna was going to laugh too, but her face contorted into a strange look of fear. She threw herself off of him to the side of the tree, where she again expelled her breakfast onto the ground.

She was wracked with shame and immediately returned to digging the bow. "Varna is sorry. Varna is just a weak woman, after all."

"Varna is not weak," Zho said. "Troon would have never selected a weak woman."

Varna said nothing and just dug away at the bow.

"Zho will go to the river and catch lunch while Varna digs out the rest of the bow."

"Varna is not hungry," she said, but it was a lie. She was famished. Every time she threw up, it left her empty and hungry, but she was afraid that if she ate, she would only throw up again.

Zho took a slender spear down to the river and made quick work of catching some fish. They used to call this the river of life, but after the flood, some called it the river of death. He looked upon the many fish that had returned to the river and wondered now if they were too hasty to leave the valley.

He carried his catch back to Mora's lodge and mounted them on spits over the fire. He was no cook and added no seasonings, but he knew when to turn them to cook them evenly. When they were done, he placed them on serving boards and carried them to Varna.

She had the bow out of the dirt and was picking off chunks of mud that had baked onto it. He thought she would have been happier to finally have the bow, but something was wrong. She sat on her knees with her head down and her back hunched over her bow. She looked up at him as he approached and he saw tears gathered around her eyes.

"Is something wrong?" he asked. "Is the bow broken?"

She shook her head and said, "Varna does not think so, but the bowstring is gone."

"Has Troon not taught Varna how to make a bowstring?"

She shook her head no and said, "Troon only taught Varna how to mount the bowstring."

"Do not worry," Zho said, "Let us go down to the river to eat this fish, and Zho will tell Varna how a bowstring is made."

Outside the cave, Mora dug up the carcass from the night before. It was as she had left it when she buried it. She lifted the bones to her nose and sniffed. The sacred soil must have prevented it from spoiling.

Pela stepped out of the cold shadow. The sun was up over the mountain and was warm against her skin. She scanned the meadow and saw patches of dirt showing through the thinning frost.

Mora joined her and said, "It is too soon for the fresh berries, but perhaps we can find some nuts or wild onions."

"Then," Yona said, "If there is little food to gather, let us at least collect the wood for Joog. The sooner we make the traps, the sooner we can eat more meat."

The tribe paused at the end of the gorge and absorbed the beauty of the waterfall.

Kendo was awed by its majesty and said, "Koro did not say how breathtaking the view was."

"It was getting dark," Koro replied. "Koro did not know."

The water tumbled down six different steps, each with its own unique character. The top was two wide sheets of water pouring over flat ledges shaped like a 'V' that spilled into each other and fell down a section of tumbled boulders then split into two separate streams that spread away from each other before widening into two wide rocky streams that came back together again for one final fall into a deep basin at the bottom where a mist undulated and glistened in the light.

It was a magnificent sight that could only have originated from some place sacred. This surely was the path to the home of the ancestors.

Koro and Brack checked the ledge to the left of the falls and found the passage they had seen the previous evening.

"It was too dark to climb last night," Brack said, "but we thought we could see enough to reach the top."

"Lead on," Kendo said.

Brack went first and climbed the few feet which he had tried in the dark. A gap between a large boulder and the wall led them up a third of the way and ended facing another large boulder. Working together, Koro put his foot in the cradle Brack made with his hands and was heaved up to the top of the boulder. From there, a narrow ledge led across the face of the wall to a deep crack that extended into the gorge wall. Koro inched across the ledge and peered into the crack.

"What does Koro see?" Kendo asked.

Koro was startled by Kendo's voice and said, "It's a narrow crevice, but looks wide enough for us to enter. It is too dark for Koro to see very far."

The dark crevice was too reminiscent of the larger cave where Joog had lost his foot. Kendo had no intention of allowing anyone to plunge blindly into the darkness unprepared.

"Wait here," Kendo said. He shimmied back across the ledge to the boulder and said, "Send up two spears. Several moments passed before Flom appeared atop the boulder with two spears and Kendo's Staff of Justice strapped to his back. He followed Kendo across the ledge to Koro and shared the weapons.

The sky darkened with gathering clouds, making the crevice even darker. A chill wind blew across the waterfall, depositing bits of mist onto the men and the ledge.

"We are almost to the top," Kendo said. "We can't stop now, but we need to hurry and search this crevice before a storm comes upon us."

A brisk wind blew across the ledge. In the distance, they could hear the crack of thunder.

A deep howling came from deep within the dark crevice. It was a low, sustained tone like the snoring of a sleeping giant, and it exhaled a cool breath that blew across Koro's face and brought chills to his spine. His knees shook as he held the spear in front of him and entered the dark lair.

After resting a moment and eating their fish, Zho led Varna up the stream to the goat he had seen. "Troon preferred spinning fibrous plant stalks into bowstrings," he said, "but Troon also said that in a pinch, a bowstring could be made from animal gut."

The goat carcass was near enough the shore that the gut hadn't already dried before he could stretch it out, but the closer he got the worse it smelled, and if it was too rotten, the gut may not be usable. He took a deep breath and delved into the animal's chest and pulled out as much intestine as he could. He used one of Mora's knives to cut away the gut and backed away from the putrid carrion.

Varna turned away and once again lost her meal into the river. She walked up river to rinse out her mouth and said, "Again, Varna is sorry. Varna has never had such a weak stomach before."

"We should get Varna back to Mora as soon as we can."

Varna heaved again and asked, "Can Zho string the bow now?"

"Zho can prepare a string for the bow. Troon liked to say that there were two ways to make a bowstring: the right way and the fast way. Zho will make a fast string while we travel and worry about making a correct string later."

Zho filled a water skin and rinsed the gut in the river while Varna rinsed off the bow. Zho laid out the gut and cut it into five strands.

They left the river and climbed one last time to Mora's hut. Three more chickens had gathered around the rooster.

Zho put the chickens into the trap he built and laid it onto one of the carriers.

Varna took the packs of medicines and instead of putting them on the remaining travois, she harnessed them onto the goats. Zho put the spears and knives on the travois, but they still had more of Mora's supplies than would fit on the goats.

Zho shrugged and asked, "Which of these packs do we leave behind?"

Varna shook her head and said, "We take everything."

"How?"

She pointed to the travois and asked, "Can Zho make another?"

"Who will pull it?"

Varna took the Travois with the weapons and tied it to the pack harness of one of the goats. "We will need to make several trips at the cliffs, but Varna thinks we can do it."

Zho shook his head in amazement and said, "Zho thinks Varna can do anything. Zho will make another travois. If we let the goats pull all of them, then Zho can work on the bowstring, and Varna can guard us with the bow."

Varna had found plenty of rope and leather straps in Mora's hut to tie the goats together in a small caravan. Zho used some salt from Mora's supplies to dry two strands of the goat gut enough to make a string that was tough and would not stretch too much. He coiled the other three strands of gut in a pouch with some salt to preserve them.

Varna carried Wull's bow while Zho twisted and stretched the goat gut into a workable string while he led them back up the mountain to the cliffs. Zho concentrated on the string he was making, but Varna watched the forest. The predator was still out there.

Zho saw the concern in her face and asked, "What troubles Varna?"

"We still do not know what killed the goat. It is still out there and Varna has a bad feeling."

Zho looked around, but saw nothing and said, "If Varna, who speaks to animals, thinks there is danger, Zho also worries."

"Varna does not speak to animals, but we do have all these goats and chickens to tempt whatever is out there."

Zho still believed that Varna was magic and communed with the animals. As they left the edge of the forest and crossed the rocky flats to the cliff, he heard something squeal behind them. He turned and looked behind and saw a flash of movement in the bushes. "Did Varna hear that?"

"It sounded like a pig," Varna said. "Did Zho see anything?"

"Zho is not sure what Zho saw, but it was bigger than a pig."

Varna scanned the forest behind them and asked, "Was it the giant goat Zho saw before?"

Zho shrugged and said, "Zho did not see it well enough to be sure, but Zho does not believe the helmeted goat would slay another goat and leave the carcass we found by the river. Besides, Zho has never seen the giant goat anywhere except high in the mountains. Something else follows us. Something more dangerous than the giant goat is behind us."

Chapter Six

The Beast That Follows

Koro sucked in his breath and pushed into the dark crevice. A flash of lightning lit the sky overhead, followed momentarily by a clap of thunder that reverberated off the canyon walls. Koro was grateful that the crevice was open to the sky and allowed him to see the flash overhead until an icy chill blew across his face and the deep moan reminded him that they didn't know what was inside the dark crack. He inched forward. It was too dark to see, so he stuck his spear out in front of him and felt the side walls with the tip.

Koro liked the ticking sound the spear made when it struck the sides of the cave. The sharp clicking sound confirmed that he was hitting stone. He feared what might happen if it hit something soft and he woke a sleeping monster. The cave moaned again and exhaled a musty odor upon him, sending a chill down Koro's spine. He clicked his spear on the wall again, but jumped when something landed on his shoulder.

"Koro is ok," Kendo said, "Kendo is right behind Koro, as is Flom."

Kendo expected Flom to announce that he was also with them, and when he did not respond, Kendo removed his hand from Koro's shoulder and turned to ask, "Flom? Is Flom still with us?"

There was no response from Flom and Kendo said, "Well, Kendo is still with Koro. Let us move forward."

Koro hesitantly put a foot forward, feeling for the ground. He tapped his spear right and left. The crevice went straight into the side of the gorge wall. He stepped forward, feeling his way with his feet and his spear, and came across an empty space to his left. The spear still tapped against the walls on the right, but nothing on the left. He reached behind with the spear and tapped the left wall, but next to him there was nothing. He tapped the spear along the ground in front of them and found the path they were on was still there, but another path fell off to the left. Pebbles scattered across the ground as he carefully slid his feet forward. The cave continued, but a branch of the cave opened to the left and fell deeper into the mountain. The cave moaned again and its breath came up from the shaft to their left.

He reached across with his spear and found the other side of the new shaft. A rock broke loose and tumbled down the shaft and he could hear it come to life. A great tumult broiled below them. Koro could hear something climb the shaft until it was upon them and struck him in the face.

Zho stood at the base of the cliff and scanned for the best way up. From there, it looked far less imposing than it had when they climbed down. He found a reasonable path that they could climb and the goats could easily follow. The goats could still carry the packs on their backs, but it was too narrow to pull the travois up the side. He stared at the extra supplies and said, "Well, this is the part where Varna volunteered to carry all the extra supplies up the cliff."

"Varna will help," she said, "but Varna will not carry them all. Zho can guard the supplies while Varna guides the goats up first."

She untied the travois and tied the lead goat's rope to a sash around her waist. She took a deep breath and started up the path that angled up the cliff. The goats followed easily behind her. At the end of the path, she had to climb vertically up the face of the cliff to the top. The goats easily scaled the wall. Their hooves clung firmly to the surface of the rock. She quickly untied the rope from her waist so she didn't hold them back. She climbed over the edge and looked back down.It was a dizzying sight that she was going to have to climb down again, and that wasn't so easy for her the last time she tried it.

She selected a large stone from the ground and pulled a stake from one of the goat's bags and hammered it into the ground. She tied the goats to the stake and pulled a long coil of rope from another goat bag. After tying the rope to the stake, she threw it over the side, but it was too short to reach the ground. She removed the packs from the last three goats and untied them from the caravan.

The thought of Troon crossed her mind and filled her heart, but she didn't have time to allow tears to collect in her eyes, so she simply whispered, "Please Troon, guide Varna." She descended back over the edge of the cliffs with the goats behind her.

Yona returned to the cave with a bundle of thin supple twigs, as Joog had requested. She carried the bundle to Joog and untied them next to him.

Joog examined the wood and said, "These are good. Building a trap is like weaving a basket, except we don't make the weaves close together." He started with a couple of long twigs and bent them into loops. "Since we have no twine, we can overlap the ends and twist them together. A knot would be better, but this will do."

Yona sat on her knees next to Joog and took twigs of her own and did as he did.

Pela sat with Brahg and paid little attention to what Yona was doing until the traps started to actually take shape. When they were done, Yona had two half globe baskets large enough for rabbits.

Pela moved to Yona's side and asked, "What do we do with them now?"

Joog tried sitting up a little straighter but fell back in his bed and said, "Joog is tired now. Let Joog rest a while and teach you later how to set the trap."

Marl patted Joog on the shoulder and said, "Joog and Yona have made some fine traps. Marl will show Yona and Pela how to use the traps while Joog rests."

⁂

Koro and Kendo were both lying on the floor of the crevice with their hands over their heads when Flom returned with a torch.

"Did you see that?" Flom asked. "Flom has never seen such creatures before. They flew like birds but had no feathers."

Kendo climbed to his feet and brushed the dust off. "No," he said, "We saw nothing in the dark."

Flom ventured forward past the shaft while Koro picked himself up. The crevice narrowed but flared out on one side. Flom climbed the crevice wall and found his way to the top. He held the torch down in the crevice so Kendo could follow.

The clouds collected into a dark mass, blotting out the sun. Lightning struck in the distance, followed by a crack of thunder.

Kendo climbed out of the crevice and surveyed the area. The gorge walls extended upwards into small mountain peaks, but he could see a valley between the peaks where the water flowed into the gorge. Sparse trees and other vegetation were scattered up and down the small peaks.

He pointed to the river valley and said, "Let us return to the water and follow the river. Kendo thinks it should lead us to a forest where we can find some shelter from the storm."

Flom asked, "Can we not take shelter in this crevice and return to our journey after the storm passes?"

Kendo looked back into the crevice. He could not see into its dark depths, but he could still feel the shaft breathing on his neck with its minions slapping him in the face as they flew past. This was not a place where he wanted to stay any longer than necessary. He did not want to admit how uncomfortable the cave made him feel, but Flom's suggestion had merit.

"Koro agrees with Kendo. That is the direction Marl suggested. We should continue on. Besides, Koro does not like the crevice. Something much worse may live down that hole."

The wind picked up and blew across the top of the crevice, and the trio could hear the howling of the wind as it blew across the deep shaft.

Flom laughed and asked, "Is Koro afraid of the wind now?"

Kendo mustered up his most fatherly voice and said, "Kendo does not think this is the time to tease Koro. If Koro thinks the crevice is too creepy, then Kendo is willing to continue on up the river looking for better shelter."

"Flom does not believe Kendo will find better shelter than this crevice. If Koro is afraid of the dark, Flom will hold Koro's hand."

Kendo said, "Flom is very kind, but Kendo does not wish to cause any undue stress to Koro."

Flom looked at Kendo sideways and asked, "Does Kendo also wish to hold Flom's hand in the cave?"

Kendo paused and said, "No, that won't be necessary, but do not go far."

Koro could see that Flom had won. In his mind, he knew that Flom was right. He tried convincing himself that it was just because his face stung from where the creatures had slapped him with their wings, but he knew it was just because it was a creepy place that he didn't like.

Flom left the torch with Kendo while he returned to fetch the rest of the tribe.

Zho remained vigilant at the base of the cliff. They both had heard something behind them and Zho had seen a flash of movement, but it hid from them. He scanned the bushes that lined the edge of the forest for any movement. Birds were the only movement he saw.

Varna reached the bottom of the cliff and asked, "Has Zho seen what follows us?"

"No," he replied, "but Zho sees the birds fly everywhere except there." He pointed to the place where he had last seen the movement.

"Then it is still there," Varna said, "watching us."

"Zho agrees, but it did not advance the whole time Varna was gone. Zho was able to finish the bow string while Varna climbed the cliff." He pointed to the completed bow that sat atop the caged chickens.

A thrill rushed through her soul as she grabbed the bow and felt the pull of the string in her hands. It was as magnificent as she remembered.

"So, does Varna know how we will carry the rest of this up the cliff?"

"Varna thinks we can tie the spears and the remaining packs on these goats, but we will have to haul the chickens up ourselves. Varna tried throwing a rope down from the top, but it was too short. Maybe if we each tie a rope to the cage, we can carry it between us."

"Zho thinks that might be too dangerous. Zho remembers Varna getting stuck on the cliff."

"Varna was stuck and almost fell coming down, but going up is much easier."

Varna tied the spears into bundles and strapped them over one of the goats' backs with Wull's bow.

Zho tied the packs onto two of the goats, then took the three travois and tied them atop the spears.

Varna tied ropes to each end of the cage. She wore Troon's bow over her shoulder and across her chest diagonally. She hung one of the ropes over her other shoulder, then tied it to her waist and waited for Zho to do the same with his rope.

With the ropes secured, they looked at each other and nodded. They didn't need to say that if one of them fell, they would both perish.

Varna went to the cliff first and said, "Troon will guide us."

Pela and Yona lay on their bellies in the meadow by the stream. Pela set her trap near the water and Yona's was in the meadow. They each held cords which they could pull to drop the traps onto any rabbit or bird that came to investigate their bait. They dug up roots near the stream for bait, but began to wonder if their bait wasn't good enough.

Marl told them they would have to lie still for a long time, but they never imagined how tedious it would be.

Pela thought animals would come to the stream for water and investigate her trap, but it had no visitors at all. She wanted to move it to a better spot, but Yona's trap had curious rabbits and a pheasant almost peeked inside. She waited dutifully, watching her trap until she heard Yona's trap fall and Yona squealed, "I got one!"

Pela jumped up to see, and as Yona had said, a rabbit was in her trap. They hugged each other with glee, but the smiles eroded from their faces as they realized what they had to do next.

Yona's lip trembled as she looked at the sweet animal and it looked back at her.

"Pela will do this for Yona."

Yona turned her back while Pela reached in through a gap in the trap and grabbed the rabbit by the scruff of the neck, but she couldn't do it either. Instead, she stuffed it into the leather sack she brought to collect roots and berries. She retrieved her trap and said, "Let us return now."

Yona saw the movement in Pela's sack and understood what she had done.

She picked up her trap and started back towards the cave.

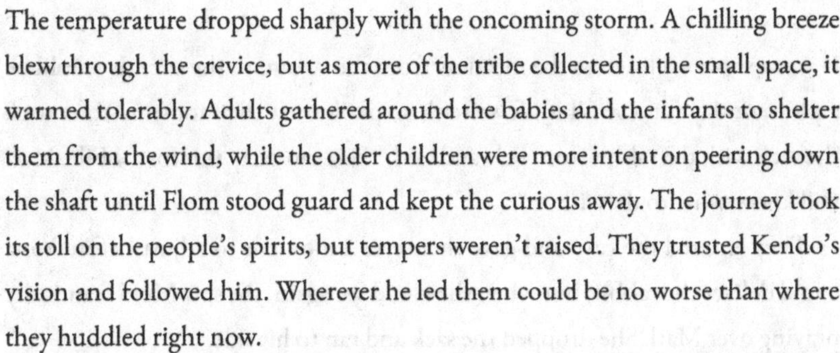

The temperature dropped sharply with the oncoming storm. A chilling breeze blew through the crevice, but as more of the tribe collected in the small space, it warmed tolerably. Adults gathered around the babies and the infants to shelter them from the wind, while the older children were more intent on peering down the shaft until Flom stood guard and kept the curious away. The journey took its toll on the people's spirits, but tempers weren't raised. They trusted Kendo's vision and followed him. Wherever he led them could be no worse than where they huddled right now.

A brief rain fell on them as the storm passed overhead. Lightning flashed across the sky, followed by thunderclaps that reverberated through the canyon and into the crevice, but the storm passed quickly, leaving blue skies in its place and the sun beaming down upon the landscape.

Kendo climbed up out of the crevice and took a second look at the valley that lay ahead of them. Steam rose from the wet ground, warmed by the sun.

Brack joined him and pointed between the mountains which guided the river to the gorge and said, "That must be the valley Joog saw."

"And the lake Marl described must lay beyond it," Kendo said. "Kendo will be glad when we can stop walking and start building."

Brack stared up at the rocky slopes that loomed over the other side of the crevice behind them. The peaks were white and barren. The trees only stretched halfway up the mountain, then thinned out to nothing.

Kendo followed Brack's gaze up the mountain and asked, "Does Brack see something?"

"No," he replied, "But Brack remembers the leopards that lived higher up in the mountains and wonders if any such beasts live in these."

<hr>

It was a short walk across the meadow from the stream to the cave. It would be a pleasant day for a stroll if life weren't so perilous at the moment. Yona took the sack with the rabbit from Pela and said, "Pela can carry this for a while. Marl will know what to do with it."

They entered the cave and gave their eyes a moment to adjust before Yona could deliver the rabbit, but when she could see again, she saw Mora frantically praying over Marl. She dropped the sack and ran to his side.

Mora heard Yona approach and said, "Marl's skin burns hot. His wounds have poisoned his blood."

Pela snatched up the sack and held it out in front of her, saying, "We have the meat. Mora can save Marl with the meat."

Mora shook her head and said, "Marl's sickness is beyond the food now. Marl needs Elk Root and red Goro Clay, but Mora has none."

"Pela knows Elk Root. Pela will go find some."

Mora said, "While Pela finds the Elk Root, Mora will go search the stream for clay."

Brahg winced as he sat up and said, "Brahg will go with Mora."

Mora shook her head and said, "Brahg is weakened and isn't strong enough."

Brahg pointed at the sack Pela held and said, "Brahg can still get strength from a good meal. Pela will cook the meat and Brahg will eat, then we will go get the clay together."

Pela handed the sack to Brahg, and he felt it move inside. Pela just shrugged her shoulders and said, "Pela must go find the Elk Root, but Yona can stay and cook the meat."

"No," Yona said, "Pela must not go out alone. Yona will go with Pela. Mora can cook the meat."

"But," Mora said, "Yona and Pela need their strength, too. Cooking the meat won't take long."

Pela looked at the wiggling bag and remembered the rabbit's eyes. She shook her head and said, "Pela is not hungry."

Yona shook her head and said, "Neither is Yona. We will return soon with the Elk Root for Marl."

<hr>

The rope dug into Varna's shoulder as the chicken cage scraped along the cliff. The goats followed effortlessly behind Zho as he followed Varna with the rope from the other end of the cage slung over his shoulder. Varna was glad she had just climbed the cliff once and knew where she would lead Zho up the side.

Zho followed Varna, keeping the cage dangling between them, but he also kept one eye below and behind them. They had no idea what was following them and didn't know whether or not it could scale the cliff.

The ledge they climbed was wide enough for their feet, but they couldn't set the cage down on its own. Varna paused halfway up and lowered the cage to the ledge, which reduced the weight on her shoulder by half and allowed them to rest a bit.

Zho felt the weight of the cage too and welcomed the relief, but he didn't want to dally too long. "Zho feels vulnerable here. Climbing the cliff is slow and hard enough by itself, but carrying the cage makes Zho feel like an easy target."

Varna twisted her head around to the left to see behind them and asked, "Does it still follow us?"

"Zho has not seen it, but Zho does not know what it is. What if it comes from the spirit world?"

"If it is from the spirit world, then Troon will protect us. Like Zho, Varna too feels uneasy hanging from the side of a cliff when we are so close to the top."

She winced as she lifted the cage on her shoulder again and resumed climbing. When she reached the end of the narrow path, the goats above them bleated their welcome return and the three that followed Zho squeezed by them and tugged on the rope until Zho loosened it from his waist. They easily bound up the cliff to join their friends.

"Zho wishes we had their feet right now."

Varna smiled as she set the cage down on the ledge and asked, "Can Zho hold the cage while Varna climbs to the top?"

Zho gripped his left hand onto the face of the cliff and his right hand onto the cage. "Zho has the cage, but do not take too long."

Varna loosened the rope on her shoulder and the cage remained on the ledge.

Zho asked, "Can Varna, who speaks to the animals, please ask the hens to remain close to the cliff?"

Varna closed her eyes and shook her head while she climbed up and over the edge of the cliff. The rope dangled from her waist as she stood up and took a firm grip of it.

"Varna has the cage now," she yelled down to him. "Varna will pull it up the cliff."

"Wait," Zho yelled back, "Just hold it from falling while Zho climbs to the top. Then we can both haul it up."

She wrapped the rope around her wrist and said, "Varna is ready."

As Varna had done moments ago, Zho loosened the rope and made sure the cage was steady before he climbed up and over the top. Once on top, he took a good hold of his rope and asked, "Ready?"

Varna nodded and together they pulled the cage up the remainder of the cliff. The cage caught on the rocks and they had to jostle the ropes to bounce the cage over the impediments. Rocks sprayed down the cliff as they tugged the cage up and over the edge.

They heard the pig like squeal again at the bottom of the cliff as the rocks rained down to the floor of the valley. The squeal was loud and pitiful, but was quickly muffled.

The goats bleated, and the chickens clucked. Zho leaned his head over the cliff to hear better, but he could not locate the beast that followed them.

The stream wasn't far from the crevice. It followed the valley to the gorge where it collected into a small pool before it spilled over the twin V shaped ledges. Kendo paused at the pool to count heads and allow the people to refill the water skins. The air was thick with moisture and their furs crackled when they moved. The men who carried the slate were exhausted, but it was too early to stop now and the terrain through the valley looked easy from where Kendo stood.

He followed the shore around the pool to the lazy stream that meandered along this new valley. The mountain range spread out right a left with wide green hills guiding the river to the gorge. Once they had entered the valley, Kendo could see that it stretched much farther than he thought it would, then it angled to the right and up into white-capped mountains.

Unlike the rocky stream that led them up the gorge, this stream had a soft bed filled with long green strands of water plants. Kendo searched for Tela and Risa in the middle of the tribe and asked, "Has Mora's apprentices learned of plants that grow in the stream beds?"

Tela replied, "Mora has told Tela about them, but Tela does not know what to look for."

Kendo pointed to the stream and said, "Perhaps you should collect some in case they will be useful."

Little Risa ran ahead of Tela to the stream bed and reached in. She pulled out several long strands of the green plants and put them in a carrying pouch. A smile that could only belong to a small child stretched across her face.

"Since Risa is so eager to help," Tela said, "Risa can collect the slimy green algae that Mora told Tela about. Risa will find it covering those rocks over there." She pointed upstream a few paces.

Risa looked at the algae and the smile shriveled on her face. Her pace to these rocks was much slower than it was when she ran to the stream. She reached in to scrape it off the rock and said, "Eeew. Risa does not like this algae." The algae shrunk in her hands as she pulled it from the water. She cupped it in both hands and placed it into the bag with the other plants. "Risa has collected the algae," she said, "but next time it will be Tela's turn."

Tela and Kendo both laughed. Kendo patted Risa on the head and said, "Risa has done a good job. Mora will hear about how brave little Risa was."

Yona and Pela returned with the Elk Root, only to find Mora praying over Joog now. Mora looked up when she heard them and said, "Please tell Mora that Yona and Pela found some Elk Root."

Pela handed the bag to Mora and asked, "What has happened?"

Mora said, "Joog now burns with the hot skin."

Pela went to Brahg and felt his face, but Mora said, "Brahg is ok so far, but Mora fears that Brahg will grow hot too."

Brahg stood up with great effort and said, "But Brahg is not hot yet. We should go find the clay Mora wanted. Mora can tell Pela and Yona how to care for Joog and Marl while we are gone."

Mora handed the slate she was using for a knife to Yona and said, "Cut a finger width of the root into pieces as small as you can make them and brew a tea with it. Strain it well and help them drink it. Mora will return as soon as possible."

Mora looked sadly at Brahg and said, "Mora is sorry that Brahg must bear this burden. Brahg should be resting, but this is too important."

"If Brahg gets the sickness too," he said, "then Brahg will also need Mora's clay to get better. Let us go now while we can."

Brahg winced as he climbed through the small door in the fence that protected the cave. The stream was across the meadow past the narrow strip of forest.

Brahg walked stiffly at first, as much from the injuries in his shoulders as from the lying down on the hard cave floor for so long.

"The best place to find the clay is in slow bends in the river where the silt deposits."

"Brahg knows just the place to look," he said. "Zho found a beaver pond near the spot where they saw the giant goat."

Mora nodded and said, "A beaver pond would be an excellent place to look."

Varna hitched the three travois back to the goats and pointed to a small rise in the snow. "Take the goats over that rise and down over the other side until Zho can no longer see Varna. Varna will wait here and kill it when it climbs over the cliff."

"If it climbs over the cliff," Zho said, "We still do not know that it can follow up the cliff."

"Of course," Varna said, "and when it is dead, Varna will call for Zho."

Zho looked over the edge of the cliff again and asked, "But what if it is a spirit or a demon?"

"Then Troon will never allow it to climb over the cliff."

Zho grimaced and said, "Varna puts much faith in Troon."

"Dead or alive," she said, "Varna trusts Troon with Varna's life."

"Yes," Zho agreed, "Varna is placing her life in Troon's hands. Zho does not like leaving Varna's fate in the hands of a spirit."

"Varna will be fine. Zho should go now."

Varna crouched down behind a small boulder with Troon's bow in her left hand and one of Wull's arrows notched and ready.

Zho took the rope to the lead goat and led the caravan over the small hill until they were hidden down the depression on the other side. He gathered the goats together and tied them to a stake. He had no intention of allowing Varna to face a demon alone, but the weapons collected on the travois were limited.

Wull's bow wasn't right yet, and Varna had all the arrows. Only three arrows, he reminded himself. He selected a spear and a long knife. Tucking the knife into the belt he tied around his waist, he felt the heft of the spear and took one last glance around the area. If the goats and chickens are attacked while he is watching over her, she will be furious.

Zho ran parallel to the cliff so he could approach the beast from the opposite side as Varna and hopefully get behind it. He hoped it would be more vulnerable from behind.

Kendo followed the river as it twisted and turned up the valley. It seemed to go on without end. The wide valley afforded them an unfettered view of where they were going as well as where they were not going. There were no secrets or surprises here, but they didn't seem to get any closer to the mountains on the far end of the valley.

The sky cleared since the brief rainstorm and the sun now beat down upon them. Some of the women, and especially the children, took the opportunity to dip themselves into the river. It was icy cold and nobody stayed long in the water, but all were refreshed when they resumed walking.

Kendo saw the sun nearing the mountains in the west and knew it would be getting dark soon. He could overlook how tired he was, but he couldn't ignore the exhaustion he saw on the tribe's faces. They came to a wide clearing next to the stream, and he said, "Let's camp here."

Kendo didn't need to direct the setting of the camp. Everyone knew what their duties were and proceeded without supervision. Brack and Koro went to the stream and scouted for fish while Wull and Flom gathered stones for a fire pit. The children still had boundless energy and splashed in the river, forcing Brack and Koro to move further upstream.

Clouds gathered to the north, but the sky in the west was clear. Kendo could see clearly in all directions. There were no trees directly over their heads to hide the saber cats, but he wondered if that only meant they would see their deaths approaching, with no way for them to fend off the danger. He rubbed his eyes and wiped those thoughts from his mind.

Wull built a large circle of stones and Flom had already filled it with wood for a fire. Brack and Koro returned with a generous selection of fish.

Kendo allowed a slight smile on his face. This was a good sign. He heard a sharp whistle to his left and saw an eagle lift itself high into the sky and fly down the valley, then turn sharply towards the west and the setting sun. To the casual observer, it was just an eagle searching the stream for a meal, but he knew in his heart that it was guiding them. The west where it turned is where they will go in the morning.

The beaver pond was no longer part of the stream. The beavers had ingeniously built an upstream dam that flowed the water around the pond and back to the original stream, leaving the pond as an adjacent feature to the stream. It still siphoned off some water into the pond, but not enough to create any significant flow through the pond. The water there was still and quiet, but not quite stagnant yet. Mora knew that the pond would eventually stagnate and the beaver would leave, but she saw signs that they were still there now, watching and maintaining their home.

The dam at the upper end of the pond was where she would look first. The beavers liked to pack mud into the dams to shore up the holes. Much of the mud she found there was debris made from decaying leaves and grass, but she found some good clay that had settled in at the bottom of the dam.

Brahg saw fish in the stream and said, "We should have brought a spear to catch fish."

"Has Brahg ever fished with a spear?" Mora asked.

"No," he replied, "but how hard can it be?"

"For someone with Brahg's injuries?" she reminded him.

Brahg tried to shrug, but his shoulder wouldn't allow him.

Mora collected the mud in a skin and said, "Let's get back now. Mora doesn't want to lose Marl or Joog because Mora is too slow."

Varna waited as Troon had taught her. Waiting was important to a hunter. The longer a hunter waits, the more he becomes part of the landscape. Even the most wary game will come to trust that a still hunter is a bush or a rock. She kept her eyes trained on the edge of the cliff and never saw Zho approach on the opposite side.

Zho was further away from the cliff than Varna was. He found a larger boulder settled down to wait. He lay on his stomach and peered around the boulder, giving him a good view of both the cliff and Varna. Troon had taught her well. Zho saw how still she remained. Only her eyes darted back and forth as she scanned the edge of the cliff.

The sky darkened overhead as the sun dipped below the western mountains. They still hadn't seen the beast. Varna hoped her eyes would adjust to the darkness. She couldn't aim the bow if she could not see, and soon it would be too dark for her to see anything. The beast would be free to scale the cliff and she would never see it, but it wasn't that dark yet.

Mora put the clay on a stone by the fire to heat it. She wished she had her cooking bowls so she could boil and dry it, but she had to improvise with what she had available.

Brahg returned to his bed. He tried to suppress the grimace as he lay down, but Mora saw it. He was glad to be back and would not be so quick to offer to leave again next time.

Mora felt the foreheads of both Marl and Joog. Their eyes were closed, and they writhed as if in dreams, but Mora did not believe they were really asleep. They were burning hot. Pela went to the gate and gathered some more snow, which Mora rubbed into their foreheads. It melted onto their skin and dripped back into their hair.

Marl came around slightly and rolled his eyes around the room. He opened his mouth to speak, but Mora put her finger to his lips and said, "Shhh. Do not speak. Eat this."

She fed him some of the drying clay. She did not believe that he knew he was eating, but his lips and throat worked automatically to swallow the dirt. Consciousness was brief for him. He closed his eyes again and rolled his head around.

Joog moaned behind Mora. Yona was rubbing the snow in his head as she had seen Mora do for Marl. Mora brushed his hair and said, "Here. Have some of this." She fed the clay to Joog and bowed her head and began praying. She sang songs and chanted prayers for their safety.

Yona and Pela set themselves up at the men's feet and joined Mora in her songs and chants. Pela kept an eye on Brahg, who now slept peacefully.

Zho and Varna barely breathed. They scanned the edge of the cliff and listened intently for any sign that the beast still followed them. The sun was nearly lost behind the western mountains before they had any sign of their foe.

Zho saw it first. He was relieved to see what looked like a man's hand reaching up over the edge of the cliff.

Varna saw the movement and drew her bow. She kept it trained on the spot where the hand was. She hoped Zho was just being superstitious when he said it could be a demon. They would know soon. It pulled itself up atop the cliff and its appearance startled her so much that she let loose the arrow and sent it flying off course. The arrow struck into the dirt in front of the demon and bounced over the edge. She didn't know what to do. She stood gawking at the hideous creature without notching another arrow. It had two heads. The larger head glanced over in Varna's direction while the other head began to wail like an injured pig.

Varna feared for Troon. It was a demon! A two headed demon! Troon would have protected her from the spirit world if he could have. If this monster did something to Troon, she would make him pay.

She broke from her frozen terror and nervously grasped another arrow and tried to notch it, but the beast ducked down below the cliff before her shaking hands could draw the bow again.

Chapter Seven

The Coming Dawn

Z ho wished he could have been wrong when he suggested that it may have been a demon that followed them, but he saw the beast as its two heads rose over the lip of the cliff. Whatever terror he felt must be little compared to Varna's when the larger of the beast's two heads looked directly at her before she loosed an arrow at it and it ducked both heads back down behind the ledge. He could still hear the smaller head wailing as he leaped out from behind the boulder that hid him and ran to the edge of the cliff with his spear held high.

Varna had never missed so badly before. Her whole body shook and had taken her aim completely off the beast and landed the arrow in the dirt atop the cliff. The arrow bounced harmlessly over the edge and the beast escaped. She couldn't control her trembling hands and clumsily tried to notch another arrow. The world spun around her as the trembling moved to her spine and her knees, and then to her eyes as darkness overcame her. She fell to the ground, unable to even beseech her beloved Troon's spirit to come and save her from the demon's grasp.

The beast's voice rose over the edge of the cliff, "Trik ga Nik da la ni ni! Trik Nik da la ni ni!"

Zho's knees weakened as he heard the beast's foreign tongue. It must be a demon. It had two heads. He saw them. What else could it be? The beast's words were unknown to him, but he assumed that it must be a curse. What else would a demon say to a mortal?

"Da la ni ni," the demon repeated.

Zho inched forward and peered over the edge of the cliff, shouting, "Go away, demon! Zho, the slayer of demons, commands it!"

Varna's head still spun as she remained sprawled out on the ground. She regained enough consciousness to look up and see Zho peer over the edge.

"Zho will not tolerate demons in our land!"

The wailing increased, and the demon began to sing, "Buwa nyok yi bey tola bah si, bey tola bah si." The wailing tapered off and the demon said, "Trik go no. Nik go no."

Zho growled back at the demon, "Zho does not speak to…"

"Shhhhh," the demon said, "Scare Nik."

Varna felt her stomach heave as she lay helplessly on the ground. She had to help Zho. Her knees wobbled as she got up and walked over to join him. "How is it we understand the demon's words?"

The demon replied, "Trik talk Grull"

"Trik?" Zho asked. "Zho has never heard of a demon called Trik."

"Trik no hear of Slayer Zho."

"What does Trik want?" Varna asked.

"Trik wants Nik safe."

"What is Nik?" Zho asked.

"No kill! No kill!" the demon pleaded, "Trik show Zho Nik." The smaller of the two heads slowly peeked up over the ledge.

Kendo walked silently through the camp. He could hear the fatigue and despair in his people's voices. The world had turned hard and cruel to them. He fought the urge to re-hash the events in his head, but couldn't completely prevent his mind from wandering. He questioned whether his people weren't supposed to survive the flood. Perhaps the great spirits had intended to collect all the tribe for the spirit world and he was defying their plans by saving them. Every step of the trip seemed to bring them face to face with harsher consequences.

He circled the perimeter of the camp. The sun had just disappeared over the western mountains and the remnants of light in the sky were fading away. Fires were set out to mark the boundary and keep the predators away, but the tribe was otherwise in the open and very visible for miles. The valley here was wide and flat, with no trees or rock features to offer shelter from either the elements or the intruders.

Kendo came across a young couple having a quiet conversation. They stared intimately into each other's eyes. He could see from their expressions that they had plans for the future. This was good. Kendo's heart was lifted to believe there was some hope for his people. He had seen the eagle fly into the sunset and believed it was sent to guide him. Only with this sign did he know which direction they would follow in the morning. He should find his place to sleep. As much as he would like to watch over the tribe all night long, he couldn't lead them without some sleep of his own.

Brahg lay nervously on the thin skin next to Marl. The pain from his wounds never left him, but it was no longer his greatest concern. He couldn't sleep, afraid that he might succumb to the burning sickness that had gripped his two friends. Their group was already small. They needed his strength to help them rejoin the tribe when they were better.

Mora was frantic. She had no intention of sleeping and hovered over the two boys, praying and chanting. She burned anything she could find that would fill the cave with either smoke or odor, hoping to keep the spirit of death at bay. There were no more healing skills left to try, that she had not already tried. The boys' wounds did not have the smell of death, but still they burned hot with the sickness. All she had left now was prayer. She prayed for the ancestors' spirits to come help her protect the young boys, but she knew they were probably busy watching over the tribe. She appealed directly to death, reasoning that he would have her spirit soon enough. He didn't need these young boys tonight.

Pela and Yona could not keep up with the frenetic Mora, so they sat out of the way and tried to echo her chanting. Pela would occasionally go to Brahg's side and feel his forehead. She still hadn't expressed her feelings to him, but he felt more than just her hand when she checked his temperature.

While Pela checked on Brahg, Yona would take a bowl outside and scoop up some more snow. She put some of the snow in another bowl to melt for drinking and rubbed the rest on the boy's heads and chests to cool them down. Pela offered some of the drinking water to Brahg while Yona dripped the water on Joog's and Marl's lips.

The two girls would then return to their places and rejoin Mora in her chanting. Pela was grateful that her man was not sick like Marl, but the same relief brought her guilt for choosing him over the other two boys, so she prayed even harder for Marl and Joog.

Mora checked their temperatures and her fear escalated. She returned to chanting with increased fervor. Her voice grew tired and hoarse. Pela insisted she have some of the water she brought for Brahg, but Mora barely sipped it, afraid she could not let her voice rest for an instant lest death swooped in to take the boys.

Varna had finally notched her last arrow and raised Troon's bow as the smaller of the demon's heads peeked over the ledge. Her trembling worsened and the arrow's notch slipped off the string.

The demon's head rose higher and higher.

Zho raised his spear and cocked his arm. "Stop! What does the demon want now?"

"Nik!" the demon proclaimed, "No kill Nik!"

The demon's head rose until Varna could see that it had its own body and was held up by larger hands. The small demon pointed to her and said, "Bah."

"Zho!" Varna exclaimed as she reached up and gripped Zho's spear to push him away. "Nik is a baby!"

Varna reached down and lifted the baby from Trik's hands and pulled it away from the cliff.

"Yes!" Trik exclaimed, "Nik bay bay." Trik showed both of his palms over the edge of the cliff, but then gripped the cliff with his left hand to remain steady. "No kill! No kill Trik!"

Zho backed up a few paces but kept his spear ready while Varna turned her back on them and cooed over the baby.

Trik climbed carefully up from the cliff and slowly stood before Zho with his eyes locked on Zho's spear. "No kill!"

He wasn't especially tall and without the second head, Trik wasn't very menacing. Zho reached out with the spear and swatted Trik on the shoulders and hips to make sure he was solid before he relaxed and said, "Trik is just a man. Why did Varna think Trik was a demon?"

Varna was too busy with Nik to pay any attention to what Zho had said, but when Trik had stood up full height, the baby reached for him and began to scream.

Trik came over and took the baby, then lifted it over his head and slipped him into the sack he had rigged on his back.

Varna laughed and pointed at them. "Zho thought you had two heads."

Trik only understood some of her words, but he saw her pointing and understood the number two. He turned his head and looked at Nik watching over his shoulder and laughed with her.

Zho thought it best to return to business and said, "We should return to the goats before something else finds them."

"The goats!" Varna yelled. "You left them alone?"

Zho moved quickly, but said, "They are not alone. They are with the chickens."

Varna picked up a small stone and tossed it at Zho's racing form. Even in the dark, she managed to whizz it by his ear. "Come," she said to Trik.

***

The tribe was exhausted and had easily fallen into a peaceful slumber. Guards were positioned around the camp, but there weren't enough men to truly watch the perimeter. A mild warm breeze blew across the camp and lulled the guards into a drowsiness that made it difficult for them to watch over the sleeping tribe.

The partial moon trekked silently across the sky, lighting the ground with a dim glow that took much patience, but the guards could acclimate their eyes to the low light. The wind was calm, but a rustling in the grass fields alerted the sentries.

Flom woke when he heard one of them call out, "Who is there?"

He grabbed his spear and joined the guard, who was staring out into the field that lay just outside their camp.

"What does Gorn see?"

Gorn shook his head and said, "Gorn saw nothing. But Gorn can hear something moving in the field."

Flom cocked his head and listened. A mild breeze picked up, and he heard rustling through the grass. He shook his head and said, "It is just the wind. Flom is returning to bed."

"No," Gorn insisted, "Gorn hears it even when the wind is calm."

Flom cocked his head again and listened. He heard something moving again, but this time there was no wind. He raised his spear and strained to see in the dim light. The tall grasses moved as if by a wind, but the air was still calm.

"Gorn thinks this place is haunted."

"That cannot be," Flom said. "It must not be. We follow Kendo's vision. The spirits brought us here. Perhaps it is them we hear and they merely watch over us from the field."

Gorn grunted. He wanted Flom to be right, so he refrained from arguing, but he didn't believe it in his heart.

"I'll take the watch from here," Flom said. "Gorn can go sleep now."

Gorn grunted again as he returned to his bed, but he doubted that he would be able to sleep.

Zho led the way back to where he had left the goats. He took long strides, hoping nothing had happened to the goats and chickens, and hoping he might arrive before something did occur.

Varna walked with Trik, cooing and playing with Nik. Nik laughed and cooed back to her.

Trik smiled and said, "Nik likes Varna. Varna is a strong woman. Trik not see woman with thuk before."

"Thuk?" Varna asked.

Trik pointed at Troon's bow and said, "Thuk jobo prindas." Trik saw the confusion on Varna's face, so he mimed shooting a bow and repeated, "Thuk jobo prindas." Then he held his hands apart to show the length of an arrow and said, "Prindas...sticks."

"Ah," Varna said, nodding her head. She lifted the bow which hung across her chest and said, "Bow."

Trik repeated, "Bo."

The conversation stalled, and Varna returned to playing with Nik.

Trik asked, "Zho let Varna with bo?"

Varna turned her attention away from Nik and asked, "Zho?"

Trik pointed ahead of them and said, "Varna's husband. Zho? Zho let Varna with bo?"

"Oh," she replied, "Zho not Varna's husband. Varna's husband walks with the spirits."

Trik turned his head forward, knowing it would hide his smile from Varna, who returned her attention to little Nik.

Flom kept his eyes on the grassy field. He could see the grass move as something passed through, but nobody was there and there was no wind. The field darkened as the moon dipped below the horizon. He could still hear the rustling in the grass, but could no longer see it move.

Something much larger and louder disturbed the grass. It sounded almost like something splashing in the water. He strained to see, but it was too dark. He waved his spear in front of him and ventured out into the edge of the field. He heard something fly by his ear and splash into the grass beyond him.

Gorn was right. The field was haunted. Flom rushed back to the tribe. Others were already up and watching the skies. Many others had heard the faint sound of the spirits flying by. They were almost perfectly silent, but when they were near enough, Flom could hear the movement of the air as they passed by his ears.

Kendo was up. He ordered the tribe to stoke the fires and plant more torches around the perimeter.

Zho arrived at the goats well ahead of Trik and Varna. There was no sign of attack, but three goats were missing. The goats with the Travois still attached remained tied to the stake, but three of the goats with packs on their backs were gone and the rope had been chewed through.

Zho had already started checking for tracks when Varna arrived and asked, "What is Zho doing now?"

"Three goats chewed themselves free and wandered off. Zho must find them."

Trik looked confused and asked, "Jork wolo?"

Varna shrugged and said, "Goat's missing."

"Goats?" Trik sounded out the word.

Varna bleated like a goat and mimed walking off.

"Zho!" Trik shouted, "Zho stay. Trik get goats."

Trik handed Nik to Varna and started looking for their tracks. Zho was glad to stay behind with Varna while Trik looked for the missing animals.

Varna bounced Nik up and down, much to his delight. She made baby noises and scrunched her face while he laughed and giggled.

"Varna is good with baby," Zho said. "It is good to see Varna laugh again."

Somehow, without even mentioning Troon, Zho had reminded her of her lost husband and she was overcome with grief again. She hugged the baby and cried quietly on his shoulder.

Zho saw the change in her and tried changing the subject. "Nik is a very nice-looking baby, but Zho does not trust Trik so much. Zho thinks something is not right about Trik."

"Zho thought Trik was a two headed demon," Varna quipped. "Maybe something is not right about Zho."

Zho just shrugged and mumbled, "Zho just doesn't trust Trik."

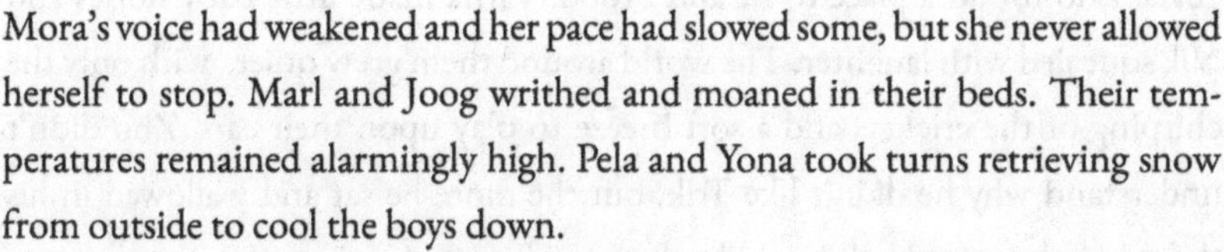

Mora's voice had weakened and her pace had slowed some, but she never allowed herself to stop. Marl and Joog writhed and moaned in their beds. Their temperatures remained alarmingly high. Pela and Yona took turns retrieving snow from outside to cool the boys down.

Marl's condition changed first. It started with a tiny cough and grew to body wracking spasms. Mora rolled him on his side to help him expel phlegm, but his coughing grew worse.

While Marl coughed, Joog grew silent. He stopped moaning, and no longer turned in his sleep. Mora listened to his chest. He still breathed, but barely. He wasn't sleeping the sleep of someone getting better. He looked more like he was settling into the final sleep of one meeting death.

Mora threw more herbs on the fire to burn like incense, but her supply was running short. Worse, she feared that Joog may die anyway, and she only prevented death from guiding his spirit to the ancestors.

As the tribe placed more torches around the camp, Kendo caught a glimpse of the spirits swooping down in the field around them. Great birds with large eyes glided silently into the grass, then lifted up from the fields with small rodents in their talons.

Kendo laughed and pointed to the large birds. The men had never seen so many hunting birds and thought themselves silly for thinking the large hunters were spirits haunting the field. The women thought they had never seen so many rodents and weren't so easily amused.

Varna continued to play with the baby while they waited for Trik to retrieve the goats. Zho found a place to sit and brood. Varna made little baby noises and Nik squealed with laughter. The world around them grew quiet, with only the chirping of the crickets and a soft breeze to play upon their ears. Zho didn't understand why he didn't like Trik, but the more he sat and wallowed in his thoughts, the more he did not like the intruder.

The peace which had settled around them was broken when they heard the long, loud cry of a large cat in the mountains. He was still far off, but Varna's last encounter was still fresh in her memory. She walked to Zho and handed Nik to him.

Zho blanched as he held the baby at arm's length and looked back at Varna.

"Hold him closer," she said. "Let him hear you breathe."

Zho was about to ask her why she would give Nik to him until she pulled the bow over her head and notched her sole remaining arrow. If the cat was coming back for her, she had a surprise in store for it. She no longer carried Wull's weak experimental bow. She had Troon's mighty bow. Troon's bow was more than a match for the cat, but she only had a single arrow and hoped that dropping one of the cats would pause its mate.

Varna scanned the hills for signs of movements. She could still remember the leopard's breath when it exhaled directly on her face during their last encounter. Maybe it will see her and remember her. Maybe it will leave them alone out of respect. She hoped it did not regret letting her live. It would not end well if the cat had returned to finish what it had left undone.

One of the goats bleated, and she knew that hunger would guide the cat to them more than respect would steer it away. It was coming. She did not know what would be in the beast's mind when it saw her, but she was certain that it would come for the goats.

Varna spoke in a loud whisper, hoping Zho would hear it and the cats would not. "Zho should go find Trik. Trik is alone out there, or worse, Trik is with the other goats."

"Zho cannot leave Varna."

"Varna has Troon's bow. Varna can protect the chickens and goats."

"But," Zho said, "Varna has only one arrow and the leopards always travel in pairs."

"Varna will be fine. Varna worries about Trik."

Zho set his jaw and ground his teeth. "Varna should worry less about a stranger," he said, "and more about us. Zho has already seen Varna stare directly into the eyes of the leopards and live. Zho thinks Varna was ready to die and offer up her spirit to join Troon. Varna is too young for that. Zho will not allow that to happen again. The leopards are in the mountains and Trik has gone the other direction. Trik will be fine."

Nik reached for Varna and started to cry.

"Take the baby," Zho said, "and give me Troon's bow. Varna was not Troon's only student."

Varna was reluctant to give up the bow, but was eager to hold Nik some more.

Brahg's fear that he may succumb to the burning sickness that was killing his friends was supplanted with a new fear as he heard Mora's chants fade over time. Where only hours before, she raised her hands and beseeched the Gods; she had come to barely rock in place and her voice had dwindled to a raspy moan. His worst fears were realized when she collapsed on top of Joog and was silenced. Yona was quick to pull her off Joog and lay her alongside the three boys.

Yona and Pela renewed the vigor in their chants as they now prayed over the boys and Mora. Brahg remained in his bed, but he too joined the girls in their chants and prayed for his friends.

Pela continued chanting while she stoked the fire and sprinkled herbs on the flames. Yona moved quicker as she fetched the snow to cool the boys. She felt Mora's forehead. Mora slept, but did not burn like Joog and Marl.

The girls were frantic. They could not lose the boys, but to save the boys, they could not lose Mora. Mora was old and her time was not far, but they could not allow her time to be tonight.

The goats left easy tracks to follow in the snow. There was little for them to eat, but they found some old grass which had been exposed by the melting snow.

They looked up calmly at Trik as he approached, but continued chewing the old grass.

"De nah," he said. "De nah." He picked up the ropes tied to their necks and led them back along the trail of footprints, which now included his own.

Nik saw Trik returning with the goats first. He enthusiastically clapped his hands, but did not beg to leave Varna this time. He returned to playing with Varna's face. She had a nose and ears like Trik's, which were fun to pinch and pull, but her skin was smooth and soft. There was something profoundly comforting about Varna, but Nik had no way to understand why. He just liked her and appreciated how safe and warm he felt in her arms.

Zho saw Trik return but only offered a half warm smile. He didn't trust Trik and wouldn't have missed him had he never returned.

Trik handed the reins to Zho and went directly to Nik. When Nik showed no interest in leaving Varna, Trik satisfied himself with nuzzling the tyke in her arms.

"Must you two coddle that child?" Zho barked. "We heard the great cats coming down from the mountains. There are only the three of us and all these delectable goats and chickens."

Trik did not understand enough of Zho's speech to respond, but Varna was quick to quip, "Does Zho really worry so about the animals and feel nothing for the helpless infant?"

Zho was struck dumb for a moment, then replied, "Of course, Zho knows the infant is also in danger, but the goats and the chickens are a meal the cats will come for when they smell it. And Zho is certain they will catch the scent if we remain here much longer."

Trik tried picking out words he could recognize, but they spoke too quickly. He had no trouble, however, recognizing the cry of a great cat and its mate. He took the reins from Zho and tied the goats back into a caravan and took the lead reins, saying, "Trik go. Zho go. Varna and Nik go."

Zho snatched the reins from Trik's hands and growled, "Zho will say when we go."

Trik and Varna looked at Zho blankly. He growled again and said, "We go."

The owls finished raiding the field and left. Kendo stood on the edge of the camp and listened. The owls were nearly undetectable in flight, but he heard something else. Further down the valley was the sound of wolves preying on the mice.

Wolves were fierce hunters. Kendo did not know whether the wolves in this valley ate the mice out of routine or desperation. He had no doubt that they might find his tribe a tasty and more filling alternative.

Flom ran up to the tribe's leader and asked, "Kendo? The women do not wish to remain here. We tried to tell them that the owls were no threat to us, but Flom thinks it is the mice that are bothering them."

"Kendo agrees. Let's pack the tribe and move out."

Flom jerked his head in acknowledgement and turned to tell the tribe, but Kendo continued, "It's funny how the valley seemed so peaceful and ideal by day and turned so threatening and angry by night."

Flom stood frozen for a moment, not sure if he should respond or wait for more.

"Go," Kendo said. "Tell the tribe to pack. We leave early."

Mora opened her eyes and saw Pela praying over her. "What happened?" she asked.

Pela replied, "Mora takes care of everybody except Mora. It is Mora's turn to rest."

Mora tried getting up, but Yona stopped her and said, "We cannot lose Mora. If we lose Mora, we will lose Marl and Joog. Mora will rest longer while Pela and Yona pray and burn the herbs."

Mora started to argue, but Brahg added, "Do not make Brahg get up from Brahg's bed to hold Mora down. It is time for Mora to deal with her own medicine."

Mora could not argue with their reasoning when they used her own arguments against her. She lay back and breathed easily, but kept an eye on the fire and smoke. She listened to their chanting and was prepared to help them if they stumbled over some of the words, but they did fine. They professed to needing her, but perhaps they didn't need her as much as they thought.

Mora wondered, as she stared up at the cave's ceiling, how her trainees were doing with the tribe. They barely knew how to gather the herbs. She had years of training and experience to bestow upon them, and she wondered now if she would see them again.

She wasn't concerned about her current condition, she was only exhausted, but there was a time when she could have maintained a prayer vigil for days without tiring. She was getting old and soon would be too old to function as the tribe's medicine woman.

She was overcome with a melancholy as she contemplated her own death and how it might leave the tribe stranded.

She remembered Koro and what a wonderful knack he had to care for his friends. He was a natural medicine man, even without the training. He had the gift.

She hoped she could live long enough to offer him some training as well.

Yona collected some more snow to help cool Joog and Marl, who both lay silent and half dead in their beds.

Mora gratefully accepted some melted snow to wet her parched throat.

The girls were doing a good job and Mora's spirit was soothed enough to slip off to sleep.

The tired tribe had mixed feelings about breaking camp and departing so soon. Even the women who were eager to leave the rodent fields behind them also felt the exhaustion in their bones. It was close enough to sunrise for Kendo to start tearing down their camp. He decided to leave without fixing breakfast, preferring not to entice the wolves with the scent of cooked fish.

By the time they began their march, the skies in the east had already lightened and Kendo could see the ground well enough to pick a path. He remembered the direction of the eagle he had seen at sunset and guided the tribe toward the break in the mountains that led into another valley through the mountains and eventually to the lake he expected to find there.

As the tribe formed up into a line, he went to Koro and said, "Kendo would like Koro to walk in the back with Wull today. Watch for anyone who is falling behind and see if Koro can help them keep up. Make sure everyone is drinking enough water. Send word to Kendo if we move too fast and need to rest or slow down."

Koro smacked Brack on the shoulder and said, "Sorry friend, today Brack will have to walk alone."

As Koro began to trot to the back of the line, Kendo shouted out, "And send Flom up here with us!"

Brack watched Koro run off to the back and said, "Brack does not know why we leave so early, but we should eat something. The tribe cannot march a full day on an empty stomach without consequences."

"Worry not," Kendo said. "When the sun is up, Kendo wants Brack and Flom to scout ahead for some food. Kendo believes a river lies between those mountains and where there is water, Brack should find something for us to eat."

Flom ran up from the back and said, "It is good that Kendo sent for Flom. Flom will protect us from flying rodents."

Brack picked up a rock and threw it at Flom, saying, "But who will protect Flom from flying rocks?"

Kendo laughed and hoped the rest of his people could find their own mirth throughout the day.

Zho was uncomfortable leading the small caravan. It placed the stranger Trik at his back. He could not protect Varna with the two of them behind him, and he could not find his way back to the cave if he walked backwards to watch them.

Neither Varna nor Trik wanted to leave Nik. They played with him constantly as they walked.

"Varna," Zho yelled back to them, "Now that we are traveling again, does Varna not think Varna can better protect the baby with Troon's bow?"

Varna scowled and gave Nik back to Trik, who promptly placed the infant in the backpack he rigged for the child. She walked to the front and took her bow back from Zho, then walked alongside the goats, watching the hills for signs of movement.

Zho's fears were lightened when he knew that Varna was armed and he no longer had to worry about her. The distance to the cave wasn't short, but it seemed to get shorter with familiarity. The sun peeked over the mountains and lit the fields, which were still covered in large patches of snow. The cave was just ahead.

They were still a few paces away from the entrance when Zho heard Pela and Yona chanting prayers inside. He dropped the reins and left the goats behind while he ran to the gate and entered the cave. Varna saw Zho bolt and followed before she had even heard the chanting from within. Trik did not know what it meant, so he picked up the lead reins and led the goats to the cave.

Mora was sleeping alongside Joog and Marl. The boys were very pale and very still.

Zho ran to Mora and shouted, "Mora! Mora! We are here!"

Mora opened her eyes and saw Zho. She was still tired, but she was well enough to sit up and say, "Did Zho find Varna?"

"Yes! She is here."

Varna ran into the cave and saw Joog and Marl. They looked dead to her. The room spun around her. She wanted to cry out, but instead her stomach heaved up and she bent over and vomited yet again.

Mora asked, "Is Varna ok?"

Zho shrugged and said, "Varna has been doing that. Zho thinks she still grieves greatly for Troon."

"Join us," Mora said. "We need more voices to pray for Joog and Marl."

"Do they still live?" Zho asked.

"Just barely," Mora replied, "but there is little more that Mora can do for them. Their fate is in the Gods' hands now."

Chapter Eight

What Lies Ahead

Mora didn't feel rested enough to resume praying over Joog and Marl, but she couldn't very well go back to sleep after inviting Varna and Zho to join her, so she got up from her bed and returned to Joog's side and chanted again with a renewed, albeit forced, vigor.

Varna didn't know why her stomach had become so weak in recent days. She had never been squeamish before, and it shamed her to have shown such weakness in front of everyone. She wiped the vomit from her mouth and said, "Certainly we can pray, but we brought Mora's medicines back with us from the old village. Perhaps something in there can help?"

Yona and Pela both stopped chanting when they heard that. Yona was the first to jump up and head for the gate while yelling, "Where?"

"Just outside," Zho said, "And there's more..."

Pela stopped at the gate and shouted, "There is a man out here! He followed you!"

"That is Trik," Varna said, "and the little one is Nik."

Trik took Nik out of his small backpack and held him to his chest while he climbed through the small door to the cave.

Yona ran outside and looked dizzily at the collection of packs on the goats and in the Travois. "Where?" she yelled into the cave, "Which one has the medicine?"

"All of them!" Zho yelled back.

"Well," Varna corrected, "most of them at least. Some have weapons we salvaged from the village."

Brahg's injuries were not yet healed, and he struggled to hide the pain as he stood to meet the newcomer. Brahg was a large and imposing man and the stranger did not need to know that he was injured. Trik watched him rise to full height and backed up to the cave wall, still clinging to little Nik.

Varna went to Trik and took Nik from his arms. "Easy Brahg. Trik is a friend now. And this baby is Nik."

Brahg wasn't interested in the baby and watched Trik with a suspicious eye.

"Don't listen to Varna," Zho said. "Zho doesn't trust this Trik either."

"Why not?" Varna asked.

"Zho does not know. It's just a feeling."

Varna took Nik over by the fire and sat down so she could rub his hands and feet to warm him.

Yona and Pela came back into the cave, each carrying one of the bundles. They lined the bundles up on the ground so Mora could look through them.

They immediately returned outside to get more bundles and heard Zho say behind them, "Zho will help."

Trik followed Zho outside and started bringing the goats into the cave.

Mora barely glanced up from the packs she was searching and asked, "More goats?"

"Yes!" Pela squealed as she placed another pack next to the others, "and chickens too!"

Mora looked at Varna and gave her a half smile. "Mora is a silly old woman. Mora thought that Varna left to join Troon in the spirit world, and instead she returns to us with goats, chickens, a man and a baby! Varna is a good hunter indeed!"

Varna giggled and said, "Varna came back with more than that. Varna came back with Troon's bow."

Mora bowed her head to acknowledge Varna's prize, then returned to searching the packs for her medicines.

***

Kendo carefully chose his path through the dark meadow. The moon was gone, but the sun was warming the eastern sky and the stars still showed him the silhouette of the valley where he led his people. The slower pace was easier on the tired tribe, but the children were still sleepy and the elders dragged their tired feet through the grass. Koro remained in the rear and offered assistance to anyone who fell behind. He carried their loads and offered encouragement until either they were refreshed enough to resume carrying their share or another straggler fell off the pace and they had to take their load back. He would not allow himself to feel fatigue.

As the sun finally peeked over the eastern horizon, Flom and Brack forged ahead in search of food. They didn't know what to expect and carried both their spears and their slings. The valley was as eerily featureless as it had been the day before. There were no trees to shelter wildlife in the ways the hunters were accustomed to seeing, but there was a river and last night's display proved there was no shortage of life. If mice could thrive, then so could rabbits and other larger rodents.

The sky had resumed its normal hue and clearly illuminated the valley ahead of them now. They had to keep to the valley if they had any hope of the tribe finding them later. Their plan was to find the river that Kendo believed would follow the bed of the valley. It was a good place to find game, and it was where Kendo was heading, so they should be able to rejoin the tribe later.

"Brack has never seen such flat land before."

"Yes," Flom replied, "Flom grew up surrounded by trees. Here there is only grass."

"Brack wonders where the birds came from if there are no trees."

Flom nodded. "Such big birds would require very big trees."

As they neared the valley between the mountains, the ground ascended slightly, and they could finally hear the rush of water. Flom pointed towards the sound of the water and Brack silently nodded his head. The grass grew to their thighs here, and they crouched down in it as they approached the water. They hoped to find some game getting water, but if not, there should at least be some fish in the river.

The ground softened beneath their feet and Brack stopped to scan the area around them. He inched forward towards the sound of the water and stopped again. He carefully placed his spear on the ground and pulled his sling from his belt. Flom didn't know what Brack had heard, but he followed suit and fetched a couple stones from the ground. Brack kept low to the ground as he slowly crept forward. Flom angled to the right, hoping he could flank whatever Brack had detected.

Brack swung his sling around his head and fired a stone into the grass ahead of him. Flom swung his sling around his head just in time to see three pheasants rise from the grass. He loosed a stone and knocked one of them off its course, but it continued on and dove into the grass further beyond them.

Flom placed another stone in his sling and followed his quarry while Brack collected his.

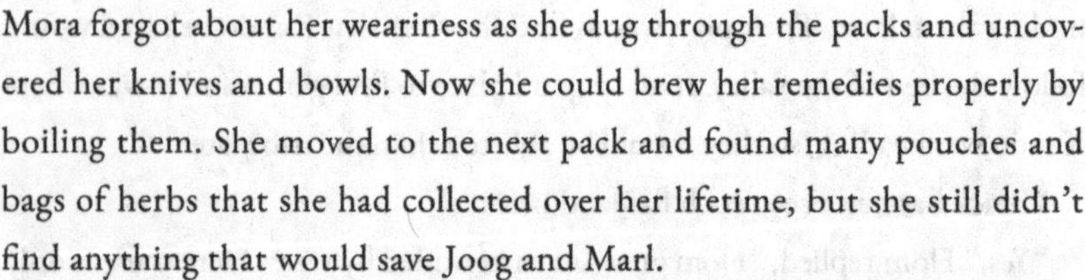

Mora forgot about her weariness as she dug through the packs and uncovered her knives and bowls. Now she could brew her remedies properly by boiling them. She moved to the next pack and found many pouches and bags of herbs that she had collected over her lifetime, but she still didn't find anything that would save Joog and Marl.

Varna saw the delight on Mora's face when she found something that she sorely needed, but she also saw the desperation as Mora continued delving through the packs, looking for something that she hadn't found yet. Varna started opening packs ahead of Mora. She removed the packs with the weapons and lined up the bags with just the stuff from Mora's hut.

Mora appreciated Varna's help and she could never properly express her gratitude for Varna fetching her supplies, but she still hadn't found anything that would help the boys and couldn't hide the fear and frustration from her face. Marl and Joog were practically with the spirits already, but Mora wasn't ready to give up on them. She went through every bag and examined every herb, knowing that what she needed must be here. Varna had brought too much stuff from her hut to have left behind the one or two critical ingredients that she required to treat the boys.

The sun was fully above the horizon, lighting the flat featureless valley and enriching the vibrant hues of the endless sea of grass. The mountains that defined the new valley were the only feature that provided the tribe with any sense of traveling. They couldn't see what awaited them in the new valley yet, but they could see the mountains drawing nearer.

Kendo forced himself to keep the pace steady, even though he could now see well enough to easily pick a path for them to walk. He was hungry, and he knew his people were as hungry as he was, so he didn't want to push them too hard on empty stomachs.

If he could have seen the valley from an eagle's eye view, he would have seen the swath of flattened grass behind them that left one river and cut diagonally across the meadow to another river. They could have remained on the first river and would have eventually reached the other river where the two merged together, but it would have been a much longer march to reach the new valley.

Having the new river to follow was comforting. Not only did the river guide them to the valley, but he knew that Brack and Flom would have also found the river and remained on its shores to meet them once they found food. He didn't have to wait long. The scent of roasting meat wafted through the tribe as they followed the contours of the river.

Kendo didn't increase the pace until he felt the tribe pushing him from behind. As a unit, they sped up to reach the source of the cooking fires that everyone now smelled.

Flom was tending the spits with dozens of pheasants and rabbits roasting over hot coals. Flames sputtered as the juices dripped off the browning game. Brack had another fire with fish roasting over similar coals.

Kendo stood aside and watched the tribe surround the two hunters. Some went straight to the spits and began divvying the prepared food, while others took a moment to slap the hunter's backs to show their appreciation. Koro joined Kendo when the last of the tribe had finally reached the scene.

"Kendo needs to eat, too," Koro said.

"Kendo will eat when the tribe is fed."

Koro knew he couldn't win by arguing, so he helped himself to some pheasant, taking two portions and bringing one of them to Kendo. Kendo could not turn down the gift; it would have been rude and his own hunger wouldn't allow it.

Brack and Flom joined Kendo and watched the food disappear.

"Maybe we should have caught more," Flom said.

"Perhaps," Kendo said, "but we don't want the tribe to be slowed down by heavy bellies. Tonight, when we make camp, we can enjoy a heartier meal."

Flom looked at Brack and asked, "How will we know where is the right place to set up camp?"

Brack shrugged and Kendo said, "This afternoon, you need only catch the game. We'll break camp and start the fires while some of the women gather the herbs and seasonings."

Flom slapped Brack on the shoulder and said, "See? Flom told Brack to season the meat."

Kendo laughed and returned his attention to his pheasant.

Varna wanted to stay up and help Mora, or at least join the others praying for Joog and Marl, but she was just too tired. Traveling all night would have been enough by itself to leave her exhausted, but believing that someone was following them and then hearing the leopards descending from the mountains had left her emotionally drained.

Nik was already fast asleep on a skin by the fire. Varna retired to a dark corner of the cave. She took Troon's bow off her shoulder and hugged it to her bosom. In her mind, she thought she could still smell Troon on the bow and didn't care if she was only imagining it. She lay down and easily went to sleep with her late husband fresh in her heart.

Trik was also tired, but he saw Varna hug the bow as she went to sleep. She was the first woman he had ever seen with a bow and the first person of any gender he had seen take a bow to bed and embrace it like a lover. She was a very strange woman and apparently a terribly lonely one.

Zho watched Trik intently as he took one of the knives from the goat packs and went to the gate, saying, "Trik de graf prindas ko thuk." It was evident from the stares that nobody understood him. "Prindas?" he asked, but nobody responded. "Bah," he muttered as he left the cave.

He entered the meadow that now only had a few snow drifts dotting the ground. The sun was brilliant and the little snow that remained was blinding. He guarded his eyes with his hand as he crossed the meadow to the forest on the other side.

In the trees, he used the knife to cut down slender twigs. The twigs were still green and flexible, which made them a little tougher to cut down, but were preferable to brittle wood that might crack or shatter. He selected only the straightest twigs he could find and shaved off any buds with the knife. After gathering a dozen such twigs, he returned to the cave. He left the twigs in a pile just outside the cave and went in.

Zho slept lightly and woke when he heard the door to the cave creak open.

Trik went to the chicken cage and selected a handful of feathers from the bottom of the cage. Most of the feathers were down and unsuitable. He examined the birds and identified some primary feathers that were loosened or broken and plucked them, much to the bird's displeasure.

Zho's eyelids drooped as he watched Trik with the chickens, and didn't close completely until Trik left the cave again.

Outside the cave, Trik selected three long strands of hair from his head, and braided them. Once braided, he plucked them and used them to tie the feathers to the notched ends of the sticks he made. With all the sticks feathered, he sharpened the other ends against a large stone until he had a dozen arrows for Varna. It would be convenient for him if Zho were impressed by his gift, but he only cared if Varna would like it.

He tied the arrows into a bundle and took them inside, where he laid them next to Varna, then found a spot near her where he could close his eyes and catch up on some sleep himself.

Mora finally found the medicines she was looking for. She set aside the leather pouches with the clay, the charcoal, and the bark from a very special tree that her mother called the old man's tree.

She scolded herself for taking so long to search the packs, but she was finally done. She had found what she needed and placed the ingredients in the mortar, which she had already found in the first pack. The three ingredients were difficult to grind, and Mora struggled with the pestle.

Yona saw the sweat dripping from Mora's temples and heard her grunting while she laboriously worked the ingredients in the mortar. "Can Yona help with that?"

A younger Mora might have argued that it was her responsibility, but old Mora was breathing too heavily to make any argument and her muscles ached too much to do a proper job. Losing her protégé to the flood was more costly than she ever imagined. She showed Yona how to twist and slide the pestle to break and smash the compounds. With Yona busy grinding the medicines, Mora went outside and collected some more snow in one of her clay bowls and put it on the fire to melt and boil.

Varna could have slept all day, but she was hungry and woke around mid-day. She went to sleep hoping to dream about Troon. She thought she felt his presence in her dreams, but his image was blurry and she was never really sure it was him. When she opened her eyes, she laid her head against the bow, which she still held against her chest.

Her stomach growled, and she sat up to do something about it. The fire reflected off the shafts of the pack of arrows that Trik left sitting on the boulder next to her.

"Zho!" she shouted without thinking, "This is wonderful! Zho has Varna's thanks!"

Zho had been sleeping, but he heard his name and opened one eye to see her approaching him with Troon's bow and a handful of arrows. She walked straight to him, leaned over, and kissed him on the cheek. He smiled sheepishly and said, "Varna is welcome." He did not know why she was thanking him.

Trik wanted to tell Varna that the arrows were from him, but he thought that maybe if he let Zho live with the lie, the truth will come out harder against him.

Trik saw Varna heading to the gate and asked, "Varna thuk prindas?"

She stopped at the exit and looked puzzled.

Trik pointed at her and said, "Bo. Varna thuk bo? Thuk prindas?"

She remembered his words and smiled. "Yes. Varna will hunt now with the bow."

"Trik go with Varna. Varna thuk. Trik watch voda pordu." He could see the puzzled look on her face, so he scratched his fingers in the air and growled like a mountain cat. "Voda pordu," he repeated, and growled again.

Varna shook her head and said, "No. Varna not hunt boda pordu. Varna is hungry. Varna will hunt for meat." Now she saw the quizzical look on his face and mimed eating something and repeated, "Meat."

Trik grabbed a large spear from the pile of weapons and said, "Trik go." He could still watch her back and keep an eye out for the leopards he heard outside.

Varna led him swiftly across the meadow to the beaver pond. She had seen the pond when she was setting traps before she left for the old village, but had never ventured beyond it. She was eager to find the giant goats Zho had observed during one of his early expeditions in this land. She hadn't really planned what she would do beyond bringing one of the beasts down and returning with some real meat, but if they were as big as Zho had said, she could certainly use Trik's help to carry the carcass back to the cave.

The beaver pond glistened in the full sun. It looked different to her. She had set traps here before, but had never caught any beaver and had concluded that the pond was abandoned. Now she saw signs that it might be occupied again. Beaver is a tasty treat, but she wanted to find one of those goats. She could return here on the way back if she remained empty-handed.

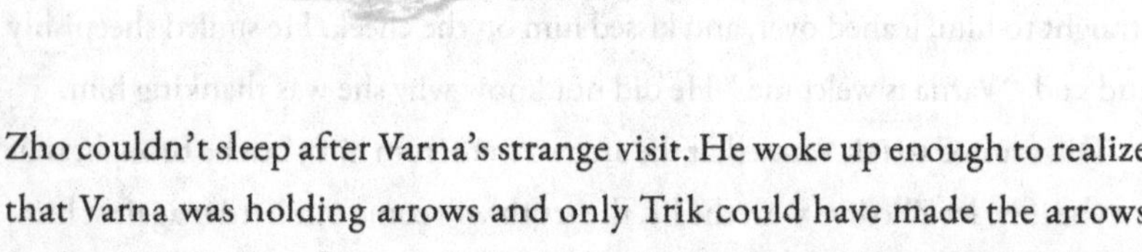

Zho couldn't sleep after Varna's strange visit. He woke up enough to realize that Varna was holding arrows and only Trik could have made the arrows for her. Zho had not known at the time why she thanked him, but Trik did. She was out there now, hunting with the arrows, and he was explaining to her that he made the arrows for her and not Zho. Zho was right not to trust him. He is trying to worm his way into their tribe and has picked on the most vulnerable member to do it.

Two can play at that game. For starters, Zho can make some real arrows for her instead of the hastily slapped together sticks he made. When she comes home empty-handed because his arrows don't fly straight, Zho will give her some real arrows and show him for the fraud he is.

But what if she doesn't come home with nothing? She is very good with the bow. She can probably compensate for his shoddy arrows and kill something, anyway. Zho laughed at the thought. The arrows she held were a mess. The feathers were falling off, and the shafts weren't uniform width. Varna was obviously being kind to accept them. Still, Zho can spend extra time to make sure his arrows are so obviously superior that everyone will be able to tell.

Nik slept by Pela's side. He stirred occasionally, but Pela rubbed his tummy and he remained asleep. Mora was by the fire preparing something from her medicines. Everything was under control here and Zho would have no problem slipping out to gather wood and make some proper arrows.

Kendo followed the course of the river. It meandered lazily along the broad valley's floor, then it led them up a gentle climb into a narrow valley between a large imposing mounting and its smaller sibling. The new valley also presented them with the beginnings of a forest of pines and firs. The forest was alive with the songs of birds and the comical antics of squirrels and chipmunks that came out of their homes to see the procession of humans passing by below them.

There was something comforting about the forest to the weary tribe. After traveling below the barren rocks of the higher elevations, and through the strange snowy fields that had led them to the broad featureless valley, they now found themselves in something more familiar. The spirits of the men and women filled with the sensation that home was near.

The valley opened up before them and showed them the source of the river. The excitement for many was unbearable. They gathered on the shore of the lake that fed the river, feeling that their journey had finally come to an end, but Kendo scowled as he looked over the lake.

An immense mountain, still covered with white peaks, stood as a backdrop to the lake. It certainly looked like a nice place to build their homes, but this did not look like the home of his visions, nor did it look like the lake that Marl had described.

An eagle descended from a high rocky peak and skimmed across the lake, looking for fish. It crossed the lake with its wings spread wide, gliding effortlessly from shore to shore, then it lifted up slightly and descended down the mountain on the other side of the lake and disappeared from view.

Kendo pointed up to a ridge that was a short way up the great mountain and said, "Brack! Take Koro and climb up to that ledge and tell Kendo if the two of you might see what lies beyond this lake. Kendo will stay and strike a camp here for the night."

Brack waved for Koro, who was still at the end of the procession, and asked, "Is this not the lake of Kendo's vision?"

Kendo shrugged and said, "It is different from Kendo's visions. Kendo does not remember the mountain being so close. Kendo also thought it would be bigger. Marl described it as an immense lake."

"And what of the spirits? Have they given Kendo no more signs?"

"They have," Kendo said.

Brack felt the great relief of the tribe. Many believed their journey was already done, but he could also see the concern etched on Kendo's brow and trusted in his judgment.

"Kendo believes we must pass beyond this lake to another."

Koro joined them and asked, "Does Brack need Koro to help scout the lake?"

"Not exactly," Kendo said. "Kendo does not wish to alarm the people, but Kendo would like the two of you to scout beyond this lake."

Brack pointed to the ridge and said, "From up there."

Koro sighed and asked, "Wrong lake?"

Brack shrugged and said, "We should hurry and see what we can learn before the day grows too old."

Mora poked at the fire. There was little she could do to speed things along; fire burns and water boils at their own pace. There were many beliefs passed down over the generations, but little was actually known of the ways of spirits and the diseases they wrought. She feared there was nothing more she could do to save Joog and Marl. It may be in the spirits' hands, and she had already pleaded with them until she had collapsed, but she would continue to do what she could. She stared into the water and saw bubbles forming in the bottom of her clay bowl.

"The water is almost ready," she said. "How is Yona doing with the mixture?"

Panic was written on Yona's face as she leaned the mortar over and showed Mora that the clay and charcoal had crushed down to a fine powder, but the bark remained fibrous strands. Tears stained her cheeks as she feared she would lose Marl and it would be her fault. "Yona is too weak to grind the bark."

"Yona did fine," Mora reassured her. "The bark never grinds the same as the earth."

Mora reached for the mortar, and Yona gladly handed it to her. The water was boiling now and Mora poured the contents of the mortar into the roiling water. She scraped the mortar with her fingers to get as much of the ingredients into the water as possible. The water turned dark and muddy.

Yona and Pela both leaned over and winced as they looked into the dark concoction.

Mora saw their faces and said, "It looks much worse than it tastes. The essence of the bark helps cool their blood, and the earth draws out the poison within them."

Yona rubbed snow into Marl's forehead and asked, "Mora thinks they were poisoned?"

"There are many ways the body can be poisoned," she replied. "Mora does not know what makes them sick, but if it is poison, this potion should help."

"What if it's not poison? What does Mora do next?"

"If evil spirits have invaded their bodies, and the earth does not draw them out, we will have one more chance to let them out, but let us hope it does not come to that." Mora remembered her training. She had the right tools, Varna had recovered them, but she had never performed the procedure and hoped she never would have to.

Varna had not seen the goat and could only trust Zho's opinion that it was a goat at all. She circled around the pond and crossed the stream to a steep rocky rise that led up the mountain. If it was a goat, it most likely liked climbing cliffs.

If she is really lucky, she will spot one of these goats on the cliff from the ground. Goats can be easy targets when they cling to the side of a cliff, but she didn't feel like she would be that fortunate. She found a spot behind a bush and crouched down. Trik joined her behind the bush and they waited.

Varna was very patient. She could spend half a day watching a trail and waiting for game to pass by, but this wasn't a known trail, and she did not know if any goats would pass this way. Worse yet, half the day was already lost. She had little time to be overly patient.

Zho set out across the meadow looking for the perfect saplings. He had a pretty good idea that he would find what he needed near the same location where they collected the wood for their spears. He walked briskly. The cutting stones clinked as the carry bag flopped against his thighs. He kept the bag slung over his shoulder and tried taming the swinging sack with his hand, but it slowed his pace. While he walked, he considered the many ways he could make an improved arrow for Varna. A straight shaft was essential, but a longer shaft carried more power with it, as did heavier wood. These were the same qualities they had looked for when they made their spears. He decided before he had even reached the woods that he would make longer, heavier arrows. He already knew that Troon's bow was powerful enough to launch them.

The woods had changed much in just the last few days. The sacred white soil was disappearing, and the trees were budding. It did not matter to him. He could still collect the wood and scrape off the buds.

He didn't know how long she would be out hunting, but the sun was already past mid-day and the best hunting usually came at sunset. This wasn't much time, and he would have to limit the quantity of arrows he produced in favor of better quality.

If only Varna could know that this was a common goat crossing, she could wait longer. If it were earlier in the morning, she could have given it more time, but there were too many unknown factors. She crept out from behind the bush that hid her and approached the cliff. The only thing she knew for sure was that goats loved cliffs. Then she remembered that she wasn't really certain that the beast was a goat.

Goats also like heights, so Varna hung the bow diagonally over her shoulders and started to climb. How many times, lately, has she found herself climbing a cliff? Trik followed behind, but Varna was in predator mode and barely knew he was there. Her focus was ahead of them, looking for any sign of movement from the rocks.

She ascended the cliff quietly. It was not as tall as the cliff that led them up the mountain, but it was sheer in the middle section. Her fingers clung to the small ridges as her feet sought solid grips beneath her. A whole herd of goats could have descended upon her while she was on this smooth section and she would have been unable to draw her bow. Traversing the cliff sideways would be no help to her, so she continued to reach up and grip the narrow edges with her fingertips while positioning her feet below her and pulling herself straight up.

At the peak of the precipice she saw a wide ledge, then the cliff continued. She climbed out on the ledge and crawled to the cliff. A large boulder at the base of the next cliff provided suitable shelter for her while she peered around its base and scanned the new bluff and was rewarded with the movement she so desperately sought.

Trik pulled himself over the edge and crawled noisily behind her, huffing and puffing.

One of the goats heard his movement and glanced their way, then bleated and bound up the hill. Varna saw three other goats follow. They were, as Zho had described; large bodied, wider than their goats but with similar hooves and with great helmets on their heads.

Varna leaped to her feet and pulled the bow, taking quick aim, then loosed an arrow up the cliff. The arrow found one of the goat's haunches. It stumbled as it tried to leap up the cliff. She notched another arrow and found the goat's shoulder, but still missed its heart. The beast lurched sideways and lost its footing, rolling down the steep wall to the same ledge that held Varna and Trik.

Trik whistled and said, "Varna is good."

"Varna is lucky."

Trik didn't know her word and asked, "Locky?"

Varna was angry at Trik for making so much noise and turned her back on him. She marched in the direction of the slain beast and said, "Varna is lucky that Trik's noise did not scare them away sooner."

Trik understood little of what she said, but he understood her tone and he heard his name in the middle of the sentence. He followed quietly behind as she approached her kill.

She knew nothing of these animals, and just because she saw it fall down the cliff did not mean it was dead. Nor did its looking like a goat mean that it was not dangerous. She notched another arrow and approached cautiously.

Trik saw her aim the bow at the dead animal. He ran ahead of her and carefully kicked the carcass. It did not move. She relaxed some until she was upon it. It was huge. It probably weighed more than she did.

Trik looked at her sheepishly and said, "Varna is locky."

Varna knew he didn't understand 'lucky', but the thrill of the hunt raced through her body and she found it difficult to remain angry with him. "Yes," she replied, "Varna is lucky that Trik is here to help carry this monster back to the cave."

She took some cord from a small purse she wore around her waist and tied the goat's feet together. She pointed to the spear Trik brought and mimed sliding it through the feet.

Trik understood and said, "Trik can help."

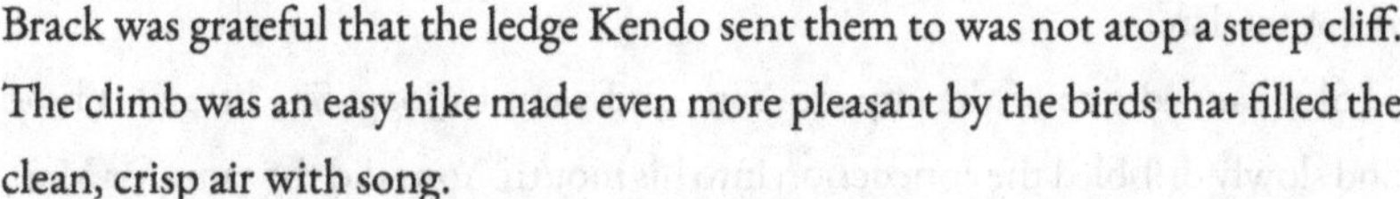

Brack was grateful that the ledge Kendo sent them to was not atop a steep cliff. The climb was an easy hike made even more pleasant by the birds that filled the clean, crisp air with song.

"This is a very nice location," Koro said. "Even the birds are happy here. Koro hopes Kendo does not lead us on a journey where there is always someplace nicer just beyond the horizon."

"Yes," Brack agreed, "this lake is very nice, but Brack trusts Kendo's vision. If Kendo does not think this is the right place, Brack will not disagree."

"Koro also trusts Kendo's vision. Already, Koro can see that there is another lake below this one. Is it not enough that we can see the lake? Must we climb all the way to the ledge?"

Brack turned around and saw the other lake. "We are almost there. We might as well continue."

"Almost there? We are only halfway to the ledge."

Brack laughed and asked, "Is Koro too tired to walk? Maybe Koro should stay with the women from now on."

"Koro will show you tired." Koro sprinted up the rest of the climb with Brack close on his heels.

As they reached the ledge, Brack grabbed the back of Koro's cloak and burst in front of him, then collapsed atop the ledge, wheezing. "Brack wins."

Koro stood over him, bent at the waist, laughing between great gulps of air, but the smile faded from his face and he pointed down beyond the lake and said, "Kendo must see this for himself."

Mora placed a medium coarse cloth over a clean bowl and poured the muddy brew into it, filtering the fibrous wood from the liquid. She stirred the filtered mix away from the fire and blew on it to cool it, then ladled it into cups for her patients.

"It is good," Mora said, "that Varna retrieved Mora's supplies. Let us hope it is not too late."

She handed one of the cups to Yona and went to Joog. She lifted his head and slowly dribbled the concoction into his mouth. Yona did the same for Marl. Both patients swallowed the liquid without waking.

"Now we wait," Mora said.

Yona softly chanted one of Mora's prayers. Her voice was barely more than a whisper until Pela joined her and their voices grew in strength. Mora sucked in her breath when she saw Brahg sit up to join them. He winced but found a comfortable enough position and added his own voice.

Zho's arrows could not have been straighter. He painstakingly scraped the bark from the surface of the wood and shaved down any bumps where buds would have created new branches. He held each arrow to his eye and stared down the shafts. They were perfect. He didn't bother collecting old dropped feathers from the chicken's cage. He plucked four strong wing feathers from each of the birds.

His arrows were longer than Trik's and he was convinced that they were straighter than Trik's. These arrows would certainly take down one of the giant goats that he knew Varna wanted. If Trik thought he could wedge his way into their tribe by making his flimsy arrows for Varna, he had more to learn about them.

Zho's hopes were dashed when he saw Trik and Varna returning with one of the great goats hanging between them. Zho looked at his arrows and wondered why he worked so hard on them. Trik waved at Zho from the meadow. Zho had to go out and help carry the beast now that they had already seen him.

Zho took the spear from Varna's shoulder and placed it on his. Her smile was immense. Even the weight of the carcass on her shoulder had not dampened her enthusiasm. "Zho should have been there. Troon's bow was magnificent. Varna saw four of the goats on the cliff, but they heard us approach, so Varna had to take quick aim to take one down."

Zho examined the goat while they walked. He only saw a single arrow and asked, "Only one shot? Troon's bow is truly magnificent."

"Well," she admitted, "it took two shots, but they only made it fall down the cliff. The fall killed it."

"Still," Zho said, "It takes a truly extraordinary bow and a highly skilled hunter to down a large animal with such puny arrows."

Varna cocked her head and looked at Zho funny while she tried to understand what he meant about the arrows.

Zho pointed to a spot outside the cave where the snow was still thick. "Let's put it there to carve."

Trik did not understand his words, but Zho's pointing finger was easy to follow. They dropped the beast on the spot Zho had selected. Trik was relieved to have the weight off his shoulder until Zho handed a knife to him and patted him on the back before trailing inside behind Varna.

Varna had not forgotten about the fates of Joog and Marl, but she had allowed the rush of the moment to supplant her feelings until she entered the cave and saw Mora praying over them.

"Did the medicine not help?" she asked.

"It is too soon to say."

Zho wanted to hear all about the hunt, but Varna joined Mora at Joog's side and added her voice to their chants.

Brack and Koro ran, jumped and slid down the mountain with a new sense of urgency.

This was not the lake of Kendo's vision and they needed to reach him while they still had light. This lake was just a stopping point for the larger lake that they saw further down the mountain. There was no doubt in their minds that it was Kendo's vision which had led them up to the ledge.

Flom pointed up the mountain and said, "Kendo, look. Brack and Koro return."

Kendo joined Flom and asked, "Why do they hurry?"

Flom grabbed his spear and said, "Maybe something chases them."

Flom and Kendo both ran to meet them, but saw nothing following them.

Brack and Koro saw Flom and Kendo approaching. They stopped to catch their breath and wait for them.

Kendo asked, "Is something wrong? You look like you had seen a spirit."

Brack spoke between heaving breaths, "Kendo must see for himself."

"What is it?" Kendo asked.

Brack responded, "We climbed to the ledge as Kendo instructed and saw..."

"No," Koro interrupted, "let us not say. Kendo's vision has brought us here. It was Kendo's vision that sent us up onto that ledge. Only Kendo will know if this was in his vision. Kendo must see it with Kendo's own eyes."

Trik had thought that he had left his life of servitude behind when he left his family and escaped the village of his birth. He crossed a lot of miles and burned a lot of bridges, trying to make his own life, but the first stop of his new life's journey had not fared much better than the one to which he was born. Now, in the next chapter of his life's story, he found himself with someone else's knife in his hand and a job they expected him to do. He saw these people as an opportunity to get the life that he wanted for himself and felt that he had already invested too much time in them to walk away now, but he would need to build relationships with more of the tribe than just Varna before he stood up to Zho. He took the knife Zho had provided and began skinning and carving the goat.

"Trik?"

The voice behind Trik startled him. Though it was a familiar voice to him, Trik did not expect to ever hear it again.

"Trik! De Nik de nub?"

Trik stood motionless, still facing the goat. He wanted to run into the cave, but did not know how many were behind him. "Neh," he said. "Nik neh de nub."

"Trik geben Nik. Geben Nik de Foln."

Trik slowly turned around and saw that Foln was alone. He pointed to the cave and said, "Aben Foln. Nik de tosh."

Trik led Foln to the gate and yelled out, "Zho! Varna! Foln is with Trik. Trik knows Foln."

Varna stopped chanting to see what the shouting was about.

Zho rose to see for himself. He wished his spear were nearer when he saw the visitor. He did not trust Trik, and he certainly did not trust any friend of Trik's. "Varna? Is Troon's bow with Varna? Trik has brought a stranger among us."

Troon's bow was near, but Nik stirred and began to cry. She could not reach both.

"Nik?" Foln said softly, "Nik? Nik geben Foln."

Nik started to crawl and Varna went to him instead of her bow. Nik stopped crying, but he blabbered on in an incomprehensible baby talk and reached his arms out for Trik and Foln.

"Varna?" Zho asked, "Does Varna have Troon's bow yet?"

"No Bo," Trik said, "Foln is with Trik."

Varna carried Nik to meet with Trik and Foln. Nik squealed with delight and reached out for Foln. Foln opened his arms and said, "Nik! Foln de Nik." Foln reached to take Nik, but Varna turned away, not sure if she should give him the baby.

Foln was a stranger here and he not only did not know these people, he didn't know what lies Trik might have told them, so he tried to explain. "Nik de Foln's tok."

Only Trik understood Foln's language. He translated, "Foln says that..."

"Neh!" Foln shouted. "Trik neh bok de Foln zeiben. Trik de sast naben."

Zho didn't understand a word Foln said, but he could tell from his voice that Foln did not like Trik and Zho liked him for that. Nik had settled down in Varna's arms, but she was aware that his eyes had never left Foln. She carried him over to Foln's side and Nik reached out to climb into his arms.

"Nik," Foln said softly, "de tok de pru."

Varna didn't need to understand Foln's language to see that Nik was fond of Foln.

Zho felt he had an ally. He wished he could hear Foln's story, but it was clear that Foln would not allow Trik to tell it. "Foln? Do you understand anything we say?"

Foln just looked blankly at Zho and shrugged his shoulders while Nik played with his long curly hair.

"Grull," Zho said. "Trik said we speak Grull."

"Grull!" Foln exclaimed, "Zu de Grull!"

Zho patted himself on the chest and said, "Zho," then he pointed to Varna and said, "Varna."

Foln similarly patted his own chest and said, "Foln," then he patted Nik on the tummy and said, "Foln's tok Nik," but then he pointed to Trik and his voice grew stern and angry when he said, "Trik de sast naben."

Trik went to Varna and wrapped his arms around her, saying, "Foln is Nik's father. Trik saved Nik from the big water, but Trik could not save Nik's mother, Deya. Trik cared for Nik after the river took us to the abandoned village. Trik tried to find Foln's village to return Nik, but Trik and Nik always lose way and return to where Varna find us. Foln blames Trik for not saving Deya and not returning Nik."

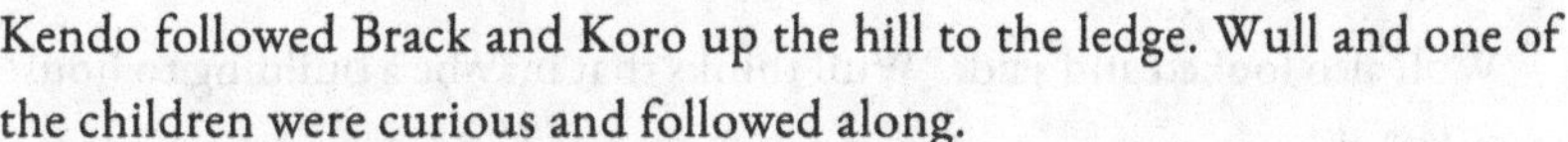

Kendo followed Brack and Koro up the hill to the ledge. Wull and one of the children were curious and followed along.

The sun had not set yet, but it was dipping low on the horizon and colored the wispy clouds a brilliant pink.

Brack and Koro refused to tell Kendo what they saw and simply repeated, "Kendo will see," when he asked.

Kendo was as tired as the rest of the tribe, but it was an easy hike. He stopped and turned around halfway up, but Koro pointed up and said, "Kendo must see the view from the ledge. The spirits must have prompted Kendo to choose that ledge for Koro and Brack to climb, and it is from that ledge that Kendo will see what Kendo sees."

Kendo shrugged and continued walking. There was something ominous in Koro's voice. Kendo had no idea what awaited him, but concern had begun to reshape the expression on his face.

Once they were atop the ledge, Kendo looked out across the lake. A smile stretched across his face as he saw the lake of his vision further down below the smaller lake.

"Kendo is smiling," Brack said, "Brack thinks Kendo sees the lake but does not yet see what is on the near shore."

Brack and Koro both pointed and Kendo focused on the tree line that stood between this lake and the next.

Kendo also pointed and asked, "Does Brack mean the rocks between us and the lake? Kendo sees no harm in the rocks."

"The sun has almost set," Koro said, "but the light is not so low yet that Kendo cannot see what we see. Look again."

Kendo shrugged.

"Are Kendo's eyes too old to truly see the rocks?" Brack asked. "Look at the rocks."

Kendo looked at the rocks again and his brow furled.

"They are not rocks at all," Koro said, "are they?"

"No." Kendo said. What he saw now were the stone tops of massive structures built by the hands of men.

Wull also looked and said, "Wull thinks that may be a building to house people."

Just as the last ray of sunshine disappeared on the horizon, something on the stone building moved and the child exclaimed, "Did anyone see that?"

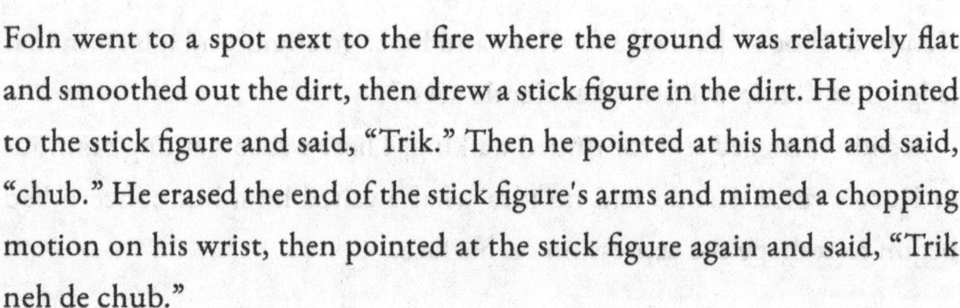

Foln went to a spot next to the fire where the ground was relatively flat and smoothed out the dirt, then drew a stick figure in the dirt. He pointed to the stick figure and said, "Trik." Then he pointed at his hand and said, "chub." He erased the end of the stick figure's arms and mimed a chopping motion on his wrist, then pointed at the stick figure again and said, "Trik neh de chub."

Zho felt vindicated for not trusting Trik. Trik still held Varna in a hug and tried positioning himself between her and Foln, but she squirmed out of his arms so she could see what he was drawing.

Foln drew three more stick figures, two large and one small. He pointed to the two large ones and said, "Foln poy Deya." He pointed to the small one and said, "Nik." He drew three wavy horizontal lines in the sand and then a curved line from Nik to the wavy lines and said, "Nik kreb de loo."

"Nik fell in the water," Varna said. "Trik told Varna that Trik saved Nik from the water."

"That must have been the flood," Zho added.

Foln didn't understand them but he drew a line from one of the stick figures to the water and said, "Deya bok kreb de loo." Then Foln erased Deya from the dirt and said, "Neh Deya." Foln drew a third line from Trik's stick figure to the water and said, "Trik bok kreb de loo. Trik poy Nik de loo, gon neh Deya."

"Nik's mother died in the flood," Zho said.

"And Trik jumped in to save Nik," Varna added.

"No," Zho said, "Trik jumped in to save Trik's hands. Why was Trik going to lose Trik's hands?"

Foln didn't understand.

"Chub," Varna said, "Trik neh chub?"

Foln reached for his knife and said, "Trik neh chub."

"Why?" Varna asked.

Foln recognized from her tone that she was asking a question. He went to the sacks with Mora's things and pretended to take items from the sacks and put them in his cloak. "Trik de sast naben."

Brahg, who had been watching quietly, said, "Trik's a thief."

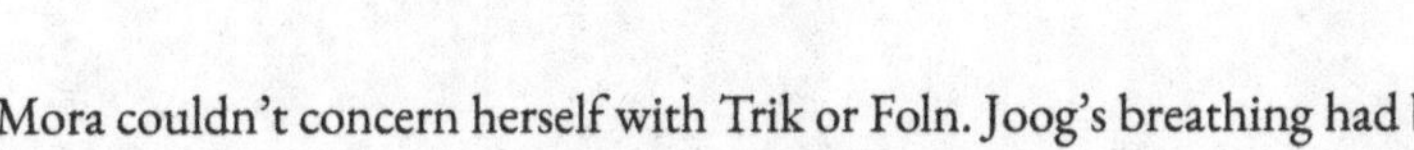

Mora couldn't concern herself with Trik or Foln. Joog's breathing had become very shallow, and she feared the medicine would not have enough time to remove the poisons from his system. She held his head in her lap, mopping a cool towel across his brow while still softly chanting for him. She was running out of options for treating him. The medicine worked on simple poisons, but if it wasn't poison, if he was being attacked by evil spirits, then she would have to resort to a very drastic procedure to flush them from his body. She didn't believe he was strong enough to survive such desperate measures.

"A thief?" Zho asked, "Yes, it all makes sense now. Zho never trusted Trik."

"No!" Trik objected. "Trik not thief. Trik blamed, but not true." Trik scanned around the room for someone to believe in him, but he could see that everyone believed Foln. Only Varna was not completely convinced, but she stood with them and did not offer him comfort.

Joog's eyes fluttered and he looked around the cave to see what all the commotion was. Mora breathed a sigh of relief and said, "We have visitors, and they are too noisy for Joog to sleep."

Zho pointed at Trik and said, "Trik will stay the night here. We will decide what to do with Trik in the morning." Zho turned to Foln and offered his forearm as a sign of acceptance. Foln recognized the gesture and accepted the forearm with his own, even though it was not his people's way.

Zho smiled and patted Foln on the shoulder, asking, "Would Foln stay and share a meal with us?"

Foln, of course, did not understand, so Zho mimed eating something. Foln smiled, which was all Zho needed to know. Zho left the cave to continue carving the goat. Foln gave Nik back to Varna and was surprised how easily his baby accepted her arms. He then followed Zho out of the cave and helped with the meat.

Mora reached for a bowl of water to give Joog, but when she held it to his lips, he had stopped breathing. She gasped as she dropped the bowl and yelled, "JOOG!"

Chapter Nine

What Lies Beyond

Kendo was still adjusting to the fact that the far off rocks by the lake were actually stone structures and not natural formations.

He had not seen any movement, but the child with them jumped up and down, saying, "Did nobody else see it?"

All eyes focused on the stone roof tops where the child pointed, but only the young boy had seen the movement.

The stone roofs reflected a brilliant white against the dark green trees that surrounded them, but shadows crept across their alabaster surface even while the small group searched to see what the child had seen.

"What did Keko see?" Kendo asked. "Perhaps it was just a bird?"

"Keko does not know what it was, but it did not fly, and Keko thinks it was too large for a bird."

"Hmmm," Kendo pondered, "We shall see in the morning what is there, but now, the sun sets and we must return to camp before it is too dark to find our way down the mountain."

The small expedition returned down the trail, but Kendo continued to watch the stone buildings as he walked, until they disappeared behind the trees a quarter of the way back down.

Tears traced jagged paths down the wrinkles that etched Mora's face as she shook Joog and screamed, "Wake up! Open your eyes and breathe!"

All attention in the cave was on her and Joog. He lay silent and cold with his head limp on Mora's lap while she hunched over him, sobbing uncontrollably. Marl still breathed, but he too slept the unending sleep of one about to meet death. Yona feared that Marl would be next and began chanting frantically, while Pela threw more incense on the fire and joined her chants.

Brahg was the only of the three well enough to sit up and understand what was happening. He bowed his head and prayed for his comrade.

Mora placed her ear on Joog's chest. She could not hear his heartbeat or his lungs breathe. She cried for him and yelled for him, but he did not hear her.

The mood of the tribe was joyous. Few had seen the concern on Kendo's face when he returned from the ridge, and he wasn't going to spoil the moment for them. The lake of his vision was less than a day's travel beyond this one and he saw no harm in starting their celebration here. They had arrived, even if they still had a little more to go.

Rabbits and quail roasted on long spits over roaring fires. There was little time to gather seasonings before the sun had set, but the women had found some wild onions and a root which was like a potato. Kendo hoped they could find enough palatable vegetation to begin cultivating, something that his people had only just started doing when his father's father was still a boy.

Many had already set up tents and lean-to shelters, but it was a beautiful clear night and Kendo thought he would enjoy lying under the stars. The moon had not yet risen, and the fires set around the camp cast a faint and dancing glow on the surrounding trees. A myriad of stars splashed across the dark heavens. Kendo looked across the lake towards their destination. The water was smooth and reflected the brightest of the stars. Glow bugs swarmed around the trees near the shore.

Kendo lay back with his hands behind his head and smiled broadly at the cosmos. A star shot out of the heavens in the east and flew overhead, leaving a thin, glowing trail behind it. It crossed over the lake and burned out beyond the other shore, somewhere over their destination. This place was magical. There was so much light to see in the darkness. Some say the stars are the souls of the ancestors. Kendo did not know if that were true, but it was a magnificent sight and tomorrow would be a historic day for their people. He wished Joog were with him to witness the end of their journey. A melancholy brushed over Kendo and left a hollowness in his chest. He did not know the fate of his son and wondered if the shooting star he saw was a good omen or a bad one.

Joog's eyes were still closed when he first felt the warmth on his face. It started on his cheeks and nose, then spread back to his ears and down to his neck. He hadn't expected it to be morning yet, but it must be because the sun shone brightly against his eyelids. The warmth he felt spread through his bones until it enveloped him, body and soul, bringing a long absent smile to his face.

He opened his eyes and saw the bluest sky he had ever seen. He sat up and looked around. The sun was low on the horizon. It was unlike any sunrise he had ever known. It was so low. It looked as if it might actually be touching the ground. He closed his eyes again and spread his arms to bathe in the warmth. He thought he had never felt anything quite so exquisite.

Rising from the soft sand where he lay, he walked towards the sunrise. He didn't know where he would go and had no destination in mind, but the warmth was intoxicating. He felt like he had always been cold to the core and had never known such warmth.

The sand squished between his toes. Even the sand was warm to him. It wasn't the hot dry sand of the desert that burns your feet. It was slightly moist, like the shore of a lake. He scanned the horizon, but he saw no water. There should be water.

A small waved lapped at his feet from behind him. He spun around and there, behind him, was the water. It was cool and refreshing, but it wasn't as inviting as the warmth radiating from the sun.

He continued walking towards the sun. It was strange that the sun neither rose nor set, but remained low on the horizon waiting for him. The water continued to lap at his feet from behind. He had walked a long distance already but when he turned around, he saw that the water was still there as if he had gone nowhere.

"No matter," he chuckled to himself. He needn't worry about where he had been, only where he was going. Only then did he realize that he actually did have a destination and proceeded towards the sun. Nothing could compare with the feeling inside of him right now. What a strange and beautiful place this was. It had everything he could want, except maybe something to eat.

The scent of fresh baked bread and roasted duck wafted past him and he knew he was wrong again. This place had everything he could ever want.

He was as giddy as a little girl and spun around in a circle, dancing through the warm moist sand. He had always been very fast and strong, but he had never been this light on his feet before. He stopped dancing and looked down at his feet. He had both of his feet. This should have alarmed him, but it felt right. He could walk again. He could even dance, and if he can dance, he can run.

Joog sprinted towards the light. The water raced behind him and the scent of food was everywhere. He ran like the wind. He had always loved running. Marl ran with him often and was the only member of the tribe who came close to his speed. They loved to race each other, whether on land or on the water, but Joog had never been swifter than he was right now.

It wasn't the sun. It couldn't be. It was bright and warm, and still far off, but he could see that he drew closer and it remained near the ground. He flew over the sand and never ran out of breath. He thought maybe if he just spread his arms, he might fly over the sand. If this was a dream, he hoped it would never end. This was like no place he had ever known.

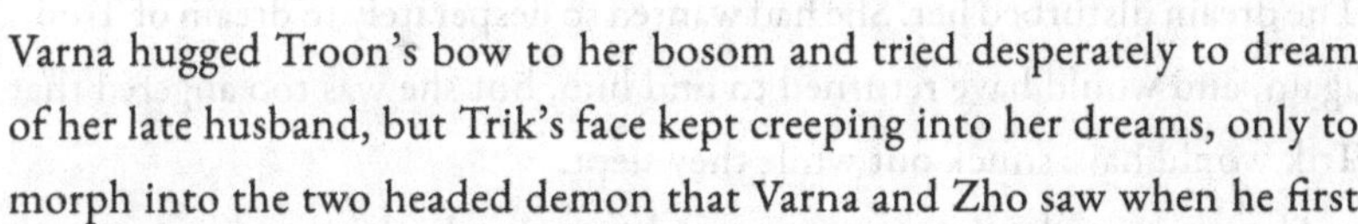

Varna hugged Troon's bow to her bosom and tried desperately to dream of her late husband, but Trik's face kept creeping into her dreams, only to morph into the two headed demon that Varna and Zho saw when he first climbed the cliff.

Nik left the comfort and safety of his father's arms and crawled across the cave floor to Varna. He played with the hairs that fell across her face. She swiped the hairs off her face without opening her eyes, and Nik gently squeezed her nose with his miniature little fingers. A sly smile spread across her lips as she opened her eyes and he cooed and gurgled with his baby talk. She couldn't help smiling and took him into her arms.

Nik nestled his head between her breasts and listened to the beat of her heart. Varna closed her eyes and tried returning to her dreams of Troon, but Nik tugged on the beads that she wore around her neck, preventing her from sleeping just yet. She stroked the back of his head. His hair was silky soft, but there was something more about him. She found great comfort in holding and caressing the baby. He looked into her eyes, smiled broadly and said, "No more. Gone."

"What?" Varna asked, "Does Nik speak?"

Nik nodded gently and said, "Varna wastes time lamenting the loss of Troon. Varna must move on, but first Varna must know who Trik is."

Varna's mouth fell open. She had never known a baby this young could speak, and for a baby to speak so eloquently must be a sign.

"Do not marvel over the baby," he said. "Varna still sees two Triks. That is Trik's magic. Varna must see the real Trik before Varna can move on."

"Trik?" she asked. "What does Trik have to do with Varna?"

"Trik weaves Trik's magic on Varna and now Varna is confused. Go find the real Trik."

"Varna does not care about Trik. Varna wants to dream of Troon."

She closed her eyes, but the baby roared, "NO!"

She opened her eyes and Nik had two heads, his own and Trik's.

Varna opened her eyes for real and sat up from her straw bed. Nik was still in his father's arms. She scanned the darkened cave and Trik was gone. The dream disturbed her. She had wanted so desperately to dream of Troon again, and would have returned to find him, but she was too angered that Trik would have snuck out while they slept.

She got up and quietly crept across the cave to the door, suddenly struck by the thought that she had to see Trik for who he really was. Her bow was slung across her back and her quiver hung from her belt. She would hunt him down.

The euphoria never waned as Joog ran, skipped and jumped across the warm sand. The waves crashed behind him and may have looked like they were chasing him, but sounded to him like children that were running along and playing behind him.

The brilliant light cast beautiful small shadows from the tiny ripples in the sand that flew beneath his feet, but the alien land was otherwise devoid of landmarks that he could use to judge how far or how fast he was running. There were neither mountains, nor trees, nor any kind of structures for him to run past, from or towards. The great light, which was his destination, was the only feature upon the great expanse and it was still far off in the distance. There was nothing here: nothing to see; nothing to hear; nothing to smell.

He stopped running for a moment and cocked his head as he examined the landscape again. He was wrong. There were things to see and smell. The sand was warm and moist beneath his feet and he could smell the salty spray of the ocean that followed him. The sky was a brilliant blue and then there was the light.

"Yes," someone said next to him, "Is it not the purest light you have ever seen?"

"Truly," Joog replied. He turned to see his neighbor. He was oddly familiar, yet Joog was certain that he had never seen him before.

The man at his side smiled and said, "Joog looks good. It is nice to have ten toes again, is it not?"

Joog searched his memory to identify the stranger. He knew him. He was convinced that he knew him, but the stranger's identity eluded him. Joog smiled and nodded as he repeated himself, "Truly."

The man laughed and asked, "Has the son of Kendo lost his ability to speak?"

"No," Joog said. He looked deeply into the stranger's eyes, searching for the spark of familiarity which haunted him. He thought he recognized his eyes and asked, "Troon?"

Troon bowed deeply at the waist and said, "At Joog's service."

"But the man before Joog is too young. How is it that Troon is here? Troon is..."

"Shhh," Troon said, "We don't speak of that here."

"But Troon was..."

Troon held his hands up to stop Joog. "Death has no meaning here, so we have no need to speak of it. Perhaps Joog should ask how it is that Joog is here. Does Joog even know where here is?"

"Joog does not know for certain where this is, but Joog has never been so comfortable anywhere."

"True," Troon said, "There is no place to compare with this, and Troon hates to impose upon Joog, but..."

"Wait," Joog interrupted, "If this is where Joog thinks it is, then why has Troon come to meet Joog? Why has Troon come alone to greet Joog?"

Troon grimaced and said, "Joog is correct. There are others who would come to welcome Joog, but only Troon has watched closely enough to see what goes on in Troon's absence. Joog's mother waits with Joog's grandparents. Joog's arrival is not certain yet, but Troon has been keeping a close eye on everyone. Things are not right. Troon hates to suggest this, but it is not Joog's time yet. Joog must return and take a message."

"No!" Joog exclaimed. "Troon cannot ask Joog to return to that half-life."

Troon hung his head and said, "Troon knows it is asking a lot, but Joog must return and warn Zho."

"Why would Joog ever want to return? Look at Joog now. In Troon's own words, Joog has ten toes here!"

"Troon understands, but Joog must warn Zho about the stranger who has visited."

Joog shook his head and said, "Joog mostly slept and was barely aware of what went on, but Joog knows that a stranger had come, and even the sleeping Joog could tell that Zho already distrusted the stranger."

"But does Joog know that the stranger stole Joog's tribal amulet?"

"Does Joog care that some stranger has stolen a worthless trinket from a dying man?"

Troon shook his head and said, "It was hardly worthless, but there is more."

"Joog does not believe that the bauble's value matters here, it certainly cannot compare with the value of having Joog's foot back."

"But, does Joog know that Varna alone knows that the stranger snuck away, and Varna alone is following him?"

"Joog did not know that, but Varna is a capable hunter. Joog is certain that Varna can take care of Varna."

"No." Troon shook his head. "Varna is vulnerable. Troon senses real danger. Joog must go back and warn Zho. Troon would do it if it were not already too late."

"Vulnerable? We must not be talking about the same Varna."

Joog resumed running towards the light.

"Wait!" Troon shouted. "Listen to Troon!"

"No. Joog thinks Troon is a test to see if Joog truly deserves to be here."

Zho hadn't trusted Trik from the start. Foln's revelation that Trik was a thief justified his feelings towards Trik, but being right about Trik didn't help Zho sleep any. He still remembered the fear he had when Trik appeared to them as a two headed demon. Awake, he could laugh at the memory, but in his dreams, the image was terrifying. His nightmares haunted him with a two headed Trik whose hands had been chopped off, but with fearsome claws growing in their place.

He welcomed the morning, relieved to be awake and free from the disturbing dreams until he looked around and saw that Varna was not in her bed. The few embers that still glowed dimly in the fire pit barely illuminated the large cave and he thought that maybe she had moved closer to the fire and he just couldn't see well enough to find her.

He poked the embers to rouse the fire. Varna was quite fond of Nik and could have chosen to share a bed with Nik and Foln, but Nik was snuggled in Foln's arms and she was not with them.

A thought struck Zho that chilled his spine. He strained to see around the cave. What if she chose to share a bed with Trik? He'd rather suffer the nightmares than that, but where else could she be? He poked the embers again and laid two more logs across the fire. He had to find her, but he shuddered to think he might find her in Trik's arms.

Life returned to the fire and light blossomed throughout the cave. She was not there. Zho might have believed she had gone hunting if they hadn't had so much meat left from last night's goat. A hollowness filled Zho's heart as he felt his soul drop from a dizzying height. Not only was Varna gone, but Trik was gone as well. He wished now even more than before that he had just remained asleep and fought the demon Trik and never woke up to learn that she had left with him.

It was evident from the snores and soft breathing around the cave that everyone else still slept. Even Mora had collapsed with Joog's head still in her lap. Marl and Brahg still lived, but Marl had yet to wake up. There would be nobody here to tell him what had happened.

He returned to his bed and closed his eyes, but could not force himself to sleep. He focused on Trik's image and begged for the nightmares but could not cross over into the dream world. His heart was struck with an arrow and the distrust in his mind grew to anger and evolved into hatred.

He did not know when sleep finally found him, but it did not comfort him with the same nightmares of the two headed Trik. Instead, he saw Trik and Varna, hand in hand, laughing and skipping across a meadow of flowers. Trik looked back at him and smiled. It was a taunt, and it vexed Zho. He did not know how to respond.

Nobody in the tribe expected to remain in the same location where they had set up camp. They knew that the lake would have to be scouted before Kendo could select the best location to build the village, but it didn't happen like that.

Night passed quietly and Kendo let the tribe sleep late into the morning. When some of them did finally start to wake, they found him having quiet discussions with Brack, Koro and Wull, but nobody was scouting the lake. Was it so late in the morning that they could have walked the perimeter of the lake already?

The women had talked themselves to sleep, sharing their opinions of where they hoped to end up and what parts of the lake they liked the best. They woke up and continued those discussions until they noticed Kendo just standing around watching everyone sleep. Something was up.

Eventually, Kendo woke the rest of the tribe and ordered that the camp be packed up again.

"We are close," he said. "Kendo promises you that we do not have far to go, but this lake is not the home of our ancestors. Kendo has seen our destination. Not just in Kendo's visions, but with Kendo's own eyes. Kendo climbed up to the ridge overlooking this lake and saw our true destination. It lies just beyond the far shore of this lake, and Kendo promises you that it is worth the journey. Let us gather our belongings one last time and take ourselves past this lake and a little further down the mountain to the ancient home where our people began."

Trik's trail was easy to follow. He made no more effort to hide his tracks here than he had made to quietly stalk the goat when they went hunting. Varna wondered what kind of man would have absolutely no training in hunting? She could understand a man who didn't like killing or didn't know how to wage war, but every boy child is at least introduced to the world of the hunt. Perhaps he couldn't learn it. Maybe something is wrong with him, yet, when he followed Zho and Varna from the village, he certainly seemed stealthy enough. Zho was right. There was something odd about Trik. Maybe she should tell Zho that she realizes that now, or maybe not.

She followed his tracks across the meadow to the beaver pond. She was a little surprised that he didn't go back to the old village. A man with no skills to hunt didn't strike her as the type who would set out on his own.

His tracks stopped at the beaver pond and paced back and forth. She could not tell how long he had dallied there, but his tracks were all over, then they changed directions when they left the pond and led her back towards the sunrise and up the mountain a bit, then back towards the cave.

His voice came to her before she saw him. She couldn't hear what he was saying and had no idea with whom he might be speaking, so she dropped close to the ground and crawled closer to the sound of his voice.

Trik leaned against a large boulder, watching in the direction of the cave. Varna made no sound, but watched and listened.

"*Trik neh de chub?*" he asked in a funny voice.

"Neh," he replied using his own voice, "Trik keeps hands. Trik keeps trinkets too."

"*Neh,*" he said in the exaggerated voice again, "*Foln naben Trik's chub.*"

"No. Trik not care what Foln wants. Foln not take Trik's hands. Foln not follow Trik. Trik will kill Foln and never see Foln again."

"*Eh? Trik naben Nik?*"

"No, Trik does not want Nik. Why would Trik want to take Nik? Once Trik kills Foln, there will be nobody left to pay the ransom."

"*Neh Nik? Trik naben Varna. Trik poy Nik naben Varna.*"

"No. Trik does not need Varna anymore. Trik has this. With this, the other tribes will see Trik as a leader of men. Trik will be someone to be respected by the clans; not someone to be trifled with. Trik will be a tribal chieftain."

He pulled a large jewel from his vest. It hung from a leather cord and sparkled in the dim light of the rising sun. Varna recognized it. Trik had stolen Joog's emblem that marked him as the chieftain's son. It was true. He was a thief.

Varna rose and aimed her bow at Trik. "So," she said, "Trik is a thief, as Foln said, and crazy too, as Varna has seen."

Trik hid his surprise and smiled sinisterly. He held his hands out from his sides with the jewel dangling from one of them. "So, Varna has caught Trik. What now? Does Varna intend to kill Trik? Trik does not think so. If Varna were the type to kill Trik in cold blood, then Varna would also be the type to know how valuable this bauble is. We could take it to another land and use it to gain much property and status. We would be lords in a new land, and they would know nothing about Varna's pathetic friends."

Varna needn't respond. The disgust that had contorted on her face told Trik that she did not share his way of thinking, but he still did not believe she would kill him. He could use that to his advantage.

"Varna thinks Trik should return to Zho. Zho will know what to do."

"Ah, yes. By all means, let us go see the mighty Zho; Zho the demon slayer; Zho who thinks Varna is just a silly girl; Zho who thinks Varna competes with Zho to be the best hunter; Zho who looks at Varna with contempt whenever Varna raises Varna's bow. Zho will know what to do, just like Zho knows how to treat Varna."

His words angered and confused Varna. "How does Trik suddenly speak our language so well?"

"Trik knows how to speak Grull. Trik has always known Grull. Trik's mother was Grull. Trik was raised Grull."

"Varna knows all our people. How is it that Varna does not know Trik, if Trik was raised Grull?"

Trik motioned to a suitable boulder and said, "Why doesn't Varna sit down while Trik tells the tale of the Grull people? Relax a bit. Varna does not need to keep that bow aimed at Trik the whole time."

"No," she replied, "Trik can start walking and explain on the way."

Trik shrugged and said, "Very well."

He started walking, but he walked slowly, always plotting and thinking how he might get out of this situation.

"Varna's people are not the only Grull. There are many Grull. It was long ago when the greatest of the Grull chieftains joined the spirit world and left the tribe to the chief's twelve sons. The chief would never pick a favorite from among the sons. The first three of them were born during the same moon, so to treat them equally, the chief hid the order of their births."

"That's all very fascinating," Varna said, "but can Trik walk a little faster while telling this tale?"

Trik took a few faster steps, but slowed back down the same pace and continued, "The chief wanted always to be fair and to be known as the fair chief. When the other sons came during the following moons, the chief hid their births and forbid celebrating the day of their births."

"So?" Varna asked. "Why do men always think the eldest son must inherit the crown?"

"It is how it has always been done. It is tradition."

"Yeah," she replied, "Like not letting women hunt."

"Let Trik finish the tale. The chief never divulged their ages to either the sons or to the tribe. Nobody knew which of the twelve sons was the eldest, so when the chief died, all twelve sons tried to rule together."

"That is sensible."

"But it wasn't," Trik replied. "It was a disaster. The brothers could not be more different and argued bitterly over how to manage the tribe until one day, the arguments between two of the brothers came to blows. The other brothers stepped in and stopped the fight. They saw that they would never agree on a leader, so they divided the tribe and left the ancestral lands to venture out into the world."

"Only men could do something so stupid for something so trivial."

"Trivial? Each brother wanted to make the tribe stronger, and each of them had a different plan to accomplish it. They gathered up whoever would follow them and set out in different directions, each anxious to prove their ways superior. In the beginning, they held gatherings where the tribes would reunite in the ancient lands and share their stories."

"How long did that last?"

"Let Trik tell the story to Varna. Eventually, the gatherings became less frequent until finally they were forgotten. Some say the Gods would one day force them to gather again and face each other, if anyone still believes in that sort of thing."

"What does Trik believe?"

Trik shrugged his shoulders, but said nothing. He still believed he would find a way out of this predicament.

No matter how much Kendo tried to inspire the tribe, the mood, while packing, remained somber. Nobody believed they would stay forever in the spot where they had set up their temporary camp, but they had gone to sleep believing that their journey was done and the morning would usher in the great rebuilding. Now they were packing their supplies so they could march onward and build a new camp beyond the lake, but nobody argued, and they kept their complaints mostly to themselves.

Kendo did not even bother with breakfast for the tribe. They were too close to their destination. Brack and Wull went ahead to scout the way while Koro and Flom made sure nobody was left behind.

The morning greeted them with the cheerful song of birds hunting the moist shores of the lake for worms and grub. A small cloud of insects formed over a marshy arm of the lake with fish eager to jump out of the water to catch them. Some of the men pointed to the plentiful fish and wondered why they would leave such a fruitful lake behind.

"Do not worry," Koro said to them, "Koro is certain the lake of our ancestors will also have fish eager to jump into our nets, but even if it doesn't, this lake will still be close enough for us to fish."

Kendo liked Koro's answer and added, "It has been many generations since our tribe has lived on a lake. All of us grew up on the river of life. Even Troon, who was so recently lost, only knew the river. Kendo expects there will be adjustments, but Kendo has no fear that we can adapt. Our ancestors lived here far longer than we have lived on the river."

"But they left."

Kendo started to turn to see who had said that, but decided it did not matter. The thought had already lingered in his mind and he was sure the words reflected what most of the tribe was thinking. "Kendo wishes the history that had been passed down to us included the tale of why we left our home. Kendo too is curious, but Kendo has been drawn to return here for quite some time. The flood was only a sign that the time was right."

They followed the shoreline, keeping themselves between the lake and the forest. The sun blazed down upon them and many took small dips in the lake to cool off. Kendo wondered whether it was farther than he had first thought, or if they just walked slower than he expected. The morning already approached mid-day before they reached the far side and saw a river flowing down and away from the lake.

The soft shore disappeared from beneath their feet and was replaced with small, rounded pebbles. Rocks and boulders of various sizes lined the sides and the bottom of the river. From where they stood at the mouth of the river, they could see a great waterfall on the far shore spilling into the lake from the mountain. Kendo wondered if this lake was also sacred. Perhaps they would return here on a pilgrimage to rediscover it.

He led the tribe along the river, heading away from the lake. It fell gently at first, then narrowed into swift currents that gurgled over the rocks until they hit flat spots and widened out into a slow, meandering stream.

Deer and squirrels came to the river and were not afraid to see the tribe.

"Look!" Flom said, "Perhaps it is time to feed the tribe."

Brack heard them approach and said, "Shhh! You are almost there. Wull waits ahead. Brack recommends we be quiet for now."

Kendo wondered why they should be silent and followed Brack. They walked ahead of the tribe and found Wull examining the stone walls of the structure Kendo had seen from the ridge.

Brack whispered, "Tell Kendo what Wull has found."

"These buildings," Wull said, "are made of stacked stones. Wull has never seen this before. Wull can see that they are many stones, but it is as if they were a single stone. If Wull hits them, they are solid and do not fall over, but the real interesting find is over there." Wull pointed to a small table out in the open between the building and the lake. "The stones in that table are too perfect. They are all the same size and shape. Wull does not believe they were plucked from the lake or were chiseled to match each other."

Kendo studied the wall of the building and compared it to the table in the distance. He shrugged and asked, "What does Wull think they are?"

"Wull does not know, but what if they are sacred? What if they were made by the hands of the Gods? Perhaps we shouldn't be here."

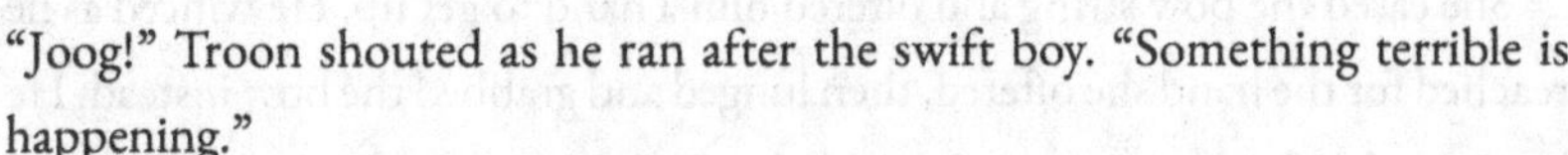

"Joog!" Troon shouted as he ran after the swift boy. "Something terrible is happening."

Troon reached out and put his hand on Joog's shoulder, saying, "Here, Joog can see with Joog's eyes."

The sand and the light faded from Joog's vision and were replaced with the sight of Varna walking behind Trik. Trik selected his footing as meticulously as he might have had they been crossing a difficult rocky field, but they only crossed the same meadow that they had all crossed a dozen times before.

He stepped slowly and deliberately through the grass while Varna followed with her bow trained on his back.

"Why has Trik grown so quiet?" Varna asked. "Is Trik's mind planning to escape before we reach the cave? Trik was so talkative about all things Grull and now Trik has nothing to say?"

Trik did not respond. She was right. He walked slowly and contemplated every opportunity to turn the tables on her.

"Varna thinks Trik is defeated and for all of Trik's fine words supporting Varna the huntress, Varna thinks Trik is ashamed, on the inside, to have been beaten by a girl."

Trik didn't respond. Instead, he fell to the ground with his foot sunk into a gopher hole. He screamed like a child and reached down to grab his ankle.

Varna pulled the bowstring taut and yelled, "Varna does not believe it! Trik walked too slowly to accidentally slip into that hole. Trik still plans to escape and fell on purpose!"

Trik just writhed on the ground, curled up in a fetal position with his hands wrapped around his ankle.

Varna circled him and yelled, "Get up! Trik's ploy will not fool Varna!"

He still did not respond and Varna yelled, "Get up or Varna will give Trik a real wound that will keep Trik on the ground!"

Trik continued to fake his injury and grimaced grandly while he climbed to his feet and hobbled two steps, then fell again.

Varna's resolve faltered. She hated it when people doubted her and now she hated herself for not believing in Trik when he might really be hurt.

She eased the bow string and offered him a hand to get up. He winced as he reached for the hand she offered, then lunged and grabbed the bow instead. He leaped to his feet and circled around behind her, gripping the bow around her neck and pulled it tightly against her throat. She reached up and squeezed her hand between the bow handle and her throat and tried pushing it so she could breathe, but he was too strong.

She gasped fruitlessly for air, and he only squeezed harder and dragged her backwards off her feet. Her strength left her as consciousness began to slip away.

He pushed her back onto her feet and loosened his grip. "Does Varna see now that Trik is in control?" He loosened the bow even further and nuzzled her neck, whispering, "Trik can do whatever Trik wants with Varna."

She was furious and stomped her heel onto his foot and smashed her head back into his face. He spun her around to throw her off balance, and they tumbled to the ground.

They rolled on the ground, leaving the bow behind. He held her in a bear hug and rolled across the ground until he was on top of her with her face pressed into the dirt. He pulled her arms behind her and tied them together with a leather strap.

She screamed and squirmed wildly, but was unable to wriggle out of his grasp.

"That should hold Varna," he said between heavy pants for air, "while Trik decides what to do with Varna."

"Trik will never get away with this," she yelled. "Zho will hunt Trik down."

"Zho again? Zho is not the great demon hunter Zho claimed to be. Zho is just a man; just one single man. Does Varna think one man can search this entire wilderness to find Varna?"

"Zho would," she said, then added with a wry smile, "And Foln will also search for Trik. Varna does not think Foln likes Trik too much."

"Bah, they will never find Trik."

"Why wouldn't they? Trik leaves a trail like a herd of buffalo. Varna didn't have to work very hard to follow Trik."

Trik lifted Varna onto her feet and pushed her back in the direction of the beaver pond. "Then if they follow Trik's clumsy trail, it will only lead them to Varna, and Varna will be near death. They will forget all about Trik when they try to save Varna."

"What will Trik do?" she asked, then she shook her head and answered, "It doesn't matter. They will save Varna and we will all track Trik down together."

"Keep walking," he said as he shoved her in the back. "Varna does not realize what trouble Varna is in. The trail will be cold and Trik will long be in the wind before Varna is saved, if Varna is saved."

"Varna will be saved. Even if the trail were as cold as the stones, Varna's Troon would still follow Trik."

Trik grabbed her shoulder and turned her so he could ask, "Where is this Troon Varna keeps whining about?"

Her lips trembled as she responded, "Varna's husband is with the spirits, but Varna is certain that Troon watches over Varna. Varna can feel Troon's presence. Troon will not let Trik get away with this."

Trik pushed her again and said, "Oh. Trik trembles at the thought of Varna's dead husband coming back to defend her honor."

Joog's vision returned to the endless sand.

"Now does Joog see?" Troon asked. "Varna is in danger, and Troon needs Joog to warn Zho."

Joog looked down at his feet and squished his toes in the warm sand. A tear collected in his eye as he nodded and said, "Joog sees. Joog does not wish to leave this place, but Joog will do Joog's duty to Joog's people."

"Joog has Troon's everlasting thanks. Fear not, Joog will return here one day, and when that day comes, Troon will have many here to greet Joog. All the ancestors will know of Joog's heroism."

Joog's head was still on Mora's lap when he opened his eyes. Mora's head had fallen to her chest and her shoulders were slouched forward. She had wept herself asleep while still sitting up and staring into his face.

Joog reached up and wiped some of the tears from her stained face. She opened her eyes and sucked in her breath. Her voice trembled as she gasped, "Joog?"

He smiled and almost imperceptibly nodded his head.

"Joog!" she shouted. "Zho! Varna! Joog returns!"

Zho was still stewing over Varna's disappearance and grumbled, "Hrmph."

Joog tried calling Zho, but he could barely manage to whisper, "Zho?"

Mora could tell that Zho hadn't heard Joog. "Zho?" she said, "Joog calls for Zho."

Zho was too wrapped up in his own thoughts to pay attention to anybody else's problems.

"Zho!" Mora shouted. "Joog calls for Zho!"

Zho looked back at Mora and reluctantly came to her. Joog beckoned him with his hand and waited until Zho was close enough to hear his voice.

"Zho," Joog said, "Zho must know about Varna."

"Yes," Zho grumbled, "Zho already knows about Varna."

"Zho knows? Then why is Zho still here?"

"Varna is a grown woman. Zho can only warn Varna not to make mistakes. Zho cannot stop Varna from making them."

"What?" Joog asked. "Varna is in trouble and Zho does not go to save Varna?"

"Zho warned Varna that Trik was bad, but Varna chose to go with Trik, anyway."

Joog's voice had grown a little stronger with each word and everybody heard him say, "Varna did not go with Trik. Varna followed Trik's trail and tracked Trik down like Varna would track an animal. When Varna saw what Trik had stolen, Varna captured him at the point of Varna's bow, but Trik is very wily and managed to escape and capture Varna. Trik will not let Varna leave for fear Varna would lead Zho to Trik."

Zho was confused. "How does Joog know about Trik and Varna?"

"Joog was with Troon. Troon watches over Varna and asked Joog to deliver this message to Zho."

Zho cocked an eyebrow at this news. His first instinct was to ignore the ramblings of a man near death, but Troon was his master and his second instinct was to heed his master's warning.

Foln was roused from his sleep by the commotion, but could not follow the conversation until Zho turned to him and mimed a chopping motion on his wrist saying, "Neh Trik neh chub. Neh Trik neh chub." He then mimed a chopping motion to his neck and said, "Trik neh... Trik neh..." Zho didn't know Foln's word for head so he simply mimed chopping the neck and pointing to his head and said, "Neh Trik." Foln understood and handed Nik to Yona.

Kendo walked out to the stone table and looked back at the structures that led them here. The table was near enough to the lake that Kendo heard the water splashing playfully on the shore. He wondered who could have built such grand structures. Even the small table was beyond his tribe's greatest creations, but the buildings were beyond comprehension. There were two stone buildings standing side by side. The one that they saw from the ridge was nearest the river they followed down to this lake, and another larger structure stood next to it. Even the roofs were made of large stone slabs.

Remnants of other structures stretched down the shoreline. Stone floors with short collapsed walls were laid out, as he would arrange a village here. The walls were barely visible through the wild vines. This was the ancient village. He walked down a lane between the ancient foundations and saw fire pits in their centers.

Some of the floors were larger than others and housed stone tables like the one near the shore. Wull entered one of these and examined the table. He picked up a sharp stone and said, "This is a tool. This table must be a place of work." He picked up a lumpy red rock from the floor next to the table. "This is a very heavy stone and is cold to the touch."

"It would seem," Kendo said, "that our village is already started for us. We can build upon these floors and be functioning before spring is over."

"Wull sees many miraculous things, the stones made by Gods; this strange rock. Wull is not comfortable building upon the homes of the Gods."

"This is not the work of Gods," Kendo said, "or it would not have fallen into such decay. This is where my vision has brought us. Kendo thinks our ancestors may have been very special, and just like we lost our bow smiths in the flood, much of their knowledge was lost when they left this place."

Kendo walked back to the larger of the stone buildings. Nobody had dared enter them yet. Stone rings were set in the floor and the top of the entrance. Wull looked closely at the rings and said, "There were doors here. The wood has turned to dust, but Wull believes these rings are hinges."

Kendo entered the dark, dusty interior. There were no more openings in the stone and not enough light coming through the doorway. Kendo went to the center while Wull walked around the perimeter.

"Wull has found a window, but stones are stacked in the opening to block the light." He pushed the stones. They were not solid like the walls and tumbled outside, allowing the sun to pour in. The center of the room was a large, round stone slab covered in a layer of dust. Kendo saw bits of color showing through the dust. He climbed down on his hands and knees and gently brushed away the dust. When the layer of dust was too thin, he blew across the stone to reveal the paintings beneath. Others joined Kendo to clean the slate. They eventually learned how to clear each section without covering their neighbor's painting.

The painting which they revealed was divided it into twelve sections. Each section had a different painting, and one of them was familiar to Kendo.

Kendo walked carefully to the base of the familiar painting. He stared at it and recited, "They shall not know what they have lost until they discover those who remember."

"What was that?" Wull asked.

"It was a proverb from the ancient book. Kendo's father used to read from the book. The book was lost in the flood, but Kendo remembers it. It had this picture in it. They shall not know what they have lost until they discover those who remember."

A loud, hideous moan reverberated outside. Kendo ran out of the structure and saw Brack pointing up the mountain. The moan repeated itself and they saw smoke rise from its location.

Someone in the tribe cried out, "It's a curse! Demons guard these lands!"

Chapter Ten

The Hunt

Zho grabbed a couple flint knives and attached their sheaths to his belt. He tied a handful of throwing spears together and slung them on his back, then chose one sturdy thrusting spear to carry. He nodded towards the weapons and said, "Foln can take what he wants from here."

Foln didn't know Zho's words, but he understood the gesture. He went to the stash of weapons, but they were all hunting tools and not what he would consider proper weapons for battling against men. He browsed through the selection and chose what he thought would work best, then went to the cave's exit.

Zho knelt down next to Brahg and said, "Zho is sorry, but Zho must leave Brahg to defend the cave. Be safe."

"Why does Zho waste time talking to Brahg now? Go!"

Zho looked over at Joog. Mora helped Joog sit up so he could wave at Zho and nod his head. Zho felt stupid for ever believing that Varna had run off with Trik. He should have known better. He didn't know if he believed that Joog had actually communed with Troon and truly brought back his warning about the danger Varna was in, but they all believed that Joog had died, and now he was back. Zho wondered if he might feel stupid, in the morning, for believing Joog's warning, but he wasn't taking any chances with Varna's life.

Yona bounced Nik in her arms. He was used to being passed around by the women, and he didn't mind. They smelled nicer than Trik and their hair was always softer. Foln took one last look at his son before stepping out of the gate. He would much rather feel stupid than feel remorse over losing her.

Zho followed Foln through the gate. The sun was already high in the sky. He had wasted the whole morning with his silly dreams and now Trik had an enormous lead on them.

Zho traced Trik's tracks leading out into the meadow, but Foln turned to the right and followed the path between the mountain and the meadow. Foln didn't know how to explain to Zho that he didn't trust the tracks that they could see going into the meadow. Trik was very wily and might have left those tracks for them to follow. Foln checked occasionally that he never lost sight of Zho for too long, but he studied the trail heading away from Foln's people. Foln knew where Trik was going. Trik was returning to his own people. Zho looked over to see what Foln was doing, but Foln didn't look like he had found a trail yet. He was scanning the ground and walking too slowly to have found any tracks yet. Zho kept following the trail that led across the meadow.

Varna wouldn't make it easy for Trik. She fought to loosen the straps on her wrists, but was unable to free her hands. Trik continued to shove her back in the direction of the beaver pond, but she dragged her feet, both as an attempt to slow him down and to create an easy trail for someone to follow.

"Now Varna goes slow looking to escape Trik."

"Varna does not want to escape. Varna wants to be here to see what Zho does to Trik."

Trik pushed her again, and she stumbled to the ground. "So much faith in Zho. And let us not forget the ghost of Troon. Varna is in such capable hands. Trik believes Zho will eventually stumble upon Varna's body, but Trik will be long gone by then."

"If Trik plans to kill Varna, then why should Varna bother walking at all?"

Trik picked her up and pointed her back to the beaver pond. "Varna is very brave and very clever. Trik will leave Varna with a chance to live, but Varna will most likely join her husband in the spirit world. Trik will see to it that Varna leaves a spectacular corpse for Zho to find."

Trik's words were meant to demoralize Varna, but she managed a wry smile in spite of them, because she really did have faith in both Zho and Troon. If they failed, she would be with her Troon, but Zho and Troon won't fail. They will find her and she will see Trik pay for his crime. Either way, she would win.

The hideous sound from up the mountain was heard by everyone. The tribe gathered on the shore and pointed to the smoke. Fears ranged from fire breathing demons that guarded this valley to giant fire golems that roamed these lands and scorched anyone who intruded them. Rumors swelled about every imaginable fire wielding monster from ancient folklore, and some new monsters that sprung from fertile imaginations. All rumors and speculation led to one unavoidable conclusion. This is what must have driven the ancestors out of this land.

"Look around you," Kendo said. "Do you see signs of fire in this village?" There were no scorch marks on the buildings.

"That only means they are not alone," someone said from the crowd. "Rock golems from the mountain may also guard these ruins."

Kendo started to reply, but he stopped. There was no sense in arguing with them. His attempts to calm them were just as much speculation as their own words of panic. "It seems to Kendo that only the truth will calm your fears. Kendo will go learn the truth. Kendo only asks that Kendo's people do not go mad while Kendo seeks out what is up that mountain."

Nobody said it, but he could see on their faces that they feared for his safety if he planned to go find the beast on the mountain. He, himself, couldn't help but wonder if the source of the smoke actually did cause the ancestors to evacuate this land.

Kendo chose Brack and Flom to join him as he searched for the source of the smoke. Wull continued to inspect the structures while Koro gathered the people on the shore. He wanted to set up camp, but nobody wanted to make this their home until Kendo returned.

Kendo followed the shore of the lake as it curved away from the ancient village, but eventually moved to the tree line where they weren't out in the open. They didn't know what awaited them, but they assumed it was watching them. None of them were prone to fears about monsters or demons, but neither were they immune to the dread of something completely unknown to them. They carried spears but had little confidence that their puny hunting weapons would be effective against whatever was up the mountain.

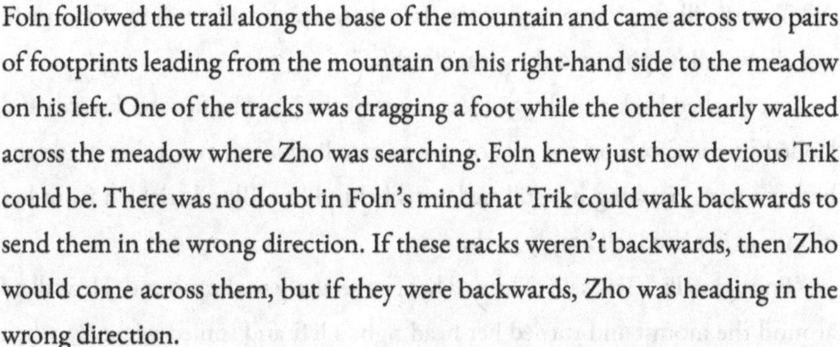

Foln followed the trail along the base of the mountain and came across two pairs of footprints leading from the mountain on his right-hand side to the meadow on his left. One of the tracks was dragging a foot while the other clearly walked across the meadow where Zho was searching. Foln knew just how devious Trik could be. There was no doubt in Foln's mind that Trik could walk backwards to send them in the wrong direction. If these tracks weren't backwards, then Zho would come across them, but if they were backwards, Zho was heading in the wrong direction.

Foln followed the tracks backwards up the mountain. It wasn't very far up the mountain when he found marks in the dirt indicating a scuffle between two people and the clear outline of a bow. This was significant. He put his fingers to his lips and let out a loud whistle. There was a struggle here, and he recognized the imprint of Varna's bow. Zho would want to see this.

He saw more tracks beyond the point of the struggle, but they were different. Neither of the tracks on the other side of the struggle was dragging a foot, however, one of them was taking smaller steps. He wanted to follow the tracks, but knew Zho would have to see this, so he whistled again and waited for him.

Once they reached the beaver pond, Trik walked Varna into the pond and through the water to the beaver home.

"We are here," Trik said. "Climb up and lie down on the beaver mound for Trik."

Varna set her jaw and stood there, refusing to cooperate.

"Come now, does Varna think that being brave is going to help any?"

Varna looked away and said, "Trik is a dead man and Varna does not wish to humor a dead man."

"Oh no?" Trik asked. "What about Varna's dead husband? Does Varna wish to humor the ghost of Troon? Would Troon want Varna to suffer?"

"Troon will save Varna, and when Trik dies, which will be soon, Troon will not allow Trik's spirit into the great afterlife."

Trik reached back and slugged Varna across the jaw. She flew backwards and landed unconscious on the pile of woven tree limbs and twigs that made the beaver's nest, crushing her still tied arms behind her. Blood trickled from her mouth as her head fell limply to the side.

"Enough talk." Trik said as he tied her feet securely to the mound. He walked around the mount and turned her head right a left and smiled wickedly when he saw she was out cold. He untied her arms and stretched them out to the sides, where they were tied securely. She would not be able to move when she recovered. Lastly, he thoroughly wet a piece of leather and tied it around her neck, securing it tightly to the mound near the surface of the water.

He stood over her and gloated, "Say hello to Troon for Trik. It should not be long now."

Trik climbed out of the pond. All thoughts of ambushing Foln were long gone now. He would make good his escape and leave them to grieve for Varna.

The beast trumpeted again. The low throaty tone echoed across the valley, but was still far away.

"I thought we'd be closer to it by now," Kendo said.

"We should be," agreed Brack.

Flom jumped up to a low branch on a nearby pine tree and pulled himself up. He climbed the tree until he could see over the other treetops. He pointed across a small valley to another mountain and said, "It has moved."

Kendo looked in the direction Flom pointed, but could see nothing through the trees. "What does Flom see?"

"Flom sees the smoke rise from another mountain, and as Kendo said, it sounded further away. It has crossed the valley to the other mountain. It must be very fast."

"Or," Brack said, "there may be two of them."

"That could be," Flom said timidly, "Or, as someone in the tribe has already suggested, perhaps the beast can fly."

Kendo shook his head and said, "Kendo will not entertain such wild speculation. When we catch the beast, we shall learn if it is very fast, or if it can fly. For now, we will alter our course to track down its new location."

"Has Kendo considered," Brack suggested, "that maybe we should stay on our original course? If we can locate where it was for the first fire, maybe we can learn what it is before we track it down."

Kendo sensed a slight fear in Brack's suggestion. He didn't want to give in to the superstition that now tried to ignite Brack's fear. His idea was sound. They should learn what they were up against. "Very well. We will try to locate the beast's previous location. It would be good to know what it is, but if we cannot find it soon, we will give up and head across the valley."

Brack and Flom each grunted their approval.

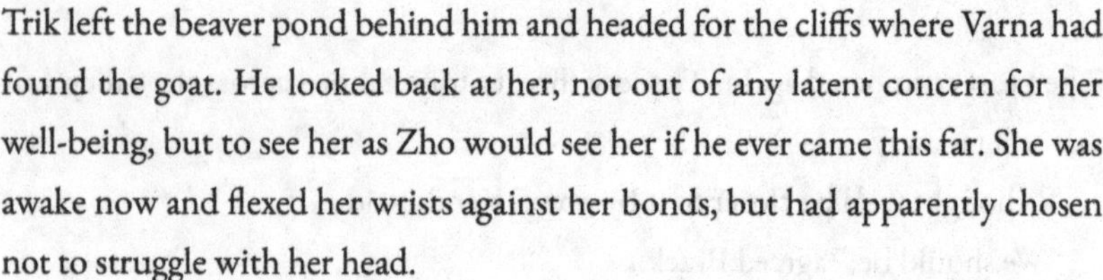

Trik left the beaver pond behind him and headed for the cliffs where Varna had found the goat. He looked back at her, not out of any latent concern for her well-being, but to see her as Zho would see her if he ever came this far. She was awake now and flexed her wrists against her bonds, but had apparently chosen not to struggle with her head.

Trik was satisfied that she would never escape her bonds and probably would not see another sunrise. He turned and scaled the cliffs. Beyond this was the home of his people; a place he swore he would never return, but now things were different. His own people had sold him to slavers, along with his mother, but he was very young at the time. They would not remember him. Nobody there would recognize him. They would only see a chieftain wearing the sacred seal of leadership. His people would not accept him out of respect for the chieftains' office, but he would suggest to them that there might be profit when his tribe joined him. Profit was a great motivator.

He had forgotten how far it was and how difficult the climb would be. He was only ten years old when he was sold to the slavers and first made the journey, but that wasn't the only time they had brought him on this trip. They made him repeat the journey several times, working for them, before trading him away when he'd grown big enough to be a threat to them.

There were two routes that he remembered. One was an easier trail that followed the foothills at the base of the mountains, but the slavers only took that route on the return trip if they were laden with heavy gold. The one that he followed crossed the plateau at the top of the cliff, saving himself at least a day reaching the canyon that led him up to the higher plains.

The canyon was the same as he had remembered. Tall steep walls that were smooth and slick where the river polished them during the winter. He thought the river would have been higher this time of year, but did not regret his fortune when he saw that it would be easily passable. He was surprised to find the remains of a campsite at the mouth of the canyon. Not surprised by the presence of the campsite, but he could tell that it wasn't one of the slaver's campsites. The ashes were cold now, but they must have been fairly fresh or the ash would have been washed away by the rains. Someone had passed through here recently, and judging by the footprints, there were quite a few of them.

He walked briskly down the canyon. The climb at the end of the canyon had spots that would be hard for him alone, but it was the easiest way up to the plains without going all the way around one of the mountains, which was a three-day hike.

He pictured his prize in his mind. He would be a prince and would be rewarded with many riches. For such a prize, he could endure any hardship to get there.

Zho didn't know why Foln had left him as soon as they had started tracking Trik, but he assumed he had his reasons. The tracks that Zho followed led him across the meadow toward the beaver pond. The track zig-zagged occasionally, sometimes leading him back towards the path where Foln went, then they turned back towards the pond.

He was almost to the pond when he heard a loud whistle. It wasn't any bird Zho had ever heard. It had to be Foln. He looked up but couldn't see him. When he heard the second whistle, he trotted off in the direction of the sound.

He found Foln pointing to where the struggle had been and the clear outline of the bow. Zho recognized the implication and was furious. Varna fought with Trik, and since she had not returned with him to the cave, she must have lost.

They followed the tracks to a large boulder where one of them had paced back and forth a considerable number of times.

From there, the tracks led down the mountain and back across the meadow towards the pond where Zho just was.

Zho overlooked the minor irritation he felt because he had already been at the point where the tracks now led. Foln was right to call for him. The scene where they struggled was too important to ignore.

Time was running short for Varna. She tried, but failed, to loosen either of her hands. The straps around her neck were growing tighter and panic was setting in as she struggled against her fate. She no longer fought to free herself. She wanted just to catch a breath.

Her heart pounded a furious beat against her eardrums. She felt her pulse throb against her temples. Each breath was a wheeze that sucked in less and less air. Panic set in and she forced her lungs to pull hard against her crushed wind pipe.

Her throat and lungs burned and her vision narrowed as the light of the world around her began to fade away, leaving her in an empty darkness. Sleep called for her. "Yes," she thought to herself, "Sleep would be better than this."

"No, love. Not yet."

"Troon?" she thought she called out his name, but she couldn't speak any more than she could breathe.

"Yes," he said, "It is Troon. Varna cannot sleep yet. Varna must remain calm. Remember Troon's training when stalking a large prey? The prey can hear Varna's pulse, so Varna must remain more calm than calm. Slow Varna's breathing and pulse so the prey knows not where Varna is."

"Varna fears it is too late. Soon, love, Varna and Troon will walk together in the spirit world."

"Not so soon," Troon said calmly, "Varna will walk with another long before Varna joins Troon beyond this life. Varna must remain calm. Not just for Varna or for Troon, but for another. Do as Troon instructs. Slow Varna's heart and slow Varna's breathing. Varna must return to the world of the living."

Varna wanted to stay with Troon. His words were a puzzle to her, and she knew not why he wanted her to stay with the living, or who he thought she would walk with in this world. "Varna will not walk with that snake Trik. Trik put Varna here to die. Varna will see Trik separated from Trik's head before Varna ever walks with Trik. If Troon ever sees Trik's head appear in the spirit world, then Troon will know that Varna cleaved it from Trik's neck, and Varna hopes Troon will kick that head as far away from the ancestors as is possible."

Troon chuckled and said, "Trik's day is coming. Varna must return to the land of the living so Troon may track down the scoundrel."

"Promise Varna then, that Troon will catch Trik, and Varna will continue to live."

"Troon promises. Troon must go now and Varna must return to breathing."

Kendo wished he could still see the smoke, but only the odor remained.

The scent of burning wood hung everywhere around them in all directions, making it difficult to locate the source. They walked thirty paces and tried to determine if it was stronger, then continued another thirty paces if it was.

Brack walked thirty paces in a tangent off their original course and called out, "This way. Brack can smell the ash in this direction. Kendo and Flom joined him and took a whiff. He was correct.

Flom walked another ten paces and pointed in front of him, saying, "There."

A ring of stones surrounded an ashen fire pit.

"This is not the work of a fire demon. This is a man's fire and those are men's footprints that circle the fire."

"And," Flom added, "they go off in that direction."

Brack asked, "Isn't that..."

"Yes," Kendo answered before he could finish his question, "that is the direction of the other smoke."

Troon's essence glided effortlessly across the landscape.

Varna's situation was dire, and he didn't want to leave her, but he made her a promise. He needed her to fight for life and not give in to join him in the spirit world, but he feared that fighting for her life would not be enough.

He peered into her future and saw only danger. A great part of his nature felt that he should have stayed to protect her, but she made him promise, and he would not break his oath to her.

He paused at the base of the cliff and looked back at her. There was no need for him to pause. He was a spirit and eyes had little meaning to him, but part of him still wanted to linger on with her.

He saw her lying atop the beaver mound. She struggled not to struggle. She was a warrior and a huntress. Such a spiritual task was not meant for warriors. It was for priests and priestesses to take on such conflicted tasks, but she tried.

As he watched her struggle, her words echoed in his head. He made her a promise.

He didn't need to follow Trik's tracks. It mattered not if Trik left footprints or if he had sprouted wings and flown over the terrain, Troon could feel Trik's malevolence as clearly as he could have smelled the musky trail of a wolverine during his life. He also found that he needn't identify Trik's particular signature. There was very little other darkness in this part of the world to mask Trik's trail, making him very easy to follow.

Troon rose up over the cliff, guided by the evil within his quarries heart.

Varna did as Troon had instructed. She calmed her heart and eased her breathing. The straps were tight against her throat, but drawing in shallow breaths as she was instructed did not force her wind pipe to close completely. She could breathe, but it did nothing to help with the mounting pain.

Sometimes when hunting, she would lie in wait for long periods and her body would stiffen and even hurt. During those times, she would imagine separating her mind from her body so she could treat the pain like it was somebody else's. She did this now and outside her body, she listened to the water that flowed slowly past the beaver mound. The sound of the water was soothing, and beyond the dam, she could hear the stream rushing by.

The sun shone brightly, and the sky had a marvelous blue cast. If it weren't for her predicament, this would probably have been a wonderful day. In fact, it was a wonderful day. She had spoken to her late husband, Troon. He still watched over her and cared for her. She knew not why he wasn't ready to accept her into his new world, but she trusted him as much as she loved him.

A small curve appeared on her lips and broke the tension on her strained face. This is how she would survive. She would remember her lover's visit and listen to the trickle of the water.

Then she heard something that was not so soothing. A grunt at first, followed by a low bark and footsteps. She cast her eyes upward but could not see. The footsteps were heavy and paced back and forth, then splashed on the edge of the water. She did not know what or who it might be until she heard the footsteps follow the shore of the pond around to her right. She could turn her head enough to see the large cat pacing at the edge of the water.

The cat saw her move and appeared agitated. It sniffed the air and did not smell death yet. The sun glinted off its long fangs as it shook its large head back and forth. It paced some more, then coiled itself to pounce. Varna could see the tension building in its muscles. Troon should have told her this was coming. She would not have sent him away so fast if she had known.

The cat's muscles jerked, but it did not jump. It coiled up to leap, and twitched as if to jump, but stopped itself. It tested the water with its paw, then circled all the way around the pond until it could see her face again. The beast let out a mighty growl as if roaring at the sun would relieve its frustrations, then it lay down and watched her. She knew it only waited for her to die, but it also wasn't sure how it would get to her. It clearly didn't like the water.

The cat flicked its tongue out from between its long fangs and waited. She no longer heard the soothing water go by, but she also was not focused on the strap digging into her flesh.

Panic spread through the tribe when they heard the beast and saw the second column of smoke. Koro had nearly quelled their fears of a winged beast that breathed fire and would come to eat their children when it had reappeared to stir up all the superstitious members of the tribe.

"This is not the end," Koro said to them. "You will see that Kendo will learn what is there and return with a very reasonable explanation."

"We have much faith in Kendo," one tribesman said, "but even Kendo cannot understand the minds of gods and demons. We have invaded their homes, and this is their warning. What will they do if we do not heed their threat?"

Wull stepped forward and said, "Wull too thought this must be the homes of the Gods, but Kendo was right to say this village was built by the hands of men. Wull has examined the structures and the tools that were left lying around. Their techniques are incredible, but with the right tools and knowledge of how it is done, even Wull could build these."

"Do you see now?" Koro asked. "This is the village of our ancestors."

"That is not comforting," the tribesman responded, "when we know that our ancestors were driven from this place, and that," he pointed up the mountain to the smoke, "is probably what forced them to leave."

His words made sense. Too much for Koro to simply dismiss. "We do not know that. Koro does not believe the Gods would give Kendo the visions to lead us here if they did not mean for us to live here."

"That's right," another tribesman said. "Kendo did have the visions. What is up the mountain is just a mystery for Kendo to unravel."

"Yes," Koro added. "Let us put our faith in Kendo's visions."

The tribe was calm for the moment, but Koro worried about the women and the children. He wondered if they might be safer waiting for word from Kendo up at the smaller lake.

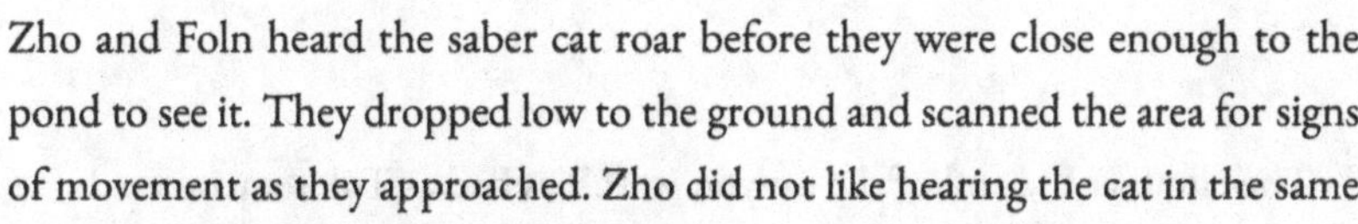

Zho and Foln heard the saber cat roar before they were close enough to the pond to see it. They dropped low to the ground and scanned the area for signs of movement as they approached. Zho did not like hearing the cat in the same vicinity where the tracks were leading them and hoped the cat would spare Varna while making a meal out of Trik.

They held their spears over their shoulders as they reached the pond and crawled around the shore until they found the cat. It lay on the edge of the pond, panting. This was odd behavior for these beasts. The one that had attacked Brahg and Marl had waited in a tree. It pounced on them when they crossed below it. Zho knew that many wild beasts were scavengers, and he did not relish the thought that it might not be alone and was waiting for its turn to feast on the remains of another's kill.

Zho had faced these big cats before, but he wasn't very familiar with them. This was not so for Foln. He knew them well. He picked up a stone and threw it across to the other side of the cat. The noise should either startle the cat to attack in the direction of the sound made by the stone, or turn and run in their direction. If it came at them, it would be in panic mode and much easier to kill, but if it attacked the stone, it would be in predator mode and they would have to attack it. He got up from his knees and crouched on his feet with his arm cocked and waited. The cat jumped towards the stone, but only took two steps, then returned to its original position by the pond.

Foln's people were warriors and not always patient. He jumped up from his crouched position and ran at the cat with his spear held high. He yelled wildly as he ran down the large cat. Zho thought he was crazy, but he wouldn't let him attack the cat alone, so he followed him with his spear also in the air.

The cat jumped and took off in the other direction. Zho was inclined to let it go, but Foln knew it might return and attack them from behind. Foln sprinted after the beast without hesitation and Zho followed Foln.

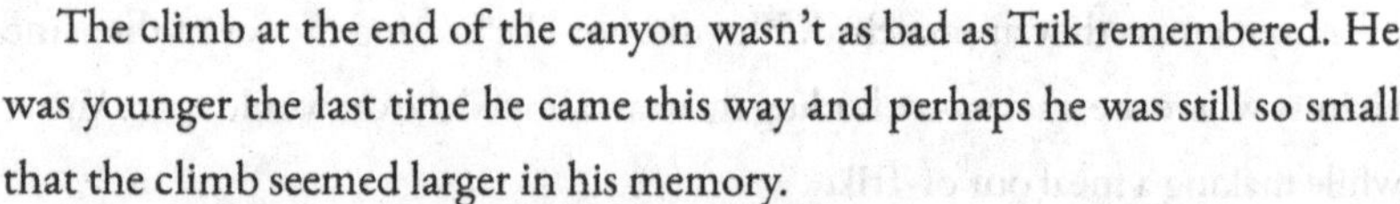

The climb at the end of the canyon wasn't as bad as Trik remembered. He was younger the last time he came this way and perhaps he was still so small that the climb seemed larger in his memory.

The musk in the bat filled cave, however, was just as he remembered it.

Once he was through the cave and up on the plateau, he scanned the area for the two different routes that the slavers had used.

The river route took them past the old lake where they had to pass through the ghost village. It was a safe and easy route, but the mountain pass was shorter.

There was a shelter in the mountains. It sat in a stone crevice and was largely protected from the weather. As far as he knew, only the slavers had ever used it.

Trik looked up to the sun. There was not much daylight left. He had no chance of reaching his people by nightfall, and little chance of even reaching the shelter before dark.

He trotted along the rocky base to the mountain and up the barely visible trail to the shelter, hoping he would still be able to find after sunset.

Troon followed Trik's anger to the canyon where the river flowed. As Troon's spirit rose up out of the canyon and followed Trik up the mountain, he sensed more evil presences off in the distance. He knew not who or what they were, but he would have to concentrate now to focus on Trik's trail.

If Trik reaches the others, he may blend in with them and Troon might lose him. He wondered what he planned to do when he found him. Who could he tell? He has only been able to communicate with those near death, and he sincerely hoped that Varna would no longer be the one who could hear him. Even if he managed to reach someone, what could they do if they were near death?

As he followed Trik and pondered the situation, memories of his old life reminded him that Mora, as medicine woman, could commune with the spirits, but she was left behind with the injured ones, and they could not track Trik down in their condition.

The saber cat was already angry that its meal was so difficult to reach. Now someone had disturbed its peace while it waited for its dinner to expire. It darted back to the tree line and sprang up a tall trunk, digging its claws into the soft bark until it was perched on a branch overlooking the two intruders. Zho saw no use in pursuing it any further, but Foln immediately began flinging stones up at the cat.

Foln pelted the cat around the head and the cat climbed up the tree to watch them from a higher limb, but Foln did not stop. Zho was stunned at first, but pulled the sling from his belt and began zipping stones up at the angry feline.

Zho connected a stone on the cat's face, prompting a particularly angry growl. Foln recognized the anguish in the cat's response and patted Zho on the back. Zho thought for a moment that the gesture meant they were done tormenting the beast, but when he stopped, Foln continued throwing stones, so Zho did the same.

The cat began stalking back and forth across its perch. It finally coiled its rear legs and prepared to jump. Foln pressed his palm to Zho's chest, and they backed away from the tree but continued slinging stones at the cat until it leaped down upon them.

Each man scattered across the ground as the cat flew down from the tree. Foln was quick to grab his spear and leap upon the cat's back. He sunk the spear deep into the cat's shoulder. Zho grabbed his spear and while the cat twisted its head around to bite the spear in its shoulder, Zho stabbed the cat in the neck.

Foln took a knife from his belt and sunk it deep into the other side of the animal's neck. The cat tried to protest, but it was unable to growl or breathe and fell to the ground, barely able to pant during its last moments.

Zho had always been a hunter. Troon had selected him as one of the best hunters that he had ever trained, but Zho had never seen anything like this before. The ferocity with which Foln had attacked the beast seemed more like lunacy to Zho, but he could not deny the efficiency of the attack or the swiftness of the kill.

Foln saw the amazement on Zho's face. He knew that not all people had his tribe's lust for the kill. It was a good kill and Zho was worthy to bask in it. Foln sunk his knife into the beast's chest and cut out its heart. He chewed a bite off the still warm heart and offered it to Zho.

Zho put his palms up and shook his head, but Foln held it out for him again and said, "Ehna. Ehna."

Zho pointed back to the trail and said, "Varna."

Foln shook his head and said, "Ehna, edu Varna."

Zho relented and accepted the heart from Foln. He sunk his teeth into the tough flesh and bit off a chunk, which he chewed. The meat was warm and chewy, but not as disgusting as Zho had expected.

Foln smiled and slapped Zho on the back, then shouted, "Ehna!"

Zho held the heart high and repeated, "Ehna!"

Foln reached out and smeared the blood that had collected on Zho's lips around his mouth and his cheeks. He smiled broadly, then motioned back towards the tracks that brought them to the pond and said, "Varna."

Varna had thought that she had heard someone's voice screaming like a crazy man. She was sure it must have been Zho driven mad by the sight of her lying limply across the beaver's home, but then she heard the same voice run past the pond and away in another direction. Zho would not have left her like this. She did not know who it was or where Zho was, but her time was up.

The straps had tightened too much for her to breathe. Even the softest, shallowest breath could not suck air into her lungs. She squeezed the air out of her lungs in what would be her last exhale, but could not draw any back in.

Her eyes fluttered and shed new tears down her cheeks.

"Troon love, nobody comes to save Varna, but Varna truly tried as Troon asked. It is too late now. The world fades around Varna. Troon and Varna will be together after all."

The footprints led Kendo from the recently abandoned fire pit down a well-worn path that cut through the thick forest underbrush. The trees grew densely between the two mountains and cast the valley in a dark shadow, but the well-cut path would have been easy to follow even at night, which was a good thing as the sun worked its way towards the horizon.

The beast trumpeted ahead of them. It was an unnervingly deep tone that rattled their souls.

"It is not a beast," Kendo reminded them. "Such a beast would not have feet so small."

Brack grunted. "Perhaps the beast is a God and we track its followers."

The trail angled up and still headed directly towards the great sound.

Kendo detected the faint scent of smoke and said, "We are close. The fire is near."

The sound bellowed before them, then the same sound bellowed behind them. Flom paused to face the rearward sound while Kendo doubled his speed. The long low blast from each direction changed to short staccato toots, and the forest was alive with movement.

Nets fell from the sky and the men were surrounded with hands tightening the nets around them.

"What is the meaning of this?" Kendo growled, but a large club slammed into the side of his head, crumpling him to the forest floor while Brack and Flom were each wrestled to the ground and bound with ropes.

Chapter Eleven

Abducted

The mountain shelter was little more than a couple mud and stone walls with a roof and a hearth in the center of the floor. Several piles of straw surrounded the hearth and served as beds. There was no window and a heavy leather skin served as a flap over the door.

The shelter was nestled into a crevice in the mountain and disguised to match the surrounding rock walls. It was hard to see by design and in the dim light of the moon. Trik walked past it until he reached a ledge overlooking the valley where his people lived. His people were nomads but they never strayed far from the valley.

He knew he had gone too far when he reached the barren ledge. It had large pine logs lying on their sides where the ancients used to come and sit while viewing the sun as it set between the mountains. Trik remembered a story about the ancients coming here to celebrate a special time of year when the sun set directly between the mountains and illuminated the entire valley with neither mountain in the shadows.

Trik saw neither the beauty of the valley nor the mystical significance that the ancients celebrated. All he saw was his failure to find the shelter. He stood for a moment, staring into the valley hoping to spot either fires or smoke, but it didn't matter. He didn't need to find them, they would spot him approaching, and they would come to him. He would show them his badge of authority and the rest would be gravy.

He turned around and headed back along the path to search again for the crevice. In his memory, it wasn't very far from this overlook. He hoped his memory served him well this time.

Zho and Foln returned to the pond where they had followed Trik's tracks. Zho was first to see Varna. She lay lifeless atop the beaver mound. A heavy lifeless weight sunk deep in his chest and pulled tight on his lungs and his feelings. He dropped his spear to the ground and wanted to rush to her side, but was unable to move.

Foln was not so emotionally affected. He crashed through the water and immediately went to work slicing the bonds that tightened around her neck. He leaned his ear close to her lips and heard no breathing. Foln looked at Zho and slowly shook his head.

Zho fell to his knees. He was overcome with grief, but an anger began to boil inside of him. Grief had taken control of his body as he knelt on the ground and sobbed uncontrollably, but his anger fought to take back that control. His hand reached out to the spear that lay at his side and gripped it. His anger found enough focus to growl, "Trik!"

Foln recognized the grief. He had seen it over and over. He cut the rest of the bonds and lifted Varna's body from the mound and gently carried it across the pond to lay her at Zho's feet.

Zho's grip tightened around the spear. He brought one foot up to the ground and while still on one knee, growled again, "Trik!"

Foln placed his palm on Zho's shoulder and said, "Neh. Varna, edu Trik."

Zho looked into Foln's face. Tears streamed down Zho's cheeks and hatred burned in his heart, but he nodded his head and said, "Varna first, then Trik."

Foln reached under Varna's body again to carry her, but Zho grabbed his wrist and said, "Neh. Zho will carry Varna."

Foln nodded his head. A slight moistness gathered in his eye, but not for the loss of Varna. He knew the power of grief and had a softness for the kind of bravery Zho showed now.

Zho lifted Varna and started back for the cave.

Foln picked up Zho's spear and followed. It would be a slow trip, but he wouldn't rush Zho now. Trik may make his escape for now and may even find his people, but Foln would find him again. And based on the anger he saw in Zho's face, there would be no place for Trik to hide from him either.

Troon was never a violent or angry man when he was alive, but following Trik's trail was changing him. Seeing what Trik had done to his beloved Varna was more than enough to make him angry, but now, following Trik's trail of malevolence as he was, he felt a whole new level of animosity coursing through his soul.

He glided over the mountain trail that led him up to Trik's hideout. Troon had never truly entered fully into the land of the spirit. He stayed in the outer realm where he could keep an eye on Varna. As he flew across the land, it occurred to him that if he had joined with the ancestors, he may have learned faster ways to cross the land. They could probably just blink and be there, or maybe they can be two places at once, but he couldn't risk the chance that maybe they couldn't come back at all, and he had too much to watch over still. He had seen many spirits enter into the light, but none had ever returned.

He could feel himself closing in on Trik. He had always felt himself gaining ground, but now it seemed much faster. It was dark and only the moon shone the way. Trik must have stopped for the night. Troon would be upon him soon and still had no idea what he would do when he got there.

Troon came upon a trail that Trik had used. Troon could practically smell Trik's presence on the soil. Troon followed the trail along the base of the mountain, but the trail continued on, yet Troon felt Trik's presence in the mountain now. He turned in towards the mountain and found a narrow crevice with a structure inside. He silently glided into the crevice and into the shelter. Trik lay quietly on a pile of straw. He slept as if he had no cares in this world. Troon would do what he could to see to it that Trik would have no cares left in this world.

Troon wrapped his hands around Trik's throat, but passed right through. He punched him several times but never met with his body. In anger, he leapt to his feet and kicked and stomped the sleeping form but was unable to even disturb him.

If Trik slept, then perhaps his dreams would be like the spirit world and Troon could battle him there. Troon tried feeling Trik outside his body, but he only felt the other malevolent souls beyond the mountain. He wasn't done trying. This was for Varna and he would never give up. He reached into Trik's body and into his mind.

He felt around for Trik's soul and yelled, "Bastard! Come out and fight me!"

His anger burst out in a string of curses, but he was a spirit and he could not reach the mortal Trik. It is not enough that he has learned to travel the mortal world. He needs to learn how to communicate, or better yet, how to become whole again, even if only for a moment.

Joog had fallen back to a peaceful sleep after delivering Troon's message and seeing Zho off to track down Trik. He was a little surprised when he felt the drowsiness tug at his eyelids, but he had been overcome with a new sense of fulfillment; something he had not felt since losing his foot.

He enjoyed the satisfaction of being able to help Varna and Troon. He did not remember the spirit world or the great shining light, but he still felt the warmth and overwhelming contentment it had brought him. He bathed now in its warmth. A broad smile crossed his face as he breathed deeply and easily.

Gone were the wheezing and shallow breaths when he barely clung to life. All was well in his life.

In his dreams he could still run and in this dream he was racing Marl as they had when they were younger. He breezed across the meadow near their old home then turned sharply before the village homes and turned again to splash along the shore of the river. Marl trailed behind but was close enough that Joog could hear his heavy breathing. The river widened when it bent to the left and the fishermen had built a pier that extended out into the river. Joog ran out to the end of the pier and leapt into the water. He was very fast in the water. Marl kept on the shore. Running on the shore was much farther and Joog's shortcut gave him a commanding lead, but Marl could cover the ground much faster than swimming and he not only caught, but passed Joog. He needed to build a sizeable lead before he entered the river, because the first few steps in the water would slow him down before it was deep enough to swim.

Their goal was to reach the rock they called Jalmoor's pinnacle. The first to climb the peak which towered over the river by almost the height of five men would be declared the winner. There was nothing more at stake; no prize for the winner; no humiliation for the loser.

Marl entered the water ahead of Joog. He was a fast swimmer, but Joog was faster. Their goal was not far. Joog's stroke was the most efficient in the tribe. He barely broke the surface when taking a breath and the rhythm of his strokes was relentless. He pulled even to Marl's hips and inched forward until they exited the river shoulder to shoulder.

They were both brilliant climbers and ascended the stone quickly. The last climb to top the peak was the hardest. Marl pulled himself up the ledge and leaned over then rolled his hips atop the stone. Joog was just a hair behind him but jumped to his feet and declared, "Joog wins!"

"No!" Marl shouted, "Marl was first to the top!"

"But Marl lay on the ground gasping for breath while Joog was the first to declare!"

The boys stretched atop the pinnacle and warmed themselves in the sun. They would rest before leaping into the river and racing back to the village.

Joog soaked in the warmth of the sun and felt a great satisfaction, but as quickly as the contentment had warmed him, he was jolted out of his dream and sat upright in his bed as he shouted into the cave, "Father!"

Fear gripped the tribe. Disagreements broke out over the source of the smoke and the impending doom it may foretell.

People distrusted what they saw and heard. They argued with each other whether to believe the stories they were told when they were children or to trust in Kendo's assessment.

Some felt Kendo was overly optimistic, but they were all afraid to trust their beliefs because that might mean the myths were true and the beasts were real.

When the second beast was heard, several members of the tribe argued that they heard two different beasts, but not everyone would believe them until they saw the second column of smoke.

Wull was quick to tell Koro, "We should go help Kendo. They might be in trouble."

"Koro agrees, but we cannot leave the women and children unguarded. Koro will take Gorn to aid Kendo while Wull takes the tribe back to the smaller lake. Set a camp in the trees where the tribe will be hidden."

Wull gripped Koro's arm in the manner with which men send other men on long trips and said, "Find them and keep them safe."

Koro nodded and replied, "Keep the tribe safe. If we do not return for you, take the tribe back to the cave with Mora and Joog. Koro hopes Wull can find the way."

Koro's statement said much about how dangerous and final his mission might be.

A chill ran up Wull's spine as he broke his grip with Koro and went to gather the tribe.

Mora had fallen asleep soon after Zho had left. She had been at Joog's side holding vigil throughout his illness. When he recovered and returned to sleep, she turned to Marl but was too exhausted to continue her vigil and fell asleep. She thought she would sleep for days, but her dreams brought her images of Kendo in a cage with his hands and feet bound. He was not alone. Brack and Flom were bound at his side along with dozens of people she did not know.

Joog's shout startled her from her rest. She sprang to his side and asked, "Is Joog well?"

Joog smiled weakly and said, "Joog is fine. Joog just had a child's dream and thought Kendo was in danger. Joog is sorry to have disturbed Mora."

Mora wasn't soothed by Joog's apology. He saw the anguish and fear grow in her face. "Mora also dreamed of Kendo," she said, "Mora saw Kendo being held captive."

Brahg stood up and stretched to test his healing wounds. "If Joog dreamed it and Mora saw it, then Brahg will go find them. Mora can see that Brahg's wounds are healed now."

"Brahg's wounds do look good," Mora said, "but what Mora saw was not a job for one man, even a man such as Brahg who counts for two men."

Joog sat up and said, "Then Joog will also go."

"But Joog cannot walk or climb," she replied.

"No worries," Joog said, "Brahg will carry Joog and leave Joog in the bushes where Joog can sound like ten men."

Mora shook her head and said, "Brahg and Joog will need Marl who still sleeps with the spirits. When Marl returns, we can all go. Then Joog will have the women to help Joog sound like fifty men while Brahg and Marl rescue Kendo."

Joog looked over at his best friend and said, "Mora's words are sound, but we do not know if Marl will return to the land of the living and we do not know how long Kendo has for us to rescue him."

"Kendo has time," Mora lied, "Mora has seen it. Mora will return to watch Kendo from the spirit world and will alert Joog when it is time."

Joog wasn't satisfied to wait, but his choices were limited. "Very well," he said, "Mora should return to the spirit world and watch over Kendo. Mora can report to us how many men are holding him captive so we can plan a strategy against them."

Mora nodded then lay back down in her bed.

Troon's senses were alive with malevolent activity. Something was going on, but he didn't know what. He heard Varna's voice call for him and started to return to her until he clearly heard Koro in the opposite direction.

He didn't actually hear Koro, of course, and what he sensed wasn't Koro's words reaching out to him. He felt a panic that originated deep in Koro's soul. Most important to Troon, was that Koro felt like he was nearby.

Troon flew down the mountain and crossed the ancient lake to Koro's spirit. Troon did not know why he could feel Koro so clearly, and hoped it wasn't because Koro had crossed over into the spirit world.

He disturbed neither air nor water as his spirit glided smoothly over the small ripples of the lake. He found Koro and the tribe hectically carrying their things up the path to the smaller lake. Koro stopped and waved goodbye as Wull enlisted Choll, the only other remaining able bodied man in the tribe, to help him lead them up the slope.

Koro started heading towards the other side of the lake with Gorn.

"No!" Troon yelled, "Come this way!"

Koro did not hear him. He headed quickly and deliberately towards two columns of smoke on two different mountain sides.

Troon flew in front of Koro and said, "Focus! Varna needs you!"

Koro did not see Troon and crossed directly through his non-corporal spirit. Koro stopped for a moment and looked across the lake wondering why he suddenly pictured something in the other direction.

"Yes!" Troon shouted. He moved himself in front of Koro again and said, "There is a man on the other mountain who tried to kill Varna! Troon cannot kill the man. Koro must come with Troon to avenge Varna!"

"What is it?" Gorn asked.

"Koro is not sure, but Koro had a strange feeling that we should go over there." He pointed to the mountains on the other side of the lake.

"Gorn agrees. We should be going away from the smoke as fast as possible, but we cannot. Kendo needs us."

Koro shook off the odd sensation and said, "Gorn is correct. Let us go."

They stayed under the trees as they ran along the base of the mountain towards the nearest column of smoke.

Zho labored to carry Varna back to the cave. His feet dragged and his steps were heavy, not from Varna's weight, but from the weight of his heart.

He had known Varna since they were children, but he never really knew her. Not until she revealed her marriage to Troon after his death did Zho truly get to know her.

The more he knew her, the more he respected her and the more he cared for her.

They left the pond and had barely entered into the meadow when Foln jumped in front of Zho and crouched low in the hip-high grass.

He motioned with his left hand for Zho to hide in the grass while his right arm held the spear poised to throw.

Zho had been too lost in his grief to have paid any attention to the field ahead of them while they were walking. He did not know what Foln had seen, but he looked now for signs of movement ahead of them.

The predatory cats are nocturnal hunters, but he has seen them lounging in the fields soaking up the sun after a full meal.

Foln crept forward and when Zho started to follow, Foln whispered, "Neh."

Zho gently laid Varna on the ground and took one of the throwing spears that were tied to his back and scanned the meadow.

Foln stayed low to the ground and crawled a safe distance away from Zho and Varna then shouted, "Bachmen Foln edubah distno pock."

Zho did not know his words but understood his tone to be both an introduction and a warning.

He had not known Foln long, and the language barrier made it difficult, but he believed Foln to be a deeply honorable and trustworthy person, yet his ferocity made him somewhat scary.

"Foln?" said a voice from the grass ahead of them.

"Bool?" Foln asked back. Foln stood, but still held his spear poised to attack.

Bool stood when he saw Foln and shouted, "Foln! Foln!"

Bool was barely three paces from Foln when he stood. A dozen more people around Bool stood and revealed themselves behind him.

"Zho!" Foln shouted as he signaled Zho to join them.

Zho stood, but did not leave Varna's side.

Foln walked back to Zho and invited Bool to join them.

Bool followed Foln and just as he started to reach his open hand forward to greet Zho, he saw Varna on the ground and said, "Ahhh." He turned his head back to the others and shouted, "Pulu!"

Pulu trotted forward to join Bool and seeing Varna on the ground, immediately headed to her.

Zho jumped in front of Varna and blocked the way saying, "This is Varna. Varna was a fierce and honorable huntress. Zho will not allow strangers to dishonor Varna's remains."

Another member of Bool's party stepped forward and asked, "Grull? Did Raas hear Zho speak Grull?"

"Grull is what Trik called our language. Zho understands the stranger Raas."

Raas walked all the way to Zho and bowed, saying, "Raas is honored to meet Zho of the Grull. Pulu is medicine woman and will not dishonor Zho's comrade."

Zho stepped aside and said, "Zho believes Pulu is too late. Varna has joined Troon in the spirit world. But Zho will trust Pulu."

Foln spoke softly to Raas, "Perdu Grull pu Zho."

"Paas da lay?" Raas asked.

Foln simply nodded his ascent.

Raas said, "Among us, only Raas speaks Grull. Foln has asked Raas to translate everything for Zho's benefit."

Foln returned his attention to Bool and began speaking.

"Foln wants to know why Bool is here with a full war party. Bool would not need so many people to track down Foln."

"There have been signs," Bool said, "Word has arrived that other tribes are returning to the ancient lands. We are investigating."

Foln plucked a blade of grass and bit the stem to suck out the sweetness. "Bool would not lead a war party to investigate pilgrims. What is Bool not telling Foln?"

Bool was hesitant to continue, but felt compelled to tell Foln, "The slavers have also been more active. Bool feared that Trik would sell the prince to the slavers and our people would lose Foln as a leader."

Pulu had been examining Varna very thoroughly and said, "Varna lives."

Zho turned his head sharply and asked, "What? Varna is not lost?"

Varna opened her eyes weakly and Pulu whispered in her ear, but Pulu did not speak Grull and Varna did not understand.

"Is the cave far?" Foln asked. "If it is near, Foln thinks we should return to the cave. There is much to discuss and consider."

Zho picked Varna up and headed for the cave. Varna wrapped her arms around him and leaned her head on his shoulder.

Fear had circulated through the tribe when they had first seen the smoke and heard the ominous roar of the unknown beast. A full blown panic settled into the tribe's hearts when they had seen the second column of smoke and heard the short staccato bursts of the beast. Something was happening and not a single tribesman thought it was good.

Convincing them to turn around and return the way they came was easy. Completing the climb up the riverside to the smaller lake was more difficult. They were tired and the panic made the travel too fast which led to some slips and falls.

"Keep it steady," Wull said to them. "We cannot carry anyone who falls and breaks their leg."

Wull's words had little effect on their gate. The beasts behind them were a much greater motivator. On the way down to the lake, if someone were to fall, others would pick them up, but Wull did not see this anymore. He saw old men and women pass by fellow tribesmen who had stumbled over the large stones of the stream. It was not their finer moment.

Troon failed to turn Koro around and there was nothing he could do to Trik, so he rushed across the land again to find Varna. The land moved swiftly beneath him. The last he saw of his love, she was tied atop the beaver mound with little hope of surviving. He never should have left her. He should have known then that there was nothing he could do to Trik and he should have remained at her side.

As his focus centered on her, he accelerated across the land until he moved without moving and was upon her in a blink. Zho carried her in his arms and they weren't alone. Her eyes were open, but they were glazed as if she were staring off into the distance.

"Troon has joined us," she said in Zho's ear.

Varna was not a medicine woman. She was a hunter and should not be able see him. Either she was so close to death, that she was already partly in the spirit world, or because she had been so close to death, part of her lingered still in his world.

"Did Troon kill Trik already?" she asked.

"What did Varna say?" Zho asked.

Varna pointed to Troon's spirit and said, "Varna asked Troon if he killed Trik yet."

"No," Troon said, "Troon found Trik but was unable to harm him."

"What did she say?" Pulu asked.

Zho stopped walking and said, "Varna says that her late husband is with us. She said that he did not kill Trik."

Pulu did not see Troon, but she had communed with the dead before and was not going to dismiss this.

Varna took a deep breath and felt a stir of life return to her. Her pupils narrowed and she said, "Zho can put Varna down now. Troon has found Trik and Varna wishes to follow Troon to his lair to kill him."

"Foln!" Pulu shouted, "Bool! The spirits have told Varna where Trik is. Varna wishes to lead us to Trik."

Foln was surprised to hear that Varna was speaking already and asked, "Is Varna well yet?"

Zho put Varna down. Her legs were wobbly, but she quickly regained her balance and said, "Varna is well enough for this."

Varna pointed up at the far mountains and said, "Troon says that Trik waits in a shelter hidden in a crack in the mountain."

"Is it near a lake?" Foln asked.

"Troon says it is near two lakes, both surrounded by mountains."

"Foln knows where this is."

Troon whispered softly in Varna's mind and she relayed, "Troon also found more of our people there."

"Then your people are in danger. Foln knows where Trik is hiding. Tell Varna's husband to go warn your people."

Troon did not want to leave Varna again, but they were right. He needed to try harder to reach Koro this time.

Troon's head spun as he zipped across the lake in a blink.

Koro no longer raced haphazardly through the forest. He sensed that he was close and slowed their pace so he could listen for signs of either Kendo or the beast. He crept from tree to tree, viewing the area ahead of him and keeping hidden by their trunks.

Troon glided to Koro's side and whispered, "Koro should cross the lake. Varna and Zho are tracking down the murderous scoundrel Trik and Koro should be with them."

Koro paused and shook his head as if an insect had buzzed inside his ear. He swiped his hand by his ear to shoo the insect away.

"It is too dangerous for Koro to continue," Troon said, "There are many evil people ahead! Koro must turn around."

Koro placed the tip of his finger in his ear and shook it. The insect sound had turned into a slight buzzing of the ear.

"Turn around!" Troon yelled.

Koro looked back in the direction of the lake, then shook his head and crept on to the next tree.

"NO!" Troon shouted. "Koro must turn around! Varna and Zho are with other hunters! Whatever Koro is doing now, can be done better with more men!"

Koro ignored the ringing in his ear and moved on.

"YOU NEED MORE MEN!" Troon shouted, but to no avail. Frustrated, Troon left to tell Varna that Koro would not be coming.

Koro remained hidden behind the trees as he stealthily made his way through the forest. He heard something ahead that sounded like laughter.

"Did you hear that?" Gorn asked.

"Shhh," Koro whispered, "That did not sound like Kendo."

Koro crouched lower to the ground and snuck towards the sound. It was definitely laughter and talking, but he did not recognize the language. As he neared the sound, he dropped to the ground and crawled.

The forest floor angled from the mountain peak to the valley with small foothills that undulated at the base of the mountain. Koro crawled up one of these hills and saw the source of the noise. He counted eleven men walking on a well-worn path. Three of those men were Kendo, Brack and Flom. Their hands were bound behind them and they were being ushered forward by their captors.

Koro and Gorn remained quiet as they watched the procession walk away from them. When it was out of sight, Gorn asked, "What do we do now?"

Koro looked back in the direction of the lake and scratched his head.

"Koro?"

Koro shrugged and said, "Koro does not have all the answers, but Koro thinks we should go to the other side of the lake."

Gorn was perplexed and asked, "Why? Shouldn't we go get Wull and some more of our men?"

"What men?" Koro asked. "All we have left are the elderly and the children."

"But what awaits us across the lake?"

Koro could only shake his head and say, "Koro can't explain it, but Koro just has a feeling. Don't ask."

Troon didn't cross the lake in a blink as he had reaching Koro. There must be more to being a spirit that he had yet to learn.

Varna and the war party had covered much ground by the time Troon found them again. They moved swiftly, but quietly and were already in the narrow river gorge. Varna was walking on her own and keeping up with the pace. Troon was relieved to see her fully revived.

"Varna," he said, "Koro does not hear Troon. Troon tried to get Koro's attention, but Koro doesn't see into the spirit world."

Varna walked right past him with no acknowledgement.

"Does Varna not hear Troon either?"

Again, she did not respond.

"DOES NOBODY HEAR TROON?" he shouted, but nobody in the war party heard him. Varna and Zho were his best and brightest pupils, but neither of them responded.

He jumped into the river and tromped around on the shore but could muster neither a splash nor a ripple.

Troon was despondent. His love could not hear him, but he consoled himself because she was fully in the land of the living again. He left for the cave hoping he could reach Joog again.

As Foln had said, he knew exactly where the shelter was. Under cover of darkness, he led the war party swiftly and directly through the gorge and the cave.

A sliver of a moon overhead barely provided any illumination in the open fields and offered them nearly nothing within the steep canyon walls. They kept to the shadows and were mostly invisible in the night.

Varna's thoughts were focused on killing Trik and retrieving Troon's bow again. She felt like it was her life's mission to always be retrieving Troon's bow. She didn't know whether Trik had kept the bow as some kind of memento of his conquest over her or a prize that he could sell, but she wished she could have had it with her when they found him so she could put an arrow in his heart.

Zho was impressed with the efficiency and organization of the war party. Bool had led them until they had joined with Foln. Now Foln led with Varna and Zho directly behind him. Bool kept mostly on Zho's shoulder with Pulu, the medicine woman, behind him. The rest of the war party kept changing formation. They were single file through the cave, naturally, but outside the cave, they spread out and undulated to match the terrain. Zho did not understand their motive at first, but they reminded him of a flock of birds. As the night dragged on, he thought he detected some purpose in their alignments. Each of them was in a position to support the other. Troon had told Zho of the ancient days when the tribe hunted giant game that required a great amount of coordination between many men. This must have been what his master was talking about. These men were experienced hunters, only they weren't just hunting some wild beast. They were hunting something that could easily hunt them back. Their positions were at the same time both hunter and prey.

Foln led them up a wide track that took them along the base of a mountain. The mountain grew steeper on their left hand side and a barely worn track formed at its base. Foln pulled to a stop and crouched on the ground. Varna and Zho instinctively crouched along with him. The war party behind them was already low to the ground. Foln pointed up ahead. Zho didn't see anything, but Foln said, "Up there, a crack in the mountain holds a small shelter."

Foln hand signaled and Bool in turn relayed the signal to his party. A slight man sprinted forward and kept low to the ground as he climbed up the steep side of the mountain. He fell even lower to the ground and crawled to the edge of the crevice. Zho didn't even see the break in the mountain until he saw the man look into it.

The slight man signaled back and Foln smiled saying, "Good. Trik is there."

Varna started to move forward, but Foln gripped her shoulder and said, "Wait."

"Why?" Varna asked, "Varna came here to kill Trik. Varna earned that."

Foln nodded and said, "Varna most certainly does have that right. Foln's people respect Varna's right for blood, but there is a larger purpose here. Foln wishes to follow Trik to his people. Foln needs to know how large their army has grown and we cannot learn that if we kill him now."

"Varna cares nothing for war parties or greater purposes. Varna only wages war on one man."

"Varna should care," Foln said, "If the rumors are true, and Trik's people plan to make war on the other tribes, then Varna's people are at risk."

Varna frowned and nearly pouted, but returned to Zho's side.

Troon flew across the terrain, still wishing he could master the speed with which he had found Koro. The sun rose over the mountains and reminded him of the spirit world where he belonged. When he arrived at the cave, he found Joog sitting up, eating and laughing with Brahg.

"Joog?" he asked, but Joog did not hear him.

"NO!" Troon cried, "Not Joog too!"

"Who is shouting?" asked Marl.

Troon went to Marl and saw that he still slept. Mora and Yona prayed over him. "Does Marl hear Troon?"

"Of course Marl hears Troon. Troon is loud enough."

"But Troon is a spirit and it is not so easy."

Marl did not respond.

"Marl is very ill," Troon continued, "and must be very near to the spirit world to hear Troon."

"Marl thinks that Marl is too young to join the spirit world, yet Marl feels something that is not so unpleasant."

Troon joined Marl in the land of the spirits. He was sitting in the desert, with his eyes closed and his face tilted up, enjoying the warmth of the light. "It is not at all unpleasant," Troon admitted. "It is where our ancestors wait for us. It is where we all go when we are done with our lives."

"Then why is Troon not there? Does Troon mean to trick Marl?"

"No, Troon belongs there, but Troon is selfish. Troon's life may be finished, but Troon is not quite finished with life. Troon still watches over the people."

Marl stood and measured Troon. "This is not the Troon that Marl remembers. This Troon standing before Marl is much younger than the Troon Marl knew."

"Perhaps so, but Troon always felt young at heart. This is a magical place. When Joog was here, Joog had both of his feet. Troon is blessed with his youth."

Marl checked his side. "Marl's wound is healed. If Marl is healed, why would Marl be here?"

"Marl's wound is festered in the land of the living."

Marl hung his head. "Then all is lost. Where is Joog? Marl would like to greet Joog again."

"Joog returned to the land of the living. Joog is there now with Brahg."

"Such a thing can be done?"

"Yes. Marl is too young to be here. Marl should grow old with Joog. Marl and Joog should find wive's and have babies."

Marl pictured running and swimming with Joog again, but this time with children in tow. "How does Joog explain the return of his foot?"

"Troon does not understand."

"To Mora? How does Joog explain to Mora that Joog's foot has returned? Mora must think Joog is quite magical."

"Ahh. Alas, Joog cannot have Joog's foot in the land of the living."

Marl looked at his side where he was punctured by the sabre tooth, then he looked at his bare feet. He squished his toes in the sand and said, "If Joog had both his feet in this world, why would Joog return to a life with only one foot? Marl would not give up a foot to go back."

"Marl might if Marl had to deliver a message. That is what Joog did. Joog returned to the land of the living to tell Zho that Varna was in danger."

"Oh yeah. Marl remembers. Troon and Varna. Now Marl understands why Troon watches over the people."

"It is true that Troon watches mostly over Varna, but Varna is still in danger. Varna and Zho are with warriors, but there are not enough of them. They need more and Troon failed to reach Koro to help them."

"Does Troon now ask Marl to return with a message?"

"Troon does."

"But Varna is not with us. How would we deliver such a message?"

"Tell Mora to reach out for Troon. Troon will guide you."

Marl was hesitant. The warmth from the light was very tempting. "Marl likes this place, but Marl does not want Joog to be alone without Joog's foot. Marl will do this for Troon and Varna, but mostly for Joog."

Koro wasn't taking any chances. After seeing Kendo captured, he exercised all the stealth he could muster to leave the forest valley and work his way around to the other side of the lake. Morning was in full bloom which made stealth even harder.

He could see the mountain on the other side of the lake. It wasn't familiar to him, yet he felt drawn to it. As he came to the ancient village, he feared Kendo's captors may be hiding in the buildings, so he slipped into the lake with only his head bobbing on the water.

Gorn did not know why Koro wanted to cross the lake to the other mountain, but he had seen the war party with Kendo in custody, and when Koro slipped into the lake, he followed without hesitation. He had never fought a man. Nobody in their tribe ever had, so hiding seemed like the best option available to them.

Once they were well past the village and the mouth of the river that fed the lake, Koro climbed back up on shore. He would have liked some trees to hide among, but this side of the lake was barren. At least that meant nobody from the other tribe could ambush them from the trees.

The lake curved around and followed the base of the mountain. Koro stopped to examine the ground. "Gorn, look at these tracks."

Clear tracks in the dirt showed that a man had come through this way. Gorn crouched down and ran his fingers through the top soil. It was soft and light. He lifted a pinch high in the air and dropped it. It scattered in even the slightest breeze.

"These must be fresh," Gorn said, "Only a day or two old."

Koro followed the footprints backwards, then turned around and followed them up the mountain. "When we came to this lake, we followed the streams through the plains to the smaller lake and then followed the river to this one. If someone knew the way, they might have bypassed the plains and come from where we were to here. They would have followed this path as these tracks have."

"Sure," Gorn admitted, "What Koro says is possible, but we already know other people live around this lake. Those tracks could have come from anywhere. Why does Koro think someone would have come this way from where we were?"

Koro shrugged. "Maybe scouts saw us coming and went this way to warn their people."

"If that's the case," Gorn said, "Then maybe we do not want to follow them."

"Yet Koro does want to follow them."

Gorn started to ask why, but seeing the perplexed expression on Koro's face, he just said, "Gorn knows. Don't ask."

"Take comfort Gorn. There is only one set of prints while we are two."

Gorn grimaced and said, "We shall see how many wait where these lead us."

Yona was wiping a cool cloth on Marl's forehead when he opened his eyes and she shouted, "Marl!"

The joy on her face was unexpected by him, but not unwelcome. He smiled as he looked back upon her face. It was dirty but quite pleasant, and her expression of love was intoxicating. Perhaps returning to the living would not be so bad.

"Yona?" he whispered.

She leaned close to hear him. She had never been this close to him before and her heart fluttered.

"Yona," he repeated. "Marl has a message for Mora: a message from Troon."

Mora still slept in the same spot where she had maintained her vigil over Joog. Yona poked Mora and said, "Mora? Troon has another message for us. Marl wishes to tell it to Mora."

Mora blinked her eyes to wake up and crawled over to Marl. She leaned over and asked, "Is Marl okay? What is Troon's message?"

"Marl will be well. Mora and Yona have taken good care of Marl, but we must prepare to leave this place. Varna is in danger. Varna is going to be captured by a warring tribe if we do not warn Varna of the danger. Mora must commune with Troon so Troon can guide us there. Troon said that Varna and Zho are with other warriors, but there are not enough of them."

"But what can we do?" Mora asked. "We are only one old woman, two girls and three recovering men. Not to mention we have some chickens and goats that we cannot leave behind."

"Mora should ask Troon."

It was mid-day by the time Wull and the tribe reached the smaller lake. It seemed a much shorter trip going down than it did going up. The area where the lake fed into the lower stream was water logged and created a marsh surrounding the stream, making it unsuitable for setting up camp. He thought he would take the tribe to the waterfall that they had seen when they came this way. It would be a good source of fresh water and should be surrounded by fairly solid bedrock since he reasoned that the water would have carried any loose soil into the lake.

Wull turned to wait for Choll to bring up the rear of the caravan, but he didn't see him. "Choll? Where is Choll?"

Men and women of the tribe turned to find Choll, but he was not there. "Where is Sara?" asked a woman in the tribe. "Sara was in the back with Choll."

Wull wanted to scout the waterfall and start setting up their camp before it got dark, but he had to follow their path to find Choll. Someone must have fallen behind and Choll was with them.

"Wait here," he said, "Wull will return soon to pick a campsite."

He weaved his way through the tribe and back into the forest that surrounded the stream. After passing the end of the line, he jumped up onto a boulder and called out, "Choll? Choll?" When he had no answer, he jumped down off the boulder and was immediately disoriented as he was covered by a net and many hands wrapped around him. He fought to free an arm but it was quickly bound by a rope and tied to his other arm. "Run!" he yelled to the tribe, "Everyone run!"

A large club was brought down on his head, but he had already raised the alarm. The tribe's first instinct was to find safety from a bear or lion. They had no experience with clashes among tribes, but when dozens of men emerged from the brush surrounding the marsh, everyone knew where the danger was. Women and children shrieked and ran in all directions. Some tried hiding, but were easily found. The few remaining elder men tried protecting the women. They had no weapons, so they raised sticks and tools used to build homes and till the soil. Their tools were no match for the experienced warriors who threw nets on them and dragged them to the ground.

One by one, the tribe was captured and dragged to the top of the stream where they were tied together in a single line.

The warrior commander stood at one end of the line and examined their faces. He saw a weak pathetic tribe with no fight in them at all, but he also saw defiance in their faces. He could tell that they would fight if they only knew how. He walked down the line and placed a pebble in a small bag for each head he counted. He had black pebbles for men; blue pebbles for women; and white pebbles for the children.

As he walked down the line he examined the elders closely and released those who were too old to work. He growled at them and pushed them away. He even wiggled his fingers like legs to tell them to go away. Two men ran away as he had wanted. The leader waited for them to take ten paces before ordering his warriors to bring them down. The warriors pulled out their slings and fired stones at the two men. Their aim was very accurate. Both of the men were struck down and one would not be getting up. The other pulled himself up from the ground and tried weaving through the field to the trees. On orders from the leader, another warrior readied a spear and threw it. It struck the old man in the small of the back and ended his escape.

The third man who was released had seen what had happened to his brothers. He did not run, but instead turned to fight the leader. The leader pulled a long blade from his belt and slit the man's belly, thus ending his escape too.

Lastly, there was one woman who was released. She fell to her knees and pleaded for her life. The leader barked his displeasure at her and severed her throat.

Now the leader looked up and down the line of people and saw an entirely different expression on their faces. He laughed at the fear he saw on their faces and licked the old woman's crimson blood from his blade. Culling the tribe served three purposes for the commander. It gave his men some target practice.

It relieved them from feeding servants who could never pull their weight, and finally, it instilled a terror in the minds of the remaining tribe making them much easier to train. He ordered his men to start the march back to their home.

Chapter Twelve

Gathering Force

Mora blinked her eyes, trying to wake herself up. She had tried saving Marl, but he was practically in the spirit world. Now he had returned to the living with a message from Troon. This was the second message Troon had sent them since his death. She lay next to Marl where she had been praying over him since he had entered into his coma and looked around the cave which had become their temporary home. The walls and ceiling of the cave danced and undulated in the flickering firelight, but hid the fine details of the stone from her aging eyes. She imagined that long ago before the fabled lands that Kendo sought even, their ancestors might have lived every day in caves just like this one.

It seemed to Mora that she hadn't spent very much time, lately, in the land of the living. In the spirit world, she was young and had perfect vision. There was a part of her that looked forward to her time when she could move on to the land of the spirits and be young again permanently, but her duties now were here with the living.

Her body ached as she pushed herself up onto her elbows. Her sight may be sharper in the land of the spirits, but her hearing was alive now with a cacophony of sounds that surrounded her. She heard Joog laughing and cajoling with Brahg. She had done everything she could think of to save him, but it wasn't her doing that brought him back. If anything, he brought himself back to fulfill a request for a dead man; a duty that he felt was his to save Varna. Now Marl has also returned from the land of the spirits and again, it wasn't due to her care. A small chuckle passed her lips as she thought that maybe she should pass from this world to the next so she could take better care of her patients. Troon had spoken to her through Joog and Marl. He needed them to do something for him and now the time had come for her to speak directly with him.

Mora took a twig of one of her more special herbs and lit it in the fire. She held it before her face and breathed in its intoxicating fumes. The pungent odor assaulted her nostrils as she pulled the fumes deep into her lungs and locked them there. She closed her eyes and felt the weight of life, that normally hung heavy from her frail bones, lift and leave her floating away from her body. She couldn't enter into the land of the spirits as Joog and Marl had, but she could see it. She saw the great light far off on the horizon. A thick fog lay between her and the light obscuring her view of the spirits homeland, but she could feel Troon's presence in the fog and called out, "Troon, it is Mora."

Troon's voice came from the fog and said, "Troon thanks Mora for coming here to see Troon."

"Marl says Varna is still in danger and Troon wants us to go save Varna. Has something happened to Zho?"

"Zho is fine. Zho and Varna have joined forces with a band of warriors and they march to find and kill Trik."

"If Varna is with warriors, then what can a small band of sick men and women do to help?"

"Troon has seen how many enemy they will face. Troon knows the war band is too small to defeat them. Troon will guide Mora to them so Mora can warn them before it is too late."

Mora couldn't help looking for Troon in the mist. She couldn't see his form in the fog, but his voice emanated from all directions within the thick cloud. She tried pushing into the fog, but her feet were stuck in the ground. She couldn't move. "Mora cannot see Troon," she pleaded, "but if Troon can see us, then Troon should take a moment to look at us more closely. Mora is old and frail. Marl and Brahg are both injured. Joog is without a foot. We will be slow to travel and we may not even be well enough to complete the voyage."

"Troon knows this. Troon wishes it weren't so, but Varna is no longer near enough to death for Troon to warn directly. Troon has no more options to tell them what lies in store for them if they attack."

"Very well. We will do what we can, but Troon must look out for our lives as much as Troon looks out for Varna's."

"Troon watches over everybody." He said the words, and it may have sounded like he watched everybody equally, but it wasn't true. He would never tell Mora, but he would sacrifice them all to save Varna. He wouldn't do so lightly, but he would do it anyway. Soon, Varna will understand why he does not let her join him in the spirit world yet. She still has much life to live, and Troon would see her live it before joining him, even though it means that she will be living her life with another before coming to the spirit world.

Koro and Gorn followed the lone pair of footprints up along the base of the mountain and quickly came across a wide track with many more foot prints. Gorn studied the tracks closely, but could not determine exactly how many men had made them. He also could not be certain which set of tracks had come first, but he knew there were far too many for the two of them to confront.

Koro looked back to the other side of the lake where Kendo had been taken hostage. There were no more columns of smoke. The lake and the ancient village were peaceful and inviting. There was no sign of the danger they had seen. He turned to look up the other mountain where he had sent Wull and the tribe to the smaller lake. Again he saw no sign of trouble. The smaller lake, as he remembered it, was a lovely little lake full of fish. He remembered seeing an intriguing water fall that he wanted to explore one day. Finally he looked back down the mountains to the far away flatlands where the tribe had started. Life was good for them before the floods came. In those days, he only needed to worry about how much food he brought to the table. He let the elders worry about why the larger game had left the valley. He was happy to fish the river and grow old. He chuckled as he thought he was too young to think about growing old and bit his lip as he reviewed all the directions they might go, but made no suggestion.

Gorn saw Koro contemplate all the places they had been and offered, "If Koro is thinking we should return to the tribe, then Gorn agrees. If Koro is looking back upon the old village and wishing that we had never left, then again, Gorn agrees."

Koro shook his head and said, "Koro wishes the flood never came, but Koro does not believe the old village still stands where we left it."

"Then we should return to the tribe and help Wull build a camp."

Koro looked back up the mountain to the smaller lake and said, "Koro thinks that is most wise, but Koro cannot help feeling we should follow these tracks."

Gorn scratched his head and looked closely at Koro's face for some signs of insanity. "Gorn likes to think that Koro's head is wise for his years, but if Koro's head allows Koro's heart to make this decision, then Gorn thinks that Koro's head has gone crazy. What does Koro think will happen if we catch up with the makers of these tracks?"

Koro shrugged his shoulders and admitted, "Koro does not know. Perhaps Koro is crazy, but we are skilled hunters. These tracks are wide and easy to see. We can climb higher up this mountain face and still follow them from a safe distance. We can keep low to the terrain and remain as quiet as mice until we learn who made these tracks."

"To what end?" Gorn asked. "When we learn whose tracks these are, what will we do with this knowledge? There are only two of us and obviously much more than two of them. We will be no better off with the answers Koro seeks than we are now. We will still have to turn around and rejoin the tribe."

Koro smiled weakly and slowly shook his head. "Koro cannot disagree with Gorn's thinking, except to say that when we learn who they are and what they are doing, Koro will know why Koro's heart tugs him there. That is something."

Gorn sighed. "Then all is lost, because Koro is truly crazy, but Gorn may be even more crazy to follow Koro. Let us hope that the makers of these tracks take pity on two completely insane hunters who are lost on this forsaken mountain."

Mora tried talking Joog into staying behind to care for the chickens and goats, but Marl and Brahg refused to leave him, and most importantly, Joog wouldn't do it. Mora did not understand their eagerness to march into harm's way and attributed it to some kind of mental defect that only men share. She would have gladly stayed behind and watched the animals. She was too old to make war and she might be too old to complete the trip, but she had no choice. She was the only one who could hear Troon's guidance.

They were a pathetic looking group. Yona fashioned a sling that Brahg could wear on his back to carry Joog. Mora worried that Joog's additional weight would be too much for Brahg to bear, but Joog only joked that he had lost at least a foot's weight since this time last year.

Pela tied their largest goat to the outside of the cave and attached one of the travois that Zho had made to its back and with Brahg's help, carried the chicken cage out of the cave and placed it on the bed of the travois.

Brahg and Marl each selected slings, knives and spears from the weapon stash and looked sadly upon the weapons they were leaving behind. Even though Varna and Zho managed to bring all of this from the old village, they could only take the essentials or they would be even slower.

Pela lifted Nik and settled him on her hip. This brought a big smile to Nik's face. He liked any kind of attention, but especially travelling.

Yona pointed at Nik and said, "Pela gets the first turn, but Yona will share the burden."

"Nik is no burden," Pela said. "But sharing would be good."

Brahg setup another goat and travois for Mora's supplies. She selected only her most important herbs and utensils. She vowed to send someone back for the rest after everything was settled.

The rest of the goats carried packs on their backs. They were tied to each other in a caravan which Mora thought this was probably unnecessary. The goats would most likely follow them wherever they went anyway, but there was nobody among them with the experience to herd them and most importantly, the ability to run them down if they wandered off.

They were ready to go.

The meadow outside the cave was a brilliant green speckled with white and yellow flowers.

Mora hung back a moment, in the shade of the cave. She took a deep breath, closed her eyes and said to Troon, "We are ready."

"Follow the path towards the mountain," Troon said. "After Mora leaves the meadow, it will turn away from the morning sun and lead Mora out of the forest towards the distant mountains. Contact Troon again from there."

They started their trek along the path. Mora looked back upon the cave. It was never more than a temporary stopping point on their way to their ancestral lands, but she felt a surprising pang in her gut like she was leaving her home behind.

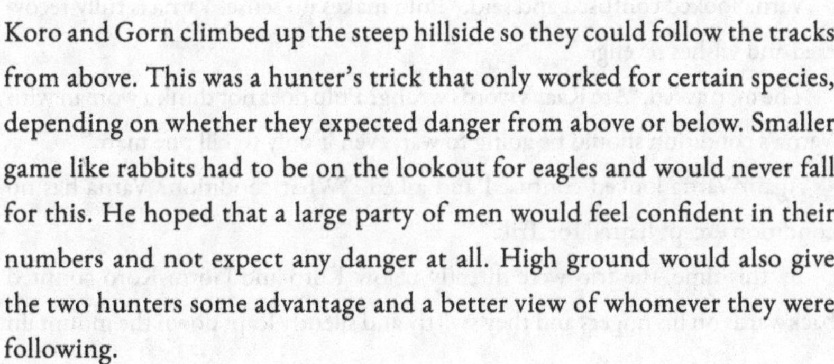

Koro and Gorn climbed up the steep hillside so they could follow the tracks from above. This was a hunter's trick that only worked for certain species, depending on whether they expected danger from above or below. Smaller game like rabbits had to be on the lookout for eagles and would never fall for this. He hoped that a large party of men would feel confident in their numbers and not expect any danger at all. High ground would also give the two hunters some advantage and a better view of whomever they were following.

The morning sun beat down upon them as they crawled along the dusty mountain side. The barren mountain offered little for them to hide behind, but their clothes were caked with mud and dirt from their trek through the lake and they had added a layer of dirt to their faces. They blended in with the mountain side, but if someone were to look for them, they would be seen.

They dare not speak for fear that their voices would carry too far down the desolate peak. It wasn't long before they saw a sentry standing guard on the path that followed the base of the mountain. He was a large man who was well armed and looked like he could handle himself in a fight between men. Gorn accidently displaced a small pebble that bounded down the mountain and the sentry looked up. Koro and Gorn froze in place as the sentry searched for something, but luck was with them as a small ground squirrel popped out of his hole and chased the pebble down to the lake.

A voice from further up the trail called the sentry. Koro was getting a picture in his mind of how much farther the rest of them were, but he still didn't know how many. He crept forward in the sentry's absence, but stopped when he saw three more figures approaching. Two of them, a man and a woman, he did not know, but between them he recognized Varna

The woman said something in a language Koro didn't understand, and then the man asked, "How is Varna feeling?"

She replied, "Varna is angry. Varna came here to kill Trik. Foln understood this and let Varna believe it would be so, but now Foln won't allow it."

The woman spoke again and the man said, "A woman in Varna's condition should not be plotting to end a man's life."

Varna looked confused and said, "Pulu makes no sense. Varna is fully recovered and wishes revenge."

The man asked, "Are Raas's words wrong? Pulu does not think a woman with Varna's condition should be going to war, even if only to kill one man."

Again Varna looked confused and asked, "What condition? Varna has no condition except hatred for Trik."

By this time, the trio were directly below Koro and Gorn. Koro counted backwards on his fingers and they swiftly and silently leapt down the mountain and pounced on Pulu and Raas, but they were immediately set upon by the sentry and three other warriors.

One of the warriors was about to bring a large club down upon Koro's head when Varna jumped on his back and yelled, "Stop!"

Kendo sat cross legged on the floor of a large wooden cage, forcing himself to remain calm when his emotions screamed for him to act out. Brack and Flom had already circled the cage testing the vertical timbers. They found no weakness in the structure but did, at least, learn the locations of the guards.

They joined Kendo and sat on either side of him.

Brack leaned over and whispered, "Brack does not know how Kendo can be so calm. Brack has never been so humiliated in all of Brack's life."

Kendo remained still and just glanced over to Brack with his eyes. "Would Brack prefer Kendo to wail like a frightened woman?"

Brack shook his head and remained quiet.

The cage was centered in a small village and was surrounded by several other wooden structures with a tall wooden fence circling the entire compound. Guards stood atop tall structures that allowed them to view over the fence while other guards walked the perimeter. Kendo's people had no word for a fort just as they had never known conflict with other tribes, but it was clear to him that these people were accustomed to a life of conflict with other people.

A commotion stirred at the main gate and Kendo saw Wull being led into the compound with the rest of the tribe behind him. They were lined up in front of the cage as Kendo, Brack and Flom had been earlier.

Three filthy men with knives walked down the line of people and slit their clothing until they all stood before him naked, with their scraps of clothing piled around their feet. A fourth man, one of the few clean shaven men Kendo had seen here, followed behind and inspected the naked tribesmen. He spent a little longer inspecting the young women and snickered to his comrades while he tested the firmness of their breasts. A fifth man followed him and handed out loin cloths to the naked prisoners. Once inspected and barely clothed, they were led into the cage with Kendo.

Kendo counted his people as they came in. He whispered to Brack, "Kendo does not see Koro among them."

Flom whispered, "Gorn is also not with them."

"Brack believes that some of the elders are missing too."

Kendo hung his head and said, "Koro would have fought them."

Flom nodded and said, "Gorn would as well."

"Brack prefers to believe that Koro and Gorn were hunting and saw them approach. They are out there still planning our escape."

Kendo looked up and said, "Kendo hopes Brack is correct about them surviving the attack, but Kendo hopes they return to Mora and Joog so our people can survive."

Flom sighed and hunched his shoulders. "Then Kendo thinks we are lost."

"Do not say that," Brack said, "We must never lose hope, but we may have to plan our own escape."

Flom shook his head and said, "But there are so many of them."

Brack reached out and raised Flom's head off his chest. "Then we wait until they are busy and there aren't so many of them."

Kendo looked deeply into Flom's eyes and said, "Brack is right. We will always maintain hope and look for our chance to escape, but today, Kendo will mourn the capture of his people."

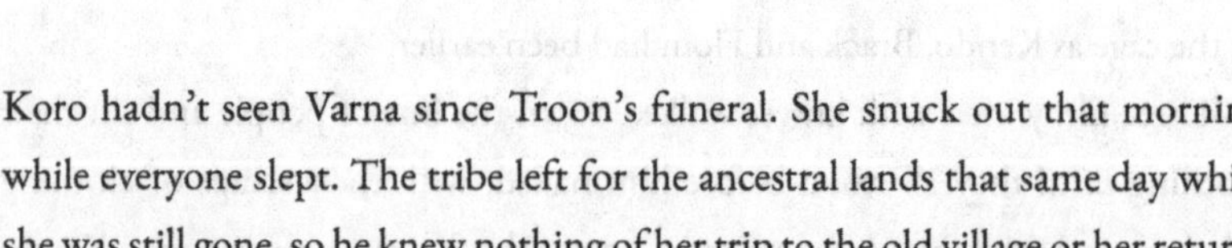

Koro hadn't seen Varna since Troon's funeral. She snuck out that morning while everyone slept. The tribe left for the ancestral lands that same day while she was still gone, so he knew nothing of her trip to the old village or her return. Most of the tribe thought she left to die, as widows sometimes do, but she was too young for that, so Zho was sent to find her. Much had happened since that time and he had as much to share with her as she had with him. She was still filling Koro and Gorn in on the story of Trik when a scout came over to them and whispered, "It is time to go. Trik has left the shelter."

The scout looked oddly upon Koro until one of the guards explained, "These are more of Varna's people." The scout nodded and ran ahead to tell Foln.

Foln was delighted to hear that there were more Grull and sent a couple scouts to follow Trik while he came to greet them. Foln gripped Koro's forearm then Gorn's and said, "Foln welcomes members of the Grull. Friends of Varna are friends of Foln and Foln's people. What news have you two?"

Varna didn't want to waste any more time recanting the events of the past few weeks while Trik was on the move. She pointed up to the rest of the war band and asked, "Shouldn't we be following Trik?"

"We have time. Foln's scouts will follow Trik. Foln would like to know if Varna's people have seen anything."

Koro nodded his head and pointed across the lake. "Our chieftain, Kendo, has been captured with two of our hunters. We had seen smoke and heard the loud trumpet of a great beast, so they went to investigate. When Kendo had not returned, Koro sent the rest of the tribe up to the smaller lake to hide while we went to help."

Some of the guards snickered at the mention of the beast, but Foln quickly glanced at them and shook his head to stop them. "The people that infest this valley have no honor," Foln said. "They are called the Griftons and they use tricks to lure people into their traps. As you have both seen, they lured and captured your leader. Foln would like to know what brought Koro here if the rest of the Grull are up on the small lake?"

"We followed tracks that went along the lake and led us to this trail."

Foln glanced from the lake to the trail and said, "We did not follow the lake very much. How did you find our tracks?"

"First," Gorn said, "There were only a single person's tracks that came up to this trail where we found many more tracks."

"And those tracks came from the other side of the lake? Foln wonders why Trik would walk around the lake like that."

Koro shook his head and said, "The tracks did not come from around the lake. We found those tracks on this side of the lake. Koro cannot explain why we came to this side of the lake. Koro just had a feeling that we should come this way."

"Don't ask," Gorn said, "That is what Koro told Gorn about Koro's feeling. Don't ask."

Koro smiled weakly and patted Gorn on the shoulder. "Gorn thought Koro had gone crazy to come here."

"No," Gorn said, "Gorn thought Koro was a little odd for coming here. Gorn did not think Koro was truly crazy until Koro insisted on following the tracks of a large war party."

The guards laughed again and this time Foln laughed with them.

Varna asked impatiently, "Now can we catch up with your scouts and follow Trik?"

Foln nodded and said, "Yes Varna, now we can go."

The master of the prisoner guards watched the tribe as they entered the enclosure and saw that they either congregated around Kendo, or nodded to him before finding their own place in the cage.

They gathered into groups: some by gender and others by age. The younger women stuck together with their arms crossed over their bare chests while the older women didn't care if they were naked.

Even while they were within their groups, individual tribesmen would pause their conversations to glance over at Kendo from time to time to see if he planned to address the situation. Sometimes whole groups would turn at the same time to see what Kendo planned to do.

The master of the guards called for the quarter master. "Was their clothing searched for any personal items?"

The quarter master had arrived with a grin on his face, but it evaporated now. He looked right and left for support from the other guards but received none.

Bring me their things and search them in front of me.

The quarter master ordered the guards to create a pile of their clothing which had been bunched into a tinder box to be burned. He stopped over and went through them one by one. He found stones and small carvings in the children's clothes and worthless jewelry in the women's, but when he came to something wrapped in the folds of a man's shirt, he pulled it out and handed it to the master of the guards.

The master of the guards knew what it was and was pretty sure whose it was.

Wearing the emblem of leadership made one a chief, but did not always make one a leader. He only had to watch the tribe to know who the leader was.

The people would eventually give away the true leadership and one of the things he hated more than anything was when the leaders remained calm in front of the other captives. It gave them a false sense of hope and made training more difficult.

He growled his displeasure and barked out orders while pointing at Kendo. Two guards entered the cage with spears pointed at the tribesmen to force them out of the way. Two other guards went straight to Kendo and dragged him out of the cage. They didn't care whether he would have cooperated or not and gave him little chance to regain his footing as they pulled him out of the cage.

The master of the guards produced the emblem that Kendo had worn until they stripped him of his clothes. He dangled it from his hands in front of Kendo and spat on it. He then pointed to a pile of stones that were as big as a man's head. The guards dragged Kendo to the pile and the master pointed again at the stones, then pointed to an empty area ten paces away.

One of the guards lifted one of the stones and pushed it into Kendo's belly. Kendo refused to grip the boulder and the master took a whip that had been coiled from his belt and laid it out flat on Kendo's back. Kendo grimaced as the leather strap dug into his bare flesh, but he still refused to take the stone. Three more lashes did not prod Kendo into taking the stone.

The master pointed to the cage and barked out some more orders. One of the guards pulled a woman from the cage. At the master's signal, the guard slugged her flush in the face. She crumpled to the ground with blood seeping from her mouth. The guard grabbed the woman's foot and dragged her unconscious form back into the cage. Kendo gritted his teeth and stared defiantly into the master's eyes, but took the stone before they pulled out another woman. The stone was only slightly heavy as he walked the paces and started a new pile.

As the task wore on, the stones seemed to get heavier to Kendo's tiring limbs, but whenever his pace slowed, the master smiled and cracked the lash on his back again. Kendo knew that the only purpose of the task was to humiliate him and cower his people. He would much rather die fighting, but he wasn't willing to sacrifice his people for his own pride. Koro was still out there. Despite what he had said to Brack and Flom, he knew that Koro would find a way to save them. Kendo only had to bide his time until then.

After completing his task, Kendo was shoved back into the cage. Several people started to come to him, but he quickly shook his head and said, "No. Leave Kendo alone for now."

Instead of returning to his place between Brack and Flom, Kendo found an isolated corner and sat with his back to the tribe. All he had to do was wait for Koro and keep anyone from getting themselves killed.

Brack whispered to Flom, "Brack should never have said that Brack has never been so humiliated."

<hr>

Varna and Foln caught up with the scouts and watched Trik from a vantage point high on the hill. The valley below was clear of trees leading up to the fort, but the trees still lined the hills around it. The grass covered valley had already lost the lushness of spring as the hot summer sun dried out the ground and browned the grass.

Foln scoffed at Trik's people. "They steal everything they know about how things are built, but never learn why. Foln would build the fort on the hill overlooking the valley instead of down the center."

Zho just grunted, not entirely sure he understood what Foln meant.

Trik was already down in the valley and walked cautiously towards his people. He did not want to appear threatening to the guards, so before he was in view of the fort, he found a large flat boulder with a bush growing on its back and stashed his weapons, including Troon's bow.

Trik steadied his nerves and walked straight down the center of the clearing. When in view of the fort, he opened his arms wide and walked directly for the warriors standing guard outside the compound and announced, "Trik, leader of the fabled Grull people, leaders of the ancient clans, bids you welcome. Trik comes to you today as the prophecies have foretold, and by fulfilling the ancient prophecies, Trik ushers in a new era of prosperity for the Grifton people."

The guard cracked open the gate and called for his commander. When the commander arrived, the guard whispered, "Don't we already have the Grull's chieftain?"

"Yes," the commander said. "Why?"

The guard pointed to Trik with his thumb and said, "This guy claims to be their leader."

The commander poked his head out the gate and looked at Trik, then motioned to someone inside the fort and said, "Kill this clown." Several warriors appeared at the top of the fence and swiftly threw spears at Trik. Four of the six spears found their mark with the remaining two at his flanks in case he fled to either side. A roar raised from the warriors as the impaled Trik fell to his knees and toppled over.

Varna watched from the hill and was horrified. Zho had to briefly cover her mouth to keep her from yelling. She turned to Zho and whispered, "Varna wanted to kill Trik!"

Zho pulled Varna close into a consoling hug and said, "Yes Varna. Zho knows this."

"It was Varna's right! Not theirs!"

"Yes," Zho said, "Varna had every right, but he is dead now. Does that not matter more than Varna's revenge?"

The sinking feeling in her gut told Varna that it was not enough, but there was nothing she could do about it.

The commander of the guards left the compound and marched out to Trik's bleeding remains. He looked around arrogantly, confident that whomever might have accompanied Trik either would not have the nerve to attack him, or would not be fast enough to beat his warriors. He leaned over and plucked Joog's emblem from around Trik's neck and dangled it from his fingers as he held his arms out wide, daring anyone to attack him.

Varna wanted to satisfy the commander's request to die. He robbed her of her vengeance. It was her blood right to kill Trik, not his. She gripped her spear tightly and started to raise it, but Foln put his hand on her wrist and said, "Neh." Foln had seen enough and signaled his war band to retreat. Varna hesitantly lowered her spear, but instead of following them back to the crevice, she slipped out of sight and snuck down the hill into the valley.

Foln had lost sight of her long before he was aware that she was no longer with them. He signaled Bool to stop the retreat and reversed back to the vantage point on the hill.

"What has changed Foln's mind?" Bool asked.

"Varna does not follow us. Foln fears Varna has slipped down the hill to raise war."

Zho grimaced and said, "Varna's blood runs hot. Varna doesn't always listen to reason."

Foln left the vantage point and led his war band down the hill to the valley. Halfway down the hill, before they had cleared the trees that lined the open grassy space, Foln heard something ahead of him and raised his spear while his company sprang into a variety of offensive and defensive positions. Varna heard them and raised Troon's bow as she entered back into the woods.

"Varna," Foln whispered, "it is us. What is Varna doing? Does Varna wish to die?"

Varna lowered her bow and whispered back, "Varna is not afraid to die."

Zho nodded his head and mumbled, "Over and over it seems."

"But," Varna continued, "Varna was not going to lose Troon's bow again." She hung the bow across her chest and said, "Varna was coming to Foln. Foln does not need to panic."

Foln left one scout hidden on the hill to watch the fort. He didn't want to be surprised by any of their patrols.

Varna surprised even herself by the depths of her disappointment.

First, Trik had befriended her and convinced her that he was a friend and she introduced him to Mora and Joog.

Zho never did trust him, but he could never explain why. They never would have known anything was wrong about Trik if Foln had never arrived.

She ran through her memory over and over and realized that they would never have trusted him if they had just trusted in Zho's feelings.

Varna dragged her feet on the ground and kicked stones as she shuffled along. Foln saved them from Trik, but he also prevented her from killing him. She was ready to do it. Trik had left her to die, and she nearly did. She was close enough to death to have seen the spirit of her dead husband, or did she imagine that? No, he was real. He told her where to find Trik, and true enough, he was there waiting for her. She should have killed him when they found him.

Koro saw how depressed and withdrawn Varna had become. He pulled alongside her and asked, "Why is Varna so sad?"

She looked up at him then flopped her head back down on her chest to reply, "Varna wanted to kill Trik with Varna's own hands."

"Why with Varna's own hands?" he asked.

"Because Trik tried to kill Varna. Trik left Varna tied up and unable to breathe."

"Koro is relieved that Varna still lives. Koro is also satisfied that this Trik is dead and will not bother Varna again."

"It is much worse than that," she said. "Varna was fooled by Trik. Varna thought Trik was good and Trik betrayed Varna."

Koro hugged Varna and said, "Does Varna not see the great irony? Trik approached those people expecting to be accepted by them. Trik believed they would invite Trik in."

"They were Trik's people," she said, "Trik was returning home."

"Even better," Koro replied, "Trik did not say that Trik was one of them. Trik pretended to be one of us. Trik thought they would believe Trik was our chieftain. Trik was betrayed by Trik's own arrogance. Koro believes that for Trik to be killed by Trik's own people was a far greater punishment than if Varna had killed Trik with Varna's own hands."

Koro was right. Varna lifted her head feeling a little better. "Varna likes Koro's words, but Varna still feels cheated."

"Koro is sorry that Varna feels so, but Trik has left this life and there is nothing more for Varna to do about it. Koro will not allow Varna to enter the spirit world just to exact vengeance upon Trik's spirit, so it is over."

Varna's face brightened considerably. "Koro is a genius. What a great idea."

"No!" Koro said, "Koro will not allow Varna to die for revenge!"

Varna shook her head and said, "Varna does not need to join the spirit world. Troon is already there and Troon will deal with Trik. Trik will never find peace."

A silence fell between them until Varna asked, "What do we do now?"

Koro looked over his shoulder at Foln and said, "We need to rejoin our people and save Kendo, but we certainly could use the help of Varna's new friends."

Foln walked with Zho. When they reached the hidden shack, he stopped and said, "We'll setup camp here. Foln will send two scouts to find Zho's people at the small lake."

Gorn said, "Gorn will go with Foln's scouts."

"Foln was hoping one of you would accompany them. We will wait here for word and decide what to do next after the scouts have seen their camp. Foln will also send a bird with a note for our commanders to send more troops."

"More troops?" Varna asked. "Foln's people lie far beyond our old village. That will take too long."

"Varna's chieftain is probably held captive in that fort. Varna saw how big it was and how many men they had within it. We need more men to breach it."

"Fine," Varna replied. "We will have more men when Foln's scouts find our tribe."

Foln smiled sadly and said, "Varna. Foln knows what it is like to want action. Foln understands how hard it is to wait when loved ones are away from us and are in trouble, but Foln will not embark on a fool's errand against trained warriors with only women and children. Foln will send for seasoned soldiers and we will have to wait here for them."

Varna looked from Foln to Zho and back to Foln again. She had no ally in this. "But that will take at least one passing of the moon."

Foln frowned and nodded his head. "It may take two or three."

"But, by that time," Varna cried, "Kendo could be dead."

"Foln knows these people. Life will be harsh for Kendo, and Foln regrets that, but they will not want Kendo dead. Kendo has value for them."

Varna was helpless. She wanted to cry but did not want these soldiers to see her tears. "Varna cannot believe that we will allow Kendo to remain captive for three moons."

Foln did not want see Varna cry either. She was a great hunter and a strong and powerful woman. Whether she knew it or not, she was a great warrior. He turned his back so he wouldn't see her face when he delivered the rest of the bad news. "It may be longer than that. In three moons, we may have winter to deal with. If winter comes in harsh, as it sometimes does in the mountains, then we may be forced to wait till spring."

Varna could not bear the news anymore and ran away from Foln and Zho. She had never been prone to emotional outbursts before, but she couldn't stop herself.

She sprinted down the path, wishing there was at least one tree she could hide behind and cry, but there were none. She ran until the path undulated downwards and she could at least hide from them below the horizon of the hill.

***

The sun was high overhead when a large clay pot was brought to the cage and bowls of soup were handed out to the captive tribe. There was little more than water in the soup, but it was all they were offered.

Brack was led from the cage and ordered to move the pile of stones that Kendo had carried back to the original location. He glanced back at Kendo and received a lashing on his back for asking Kendo's permission, but he saw Kendo nod his head and he moved the stones as requested.

Three women were taken from the cage and given tasks to gather herbs. Ropes were tied to their ankles and guards watched every move. They had no desire for the whip and simply did as they were requested.

Two other women were taken to a cooking area with clay pots filled with water. The guard that watched them mimed a few actions and made it clear to them that if they did not make the food, their people would not eat.

The cooking area had a small store of baskets half filled with wilting vegetables and some buggy grain. A tray of leftover meat bones was placed on a table for them.

The two women looked forlornly at each other and shrugged their shoulders then set about their tasks.

One of them took the grain and began kneading it into a dough for bread while the other shooed the flies off the meat bones and dropped them in the pots of water. She then went through the vegetables and tried separating the rot from the almost edible and prepared a soup for her people.

Brack finished moving the stones and rejoined Flom in the cage. "They're slavers."

"Yes, Flom knows this."

"We must do something."

Flom looked at Kendo who still sat alone in the corner. "Flom thinks Kendo wants us to stay alive until Koro can mount a rescue. We will do what they ask and keep physically alert until that time."

Brack grunted and said, "Don't look for Kendo when it is your turn."

"Flom won't. Flom wonders if they know that moving the stones will only make us stronger?"

Night was setting and Varna remained in a funk. She sat alone and nibbled at her food but mostly pushed it around on the board Foln had given her.

Foln came to see her with Raas in tow.

"What's the matter?" Foln asked. "Does Varna not like Foln's people's cooking?"

Varna looked up and tried to force a smile. "No. It's not that. The food is good, but Varna does not feel much like eating."

"Ahhh," Foln said while nodding his head. "Foln understands. Varna is not in the mood to eat, or drink, or laugh, or even go on living. Is this all because Varna was cheated out of a kill?"

"Varna wanted to kill Trik. Even Foln admitted that Varna had the right for blood, but it is more than that. Varna has been sad and alone since Troon was taken to the spirit world."

Foln sat down next to Varna so she would not have to crane her neck upwards to speak with him. "But Varna is not alone. Varna has Zho and Zho cares much for Varna."

"Zho is Varna's brother. Troon was master to us both."

Foln raised an eyebrow and asked, "Troon was Varna's father and husband? Foln must not understand the Grull way."

"It's not like that," Varna defended herself. "Troon was our master. Troon taught us to hunt, but Zho did not know that Troon taught Varna. Troon was Varna's secret master and later became Varna's secret husband."

"I see," Foln said. "And now Varna is without a husband. Foln sees how that can be lonely, but Foln still think's Varna should eat. If not tonight, then in the morning. Varna can sleep in the shack with Pulu. Foln will sleep under the stars with the men."

Foln took the board of food from Varna and left her to go to the shack and make herself comfortable. He didn't order her to sleep now, but she felt it was expected of her and went directly to the shack.

Pulu was already there fluffing up a pile of hay. Pulu looked at Varna warmly as she lay down on her hay. Something about her stare left Varna feeling self-conscious, but she ignored it and lay down on one of the other piles of hay. She closed her eyes and fell swiftly asleep.

Varna wanted to dream of Troon. She wanted desperately to watch Troon terrorize and defeat Trik, but she was alone in her dreams. She was usually an early riser, but didn't rise this morning until she was wakened by the clacking of wood and grunting of men.

She left the shelter and found Foln's soldiers training. Zho was with them learning the ways of fighting against men. Varna picked up a spear and joined Zho. She lifted the spear and swung it like a staff as she had seen the men do.

Zho placed the butt of his spear on the ground and asked, "Does Varna wish to spar?"

A smile crossed her face as she jumped in front of him and prepared to do mock battle, but Pulu jumped in front of her and said, "No training for Varna!"

Varna looked around and saw many puzzled faces. "Why should Varna not train? Why would Pulu object when nobody else does?"

"Pulu knows what they do not. It is not possible for Varna to train because it is not possible for Varna to go to war."

"Varna will so go to war! Varna is already an accomplished hunter. Varna will defend Varna's people and rescue our chieftain."

Pulu looked at the war band. Even Foln was puzzled. She looked again at Varna's determination and then at Raas, the interpreter. "Come with Pulu. Pulu will explain."

Varna did not want to go and even Foln did not know what was on Pulu's mind, but he trusted her judgment and nodded his head suggesting Varna should go along.

She followed Pulu back to the shelter where they could talk in relative privacy. Pulu whispered something to Raas and he jerked his head in agreement.

Varna entered the hut and sat down on the straw. "What is so important that Varna cannot train?"

"Our people," Pulu began, "are warriors. We deal out many deaths, but we don't do so lightly. We actually have the greatest respect for life. We honor our warriors, but we also worship our mothers and their children. We do not send children off to war until they are grown men..."

"And," Varna interrupted loudly, "Varna is not a man, so Varna cannot go off to war? Varna is strong and will defeat many men."

Pulu raised her hands in an effort to calm Varna. "No. That is not what Pulu was saying. Pulu has no doubt that Varna would be a proven warrior against men. Please calm Varna and hear Pulu. We do not send our children off to war until they are grown men and women, but we never send them off to war while they are still children, and we never send their mothers off to war. The only reason that we have very few women warriors is because we place so much value on life and on motherhood. This is why Varna cannot go to war."

"What?" Varna shouted. She looked alternately at Pulu and Raas.

Raas shrugged his shoulders and pointed to Pulu saying, "Raas has no say in this. Raas is only interpreter for Varna and Pulu."

Varna was outraged and cried out, "Pulu thinks Varna should not go to war because Pulu wants Varna to remain behind so Varna can breed children? Varna is not a goat or chicken to be bred that way."

Pulu shook her head and said, "That is not what Pulu is saying either. Does Varna not know?"

Pulu looked deeply into Varna's eyes and saw only confusion.

Varna looked at Raas again, but still he did not know what was in Pulu's mind. "Tell Varna," she pleaded, "what is it that Pulu thinks Varna does not know?"

Pulu looked at Raas pleadingly and he reaffirmed his promise to keep their conversation secret. She turned back to Varna and said, "Varna is already with child. If Varna does not know, then surely Zho does not know either."

Varna was stunned. Her mouth fell open, but she could not speak.

"Does Varna wish Pulu to tell Zho for Varna?"

"This cannot be," Varna argued, "How can this be so? What makes Pulu think this?"

"Oh," Pulu said softly, "Does Varna not know how babies are made?"

"What?" Varna spat back. "Of course Varna knows about babies!"

"But Varna is surprised by the news. Pulu will tell Zho if Varna is too embarrassed."

"Why does Pulu insist on telling Zho? What has any of this have to do with Zho?"

Zho had come to the doorway to see what the shouting was about and asked, "What is it that Zho does not know?"

Pulu looked up at Zho, but would not say, and Raas was sworn to secrecy.

Varna stood and lightly said, "Pulu says that Varna is having a baby."

Zho's mouth parted and he said breathlessly, "A baby? Is Pulu sure?"

Pulu nodded and said, "Pulu is sure. Varna is having Zho's baby."

"No!" Varna shouted, "Varna is not having Zho's baby! Varna is having Troon's baby!"

"Ahhh," Pulu said remembering Varna's dead husband.

Zho shook his head in astonishment and said, "At Troon's age? Varna is having Troon's baby? Troon is truly Zho's master in all things."

"This is good," Pulu said, "It is no longer a secret now. Foln should know. We should return Varna to your people to have this baby. Pulu will tell Foln."

Pulu had to shade her eyes from the sun as she left the shack and stepped out of the shadowy crevice. She walked down the path a short ways and found Foln talking with Bool.

Bool nodded his head as Foln spoke, then pointed to the edge of the lake where he saw two scouts returning from the ancient village with Gorn.

Pulu knew the scouts would have important information for Foln, so she waited her turn behind Bool.

The scouts were accustomed to running and jogged up to Foln, only slightly winded. Gorn ran to give his news directly to Zho, but when he found Zho in a private conversation with Varna, he returned to Foln and the scouts.

"What news have you?" asked Bool.

"We followed the river from the ancient village to the higher lake. Many people had gone that way. We found tracks going in both directions. Further up by the smaller lake, we found tracks for many warriors too. The Grull people were attacked, but there was no contest. They were taken prisoner. We counted four elders that were slain."

Foln scowled as he heard the news. Zho and Varna should be told. The scouts waited patiently for instructions until Foln dismissed them.

Foln turned around and scanned the area for Zho and Varna, but only saw Pulu waiting patiently to speak with him. He turned back to Bool and said, "Go find Zho while Foln speaks with Pulu."

Bool nodded his acceptance of his orders and moved to leave them, but Pulu reached out for Bool's arm to hold him while she said, "Foln may wish to hear Pulu's news before Foln sends Bool to share word of the Grull's fate."

Gorn said, "Gorn knows where Zho and Varna are. Gorn will get them," but Gorn paused, instead, to see why Pulu held up Bool.

Foln looked at Pulu curiously, then at Bool who only shrugged. "Very well then. Tell Foln what has Pulu so concerned."

Pulu let go of Bool's arm and said, "If Foln tells them now, Varna will want to take immediate action."

"Yes," Foln agreed, "Foln has seen how passionate Varna is. It is not such a terrible thing. Varna reminds Foln of a younger Foln."

Gorn nodded his head and said, "Gorn too wishes to act, as will Koro and Zho."

"Varna will not wait," Pulu continued, "Varna is too impulsive and will sneak off and get killed trying to rescue the Grull people."

"Foln will try to talk sense to Varna, but ultimately, it is Varna's right."

"It is all our right," Gorn said, "to save our people."

"Yes, yes, yes," Pulu said impatiently, "As it was Varna's right of blood to kill Trik, but Foln denied Varna of that. Does Foln believe Varna will allow Foln to deny Varna again?"

"Losing Varna would be a great loss," Foln said, "but Varna has already honored Foln by accepting Foln's advice. Foln is not comfortable lying to such an honorable warrior."

Foln thought he had spoken the last word and gently nodded his head to tell Bool to carry his message, but Pulu grabbed Bool's arm again and said, "Varna cannot be a warrior in this. Varna has a higher responsibility. Varna is with child."

That spun an entirely new slant on the conversation. Foln understood exactly what had Pulu so agitated now. "Foln will not lie to Varna, but for Varna's own sake and that of Varna's child, Foln might be slow in revealing the truth. Bool, tell the men only that we leave immediately. We will return to our friends' cave to wait out the winter. Select four scouts to remain here. Foln will send two more scouts back here when they know where the cave is."

Gorn saw the change in Foln's expression, but he did not completely understand the implication. Foln said, "Foln asks that Gorn hold off telling Varna what has happened until we are closer to the Grull's cave, for Varna's sake."

Gorn still did not understand, but he agreed for the moment.

Bool started to trot off and Foln added, "If Zho or Varna ask why Foln has decided to leave so abruptly, tell them that Foln is anxious to see Foln's son again."

Joog hung in the sling Yona fashioned with his arms wrapped around Brahg's neck. Brahg would have carried him like that all the way without complaining, but the wound on Brahg's shoulder was just below one of Joog's arms and Joog could feel Brahg wince from time to time.

They had barely passed the site of the slate deposits and turned towards the west when Mora said, "Mora needs to reset the chicken's cage before it falls apart."

Brahg found a tree stump where Joog could sit and went to help Mora.

Marl was also going to help with the chicken coop, but Joog motioned for him and asked, "Can Marl help Joog a moment?"

Yona would have joined Joog, but she saw him call for Marl and took Nik from Pela instead and said, "Yona's turn." Nik squealed delightfully as she bounced him up and down. When she saw Marl leave into the woods after Joog had whispered something to him, she took Nik with her and joined him on the stump.

"Yona looks good with Nik. Yona will make a fine mother someday."

Yona looked wistfully at Marl as he tramped through the trees examining fallen limbs and wondered if that day would ever come.

Nik reached out for Joog and felt the whiskers on his face. Joog crossed his eyes and made a silly face. Nik erupted in laughter and nearly flew as he jumped into Joog's lap. Joog bounced him up and down on his one good leg while Nik flapped his arms up and down and spoke some gibberish baby language.

Joog responded, "Goo baba ga goo boo da."

Yona smiled and said, "Joog is also good with babies. Someday Joog will…"

Before she could finish her thought, Marl returned with a sturdy branch that was thin and straight and almost as tall as him. "Is this what Joog wanted?"

Joog gave Nik back to Yona and accepted the branch. He pulled himself up onto his one foot and leaned on the branch. He gripped it with both hands and pulled it tight to his chest and tried taking a step, but that didn't work. "It's too long," he said. "Can Marl take this much off?" He held his hands out almost as long as his foot.

Marl retrieved a knife from one of the goat's packs and began gnawing and chopping off the end.

"The chickens are ready," Mora said behind them. "What is Marl doing?"

Joog replied, "Marl is making a walking stick for Joog. Joog wishes to save Brahg's strength for the climbing."

Brahg said, "That is not necessary."

Joog shook his head and said, "Brahg is too good a man to ever admit what a burden Joog is, but Joog can feel the wounds on Brahg's shoulder. Besides, it will be good for Joog to walk the easy trails. Please allow Joog to feel a small amount of independence. Fear not big man, Brahg will still have plenty of work carrying Joog."

Joog placed the shortened stick under his arm pit and hopped along using it as a crutch.

"Wait," Yona said, "That cannot be very comfortable. Let Yona help." She handed Nik back to Pela and went to her pack on one of the goats. She pulled out a length of leather cord and a small skin which still had the fur on it. She carried the skin to Joog and tied it atop his walking stick. "That should help."

Joog tried it out under his arm and smiled. "That is much better. Joog thanks Yona."

Zho became hyper attentive to Varna's every need. She carried Troon's child and if her foot were to slip on a pebble, he intended to be there to catch her. If there were a river to cross, he would carry her. His eyes never roamed from her.

Varna knew nothing about having a baby or raising a child. She kept close to Pulu and pelted her with questions. "Is Pulu sure that Varna is having a baby? How does Pulu know this?"

Pulu just smiled and replied, "Pulu wonders how Varna did not know. Did Varna's mother never tell Varna about babies?"

"Varna did not know Varna's mother. Varna was raised by the tribe without parents."

"Has Varna noticed that Varna's clothes fit more snugly?"

"Sure," Varna said, "Varna has seen this, but Varna has been eating much in grief since Troon's death. Varna still has dreams of that day."

"Losing one's mate is never easy," Pulu said, "and seeing it is even more horrible. If it is not too difficult, can Varna tell Pulu how Troon died?"

"We were in the cave. Our people don't usually live in caves, but it was a temporary shelter between our old village that was destroyed by floods, and our destination in the home of our ancestors. The men were off scouting for the ancient homeland leaving the women and children alone in the cave with a few elder men when we were attacked by a pair of great cats. Troon was the oldest in the tribe, but Troon never hesitated to protect us. We had lost Troon's great bow in the flood leaving Troon with only a flimsy wooden spear to fend off the cats, but it was not enough. He fought to keep them away from us, but they beat him and dragged him off into the fields to kill him."

"What a tragic loss," Pulu said, "but also a very fine heroic way for a noble warrior to die."

Varna barely heard Pulu as she reminisced. Her voice was almost monotone and tears streamed down her face as she continued, "Varna is good with bows, but we had no craftsmen to make one. Troon told Wull how bows were made, but Wull needed practice making them. Wull's first bow wasn't very good, but Varna tried to kill the cats with it anyway. It just wasn't Troon's bow. It had no power and its arrows just bounced off of them. Varna followed the cats out to Troon's body and offered to join Troon in the spirit world. Varna was closer to the cat than Varna is now to Pulu. Varna could smell Troon's blood on the cat's breath. Varna knows not why, but the cat would not take Varna."

"Some say that the animals respect humans with great courage and they can honor us by either letting us live or taking us in battle. Pulu thinks that perhaps the cat could smell the baby within Varna and chose to respect Varna by letting the baby live."

The first time Joog and Marl climbed the mountain to scout the pass, they practically raced up the slope, but that was before their injuries. Brahg and Marl could have gone faster, but neither wanted to leave Joog behind, and even though they wouldn't admit it, they hadn't recuperated enough to charge up the mountain yet either. Joog insisted on hobbling along with his makeshift crutch and Mora could only go as fast as her age allowed. Even Yona and Pela were slowing down as they learned that little Nik's weight seemed to grow heavier as they went along. Only Troon wasn't hampered physically. Their slow pace was killing him. He could certainly get there much faster on his own, but he could do nothing without them and had no choice but to wait for them.

The goats didn't care. They were glad to be out in the sunshine and bleated there approval along the way. The packs on their backs and the travois they pulled along did little to dampen their spirits, but it did slow them down a bit. The chickens would have been truly slow if they had been free to sample the seeds and insects along the way, but they too were glad to be out of the cave and in the fresh air.

Nobody in the troop was moving very fast, and regardless of how fast Troon could travel on his own, having to find quiet places with a little shade where Mora could enter into her trance to contact Troon also slowed them down.

"Mora," Brahg said while pointing ahead, "Brahg sees a small hollow under a rock up there. Mora can check with Troon again."

Mora didn't feel that they had gone far enough yet to check with their guide, but she welcomed an opportunity to take a short break off her feet. She sat cross legged under the overhang of the rock and took a deep cleansing breath. A cool breeze swept across her face and licked off some of the moisture around her neck. She closed her eyes and let the world slip away.

"Why must you take so long?" complained Troon.

"We are not spirits with boundless energy. Look at us Troon. Troon will see an old woman with three injured men and two young girls."

"Troon sees that Mora has brought goats and chickens. Did Mora forget to bring Mora's hut too?"

Mora shook her head and said, "Has Troon forgotten what it meant to be alive already? What good would we do to save our people if we cannot sustain the tribe? These aren't just goats and chickens. These are Mora's herbs and supplies. These are milk and eggs. Mora wishes we had just one fully whole man to send ahead, but we do not."

Troon growled, "Varna is doomed."

This upset Mora more than it should have. She knew all along that Troon was only concerned about Varna, but she didn't need him to place guilt upon them. "Perhaps Troon should not have died and left Varna alone."

"How can Mora say that? Troon did not plan to die. Troon tried to protect the women and children, and that includes Mora. What happened was out of Troon's control!"

"And Joog did not plan to lose Joog's foot either. Troon knows what is going on here, yet Troon expects us to run up the mountain like we were all young and healthy. We would not have been left behind if we had not been dealt such an unfortunate hand. Mora is sorry that Troon had to die, but Troon was relieved of his burdens while we must still live with them."

Troon scowled and said, "Whenever Mora is ready, there is a river and a gorge up ahead. Follow the river into the gorge and it will take us to the high plateau where Varna is."

Foln set out, on their trek down the mountain, thinking they could reach the river in time for their mid-day meal, but Pulu kept on his heel and tugged back on his pace. Pulu had no doubt that Varna was strong enough to keep up with any pace Foln and Bool set. She knew that Varna would push herself to excel and never allow herself to show any extra effort. Pulu did not know how much the baby could survive and she would not allow a pregnant woman to put the baby in jeopardy.

The sun pushed past high noon and they still hadn't reached the river yet, but Foln stuck to his plan to have their meal on the river. It would just be a little later than he had expected. He didn't blame Pulu for holding them back. He respected Varna's condition as much as all his people, but he was looking forward to some food. Soon, he reminded himself, they need only traverse the cave and they will be there.

Mora heard the splashing of the river ahead of them and said, "That must be the river Troon told Mora about. Let's water the goats and have some lunch while we are there."

Marl led the goats to the edge of the river. They were thirsty and needed no prodding. He lifted the chicken cage with Brahg's assistance and placed it on some stones where the river was especially shallow so they could have some water through the bars of the cage. One of the chickens jumped into the corner of the cage where the water ran the highest and squatted down to soak her feathers and bathe off the dust of the cave.

Yona strolled out into the cool water and dipped Nik's feet into it. Nik squealed and reached for the water. Yona ventured a little deeper into the river until the water reached Nik's waist and he splashed his palms on the top of the water.

Brahg elbowed Marl who had been watching Yona with Nik and asked, "Why is it that women are always so good with babies?"

"Marl does not know."

Brahg smiled and shook his head mildly. "They must be born with it."

"Yeah," Marl admitted. "They look different when they are with the babies too. It's like their smiles come from deep inside of them."

Brahg just nodded in agreement while he watched and smiled. He saw a smile on Marl's face and thought it too came from deep inside. He glanced over at Pela to see if she too had the same radiant smile from inside of her. Pela had been watching Brahg and Marl and quickly darted her eyes away from them when he caught her staring, but not so quick that he did not catch a glimpse of that same inner happiness he saw in Yona.

Marl broke his gaze from Yona and looked up the river. It was a good river with a strong deep current. "Marl is going up stream a bit to find some fish for lunch. Maybe Brahg can start a fire while Marl is gone?"

"Yeah," Brahg said somewhat hoarsely, "Brahg can do that."

<hr>

The river was a welcome sight to Zho. It meant most of the climbing was behind them. He didn't have to worry at every turn that Varna might slip and fall. Varna hoped it would be the end of Zho the mother hen. Foln was impressed with

Zho's concern over the baby, especially since he did not believe the Grull shared his people's deep reverence for motherhood.

Varna maintained that she was the same as ever and nothing had changed, however she indulged herself by walking out into the river, unwilling to admit even to herself that her feet felt tired and swollen.

Foln would never tell anyone that he saw the relief in Varna's face and he would never have to. He would have ordered the party to rest here on her behalf, but he would not have to this time, because he had already said they would break for lunch at the river. It was past noon, but the sun was still high in the sky and beat down mercilessly upon them. He looked up and shaded his eyes with his hands. "Bool, find us some fish. Foln welcomes the break but does not want to waste our daylight. If we hurry, we might still make it to the cave tonight."

"Neh," Zho said, "Bool is a warrior. Allow the hunters among us to catch our lunch."

Koro and Foln quickly jumped up at Zho's side and nodded their approval.

"Very well," Foln said, "We will let the Grull prepare our..."

Foln stopped mid-sentence when one of his advance scouts came running back from down river waving his hands to signal everyone to be quiet. The scout came directly to Foln and whispered, "Smoke! We smelled smoke ahead of us. Nerg has continued forward to see what is there."

Foln didn't wait for Nerg's findings. He knew what people frequented this trail and growled, "Slavers!"

"Slavers?" Zho asked. "I thought Trik's people were slavers and they are behind us."

"Neh," Foln said. "Trik's people are opportunists. They will steal your gold and your technology and then trade your people to the slavers to save their own hides. Trik's people are bad, to be sure, but the slavers are worse. They will sell your people like cattle."

Zho's face went slightly blank as he absorbed the information.

Foln grabbed his spear and began running down river. Zho shook off the shock that there were worse people than Trik's and followed Foln with Koro close on his heels.

Flom remained behind and pointed to the high walls of the gorge saying, "This would be a terrible place to be caught by surprise."

Bool slapped Flom on the back and said, "Now Flom is thinking like a warrior!" He then signaled the war band to split up. Half of them would take defensive positions and watch the high points of the gorge while the other half would follow Foln.

Foln slowed down when he had gone far enough to smell the smoke himself. The river and the gorge wound back and forth like a snake. Nerg waited at the last of the bends, peeking around the smooth wall where the river left the gorge and spilled into the forest.

Foln stayed low to the ground and crept up behind Nerg. "Is it Slavers?"

"Neh. Nerg does not know who they are, but they do not appear like warriors, except for the giant maybe."

"They have a giant? Let Foln see."

Nerg moved out of the way and let Foln take his place. Foln peeked around the edge of the canyon and saw Brahg carrying a log from the forest to the fire. The log was as big as Foln. Foln had only seen Brahg in the dim cave and mostly lying down on his back. He turned and jerked his head for Zho to join him. "Is that Zho's giant?"

Zho peeked around the corner and yelled, "Brahg!!" Brahg nearly dropped the log on his feet as Zho appeared out of nothingness and ran towards him.

"Those people," Foln explained to Nerg, "are the Grull we left at the cave. The last Foln had seen them, the giant was badly injured and confined to his bed. It would seem that the giant Brahg has healed nicely. Go get Bool and bring the rest of our party to them."

Brahg recovered from his surprise and lifted Zho in the air in a great bear hug.

Mora heard the commotion and came to see who it was. "What is Zho doing here?"

Zho broke his hug with Brahg to hug Mora. "Zho returns to wait out the winter in the cave with Mora."

"Why is Zho not in the home of our ancestors? Where is Kendo?" she asked.

"There is much news," Zho said, "and not all good, but we have time for that. Foln is with Zho as are many of Foln's friends for Mora to meet. They will be staying with us."

"For the winter?" Mora asked. "In that cave? More people? Mora hopes they can hunt." She turned and cupped her hands around her mouth and yelled, "Pela! Yona!"

Foln came out from behind Zho and said, "Mora looks well."

"Mora looks like a shriveled up grape. Mora would look better if we had known you were coming and had not walked ourselves to our deaths."

Brahg joined them and asked, "Did Foln catch Trik?"

Foln just stared at him for a moment and said, "Brahg is much bigger when Brahg is not lying down."

Brahg smiled. He liked people's reaction to his size.

"Yes," Foln eventually replied, "We caught up with Trik. Varna wanted to deliver the killing blow, but Trik's own people robbed Varna of that right."

Brahg frowned and said, "Brahg would have liked to rip his arms out."

Foln paused and marveled at the image in his head. He had no doubt that Brahg could pull a man's arms out of their sockets.

Nik squealed when he saw Foln. Yona and Pela walked a little faster to bring him to his father.

"Why has Zho returned?" Mora asked. "Why is Zho not with Kendo building our new home? Have the ancestral lands rejected our people? Where is Kendo?"

"Slow down," Zho said. "Mora asks too many questions too fast. We were not alone in the ancestral lands. Trik's people were already there. Foln can tell Mora about Trik's people. Zho only knows that they took Kendo and our people as prisoners. Foln has sent for Foln's armies to help us save them."

Mora raised her eyebrows as she looked again at Foln playing with Nik. "Foln has armies?"

Foln shrugged and said, "Foln is not a simple farmer."

Zho whispered, "Zho heard someone call the baby a prince."

"Why would Foln's armies help us?"

"Like the Grull," Foln said, "Foln's people, come from the same ancestors. Your ancestral home is also our ancestral home. We are called the Pallerax people and we too felt the calling to one day return home. We have always had a code by which we live. We will always stand up against the Griftons and the Bolerons. They too come from the same ancestors, but they have no honor. We know of nothing that has less honor than slavery."

"Slavery?" Mora gasped. "Is that what has become of our people?"

Foln shook his head and tried to look reassuring. "Not if Foln can help it."

"Then why does Foln return if our people are still there?"

"The Griftons have grown in numbers. It will take an army to defeat them and it will take time for Foln's army to get here. We will attack in the spring after the snows melt."

"The snows?" Mora asked.

"That's what they call the sacred white soil we discovered when we arrived here," Zho replied.

"But if we wait until spring," Mora cried, "Something might happen to our people."

"Kendo is strong," Zho said, "Kendo will keep our people alive."

"Mora must have faith," Foln said, "but to be sure, Foln has left scouts to watch over them. They will get word to us if anything changes, but Foln feels certain that things will remain as they are until the Bolerons arrive. When that day comes, Foln will have a surprise waiting for them."

Varna walked along the river to hug Mora. She wrapped Mora in her arms and began to squeeze, but Mora backed away, careful not to hug too hard. Varna looked at Mora with surprise and asked, "Mora knew?"

"Of course Mora knew, and now I suppose Varna cannot keep it a secret any longer."

Varna blushed and said, "Everyone knows. How did Mora know when even Varna did not know?"

Mora just smiled and kept her knowledge to herself.

The End

The Original Short Story

The Calling of the Grull, book one of The Valley of Hope series, began as a short story competition. Writers were challenged to write a short story in 800 words or less regarding snow. The following clip was my entry. It didn't win, but I did get some nice comments including one reader who wanted more. Around the time I had started writing my fourth book, I started releasing a select few of my short stories, and thought, almost on a lark, that I might try turning this story into a novel by releasing a new chapter every month. I was surprised at how well it was accepted, so the story was greatly expanded.

The Sacred Soil

Laughter echoed off the cold canyon walls. Kendo picked himself up off the ground and brushed the cold white stuff off his backside. He surveyed the paltry remains of his tribe. It was the first time they had laughed since their homes and crops were destroyed by floods. On another day, he might have admonished them for laughing at him, but not today. What would be the point? They climbed the sacred mountains searching for the fabled homes of their ancestors.

They were tired, cold, and hungry. They could use a good laugh and he laughed along with them. But he couldn't laugh too long, they needed to find a new home, and something to eat.

"It is good to hear you laugh my friends, but we must climb these mountains to find the home of the old ones; a land which has been told to us in our sacred songs. I fear we do not have so much time to laugh at an old man's clumsiness."

Kendo turned and headed once more up the mountain, and once again, his feet skidded out from under him and he crashed to the ground. "This land is hard to walk on."

Someone in the tribe said, "Perhaps you are doing it wrong."

Kendo brushed himself off again and asked, "Do you suggest Kendo does not know how to walk?"

"We certainly weren't suggesting Kendo does not know how to fall!"

The tribe erupted in laughter again. A young boy fell to the ground and rolled around laughing, then leaped to his feet and yelled out, "Hey, this white ground is very cold, but it is also very soft."

Kendo responded, "It is not so soft as you might think, little one."

Mora, the medicine woman, beckoned to the young boy, "Bring me some of that white ground."

The boy scooped up a handful and took it to the gnarled old woman. She took a pinch of it and tasted it. "Ooh, it is very cold," she said, "but it has no flavor." She turned and pointed into the tribe. "Ragna, does your child still burn?"

"Yes Mora, he does."

"Bring him to me." Mora took a handful of the white dirt from the boy. It was even colder than her first taste. She rubbed it into the baby's forehead, but it disappeared.

The crowd hushed. They had never witnessed such powerful magic from Mora before. She kissed the baby's forehead and said, "He feels better. If he gets hot again, rub some of the white dirt on him like I did." She turned to the boy and said, "Give him the rest of your dirt."

"I can not!" the boy cried out, "It is gone!"

The tribe was stunned.

Kendo stepped into the hushed crowd. "This must be sacred dirt. That is why it is so white. We are not allowed to own it, but the spirits allowed us to soothe the baby with it. We must be close to our destination now."

Mora asked, "What if we are not allowed to walk on the sacred dirt? Is that why you fall?"

Kendo stood tall and said, "If we are not allowed to walk on the sacred dirt, then we will humble ourselves before the spirits of our ancestors, and we will crawl on it."

A loud crack, followed by *oohs* and *ahs*, was heard on the other side of the tribe. The crowd parted and two of the tribe's hunters approached each carrying a rabbit.

"So," Kendo said, "it looks like we shall have some meat tonight. How much water do we have left?"

"Very little," the water porter said, "The floods spoiled our river and we could not refill our water skins."

Kendo frowned and asked the hunters, "Has anyone seen any sign of water?"

"No," a hunter said, "Not since we climbed above the stone quarry."

Kendo scanned the valleys below them. "If only we could find some water, we could use these rabbits to make enough stew to feed us all."

Mora could still taste the dew from the baby's forehead on her lips. "I think," she said, "that the spirits of our ancestors have provided sacred water for our stew."

Kendo looked around but saw no water.

Mora waved her arms to indicate the white dirt that lay everywhere. "When I put the sacred dirt on the child's forehead, it turned into water."

Kendo looked at his medicine woman, then at the starving tribe and asked, "Can we use sacred water to cook our food?"

Mora asked, "Can we turn down a sacred gift from the spirits?"

The tribe found shelter in some rocks and set up camp. They ate stew and told stories into the night. Tomorrow would be a new day.

About the Author

Jonni Jordyn was born in Oakland, California in 1957. She started writing at an early age, writing music, poetry, short stories, radio, film, and stage scripts. She didn't start writing novels until later in life, after she retired from playing music, and found herself travelling away from home for extended periods.

She currently lives in Denver, Colorado

www.ingramcontent.com/pod-product-compliance
Lightning Source LLC
Chambersburg PA
CBHW010558310726
48969CB00009B/2473